Steel & Spellfire

ALSO BY LAURA E. WEYMOUTH

The Light Between Worlds
A Treason of Thorns
A Rush of Wings
A Consuming Fire
The Voice Upstairs

STEEL & SPELLFIRE

LAURA E. WEYMOUTH

MARGARET K. McELDERRY BOOKS
New York   Amsterdam/Antwerp   London
Toronto   Sydney/Melbourne   New Delhi

MARGARET K. McELDERRY BOOKS
An imprint of Simon & Schuster Children's Publishing Division
1230 Avenue of the Americas, New York, New York 10020
For more than 100 years, Simon & Schuster has championed authors and the stories they create. By respecting the copyright of an author's intellectual property, you enable Simon & Schuster and the author to continue publishing exceptional books for years to come. We thank you for supporting the author's copyright by purchasing an authorized edition of this book.
No amount of this book may be reproduced or stored in any format, nor may it be uploaded to any website, database, language-learning model, or other repository, retrieval, or artificial intelligence system without express permission. All rights reserved. Inquiries may be directed to Simon & Schuster, 1230 Avenue of the Americas, New York, NY 10020 or permissions@simonandschuster.com.
This book is a work of fiction. Any references to historical events, real people, or real places are used fictitiously. Other names, characters, places, and events are products of the author's imagination, and any resemblance to actual events or places or persons, living or dead, is entirely coincidental.
Text © 2025 by Laura E. Weymouth
Jacket illustration © 2025 by Fernanda Suarez
Jacket design by Debra Sfetsios-Conover
All rights reserved, including the right of reproduction in whole or in part in any form.
MARGARET K. McELDERRY BOOKS is a trademark of Simon & Schuster, LLC.
For information about special discounts for bulk purchases, please contact Simon & Schuster Special Sales at 1-866-506-1949 or business@simonandschuster.com.
Simon & Schuster strongly believes in freedom of expression and stands against censorship in all its forms. For more information, visit BooksBelong.com.
The Simon & Schuster Speakers Bureau can bring authors to your live event. For more information or to book an event, contact the Simon & Schuster Speakers Bureau at 1-866-248-3049 or visit our website at www.simonspeakers.com.
Interior design by Irene Metaxatos
The text for this book was set in Adobe Garamond Pro.
Manufactured in the United States of America
First Edition
10 9 8 7 6 5 4 3 2 1
Library of Congress Cataloging-in-Publication Data
Names: Weymouth, Laura E., author.
Title: Steel & spellfire / Laura E. Weymouth.
Other titles: Steel and spellfire
Description: First edition. | New York : Margaret K. McElderry Books, 2025. | Audience term: Teenagers | Audience: Ages 14 up. | Audience: Grades 10–12. | Summary: Disguised as an Ingenue with limited magical abilities, powerful mage Pandora infiltrates the royal court to escape her past, but when a killer mimics her powers and begins murdering other Ingenues, Pandora must join forces with Royal Guard Kit Beacon to claim her freedom.
Identifiers: LCCN 2024041674 (print) | LCCN 2024041675 (ebook) | ISBN 9781665959759 (hardcover) | ISBN 9781665959766 (paperback) | ISBN 9781665959773 (ebook)
Subjects: CYAC: Fantasy. | Magic—Fiction. | Courts and courtiers—Fiction. | Murder—Fiction. | Interpersonal relations—Fiction. | LCGFT: Fantasy fiction. | Novels.
Classification: LCC PZ7.1.W43761 St 2025 (print) | LCC PZ7.1.W43761 (ebook) | DDC [Fic]—dc23
LC record available at https://lccn.loc.gov/2024041674
LC ebook record available at https://lccn.loc.gov/2024041675

Steel & Spellfire

THE MAGE LAWS OF HESPERID

~FOR THE PROTECTION OF ITS PEOPLE~

Every mage must have their proper patron, either freely chosen or assigned by those in governance.

The binding rite, which fixes mage to patron through bonds of spellfire and obedience and which tempers wild magic, must be undertaken by the age of thirteen, lest a mage grow too great in power and become a danger.

Aside from the binding rite, magic must never be exercised upon another person, regardless of intent. It may not be used consciously or unconsciously; not to harm, not to help, not to heal.

Any contravention of the mage laws is punishable by death.

1

LITERALLY NOT LIKE OTHER GIRLS

At the Bellwether School for Young Ladies, the air smelled of white jasmine and roses, no sound louder than a mild laugh was ever heard, and all aspects of life proceeded according to plan. It was a place of restraint and beauty, of potential and expectation, built on old money and designed to nurture sweetly talented blossoms until they were ready to open into the full flower of love.

"*Shit,*" Winifred Harper swore softly and devoutly at Pandora's side in the quiet ground-floor hallway of the school. "Sheesen. Shestra. Shinghaijao."

They stood together, waiting for the last of the year's Ingenue examinations to wrap up. Eight girls had completed their course of study with the Bellwether sisters this year, and there were only six places for Bellwether Ingenues at court. Everyone was on tenterhooks. Winnie had already torn her handkerchief to pieces in an attempt to vent her nerves, so now Pandora's ears must pay the price. Admittedly, it was at least a testament to Winnie's facility with languages that she could curse fluently in not only her native Hesperidian, but in Oberin, Hochvelt, and Coven as well.

"Stop it," Pan hissed, though she shot Winnie a sympathetic look. Winifred jerked upright at once, shoving the ruined kerchief into her pocket as her eyes went wide with panic.

"Did Miss Alice see me tearing up my things? Or worse, did she hear me?" Winnie cast a surreptitious glance down the hallway to where the younger of the Bellwether sisters stood watch, reserved and resplendent in a matron's black silk gown. "Oh, Pan, what if she did? What if I was going to get a place as an Ingenue but she's just changed her mind? I can't go around behaving like this at court—she's sure to fail me now, and you know I need this, my family's counting on me."

"You have to stop worrying," Pan said, slipping an arm around Winnie's shoulders. Snub-nosed, red-haired, and perpetually eager to please, Winifred Harper was by far the friendliest and most charming of the girls in Pandora's year. And it was true that her family depended on her—the Harpers were insignificant in the grand scheme of things, with just enough minor titles in the family tree and just enough money in the bank to render them respectable. They needed Winnie at court and well matched if they were to rise and had paid dearly to send her to the Bellwether School in pursuit of that aim.

"See?" Pandora said, giving Winnie a squeeze as the door to Miss Elvira's office opened and one of their classmates emerged, ashen-faced and stricken. A faint smell of sick wafted out along with her, and Miss Elvira's voice cracked through the air, sharp as a whip.

"Alice! Send one of the maids in *at once*."

"Bad luck, Edith," Pan offered, tightening her protective arm around Winifred as the other girl passed them by. "Sorry you didn't do better, but maybe others will be worse."

In response, Edith gave Pan a truly vicious stare and stalked away.

"Ugh," Winnie said, shivering beside Pandora. "I wouldn't want to be on Edith's bad side, not for anything. You didn't . . . you didn't *do* something to help her fail, did you, Pan?"

Pandora widened her eyes, the picture of wounded innocence. "Winifred, how dare you imply such a thing? What have I ever done to make you believe I could be so ruthless?"

A memory of the previous evening flashed across Pandora's mind. She'd gone to Edith's room just before midnight, knowing the other girl would be up studying the history of their small but powerful homeland of Hesperid and practicing her parlor magic. Why Edith wanted a place as an Ingenue so badly was anyone's guess—her family was fabulously wealthy, but perhaps they thought gaining a title would be a feather in their collective cap. At any rate, Edith certainly didn't *need* access to court like some of the other girls did, and so Pan had paid her a visit with a smuggled bottle of summer wine under each arm. It wasn't Pandora's fault if Edith didn't know her limits and couldn't hold her wine, and if every other girl at the Bellwether School knew that weakness.

Winifred looked unconvinced by Pandora's protestations of guiltlessness. "You know, sometimes I think you might be the most frightening person here. More than Miss Elvira, even."

You don't know the half of it, Pan thought grimly as a twist of pain knotted up inside her. She pointed down the hallway to where two other girls were speaking with their heads together.

"You think *I'm* frightening? Cecily hasn't gone in yet, and Imogen's cornered her. That won't end well."

If Pandora was honest, it was Imogen Hollen she'd have loved to cut out of the Ingenue runnings. But Imogen was unassailable. Willowy and exquisitely fashionable, with a wealth of golden hair, sea-green eyes, and the faintest possible scattering of freckles which kept her from untouchable perfection, she stood an enviable six inches taller than Pan and never faltered in her poise or her determination to secure a place at court. Now, as Imogen spoke to Cecily in low tones, the other girl's face slowly grew paler and more anxious. At last, Imogen pressed something into Cecily's hand the moment before a maid emerged from Miss Elvira's study. This time, a smell of lemon polish wafted out, along with a palpable air of annoyance.

"Cecily Sharpe!" Miss Elvira snapped, and Cecily hurried through the door, gathering up her skirts and looking on the verge of tears.

Though each examination was meant to last an hour—Pandora had volunteered for the first slot, and Winnie had gamely taken the second—Cecily was ensconced within Miss Elvira's study for no more than ten minutes before a gale of sobs rang out, and she was escorted away in hysterics by the long-suffering Miss Alice.

"I only wish it had been Imogen who fell to pieces, not Cecily, but Gin's a fortress," Pandora said with a stifled sigh as she watched the beautiful girl down the hallway toss her head and leave the corridor, headed for the front parlor, where the rest of the hopeful Ingenues were waiting. It was certainly the more mannerly thing to do, sitting and taking tea or amusing themselves with parlor magic as everyone else completed their examinations and fate was decided. Pandora was surprised that Imogen had hung back in the corridor—normally she was the picture of propriety, while Pan and Winnie were considered the least genteel contingent of their year.

"Come on," Pandora said, taking Winnie's hand. "Time to go give the impression that we don't care what comes next, or whether we've wasted the last five years on a pointless exercise."

Though Pan would never own it to Winnie, her heart was in her throat. Whatever the rest of the girls' reasons for wanting to secure a place at court, her need was greatest. She couldn't afford to fail. Not after the effort she'd put in and the strain five years at the Bellwether School had been.

"Hello, darlings," Imogen said coolly from her place at the tea table as Pandora and Winnie entered the room. "Refreshments while we wait?"

She poured out two cups with perfect grace, serene and lovely in fine lace and lavender watered silk. Imogen looked like a painting. She looked like everyone's image of an ideal Ingenue. She certainly did not look like the sort of person who'd just terrorized one of her classmates into a breakdown.

Knowing full well that Pandora only ever took her tea black, Imogen smiled while stirring four lumps of sugar and a generous helping of cream into each cup. Pan couldn't help but hold a grudging respect for the varied and creative ways in which she'd been snubbed over the years, even while she chafed under the constant goad that was Imogen Hollen's attention. For all their time at the Bellwethers', Pan and Imogen had been sworn rivals. By far the most adept with parlor magic of the girls in their year, they'd sparred with magic and words and deportment, each determined to come out as the superior Ingenue. So as Miss Alice and Miss Elvira swept into the room, Pan sipped her tea with what she hoped passed for elegant unconcern, while struggling not to pull a face over the sickly sweetness on her tongue. She would not give Imogen the satisfaction. Beside her, Winnie stiffened visibly, a bundle of nerves, and her teacup clattered against its saucer.

Never one to miss an opportunity for display, Imogen rested a hand on the tabletop as a small magic-wrought butterfly appeared on her palm. It fluttered upward and alighted on Miss Elvira's shoulder. The eldest and sternest of the Bellwether sisters smiled indulgently, only ever a soft touch where Imogen was concerned. The sisters had ambitions for Imogen, Pandora knew. She'd overheard them talking once—Pan discovered during her first year that the broom closet adjoining the Misses' office was an excellent place for eavesdropping. Imogen's parents, it seemed, were close with the royal family, and she'd been in and out of royal estates since leaving the nursery. The Bellwether sisters cherished hopes of a match to Prince Theo, despite rampant rumors that the heir to the throne was little better than a feckless libertine. His character was of no import, however. Were Imogen to be bound into the royal family, it would give the Bellwether sisters that much more opportunity to foster ties between Hesperid's sovereigns and their school. Just as Imogen and Pan were sworn rivals, the Bellwethers were in constant competition with a larger institution called Grace College. While many facilities for the training of Ingenues existed across Hesperid, and private tutors could even be hired for outrageous fees, Grace and the Bellwethers stood head and shoulders above the rest when it came to turning out successful mages who would serve as an ornament to the highest ranked and most privileged families.

What Imogen thought about being used as a pawn in this game, Pandora had no idea. She was a perpetually closed book. Pan, quite frankly, found it all appalling. Unlike the other girls, Pandora was not breathlessly awaiting binding and marriage to a patron and spouse all rolled into one perfect package. She did not relish the idea of surrendering even a spark of her highly restrained power. Her schoolfellows might look over the society columns and compare notes on eligible patrons while giddy and giggling, but Pan did not view patronage as a laughing matter. She knew all too well how a binding could be used against a mage, subjugating both them and their magic until they were little better than a puppet in their patron's hands.

Pandora had already been bound. Was still bound, though she'd escaped her patron's influence and never breathed a word about her binding to anyone. So, no. When it came to patronage, she was nothing like the other girls. They were going to seek out bindings and new lives. Pandora, meanwhile, was hoping to force a reckoning. To track down the person who'd claimed her in childhood and somehow shatter the tie between them.

If she meant to accomplish that, she'd have to win access to society's glittering first set, which lived in a whirl of gaiety and wealth and power on Palace Hill.

Imogen's scarlet butterfly fluttered its wings on Miss Elvira's shoulder and vanished when its maker's magic ran its limited course. Not to be outdone, Pandora thought of flowers, and a rain of golden petals drifted gently from the ceiling. They filled the room and, where they lit upon tables or settees or lace-draped shoulders, evaporated in little puffs of silver sparkles, leaving a heady floral scent lingering on the air. Pandora did not need to set her hand on the tabletop to focus her attention as Imogen had done or to subtly demonstrate that it was her magic at work. Everyone in the room knew her magecraft and envied it. For perhaps Pandora Small was stubby and plain and in many ways common, but her parlor magic was a thing of beauty. Even Imogen, her nearest rival, could not hold a candle to it.

Pain lanced through Pandora, burning its way from the crown of her head to the soles of her feet, but she tamped it down ruthlessly, her face an emotionless mask. Miss Elvira frowned a little at Pan's display—the eldest of the Bellwether sisters had no magic herself, instead instructing the girls in deportment, Hesperidian history and economics, and delicate arts such as drawing, needlepoint, dance, and genteel conversation. Miss Elvira *did* have the magesense, however, and her capacity to hear magic kept the girls in line, forever afraid of being caught using their power for mischief.

Miss Alice, by contrast, smiled and nodded to Pandora. She taught the girls how to hone and shape their magecraft, readying them for their roles as display pieces and objects of conversation in elevated households, as well as for an Ingenue's more useful undertakings on behalf of her patron—divination of truth, the harmonious unifying of two parties who were at odds, the amplification of pleasure, and a dozen more feminine and magical skills. Miss Alice's own magecraft was understated and exquisite, her tutelage indispensable.

"All right, *enough*," Miss Elvira ordered as several of the other hopeful Ingenues set off bits of parlor magic, vying for attention. A spellfire songbird's rill of music died away, and a flickering aurora vanished from overhead. But the glint of silver left by Pan's magecraft still shone on every surface, and the scent of flowers lingered on the air.

I'm coming for you, Pandora thought, sending the warning out through the streets of the capital city of Valora, toward the bright hill where the wealthy and ennobled resided. *I will find you, and I will win back my freedom, even if I kill us both in doing so.*

"As you know," Miss Elvira said sternly, "this year we've had eight girls complete their course of study with Alice and me. You're all to be commended for your diligence, discipline, and hard work. In the past—before the wellspring, when mages were rarer and less in power—we had fewer girls ready to become Ingenues than spaces allotted to us at court, which made our students' lives easier. Now we must choose between eminently qualified young ladies. Regardless of the decision Alice and I have reached, every one of you should be proud of what you've accomplished. Whether you join us at court or not, you'll undoubtedly find yourselves sought out by patrons of fortune and quality."

Lambs to the slaughter, Pandora thought, while smiling prettily at her peers. Beside her, Winifred had gone dead pale. Squeezing her friend's hand beneath the table, Pan offered reassurance under her breath. "Steady on, Winnie. Whatever you do, just don't fall apart now. You're so close."

Worry bit at Pan. She knew what waited for Winifred if she failed to gain an Ingenue's position. Families always had an alternate match arranged for their darling would-be Ingenues, should the worst come to pass. They strove for the greatest advantage that could be gained without access to Palace Hill. In Winifred's case, this would mean marriage and patronage from a man three times her age, who'd wed and been made widower by two other mages. He'd driven his wives into early graves, most people said, by pushing them to the limits of their small magic in order to satisfy his own lusts and impress his peers. Even if Winifred survived the man's hard usage, it would do her no good—a mage with a single binding died within hours of their patron's passing. It was a death sentence that only ran one way, for patrons suffered no such fate upon the death of their mages. And while boys born with a gift for magic were bound first to an apprentice master and then to a wife, thereby circumventing premature death brought about by a single binding, girls were not. Those of them lowborn were bound to an employer. Those of them highborn became would-be Ingenues and were bound to husbands. In some households, when the master died, both the mistress and half the household staff were killed by his passing.

"Pandora," Miss Elvira snapped, catching Pan murmuring reassurances to Winnie. "Would you care to address your comments to all of us?"

"Certainly." Pandora smiled more charmingly still, sweet as the tea Imogen had given her. "I was only telling Winifred that whatever comes next, it's been a pleasure and an honor to spend the past five years with her, and I'm sure I feel the same way about everyone else."

From her place on a settee beside the window, Edith scowled and muttered something inaudible. Imogen's green eyes flashed from Edith to Pandora, and what might have been the ghost of a smile played at the corners of her perfect mouth. Both Pan and Imogen were well aware of their status as the fiercest contenders in the room—tigers biding their time in a pride of housecats.

"What a lovely sentiment," Imogen said, smooth as silk. "Perhaps applause are in order, for all of us. A celebration of who we've become."

As one, the eight girls began their applause, but in the way of Ingenues—rather than clapping vulgarly with their hands, they created a rain shower of magic, which filled the room with its exultant sound and never dampened a single surface. Gray clouds billowed just beneath the ceiling, and an earthy scent of petrichor rose on the air.

"Oh can we just get this over with?" Winnie moaned under cover of the noise.

With a sympathetic look at Winifred's wan face, Miss Alice moved to her sister's side. "Tonight, we'll be saying goodbye to two of you as you return to your families. And tomorrow, the following girls will join us for the summer on Palace Hill . . . Imogen Hollen."

No surprises there. Neither Pandora nor anyone else ever doubted that Imogen would secure her place.

"Eleanor Wellesley."

Eleanor glanced up in shock. She was a silent, proud girl who kept mostly to herself. Not out of choice, Pandora often suspected, but out of necessity. Eleanor came from a long line of gifted mages, once celebrated servants of the court, now entirely out of favor. Six years back, when the wellspring—a catastrophic fount of magic located somewhere beneath the great city of Valora— broke open, a

Wellesley had been executed for tearing apart the earth and unleashing that flood of wild magic. The stain of high treason did not wash out easily, and the Wellesley name had been tainted ever since. Pan had made occasional overtures to Eleanor over the years, but the girl was difficult to draw out of her shell.

"Mamie Hawthorne."

A good-hearted girl with a family who'd made their fortune in trade, Mamie reached out and impulsively took Eleanor's hands in congratulations. Were her family's status what it had once been, Eleanor might not even have acknowledged Mamie on the street. Now a relieved and happy look passed between them.

"Winifred Harper."

"Oh thank the *gods*," Winnie blurted out fervently, and the assembled girls couldn't help the wave of laughter that rose from them. Even Miss Elvira, staid and strict as she was, showed a flicker of amusement.

"Leslie Moran."

Leslie sank back against her armchair, transparently overcome by relief. Pandora remained straight-backed and motionless, refusing to look at Edith or Cecily. It was down to the three of them now, and it was conceivable, *just* conceivable, that Miss Elvira's pointed dislike might win out over all Pandora's accomplishments. Pain bit cruelly at Pan from the inside, but that was nothing out of the ordinary—she was accustomed to its constant presence. It was only anxiety heightening the sensation, dragging her perpetual discomfort to the forefront as worry lowered her defenses.

"Pandora Small," Miss Elvira said, unable to hide a slight note of distaste in her voice.

Once again, applause fell like rain. And for the briefest moment, Pan felt a stab of pity for the girls she'd beaten out, and for the newly minted Ingenues she'd spend the summer with as well. At her heart she was nothing like them, with their luxurious childhoods and ambitions of romance and social achievement. Whatever they'd won in seizing hold of this distinction and gaining access to court, Pandora knew she'd far outstripped them all, through the simple act of convincing the world that she was biddable and bindable, and could ever be delicate and decorative and desired.

I'm coming for you, she thought at her patron once more. *And I will see you suffer.*

That night, Pandora was tormented by pain and the whispers of a half-forgotten voice. Already aggravated as she was by worry and uncertainty, relief and anticipation had riled her internal complaint further yet, so that she was hard-pressed to sit and smile through the celebratory dinner the Bellwether sisters hosted for their eldest and most-talented students. Edith and Cecily had taken leave of the school at once, unable to endure an evening of fêting those who'd gained what they'd lost. Pandora wished she'd been able to bow out as well but sat sandwiched between Winifred and Leslie, daintily consuming clear soup, roast partridge, and raspberry blancmange, while setting off an occasional strained piece of parlor magic.

"Have you got a headache, Pan?" Winnie asked sympathetically as the dessert plates were cleared and tea was brought out. Pandora, who'd discovered in her first year that headaches made a convenient excuse for becoming pale or slow when her secret agony grew unbearable, nodded. It was a mark of distinction in an Ingenue to be a little fragile—as if their magic burned too brightly, leaving them scorched by its presence. There were hard limits to their power, after all, with dire consequences for those who held more of it than was considered right or natural.

"Go on upstairs," Winnie said, giving Pandora's hand a kind pat. "I'll tell everyone the excitement today was too much for you."

Once again, Pan nodded mutely. Truthfully, she could hardly speak past the hurt beneath her skin or hear past the wordless whispers filling her mind. It was an effort just to keep herself from breaking out in an unladylike sweat. Winnie, by contrast, was sparkling-eyed and bright, triumphant over having won the place as an Ingenue she'd striven so hard for.

Slipping away from the table while the Bellwether sisters' attention was elsewhere, Pan drifted upstairs and carefully locked the door to her room behind her. In a moment, she was at the bureau, rifling through drawers with trembling hands, tearing off her gown, her stays and petticoats and filmy underthings, and pulling on a set of rough trousers and a homespun shirt that felt like a second skin. The window was open, letting in a breath of balmy, late-spring air and an earthy scent of filigree ivy, which climbed the school's mellow stone walls. At the last moment, Pandora remembered her hair—it was pinned up in one of the arrangements prospective Ingenues were taught that gave an impression of ease and carelessness despite taking the better part of an hour to create. Sending rhinestone-studded pins scattering in every direction, Pandora pulled a face at herself in the mirror. Good. Back to looking like the monstrous thing she truly was.

It wasn't fully dark yet. Dusk was falling slowly over the city, but Pan was willing to risk the leftover remnants of light. Trusting her weight to the thick stalks of ivy as she'd done a thousand times before, down Pandora went, putting four blocks between herself and the Bellwether School before hailing a hansom. A terrible heaviness lodged in her chest. There'd be no time for this sort of escapade once she was on Palace Hill—Ingenues were kept busy with endless rounds of teas and luncheons and balls and theatrics, on their feet and swept along in a fever dream of levity from sundown until the small hours of the morning. Pan would have to manage without her occasional escapes, her forays into the less desirable parts of the great city of Valora, her pilgrimages back to the seedy sort of places she'd once looked to for freedom.

Scrambling out of the hansom at the edge of a busy, unkempt market square, Pandora stopped, taking stock of her surroundings. The daylight stalls had been shuttered an hour ago, but night vendors with peddling carts had taken their places. Gas lamps flared around the square's perimeter, flooding the space with wan, uneven light as the moon rode overhead, a sickly waning thing that did little to penetrate the fetid lowland mists that descended on Valora's seedier districts each evening. Immediately Pandora felt wariness wash over her. Though the square itself was bright enough, and full of nocturnal activity and life, it was the outskirts and the shadows she was concerned with.

Refined girls and their parlor tricks were not the only form of magic in the nation of Hesperid. Not since the wellspring had been torn open six years back, flooding the capital and the countryside around it with unchecked power.

Systematically Pan began to prowl the edges of the square, feigning interest in cheap trinkets or treats as she kept her attention focused outward, on the dark alleyways and twisted lanes that joined up with the square like strands of a spider's web. She'd traveled halfway around the perimeter when something at the square's heart made her turn.

A commotion, at the head of one of the alleys that terminated in the square. Eagerly Pandora peered around a roughly dressed miner who'd come to browse the same cart she was standing at.

But Pan's heart sank as four uniformed members of the Queen's

Guard materialized from the alley, a young girl with blank eyes walking in the midst of them. The Guard members were immaculate, the picture of self-assured justice in their crimson and silver jackets, while the girl by contrast was ragged and filthy. A small gaggle of people trailed in their wake—a man and a woman and three young children. The woman was wailing, the man ashen-faced and stricken, while the children looked only confused. Last of all came a priest in midnight-blue robes, his eyes flashing with righteous fury as he herded the stricken family ahead of him.

Inside Pandora, the constant pain she carried twisted and magnified itself, becoming agony. The whispers at the edges of her hearing escalated, until perversely, she yearned to listen, to reply, to reach back through memory to touch their source.

"Caught another one, have they?" the bearded and dust-spackled miner at Pan's side said gruffly. "That's the third this month. You'd think they'd know better by now."

Pandora wanted to leave. She wanted to return to the stifling, lovely confines of the Bellwether School, which even the wellspring had done little to alter, and bury her head under silk-covered pillows. She wanted to flee, losing herself in the labyrinth of Valora's lower streets and squalid districts, vanishing into the tawdry slums that had once been her home. Anywhere would do, so long as she was not *here*.

Above all, she wanted to give in to the pain at her core and the beckoning voice that haunted her.

But Pandora owed it to the girl to stay, and so she stood just where she was, rooted to the spot. She watched as the guards led their prisoner to a raised platform at the square's center, atop which stood a gleaming steel box. It was a perfect cube, with dimensions of four feet to every side. There were no windows, only a single small grate of the finest possible steel mesh. One side was hinged, so that it could swing open and shut, with a hasp opposite the hinges, ready for a heavy padlock.

Over the last half dozen years, such things had become commonplace in Valora, though beyond the capital, in the remainder of Hesperid, they were more a rarity.

The guards muscled the girl up onto the platform, and she began to sob, not desperately but wearily. She was a few years younger than Pan, and sick guilt churned in Pan's stomach. It was only Pandora's status as a protected and privileged soon-to-be Ingenue that stood between her and this child's fate. Only they were granted a temporary exemption from the requirement that all mages be bound to a patron by thirteen, to check the further development of their power.

Pandora did not require an Ingenue's reprieve in regards to the binding law. She'd been bound as far back as memory served her. What she needed was an Ingenue's access to Palace Hill.

"Your attention, please." It was not the guards who spoke, but rather the priest, who stepped forward and stood at the base of the raised platform, a zealot's holy flush coloring his face. "It is my privilege to represent the joint interests of church and state, and to inform you that this girl has been found guilty of breaking not one but both of Hesperid's mage laws. Not only is she fourteen and still unbound to a patron as the law requires, but she recently made use of her power upon another person. The exercise of hellfire in such a way, regardless of the outcome, is strictly prohibited by both the queen and the Higher Gods. It is an offense against your sovereign, against your deities, and against nature."

"I heard about this one," the vendor behind the peddling cart whispered. She was a thin, haggard-looking woman, with dark shadows beneath her eyes and a tight set to her mouth. "An awful thing.

The girl's father's a miner. He had the lung sickness they get down in the pits sometimes, but the whole family depends on him to earn. So the girl held off on her binding, hoping that if she waited, she'd grow far enough in her power to be his cure. And she did it—she mended him, but she'll pay for it now with her life."

"Doesn't matter why she did it," the rough-dressed miner said with a scowl, showing no compassion for his comrade's family and fate. "The mage laws are for the protection of us all. It only takes one mistake, one slip of control, and a mage like her could kill herself and anyone within a stone's throw. Everyone knows spellfire's that tricky."

As he spoke, Pandora felt her pain grow acute. Spellfire was everywhere in Hesperid and always had been—in the water, in the soil, some said even in the air. A little of it was needed for life. A little more, and you became a mage, someone who could bend their excess of spellfire into magic. Magecraft had been limited in the world before Valora's recent flood of power and hadn't required governance. But along with the wellspring came not only a stark increase in the sheer number of mages, but in their capabilities. For two years after the wellspring tore open and released its flood of spellfire, those with a knack for magic had struggled to cope. They'd lost control, causing their own deaths and many others. Only Queen Maud's enactment of the mage laws, to bind magic workers and prevent the full growth of their power, had restored order. Worse still, the glut of spellfire bred monsters, pooling in places where it went unchanneled and shaping its raw essence into inhuman creatures of malevolence and insatiable hunger, which stalked the edges of Valora and preyed upon her citizenry.

Hellions, the church called such beasts, as they insisted on referring to the element that fueled magic as hellfire. Hellions were considered demonic and clearly tied to the wicked Lower Gods, rendering spellfire wicked too in the eyes of the church. Though no one asked to grow into a mage's gift, those who did were viewed as suspect and dangerous, requiring careful handling to prevent damage to the well-being and faith of the general populace.

Watching the priest and the guards and the girl about to receive their discipline, Pandora thought she would take an encounter with a hellion over confinement in a steel box any day.

A metallic clang resounded in the market square as one of the guards swung the door to the box open. The mage girl was forced onto her knees and made to shuffle forward, into its steel interior. One last charged look passed between her and her family, and the door was shut, a padlock fitted into place.

Pandora had seen mages being executed before. It was a cruel and inhumane punishment—though no one was certain why, steel and spellfire existed in opposition to each other. Spellfire could not seep through steel and enter a mage's body, as it could through stone or brick or wood. And steel could not be damaged by spellfire, proving impervious to magic.

"Do you think she'll linger?" the miner asked, half curiously. Some mages lasted a day or two after confinement to a steel box, spending their magic bit by bit trying to escape. Sooner or later, every one of them died of caster's fatigue when the steel kept their spellfire from being replaced.

Pandora knew the answer to the miner's question. She'd seen it in the final look that passed between the girl and her mother, before the box was shut. Now, as if in answer to Pandora's knowing, a blinding flare of blue-white light flashed from the box's small mesh grate, followed by a percussive sound.

A quick death, Pandora thought, as her heart ached and ached within her. That was the last gift the mage girl on the platform was giving to her family. First life for her father, then a quick death for herself.

The miner made a disparaging sound. "And *that's* why her sort are a danger. Only a moment in the box and she went off like a bomb. A patron would've kept her honest, and under control."

Pandora bit back the sharp words already on her tongue. Even the silliest and most pampered of girls at the Bellwether School could keep her magic in check for more than a moment and manage it in the throes of hysterics, too. The girl in the box had not died so quickly for want of control. She had chosen it, as a final mercy for those she loved.

"Better she'd been born with her power and snuffed as a babe in arms, than that her parents should live through this," the vendor said sympathetically.

A barely suppressed shudder ran through Pandora. Snuffing, though not legally prescribed in the wake of the wellspring, was not forbidden, either. Most mages grew into their power slowly, beginning to develop it around five or six, once they were capable of controlling its first nascent embers. But sometimes—rarely—a child was born already imbued with enough spellfire to work magic. They were a danger to others and to themselves, for even the limited magic possessed by Pandora's fellow Ingenues could be destructive if not channeled properly. The mage laws were mute on the subject of such children, dictating only that a mage must be bound to a patron before the age of thirteen or before their power grew beyond control. A babe in arms could not control its spellfire; neither could it undertake the act of power necessary for mages to bind and subjugate themselves to proper patrons.

So by law, such children's fate was consignment to a lingering, lonely end in a steel box. In practice, numerous discreet doctors and midwives offered the service known as snuffing—a quick and painless death for newborn things Hesperid's people did not know how to raise in safety.

The priest climbed the platform at the square's center and loosed the padlock, then swung open the door to the steel box. Inside, there was nothing but gleaming blue ash—the usual sign of a life ended by spellfire. A keening sob rose from the girl's mother as she crumpled to the ground, and the man who'd been cured by his daughter's illicit magework gathered the remainder of his children close.

They were broken. Broken by magic, broken by spellfire, broken by the mage laws that had been meant for protection but nevertheless held part of Hesperid's populace by the throat. And Pandora could not bear it. Turning her back on the scene, she strode down the nearest dark alley, hot tears blurring her vision as insidious whispers rang in her ears. There was so little to separate her from the girl who'd been reduced to ash. Only a few fragile twists of fate. But for them, she'd be—

Pan stopped, pressing her forehead to the cool stone of an abandoned tenement's wall. A thick, toxic sense of despair weighed her down, joining with the pain that perpetually echoed through her bones. What was the use of all she'd done over the past five years, dedicating herself to a decorous world of frivolity and artifice in an attempt to right one wrong? Hesperid was a hotbed of injustice, and the city of Valora especially steeped in it. Even were Pandora to succeed in finding and confronting her shadowy patron, it would be no more than a drop in a vast sea of suffering. Why bother? Why carry on, when the upstanding and virtuous people of Hesperid would prefer girls like Pan did not exist at all, and the less scrupulous, more grasping souls among them sought to use her kind to their own advantage?

A sudden image flashed across Pandora's mind, of the girl being forced into the box. Hard on its heels came a new vision, this time of herself on the roof of the four-story tenement she stood beside. It would be so easy to climb the stairs inside and get out under the night sky. So easy to stand at the edge of that roof, with blank space before her. The simplest thing in the world to lean forward and trust herself to the air. No more mage laws. No more life of constraint and falsehood. No more guilt and fear and pain.

Abruptly that very pain jolted within Pandora, sending a shock of clarity running through her like lightning. She was not prone to despair, not even in her darkest moments. If there was one thing that defined her existence, it was a dogged tenacity and refusal to give up once she'd fixed her mind on a goal.

A fog seemed to lift from her as she came to the realization, and dimly Pandora grew aware of an eerie, mournful song filling the air around her. It had all but drowned out the creeping and familiar whispers she battled every day—this new song sounded like wind over an open grave, like the crack of ice about to give way underfoot, like the sensation of a thousand sleepless nights made audible.

Lifting her head from the tenement stone, Pandora turned.

And found herself face-to-face with one of Valora's monsters.

Such creatures haunted the impoverished lower city in great abundance, though they grew scarce on the lofty summit of Palace Hill and in the farther reaches of Hesperid. They took manifold shapes, with some more common than others. The demon that hovered a mere six inches away from Pandora was a Fell—a wraithlike, shadowy being limned with blue spellfire, the only thing of substance about it a bone-white face. Merciless black eyes stared back at Pandora, and she met the monster's gaze without faltering, despite the numbing, disorienting song proceeding from a gaping mouth lined with fish-hook teeth.

The better to feast on her flesh and blood after the Fell had sung her to death, breeding despair until she could not bear to live and did the creature's dirty work herself.

"No thank you," Pandora murmured with a shake of her head.

The Fell floated backward a foot, confusion written across its unnatural face. After a moment, it seemed to decide. If this little morsel of a mage could not be moved by the usual song, something *un*usual was required. Opening its wicked mouth wider, the creature sounded a wild, vicious cry.

Ghost lights flickered into being several derelict buildings down, in the empty and disused woolen mill at the terminus of the alley. Three more Fells floated in the mill's shattered windows, framed by fangs of long-broken glass. They joined their singing to that of the creature before Pandora, and involuntarily she stumbled backward, coming up short against the tenement wall. The weight of the Fells' combined magic was crushing her—it would lead her to the grave. No, she would seek the grave herself, she thought dully. Surely death would be a release. From struggle, from deceit, from pain—

And once again, that proved the Fells' undoing. For Pandora's pain blazed into an inferno, until she was gasping with it, doubled over with the effort of keeping it in check. The whispers grew loud, a sibilant hiss to counter the Fells' song.

Come back to me, they called. *Come back to me.*

Curious again, the first and nearest of the Fells drifted closer, lowering itself until its haunting face swam before Pandora.

Are you mine? the creature asked in an icy voice, the words not audible, but manifesting in the troubled depths of Pandora's mind.

"No," Pandora said through waves of pain and a mist of scalding tears. "Not yours. Not ever. I am *no one's* now."

She voiced the declaration defiantly, aiming it not just at the Fell but at the whispers clouding her perception. At her core, something splintered, and Pan gave in. She let go of her iron grip on the agony writhing inside her. It tore from her as a javelin of blue spellfire, rendering the nearest Fell ash in an instant. Pandora's power only grew in force as it traveled, tearing up a great swath of cobblestones while it arrowed toward the remaining Fells and their lair.

The creatures had no time to flee. Shrill calls of panic died on their lips, drowned out by the sudden roar of collapsing masonry and shattering timbers. Pandora was not one for explosions—she didn't like debris flying outward, leaving a mess and causing unintentional damage. Instead, she *pulled* the mill inward, folding it in on itself like a collapsing house of cards. In the span of two breaths, all that remained of the deathtrap set by the Fells was a stretch of ruined cobblestones, a heap of settling rubble, and a shimmer of blue ash still hanging on the air.

At once Pandora's pain lessened and grew quiescent, retreating back inside to nestle at her core. It was her constant companion and a perpetual reminder of Pandora's deepest truth: that she burned with an impossible ocean of spellfire. She should never have been allowed to live. For Pandora had been born a mage like no other, and every year her power grew. She was near as much a monster as the Fells she'd destroyed—more so, perhaps, for while they could damage only one soul at a time, if Pandora was ever to lose control, she could make a crater of Valora, reducing the entire city to ash.

Come back, the whispers called mournfully one last time, before falling silent. *Come back to me.*

On instinct, Pandora stepped forward and picked through the rubble she'd created, searching for something. After a quarter of an hour of moving slowly and systematically through the ruins, at last she found what she'd been looking for.

A human hand stretching out from beneath the rocks, long dead already with the flesh gone cold and gray and the beds of the nails stained spellfire blue.

It was not only Fells that had used this place as a killing ground. They consumed their prey entirely, feasting on flesh and blood, but scorned anything already dead. This body, Pandora knew, had been hidden in the mill before the Fells polluted the place with their presence. She found such remains often—mages, drained of their spellfire and left where anyone other than Pan might assume they'd fallen victim to the vicious creatures that plagued Valora's streets.

Pandora knew better. She knew what it looked like when a fellow magic worker's spark had been fatally stripped from them, dragged out by a stronger and entirely human power. Not only did she know the look of it, Pan remembered the feel of it, like poison in her blood and slow rot in her bones.

Straightening, she let out a trembling breath. Her patron had been here. Not recently, but a week or two ago. And, like a moth to flame, Pandora was drawn unconsciously to places that bore signs of her patron's presence. Hard as she tried to quench the seductive whispers within her, much as she fought against the subtle pull to sites that hid her patron's victims, Pan could not fully escape. The binding she still bore was intact, only blocked, so that she could not be commanded or overpowered directly. But through indirect means, a mage greater than Pandora still played her like a fish on a line.

Time to make herself small once more, and delicate and harmless. Time to lie with her words, her actions, her very way of being. Because while tomorrow she would join the ranks of Hesperid's highest court, Pandora Small was no true Ingenue. She was the thorn among roses and the serpent in the grass, neither monster nor girl but something in between. She was Hesperid's greatest fear: a true mage, imbued with unchecked power and left to her own devices. Were it not for the fact that someone worse and stronger than her haunted the halls of Palace Hill, nothing would induce her to risk a sojourn there. The Queen's Guard was everywhere on the Hill, and Her Royal Highness, Maud Hera, sovereign of Hesperid, was no friend to mages.

But Pandora had been toyed with and tormented and halfway to free long enough. She wanted to taste life untainted by her patron's insidious influence, even when all she saw of it now was the aftermath. While the other Ingenues hunted for their patrons, Pandora would hunt for hers as well. And when she found them, she would not be bound and wed. One way or another, she would sever the tie between them, even if it meant doing the unthinkable and transgressing the second mage law to use her magic for murder.

Come back to me, the baleful influence within Pandora whispered again.

Soon, she thought grimly. *We'll meet again soon. And when we do, one of us will pay for this binding with their life.*

2

AN ORNAMENT TO HIS PROFESSION

For a panicked moment upon waking, Beacon thought he'd been ambushed by a spellfire creature. Hellions, the Queen's Guard and the church called the menagerie of ravenous magical beasts that plagued Valora's streets since the wellspring. Beacon's head was splitting and his stomach churning just as it did in a hellion's presence. But then it all came crashing back—the letter he'd received from home the night before, followed by an impromptu, ill-advised visit to the Guard barracks down in the lower city. He'd wanted to blow off steam, and the younger guards had been all too happy to oblige, toasting him raucously well into the early morning hours.

Still willing to hobnob with the riffraff, Beacon?

Not too high-and-mighty now you're posted to Palace Hill?

Beacon, who'd seldom drunk with the others while he'd been housed at the main barracks, raised pint after pint with them this time, trying to drown out what he'd read between the lines of his younger sister's note. Misery. Suffocation. Despair. By the time he left the barracks, he'd been well and truly off his head, stumbling back up to the royal compound on Palace Hill and his quarters there.

Even now he couldn't shake the thought of Everly as he'd last seen her a year ago—wan and frightened, unable to avoid the fate laid out for her. The day Everly was bound to Baron Rockford as a minor mage in his household was the day Beacon shook the dust of their village off his feet, setting out for Valora and a trainee's position in the Guard.

Sitting up and wincing as the pain in his head redoubled and his stomach turned over, Beacon pressed one hand to the scar in the left hollow of his throat. A whorl of slick, damaged skin that forever reminded him of his failure with Ev. Bindings between blood kin were difficult magework and generally frowned upon, but Beacon and Ev had been desperate enough to try. Though it was Everly's magic that must make the binding, Beacon always felt the failure was his fault in some way. If he'd been stronger, better, more devoted, surely Ev's spellfire would have cleaved to him. Surely he'd have been able to save her.

Crossing the tiny private room he'd been assigned upon arriving at Palace Hill, Beacon crumpled the letter with one hand and tossed it into the wastebasket. No time for brooding. He had another stultifying day on the Hill to get through. At least when he'd been a Guard trainee and a newly minted patrol member down on the city streets he'd felt *useful*. Like he was doing something worthwhile in tracking down and dispatching hellions. That, to Beacon's mind, was a worthwhile occupation. It was why he'd joined the Guard in the first place. While he could not agree with all of Queen Maud's reforms in the wake of the wellspring, in this, at least, he thought highly of her: that she'd immediately seen the threat hellions would pose to Valora's unsuspecting and unprotected populace. Accordingly, Maud had drastically expanded and retrained her personal guard, transforming them into a force fit to fight demons wrought of spellfire. Their second purpose, Beacon preferred not to think about, for it was the Queen's Guard that tracked down and prosecuted rogue mages. That was none of Beacon's business, however. He was a blunt instrument meant for one thing and one thing only—destroying hellions. Or rather, he had been until recently.

The transfer to Palace Hill, which came a few weeks back, had at first been a surprise and then an embarrassment. It hadn't taken Beacon long to realize that with the court social season approaching, he'd been posted to the Hill not because of his distinguished service to Valora's populace in the lower city, but because of his looks. He was tall and broad, easy on the eyes, and wore the uniform well. That, it seemed, was the sole requirement for many of the palace guards.

Time to put on a show, then.

After he spent a few moments upright, the throbbing in Beacon's head subsided a little. He did the necessary in the chamber pot and pushed it back under the bed with one foot, then set about shaving with the warm water that appeared on his washstand every morning. Palace Hill, although an unwelcome posting for him, did have its comforts. Looking creditable, even if he felt like death warmed over, Beacon pulled his uniform from the wardrobe and made himself smart.

Outside the confines of Beacon's small, spare room, second bell rang, reverberating through the palace and across its grounds. He'd have just enough time to visit the Guard commissary, kept separate from the palace kitchens, before reporting to his immediate superior for the day.

The commissary was never quite quiet or busy—an in-between place scattered with tables, it was always half-full of Guard members going on or off duty. At the counter, Beacon nodded to the stocky, gray-haired woman serving oatcakes and strips of bacon and cups of haxberry pudding.

"Something to eat?" she asked, and Beacon cringed inwardly. Absolutely not.

"Just kantha," he said. "One for myself and one for Captain Tanner."

"Bitter or sweet?"

"Bitter for me, half-sweet for the captain."

With two steaming waxed-paper cups in hand, Beacon made his way through back corridors, where servants bustled here and there on vital business, such as bringing the titled and moneyed palace residents their luxurious breakfasts in bed. At Captain Tanner's door he stopped, having to shift the cups about to free up one hand to knock.

"All right, Beacon, come in," the captain called.

Though little about the Palace Guard had impressed Beacon thus far, Captain Tanner certainly did. Her study was fiercely tidy, lined with bookshelves covered in volumes on protocol and magecraft, history and statesmanship. A neat, dark-haired woman with streaks of silver in her hair, her sandy skin and teardrop eyes were a testament to her family's roots in Hesperid's southern regions.

"You asked me to come for my assignment early this morning?" Beacon asked, setting one of the cups down on Captain Tanner's desk.

"Thank you for this," Captain Tanner said, taking the cup and sipping appreciatively. "You have the magesense, don't you, Beacon?"

"Just a little," he answered, flushing. "Nothing worth mentioning."

It always made him awkward to speak about it. Only a handful of people could sense the presence of magic—for most who could, it was detectable as visible auras or rills of sound or wafts of scent.

Everly was the sole person to whom Beacon had ever explained his magesense, because it seemed an oddity to him and made him uncomfortable. While others saw or heard or smelled manifestations of magic outside themselves, Beacon *felt* it. Magic for him was a matter of the nerves. Hellions, with their malevolent hunger, worked on him like headache or sickness. Everly's magic was the stir of a gentle breeze. Other mages were a sensation of damp or dizziness or sudden fatigue. There were dozens of ways for it to manifest, and all of them left Beacon on edge. Since joining the Guard, his discomfort with the acuteness and specific manifestation of his sense had only grown. He ought to have reported it upon first joining up, but they'd have made him a magefinder for certain if they'd known how well he could sense even a spark of latent spellfire. And that was the one role Beacon could never tolerate.

"A little will do," Captain Tanner said. "We have an influx of Ingenues arriving this morning, and not quite enough guards available to test their parlor magic. That will be your assignment for the first half of the day. Afterward you can return to your usual station."

"Test their magic?" Beacon asked with a frown. "I thought the girls have all been put through years of examinations. What is there to test?"

"It's accepted practice to test the extent of each Ingenue's power one last time before admitting them to the palace for the season. You know how careful we have to be. Every mage, from Ingenues to personal clerks and members of the palace mage corps, is thoroughly vetted, and never allowed on palace grounds without Guard approval."

The mage corps, primarily composed of weather workers, was a little overzealous in Beacon's private opinion. They were tasked with ensuring sun and clear skies on Palace Hill at all times save in the hour before dawn, when a gentle rain soaked the pleasure gardens and avenues. But Beacon, raised on the sweltering western banks of the swift-running Hesper River, found the Hill too cold for comfort, even at the height of summer.

"All it would take," Captain Tanner went on, with a warning in her tone, "is one rogue mage gaining access to this compound, and chaos would ensue. Imagine if something like that happened and the royal family ended up in harm's way. It's our job to stop such things before they happen."

"Understood," Beacon said. Reluctantly he added a loathsome suggestion. "But wouldn't a magefinder be better suited to the job?"

Captain Tanner raised an eyebrow. "We all know the ruthlessness that's required of magefinders. Valora's first families are adamantly opposed to their daughters coming into contact with that section of the Guard."

Beacon was hardly surprised. Many of the magic workers tracked down and punished by magefinders were little more than children. If you were not callous and uncaring upon becoming a magefinder, you either became so by necessity or washed out of the Guard entirely. The moment the extent of Beacon's magesense became known, he'd be given a choice: join the magefinders' ranks or be dishonorably discharged from the Guard. It was not quite the same fire-and-frying-pan dilemma of a forced binding or a steel box that mages faced, but it was Beacon's equivalent.

"What am I expected to do?" he asked.

Captain Tanner passed Beacon a page with the morning's brief on it. He scanned it quickly, the frown deepening on his face as he did so. Beacon couldn't help but envision his sister being subjected to this same test, meant to determine the exact limit of an Ingenue's power, and as he did so, his temper mounted.

"Is this fair to the girls?" Beacon asked, struggling to speak evenly. "You said we're to keep the royal family out of harm's way. What about the Ingenues? It seems like this is just shoving them into the path of potential harm."

"Which is why you're on hand," Captain Tanner reassured him. "You watch, see what the girl's response is, and the moment you're sure she's not possessed of more magic than she's letting on, you step in and play the hero. Don't tell me *that* doesn't at least appeal to you, Beacon."

His frown grew into a scowl. "Begging your pardon, ma'am, but it doesn't. Not if it means toying with someone else's safety."

Captain Tanner sat straighter in her chair, becoming severe. "What we're interested in is the safety of everyone on this hill—the entire governance of Hesperid occurs here. It's very rare for any of the girls to actually come to harm when we put them to the test, you know. In their own way, they've been as well trained as you have. They know their limits, know what's expected of them. And you, as a member of the Guard, should know when to intervene. Or do you think that's beyond you?"

"No," Beacon admitted reluctantly. "I just don't like it."

"Well," Captain Tanner told him, her voice stern. "I don't expect you to like your orders. I expect you to carry them out."

"Understood, ma'am," Beacon said, getting to his feet. "I will, as always, endeavor to be a credit to the Guard."

"The Guard, Ellis Beacon," Captain Tanner called after him as he left her office, "doesn't deserve you."

An hour later, Beacon stood in the sunshine on the long, looping gravel drive before the palace. The palace itself sprawled out behind him, an opulent compound of yellow stone and sparkling glass, surrounded by jade-green pleasure gardens and labyrinths, all spangled with glistening pools and fountains. The luxurious environment was, in places, scattered with incongruous earthworks and half-finished plantings, as well as incomplete wings of the palace surrounded by scaffolding. Prior to the wellspring, the royal family's residence had been a relatively modest hill fort. But the glut of spellfire suffusing Valora was good for more than just churning out monsters and rendering unsuspecting children mages. It had brought vast wealth to Hesperid, as it was harvested, stabilized, and sold off to countries with little to no spellfire of their own. The improvements to Palace Hill, now considered Hesperid's crown jewel, were a testament to the country's newfound riches.

Before Beacon, Palace Hill sloped downward to the remainder of Valora, the hillside of the upper city dotted with private residences of highly favored nobles and merchants who had occasion to visit the palace without fully joining life at court. Beyond that, at the base of the hill, the lower city sprawled out, a tangle of streets and districts stretching across river lowlands nearly to the horizon.

From up here, it was easy to imagine yourself set apart and untouched by whatever happened below. Beacon didn't like that. He didn't like the distance or the sense of looking down on what he considered the true Valora. But for now, he had other things to focus on. Carriages were visible on the road snaking up to the palace grounds—loaded with frilled and flowery Ingenues, no doubt, who would arrive at the palace and be sought out and bargained over like cuts of meat in the lower markets. The role of the Ingenues predated the wellspring and was an intoxicating blend of debutante and courtesan. Little wonder they'd been allowed to persist, the sole exception to Valora's draconian new mage laws. Even noble-born and wealthy boys were required to be bound by thirteen, though for them patronage also took the form of a political or mercantile alliance and apprenticeship. The potential for an early death due to the patronage bond was mitigated for them by a later, secondary binding to a suitable wife.

"Here they come," a taciturn and grizzled guardsman said, taking his place at Beacon's side. "Fortieth time I've seen those carriages arrive, and it never seems like anything but a lot of nonsense."

He held out a hand to Beacon, and Beacon shook it heartily.

"I'm Dawes," the man said. "You and I are to put some unlucky girl through her paces this morning."

Beacon glanced about and realized that the guards standing in wait had all paired off—it only made sense, to have two of them to confirm one another's perceptions of the girls, if the Guard meant to be so careful without relying on actual magefinders.

"Have you—have you ever had a girl injure herself?" Beacon asked, unable to shake the worry that had been nagging at him since arriving in Captain Tanner's office.

Dawes nodded. "Fifteen years back they sent me a pretty little thing, but she was nervous and spent too much of her power. Worked herself right into caster's fatigue. They keep vials of spellfire on hand for cases like that, though, and we sorted her out all right. And it wasn't one of mine, but three years ago, a girl from one of the lesser merchant families was found to have too much spellfire to qualify her as an Ingenue. Her school should've seen it, but it either went overlooked or they didn't much care. She was given a choice—a steel box, or be bound then and there to a patron of the Guard's selection. Not much of a decision to make, is it? The girl panicked and lost control of her spellfire. Killed two guards along with herself when she slipped her spark. Terrible day, that."

Beacon's temper, which had briefly subsided to a low ebb out in the sun and fine air, flared up again. But there was no time for more talk between the two of them. A row of carriages was pulling up the drive, twenty at least, with school insignias on the doors and a train of wagons winding around the back of the palace in their wake, laden with trunks and travel cases. All at once, the quiet morning erupted into chaos. Doors opened and girls spilled out, their bright laughter and breathless chatter ringing through the air. The drive became a dazzling garden of colors, each of the girls dressed in whatever they felt showed them to the best advantage. Several of them were already gleefully gossiping about the wellspring—Robert Wellesley, the mage who'd attempted to destroy the capital by opening the spring, had gone to his steel box refusing to give up its location. A rumor persisted in the lower city that it was somewhere beneath Palace Hill and that whoever found it and allowed Valora to better channel its vast magic would be greatly rewarded.

It all seemed so awfully tiresome to Beacon. So pointless. In a world where mages now died for lack of control over their own power, or were killed for wishing to remain free, and where hellions prowled the streets, what was the *use* of carrying on like this? What was the good of pretending life in Valora was glad and normal? If the wellspring hadn't been found yet, it never would be. All that was left was to learn how to live in a city suddenly rife with lethal magic and spellfire demons.

"All right," Dawes said at last. "Let's go find our girl. She's one of the Bellwether lot, over there, by the carriage with the rising phoenix on its side."

Beacon trailed in Dawes's wake, doing his best not to look too closely at any of the Ingenues or to seem anything but a professional, a piece of set dressing. Nevertheless, several of the girls put their arms around one another and giggled as he passed or whispered behind raised hands while their eyes followed him.

Not for you, he thought sullenly. *You're meant for finer folk.*

Dawes stopped before the phoenix-marked carriage and read off a name while Beacon stood with his gaze fixed stubbornly on the ground.

"Pandora Small."

A girl came forward slowly, a little shyly, Beacon thought. She was more simply dressed than the rest of the would-be Ingenues, in a tidy gown of ivory muslin trimmed with cottage lace. There was nothing exceptional about her—she was a small thing, pocket-sized really, at several inches below five feet, and her stature coupled with her drab brown curls and plain face put Beacon in mind of nothing so much as a field mouse. She would not be the prospect gentlemen vied for, he was certain. If she was lucky, this mouse before him would garner one respectable offer of patronage and marriage and have no choice but to accept. Life had not fixed her with a face or form that would allow her to choose.

"Miss Small," Dawes said politely. "I'm Dawes. This is Beacon. We have a few questions for you to answer before you're given the run of the palace. If you'll follow me?"

"Certainly," Pandora murmured.

With a long-suffering sigh, Beacon brought up the rear as she fell in behind Dawes. The test of her parlor magic would be a trial for this reserved, unextraordinary girl. Beacon only hoped she wasn't prone to swooning or weeping or fits of hysterics. Everly never had been, and he didn't know how to handle such feminine bursts of passion.

"Lucky you, Pan," a red-haired girl with a snub nose called after them as they started for the palace. "If someone served me your guard on a plate, I'd eat him right up!"

To Beacon's surprise, the mouse showed a flare of humor. Mincing a few steps forward, she linked arms with craggy, taciturn Dawes and glanced back coquettishly at the other girl.

"Oh, you're absolutely right, Winnie, he's a tempting dish if I ever saw one. Perhaps later I'll take a bite."

A gale of laughter rose from the red-haired girl and a few of her lingering peers. For his part, Beacon grew more sullen than ever. Palace Hill was a place of consumption—just as he and the rest of the Guard and the servants were commodities for the wealthy to use at their discretion, so too these foolish, gifted girls would find themselves bartered away, sold off and bound to the highest bidders.

But first, a test. To prove not their power, but their comparative powerlessness. Five paces ahead, the mouse let go of Dawes and shivered as they stepped into the shadow of the palace.

3

THINGS THAT BURN

The substance of the palace's parlor exams was a closely guarded secret. Though every Ingenue endured them, those who came out on the other side viewed keeping the secret as a badge of honor. Accordingly, Pandora had been able to ferret out very little information about them.

It is a test of the limits of your magic was all Miss Alice had been willing to say.

I couldn't begin to guess—no one in my family's ever made it to court before had been Winifred's response when Pan asked her about the exams.

Desperate, she'd even attempted to sound out Imogen on the subject. Gin had done nothing more than give Pandora a mocking look, which as good as said, *Wouldn't you like to know?* It wouldn't surprise Pan in the least if Imogen knew exactly what the parlor exams entailed. It would not surprise her either if Imogen had no idea whatsoever and was only needling Pan for fun.

She'd have done the same, were their positions reversed.

Either way, Pandora walked into a small, windowless stone room in the company of two uniformed guards and cursed her own ignorance. Pan did not like unknowns. She especially did not like facing them in the presence of two people who could have her confined to a steel box on the strength of a single word. Though a steel box alone was not enough to contain Pandora and her magic, breaking out of one would render her infamous and put her at odds with all of Hesperid. Pan knew that rather than confirm to all the world who she was—someone monstrous and unnatural—she would turn her magic in on herself if boxed. It would be a death sentence not by necessity, but by choice. A grim decision she'd made years ago and always held within herself.

"Am I not to have a chair?" she asked irritably as the younger of the guards gestured to her to stand against the wall opposite the little room's door. She hoped the inquiry came out as snobbish and disdainful—truly, it proceeded from an abundance of nerves. Standing did not do her any favors. It felt too much like being poised for action and riled her latent spellfire. The *last* thing she needed just now was to have her power agitated.

"I'm afraid not, though we won't keep you for long," the younger guard said apologetically, retreating to his own seat on one side of the door. His compatriot was seated on the other side, the two of them flanking the exit, and a horrible feeling of doom prickled down Pandora's spine. The two wooden chairs the guards occupied were the only furniture in the room.

"This is all very uncivil—I shall register a complaint as soon as I'm granted access to court," Pan said, directing her comment solely to the older guard this time. The younger of the pair didn't deserve to be spoken to—he was, as Winifred had so loudly pointed out, upsettingly beautiful. No more than a year or two older than Pan, but an easy foot and a half taller. Broad-shouldered, trim-waisted, and while the carefully tailored Guard uniforms elevated most of their wearers, somehow this ridiculous boy managed to improve the uniform with his presence. He was so clean-shaven his face looked like a delicacy—something cool and silky and sweet, like blancmange or an exquisitely blended iced kantha and cream. Pandora was flooded by a sudden and humiliating desire to put her mouth to the line of his jaw.

Gods above, she thought viciously. *Collect yourself, you stupid girl. He may not be a magefinder, but his entire job at the moment is to ensure you're barred from court and sent off to an agonizing death.*

"You may certainly complain if you like," the older guard, Dawes, said evenly. "It won't make any difference. Here on Palace Hill, we do things our own way. Now, my partner Beacon has some questions to ask you. Don't you, Beacon?"

"Yes." The younger guard removed a small, hand-sized dossier from the pouch on his belt. "Your full name?"

Beneath her filmy layers of underthings, Pandora began to sweat. Knots were growing inside her as her spellfire gathered force and began to twist and ache and burn.

"Pandora Small."

"Parentage?"

"Unknown." Miss Alice had hinted often over the years that Pandora might be highly born. If so, Pandora's life before the Bellwether School was more of a puzzle than ever—who, possessing both wealth and status, would ever surrender a child to the sort of patronage she had endured? Whoever Pandora's parents were, she was certain she never wanted to meet them. To her mind, they had failed her in every possible way.

"Fortune?"

"None."

Both the guards glanced up in surprise.

"I'm a scholarship student," Pandora explained. "My position and personal effects are paid for by an anonymous benefactor, who makes additional donations to the school annually in my name."

She knew what they'd immediately think. That she was a bastard. The illegitimate get of some noble here on Palace Hill. It was the conclusion everyone jumped to. The thing Miss Alice hinted at. In truth, Pandora had no idea who paid for her place at the Bellwether School and stubbornly refused to ask questions in that regard.

"Miss Small." Beacon seemed distracted. He kept glancing at the door, and one of his feet tapped a barely audible tattoo on the stone floor. "Are you currently bound to a patron?"

"No," Pandora lied blandly.

"Have you ever made use of your magic on another person?"

"No," she lied again.

Behind the closed door, a scraping, grinding noise was rising up, drawing closer by the moment. Both guards shifted in their chairs, and Pandora balled her hands into fists, hiding them in the folds of her skirts as she dug her nails into her palms.

Stay calm, stay focused, stay in control. No matter what, you cannot *lose control.*

"Have you ever intentionally misled anyone regarding the extent of the magic you possess?"

Pandora dragged her gaze up to the beautiful guard's, willing herself not to falter as spellfire roiled within her. The boy was inscrutable, damn him, as unreadable as one of the carved stone statues outside the palace, which depicted Hesperidian heroes of yesteryear.

"I've never lied about my magic," Pan said, as if she wasn't lying right now with her whole being, by keeping herself compressed and bottled up, folded inward a thousand times until no one could see the true extent of her.

The rough grinding noises were at the door now. Pandora's eyes flickered to it, and her spellfire surged so painfully, she let out a strangled gasp.

With a splintering crash, a Grim broke through the doorway, sending fragments of wood flying and filling the enclosed space with a bone-rattling growl and a stench of cold earth.

Grims were the dullest breed of hellion—low-slung, heavyset creatures with wide, gaping mouths and raking claws. If they put Pandora in mind of anything, it was perhaps a badger or a toad. This particular Grim was sizable, standing as tall as Pandora, and though the guards sprang to their feet and drew their pistols as the creature burst in, neither of them moved to intercept it.

Pandora stood facing the Grim alone. Its attention had fixed on her at once—a toothsome morsel, laid out for it like a tempting cake. Pan could feel the blood drain from her face, and her hands begin to shake as it stumped forward. Her spellfire was an inferno, the pain so great, she couldn't help the half-hysterical sobs that began to rise from her. The creature stopped within a foot of Pan, its broad mouth snapping and a film of spellfire dripping from its jaws.

"Don't," Pandora whispered desperately as a sound of flames filled her ears and blue sparks danced across her vision. "Don't, don't, don't, don't."

Come back, her patron's echo beckoned, twining itself through the roar of fire only Pandora could hear. *Let go. Rise in power. Come back to me.*

The Grim pressed its snout to her middle and took in a long draft of her scent. Everything in Pan revolted—she hated hellions with a passion to equal the force of the spellfire she contained. She wished every last one of them dead and in ashes, and even as she thought it, the spellfire in her gladdened and began to take shape.

A helpless sound escaped Pandora as she fought to keep her power in check. Whispers bounced from the walls and ceiling, until the room seemed full of them.

At least not a weapon, Pan thought at her spellfire as it seared through her, running like lightning in her veins. *At least be a ward.*

With a shrieking roar, the Grim rose up on its hind legs. It towered over Pandora, and she knew what would come next. How it would bear down on her, those wide, rending jaws aiming for her head. Behind it, she had the dim impression of a struggle between the guards, as the beautiful boy called Beacon started forward with a hoarse cry and his partner held him back.

Pan's magic reached a fever pitch. It sang through her until she was nothing but spellfire, a spark herself, a creature of flame, a raw ember of power.

Yes, the whispers sang in counterpoint. *Let it burn.*

With startling swiftness, the Grim lunged for her—

And met the impenetrable barrier of Pandora's ward. A gleaming shield of blue spellfire circled her, encasing Pan in a hemisphere of unbreachable power. For an instant, the Grim raged at its perimeter, but Pan couldn't let the ward stay. No proper Ingenue could cast a shield like that, able to foil hellions and even (for Pan had been tested on it a hundred times over the years) weapons of steel. With another wrenching sob, Pandora dragged her power back.

The ward fizzled and died, and horrific pain flooded her as the glut of spellfire she held returned to the fragile cage of her body. As she crumpled to the floor, Pan felt the Grim's claws rake her upper arm, rending delicate muslin and skin with the greatest of ease. But the pain of it did not even register, so consumed was she with the wretched burning of her spellfire and the whispers that now obscured all other noise. She could not let her power go—could not, but something must give, and so Pandora released the raw emotion trapped within her chest. She abandoned herself wholly to frantic sobbing and trembling, the apparent frailty of her exterior a perfect mask for the titanic battle occurring within, and which, inch by slow inch, Pandora was winning.

She was the master of her own spellfire and her mind. Potent and wild as her magic was, she'd never yet allowed it to best her and never would. Insidious as the whispers were, she refused to heed their siren call.

In the fraught instant after the Grim tore at her, Pandora was aware of a sudden presence inserting itself between her and the beast. The young guard, Beacon, had hurled himself forward the instant he was allowed, throwing himself bodily between Pan and the outraged hellion. Through a veil of tears she saw him close with the Grim, deftly avoiding its claws and teeth, shockingly light on his feet for someone so large. In seconds the boy had overthrown the beast, taking advantage of a distracted moment to drive his shoulder into its side and knock it from its feet. No sooner had it fallen than he descended on the creature, plunging the naked blade of his steel short sword into it over and over again, until the Grim burst into a fall of ash.

"Well," Dawes said, sucking on his teeth. "That's done, then."

Pandora choked on her sobs. Done? But had she passed the parlor exam, or would she be consigned to a steel box? Had either of them noticed the quality of her brief ward or heard or seen some scintillating note or vibrant color that testified to the true force of her magic?

"Unless you've any objections, Beacon," Dawes said, "I'll go give notice that Miss Small's to be granted access to court. Welcome to life as an Ingenue, Miss Small."

A wave of relief washed over Pandora, so great that it dulled the edges of her pain and calmed the last of her hysterics. She drew in a shuddering breath and dabbed at her face with a handkerchief, giving Dawes a watery smile.

"Thank you, sir. It's all I've ever wanted."

The gruff older man turned to Beacon, who'd cleaned and sheathed his sword and stood brushing ash from his uniform.

"Escort Miss Small to the infirmary, get yourself properly cleaned up, and report to your usual station."

Beacon nodded. Turning smartly on his heel, Dawes left.

Silence fell in the little room, broken only by an occasional sniffle from Pandora.

"Miss Small," Beacon said when she'd sufficiently collected herself. "May I be of assistance?"

Pan glanced up, only to find him standing over her, one hand outstretched. She still sat in a pathetic heap of muslin and tears and felt weak as water after battling so hard with her spellfire. Without a second thought, Pandora took the proffered hand and let herself be pulled to her feet.

Briefly she stood before the guard, her hand still in his, and searched his face. This close, she could see what she had not before—the faint spiraling scar in the left hollow of his throat. Pandora was taken aback. Though he was young for it, the boy had obviously attempted to become a patron only to have the binding fail. The mage had likely been family, then—such bindings were difficult to work, though when they took, they functioned with greater potency than most.

For a moment Pandora regarded Beacon, and he looked back at

her. Then his face tensed, and a shadow of pain crossed it. A wordless, discomfited sound escaped the guard, and Pandora glanced down in embarrassment as he withdrew his hand from her own.

But any embarrassment immediately gave way to icy panic. Where Pandora had touched him, Beacon's hand was seared, his palm flushed cherry red with violent blisters already rising from the burn.

Touch.

His magesense was touch, or something very like it—a rarity Pan had never encountered before. For all the years she'd fought valiantly to keep her rampant spellfire trapped within her, invisible and inaudible and undetectable, at last she'd been betrayed by her very skin.

4

SPECIAL REQUESTS

Beacon had felt everything.

Not just the heat of Pandora Small, but what lay beneath her surface—a swirling vortex of power and pain that left him dizzy in the aftermath of their touch. She was, according to Hesperid's laws, an abomination. The precise thing that the strictures governing mages were meant to snuff out. With power like that, the girl could make a crater of Palace Hill without thinking. She could take half the lower city with it as well, if she was quick and clever and bent herself on destruction.

And he had thought her a mouse.

He turned away immediately, ignoring the sharp burning of his hand and clearing his throat. Fear upended Beacon's stomach. He'd faced many a ravening hellion since joining the Guard, but never had he been in such danger. Alone. In uniform. And now party to this deadly girl's secret.

When the silence and tension in the room grew unbearable, he had no choice but to turn toward her again. She did not look dangerous. She looked small and frail and unspeakably tired, with her sad dark eyes and blood staining the ruined sleeve of her gown.

"I'm sorry," the girl said, her voice breaking on the words. "I didn't mean to."

Beacon was entirely at a loss. He didn't know what to do with her. Had she threatened him, his training would have taken effect. He'd have fought to his last gasp to get away, to sound a warning, to have her apprehended. An apology set him off balance, and if the Guard had taught Beacon one thing, it was that when confusion set in, you could do a good deal worse than following orders.

"Miss Small," he said stiffly. "I'll escort you to the infirmary, if you're ready."

Pandora took his proffered arm and cast a bewildered look up at him, but Beacon was stone-faced. He had no intention of meeting her eyes or allowing her to see the way she'd rattled him. Several times as he led the girl through the palace corridors, he felt her gaze on him but kept his attention fixed rigidly ahead.

How? How was she doing it? Even at such close proximity, he couldn't feel so much as a hint of her magic. He'd sensed a bit of it when she cast that ward—just a slight warming of the air, and it had puzzled him how someone with so little detectable spellfire could raise such a steadfast shield. But the magework hadn't lasted more than a moment, and then he'd been assured. She was what she claimed. A sparkling Ingenue, brought up to serve a husband and patron, possessed of manners and wit but no real power.

Now Beacon was entirely at sea. What *was* she? Not an Ingenue, though she'd spent five years preparing for the role. Not a mage like any he'd ever known. Not a threat, either, at least not in this moment, as she walked demurely at his side.

The open doorway to the infirmary loomed ahead, and Beacon ushered the girl in. Immediately a neatly clad nurse hurried over to them, clucking her tongue in sympathy.

"Oh, my lamb, whatever have they done to you? Ridiculous guards and their exams—every one of them ought to be subjected to the same thing. Stood up weaponless and anxious and made to face down a hellion in no more than lace and silk. But we'll have you sorted out in a heartbeat, don't you worry. By the time I'm through, there won't even be scars left to tell a story over."

Pandora seemed to shrink, melting into the nurse's motherly care. The heavyset, middle-aged woman was about to guide her away when Pandora stopped abruptly. Beacon stayed rooted to the spot as she turned, fixing him with another penitent look from her dark eyes.

Plain, he'd thought her at first glance. Unexceptional. What a fool he'd been.

"The guard who brought me in. Beacon," Pandora said softly. "He's injured his hand. I'm all right, but he needs to be back on duty. Can you see to him first?"

To Beacon's great discomfort, the nurse turned her fussy attention to him, surging forward and taking his hand in her own. She gasped at the sight of the burn, and Beacon, hardly a quick wit at the best of times, was surprised to find himself ready with a lie.

"Spilled kantha on it this morning," he muttered. "Just as I was taking it off the burner. But I didn't have time to get it tended before my duty shift began."

The nurse clucked again and began to chatter, voicing her disdain for the Guard in general and Beacon's superiors in particular. He sat silently as she covered his hand with salve and bandaged it neatly, giving him strict instructions as to how to tend the injury himself. All

STEEL & SPELLFIRE

the while, Pandora kept her eyes fixed on the floor. Beacon stole half a dozen glances at her over the nurse's shoulder, but she never looked his way. She'd retreated into herself entirely, any hint of her true character hidden as deeply as her spellfire.

"On your way, then," the nurse said, practically sweeping Beacon out of the door. "I've got to fix up our little lamb here, and you have plenty to keep you busy today, I've no doubt."

With a last look back at the silent Pandora, Beacon had no choice but to stride away, returning to his regular patrol with this new secret like a millstone around his neck.

The parlor exams had failed this year. A mage possessed of shocking and unfettered power had gained access to Palace Hill, and it was Beacon's fault.

To Beacon's great chagrin, he found himself assigned to all the most visible tasks the Queen's Guard undertook, intended as an ornament to the palace. For the afternoon, he patrolled the pleasure gardens while jubilant and effusive Ingenues explored the grounds. Several cast sly remarks his way; more cast sly glances. Beacon tried to ensure his bandaged hand remained in sight at all times, thinking the sign of weakness would put off this pack of exquisitely dressed jackals. Not so—in fact, three of the girls approached him in paroxysms of sympathy, offering the services of their families' personal physicians and inquiring as to the nature of his injury. Surely he'd been terribly brave and wounded in pitched battle with a hellion.

Burned it on kantha, Beacon answered flatly each time, as dull and insipid as he could possibly make himself. No doctor, thank you, he had the palace infirmary at his disposal. No, he most certainly did not need a fruit basket or a cage of songbirds or a puppy to cheer him up. He didn't care for fruit (he did, actually, but not under the circumstances), and animals were forbidden in the Guard quarters (besides which, he preferred cats). Yes, he'd be more careful in future. No, he didn't like kantha particularly (he did, once again, and drank far more of it than was good for him), so there was no use sending him an assortment of the finest brews made from roots grown in Hesperid's misty, humid south and dried on the central plains. Wasn't that the master of ceremonies, by the way, come to usher the young ladies indoors for an elegant tea?

Offered a temporary reprieve, Beacon retreated to the commissary to eat a solitary and early dinner. But the unwanted attention of the Ingenues had done one thing, at least—it had taken his mind off Pandora Small, who had not been present in the gardens. Left to his own devices, Beacon had nothing to do but brood, remembering the lightning-strike impression of the girl's power as his hand seared. The debilitating, momentary surge of pain that came with it. The look in her dark eyes as she'd apologized to him. For what, though? For the burn? For the unexpected revelation of her true nature? For making him a liar on her behalf?

Even if he wasn't lying with words, he was certainly doing so through oversight, just as he did by failing to disclose the true scope of his magesense. By rights, Beacon ought to have left the infirmary and gone straight to Captain Tanner, revealing what he knew about Pandora and leaving her to the judgment of the Guard. But he hadn't. It wasn't even a matter of protecting himself and keeping his own skill hidden. Though Everly was nothing like Pandora Small, he couldn't help comparing the two.

It was why Beacon couldn't bring himself to do what was necessary and report what he knew about Pandora Small. He'd already watched Everly face the impossible choice of a steel box or a forced binding, thanks to his own failings. Repeating history by subjecting an Ingenue to the same was more than he could stomach.

Clearing away his half-eaten dinner, Beacon moved to his next post.

There was a musical reception in the palace's sprawling conservatory that evening. The place was thick with palm fronds and redolent with the aroma of orange blossoms, magelights sparkling among the trees and spangling the glass overhead as a few closely watched members of the palace mage corps worked their subtle magic. Every one of them had their match—a patron in the Guard's scarlet and silver who permitted and grounded their magic. The conservatory doors had been thrown open to the gardens beyond, until it might have been difficult to tell where glass and magic ended, and sky and stars began. Might have been, because the magework being done indoors jangled at Beacon's sense, subjecting him alternately to chills and dizziness and gusts of unwarranted wind.

A Corinthian septet began to tune up their instruments, filling the air with a sweet, mournful sound. Beacon stood at his assigned place near a potted lemon tree, keeping careful watch over the proceedings. Nothing amiss. Nothing untoward to see. Just a ridiculous room full of ridiculous people, enjoying an evening so expensive, the cost of it could feed the rest of Valora's population for a week.

A rill of heady laughter drifted over to Beacon, and he glanced at the conservatory's main entrance. A gaggle of girls stood on the threshold, dressed in silks and glittering jewels, their chaperones standing indulgently by. At their center, arm in arm with the red-haired Ingenue who'd called to her on the palace drive, stood Pandora Small.

At first, she seemed just as Beacon had thought her that morning. Unimpressive. Mousy. A little dowdier than her peers, in ivory silk this time, rather than muslin. Her gown was plainly cut, trimmed only with tiny, embroidered forget-me-nots at the sleeves and neck and hem. She wore no jewels except for a thin chain bearing a silver evening-star pendant—Hesperid's national emblem. The girl's lusterless brown hair was bound up but unornamented, whereas the others had decorated themselves with feathers or flowers or gems. She looked like a country cousin, come to Valora to see the sights. Not like a pampered and petted Ingenue, trained to claw her way up the social ladder by her charms and smiles and gentle magic.

And yet. As Beacon watched the girls float into the room, taking in the sights with wide bright eyes and keeping up a constant flow of conversation, he realized Pandora *was* exceptional. She had a certain reserve about her—a way of holding herself slightly apart from her peers, even when she was in the midst of them. Her gaze as she observed the room was more guarded than theirs, sharper, warier, as if she was a wild creature stepping into an untested forest glade. And where the others chattered or minced or proffered elegant, wordless smiles, Pandora, it seemed, had no interest in performing. She radiated an unusual confidence—here she was, small, tidy, and unremarkable, but she would not change herself. You must take her as she came.

Beacon swallowed and tore his eyes from Pandora. The royal family was sweeping through the door now, and the music would begin the moment they were seated. Queen Maud walked at their head—an ordinary-looking woman of medium height, who would have been indistinguishable from any other palace matron were it not for the diadem of sapphires and diamonds she wore. The prince consort steered the queen through the gathered crowd, as he was rumored to direct her in all things. Publicly, Maud was called the savior of Hesperid and credited with the preservation of the country thanks to the mage laws that had prevented a plague of undisciplined magic workers. Privately, most believed the mage laws had been the prince consort's work.

Behind his parents followed the royal couple's only child—Theo, heir to the throne, no older than Beacon but a wild-hearted libertine, according to everything he'd heard. They moved steadily to the front of the conservatory, bypassing little knots of staring Ingenues and bored courtiers and rows of nobility who'd already been assigned seats. Only Theo stopped once, to greet a particularly lovely Ingenue near Pandora. Beacon overheard a scrap of their conversation, though he remained stoic.

"Imogen," Prince Theo said in a mocking voice as he bowed over the golden-haired girl's hand, brushing it with a kiss. "Come to torment me as promised, I see."

The golden Ingenue raised one eyebrow, a perfectly studied gesture of refined amusement. "Do I torment you, sir? It's certainly never been my intent to cause you pain."

"Oh come off it, Gin," Theo said, suddenly growing familiar. "You know damn well—"

The septet's discordant sounds swelled, drowning out their words. After a moment, Theo rejoined the royal party, which swept onward to the head of the room. Tonight, the seating arrangements were based on precedence. The royal family occupied spaces closest to the musicians, with the highest-ranking members of court behind them, trailing all the way back to the farthest third of the conservatory, where the Ingenues and their chaperones were seated. It was a pointed reminder to the girls—whoever their families were, they had not ensured their own places yet. Who they became, and what degree of respect or fortune they earned, depended on them. If they wished to rise, they must be matched well, for a failed Ingenue was never welcomed at court again.

Queen Maud stopped at the conservatory's front to speak with several courtiers, and Beacon's gaze strayed instinctively back to the group of Ingenues he'd seen Pandora with. She was no longer there. Frowning, he scanned the room quickly, his pulse rising as he found no sign of her. Curse the girl, she was so small she could be anywhere, hidden by the more ostentatious crowds. She could have left entirely and been prowling the palace corridors unattended. She could—

A glimpse of ivory. Beacon watched, and the course Pandora was bent on did nothing to still his nerves. She was walking, slowly and carefully, to the front of the conservatory. Moving among the nobles whose places she had no right to bypass. With a slight smile on her face, she made her way, and Beacon's heart beat like a forge hammer as he felt the air in the conservatory warm by a degree. Was it only his worry causing him to sweat, or was the wretched girl planning something? Was what he sensed her prodigious power building, ready to blow them all to pieces at the behest of some disgruntled foreign principality or irate shunned lord? Starting forward, he began to push his way through the froth of waiting finery, no one permitted to claim their seats until the royal family had done so. For a moment, he lost sight of Pandora and swore beneath his breath.

Where was she? What had he done?

"Captain Tanner," Beacon called as quietly as he could while still ensuring he claimed her attention. His superior was on duty herself this evening, never one to trust the safety of Hesperid's ruling family to others when she might oversee it personally. Hearing him, Captain Tanner left her post at once and hurried to his side.

"Beacon," she said tersely. "What's gone wrong? Should we clear the room?"

A "yes" waited on his tongue. But the moment he spoke, Pandora's fate would be sealed. He'd have to report on what had roused his suspicions, and while he could lie by omission, Beacon was far from skilled at direct falsehood. Captain Tanner would see through him in a moment if he tried to obfuscate.

Where was she, where *was* she?

A gap formed in the crowds, and Beacon went faint with relief. At the front of the conservatory, Pandora stood with the septet, speaking animatedly to them as the flautist nodded and smiled.

A request.

She'd been making a request of the musicians.

A little gauche and presumptuous to be sure, when the music set would have been planned out weeks ago. But nothing dangerous. Nothing like what he'd feared.

"I'm sorry, Captain," Beacon said, straightening. "I thought I saw something, but I was wrong."

Reaching up, Captain Tanner placed a reassuring hand on his shoulder. "Don't apologize. I'd far rather have you act on false suspicion than keep quiet from doubt, only to have disaster follow. You did the right thing."

Beacon fought back a wince. Had he done the right thing, even once that day? He was far, far from certain.

That night, after the music and his duty shift had ended, Beacon was eaten up by worry. As much as he hated the idea of Pandora loose on Palace Hill, and himself solely responsible for her presence there, neither could he bring himself to turn her in. He was caught between public duty and private principles. Out of uniform, Beacon paced the confines of his small stone room. A growl of frustration escaped him as his burned hand twinged, a visceral reminder of all he'd sensed in Pandora. He could not shake the way he'd felt during that brief moment of contact, or the fear that had risen in him when he thought she might be moving with ill intent.

He needed an outlet. And late as it was, Palace Hill offered none. Beacon only ever felt truly calm, truly centered, truly at peace, when he had a hellion at the end of his steel-loaded pistol or beneath his short sword blade. Never minding the civilian clothes he wore, he buckled his weapons belt back on decisively and made for the door.

"Oh," a gentle voice said as Beacon swung the door open abruptly. "I'm so sorry, I was just about to knock."

There she stood. Pandora's ivory gown was wrinkled from wear now, and somehow amid his panic in the conservatory, Beacon had failed to notice the bandage on her left arm. They were a matched set, him with his hand, her with her arm. She held a small brown-paper parcel and flushed as Beacon gazed sternly down at her.

"I wanted to bring you something," she said, and offered the little parcel. "It's salve, for your burn. I'm sure the palace infirmary's marvelous, but there's a chemist down in the city I've always bought things like this from. I had one of the servants go—they wouldn't let me leave on my own."

Beacon took the packet and said nothing. He'd learned years ago that silence, joined with his height and unreadable face, was often his best defense.

"I'm awfully sorry about what happened this morning," Pandora went on, biting at her lower lip and looking contrite. "I've never . . . I've never hurt anyone like that before. I'd have been far more careful if I'd known. And look—I'm being careful now."

Softly she brushed her fingertips to the back of Beacon's unbandaged hand. Heat seared through him, though it had nothing to do with Pandora's spellfire. In fact, he could feel hardly any of her power—only the faintest possible hint of warmth. And he found it maddening, knowing who she was yet not being able to sense the full breadth of her.

"I'm sorry too," Beacon said gruffly. "I should never have let Dawes hold me back, and allowed that Grim to get so close. It was stupid of me—if you'd been anyone else, the beast could have killed you."

He spoke the words unthinkingly, and Pandora's gaze shot up to meet his, her lips parting in a muted gesture of surprise. It was the first time he'd acknowledged what he'd sensed—the deadly secret that she knew he was party to.

"Why don't we call things even between us?" Beacon said. "First blood drawn by both and so awarded to neither."

"Are we sparring, then?" Pandora asked with a lift of one eyebrow. She glanced down the empty corridor cautiously, and Beacon knew what a risk she was taking in being there with him. Though the Ingenues might giggle and flirt, none of them would dally with him in seriousness. To be caught in company with a lowly guard would ruin them for a nobler patron and result in expulsion from Palace Hill, along with the forced binding that was required.

Although there'd be no forced binding for Pandora if she was caught. Her power was far too great for simple patronage. Only death behind steel would suffice.

The idea of her with a patron was a heady one, though. For an incandescent moment Beacon imagined what it would be like to hold Pandora's binding himself—to feel her magnificent power always and be the anchor that balanced and steadied it. He shook the thought off with an inward effort. Not for him, he reminded himself. None of them were for the likes of him. But *especially* not her.

"We're not sparring," Beacon said, a rebuff in his tone. "Not yet, at any rate. I don't close with an opponent until I've taken a full measure of them. And I haven't managed that with you."

"Is there any way I might help hurry the process?" Pandora asked in her low voice, looking up at him through silken lashes. "Only I do love a challenge."

Beacon fought back a groan. He should not be standing here. He should not be speaking to her. He should not be entertaining her company or granting her access to Palace Hill through his sins of omission. He should right this whole day of wrongs, letting his word be the thing that consigns her to a steel tomb. Duty should supersede principle, at least in regard to Pandora Small.

Instead, Beacon reached up and gripped the door frame, ducking an inch or two to breathe in her sweet lily of the valley scent, hoping desperately for a stronger suggestion of her power as well. But she was parsimonious with it, this little minx of a mage, keeping it locked away in some fathomless internal vault. Beacon wanted it—he'd been denying the truth all day, but here it was; he ached to feel the true extent of her again. Because in that one fraught moment when they'd clasped hands, before she'd realized he knew her fully and before he understood that her touch could burn, he hadn't been afraid. He hadn't been ridden by doubt or plagued by suspicion.

All he'd felt when joined to Pandora's power was ecstasy.

"There is one way you might help," Beacon said, hating himself for his weakness even as he spoke the words. "You could come with me to the lower city. You could show me what you can do."

5

A DANCE OF SPARKS

Pandora did not know what to make of the company she was keeping. The Queen's Guard represented everything she feared. Power meant to govern and subjugate her own. Enforcement of the mage laws. The specter of a brutal death by her own power, cowering in a steel box and making an end of herself to spare Hesperid the full knowledge of who she was and what she could do. Even now, having become an Ingenue by Beacon's forbearance alone, she found herself mistrusting him as they walked through the midnight streets together.

Pan was wearing her concert gown still, carrying the drab green cloak she'd swathed herself in to pass for a serving girl when Beacon smuggled her off Palace Hill. They'd used a small, rusted back gate watched over by a single sleepy guard, who hadn't given a second look to a member of his fraternity slinking off into the night with a servant. Being in her gown rather than the clothes she disguised herself in on the streets made Pandora feel awkward and conspicuous.

Being beside Beacon, who garnered appreciative sidelong glances even out of uniform, added annoyance to her discomfort.

"Where are we going?" Pan asked irritably as Beacon strode through the market district. They were still in the safer, affluent areas of Valora, around the base of Palace Hill. Every confluence of streets had its Guard outpost, occupied by two or more guards, and while the shops were closed, here and there clubs and cafés remained open until dawn, their windows and doors thrown wide to spill out light and music and laughter.

Beacon seemed oblivious to the fact that Pandora was forced to take two steps to every one of his, and that she was breathless with the effort of keeping up. Gathering her skirts, Pan gritted her teeth and broke from a hurried walk into a reluctant trot. Miss Elvira would be furious if she saw one of her protégés all but running through the streets.

"We're headed to the Fuller's Quarter," Beacon said. "We might as well make ourselves of use and find some hellions. I normally hunt down a few on my off hours, and it's the only way for you to show me that spellfire of yours safely. You need something to aim it at."

Though his words sent a prickle of warm anticipation up and down Pandora's spine, they did nothing to allay her underlying suspicion, or her annoyance over the pace he was setting. Slowing to a reasonable walking speed, she let him march on ahead, his every step brisk, measured, and businesslike. After a minute, she saw the guard cast about himself and find her missing. From a hundred yards back, Pandora gave him a long-suffering look.

Beacon returned to her and at least appeared apologetic.

"I'm sorry," he offered. "Was I going too fast for you?"

"Too fast for any normal person," Pandora groused. "It's hardly my fault you're some sort of giant."

Beacon raised an eyebrow. "Well now, that's an instance of pots and kettles. When I first saw you, I thought you looked like nothing so much as a mouse."

"A *mouse*?" Pan could feel her overactive spellfire stirring within her, looking for any excuse to seek egress. "I beg your pardon! I'll show you just how much of a mouse I am once we find ourselves a hellion."

"Good." Beacon grinned suddenly, unbothered by Pandora's temper. "I'm looking forward to it."

Again, confusion. He was eager to see the very thing anyone else in Hesperid would believe made her monstrous. As the shadowy, temptingly stocked windows of the merchants' district faded into seedier watering holes and houses of ill repute, Pandora began to wonder if there was something not entirely right about the guard walking conscientiously at her side.

"So, you make a habit of hunting hellions, do you?" she asked, trying to get a measure of him. All Ingenues learned that a wealth of information could be gleaned about anyone through seemingly polite small talk—the art of extracting personal details was, in fact, part of their education. They could, too, perform an intricate piece of parlor magic that allowed them to ascertain truth or deceit in what they were being told. Outside of classes, Pandora had never bothered with it before. It felt, to her, like cheating, and very much like a contravention of the second mage law.

In practice, a great deal of what Ingenues did toed the line of transgressing the second mage law. But given who they were, their long history at court, and the supposed limits to their power, both society and the Guard overlooked it all. Pandora's well-bred, well-trained, and well-dressed peers were, in many ways, Hesperid's lingering great exception.

Beacon gave Pandora a searching, sidelong glance. "Before I was posted to Palace Hill, I patrolled the streets down here in the city, tracking and dispatching hellions. I found that work rewarding. Safeguarding the people of Valora is why I joined the Guard in the first place. Not to stand about being decorative in the palace."

Pandora smiled in amusement at the frustration that colored his words. The boy clearly had little liking for his present role. Interesting. Interesting indeed.

"How awful for you," she said with exaggerated pity, keen to put him off balance. "Here I've spent five years earning the right to stand about being decorative in the palace, and you'd rather do anything else."

"I—I meant no offense," Beacon stammered. "It's only that—"

"Don't dig your hole any deeper," Pandora said, but her amused smile never slipped. "As a matter of fact, I spend my nights hunting hellions too. Some of them, at least."

"You do?" Disbelief wrote itself across Beacon's face as he glanced down at her again, taking in her demure gown, her smallness, her carefully dressed hair. "Well that's . . . unexpected."

Pandora nodded her assent. "I'm sure it is. However, it does often take time to find the beasts I'm looking for. I haven't got the magesense to guide me, after all. It'll make a pleasant change, having you lead the way to what we're after."

Beacon went red, shy as a schoolgirl about his magesense, and Pandora swallowed a laugh. Though many Hesperidians considered anything related to spellfire—either magic or the magesense—to be an intensely private subject, Ingenues did not have that luxury. Modesty about one's magecraft was decidedly *not* an Ingenue's virtue.

They were well and truly into the derelict Fuller's Quarter now, surrounded by sparsely inhabited tenements and abandoned mills and

STEEL & SPELLFIRE

factories. In the years since the wellspring opened, many people had fled Valora, which had become the most dangerous place in Hesperid. Others doggedly remained in the city, clinging to a belief that just as suddenly as the monsters stalking their streets had appeared, they might disappear again. For those who stayed in the run-down and poorly patrolled lower city, *anywhere but here* had become a grim, tongue-in-cheek motto. Anywhere but here was safer. Anywhere but here was wiser. Yet for many of those who'd been born and raised in Valora, they'd rather die than end up anywhere but here.

Halfway down a twisting lane that smelled of boiled cabbage and old rubbish, Beacon stopped abruptly and pressed two fingers to his temple with a grimace.

"There's something that way," he said, gesturing to a nearby crossroads. "More than one something, I should think. Two or three, but no more than that."

"Can you tell what they are?" Pandora asked curiously.

"No." Discomfort strained his voice. "Only a guess as to numbers."

"How do they feel?" Pandora pressed. "I know your magesense is touch."

"Touch sometimes, but more than that. It's nerves—things you feel with the body. You're heat, obviously. And hellions are a sick headache. Bit of a disadvantage when you're fighting them, but I've always muddled through."

Pan wrinkled her nose sympathetically. "How unpleasant. I'm sorry."

Beacon shrugged. "There's no changing it. Shall we?"

In answer, Pandora stepped lightly forward, down the alley to which he'd pointed. It terminated in an unexpectedly familiar place—the open, cobble-strewn square crowned with the ruins of the mill where Pan had extinguished a coven of Fells only the night before. But the location made good sense. In places where spellfire accumulated abundantly enough to generate hellions, it often bred them regularly. The flow of power through Valora could not be stopped, and the only way to deal with the monsters it created was to put them down systematically, as they came into being. As such, Pan had a habit of going back to places where she'd found hellions before, to ensure new ones had not risen since she last played angel of death.

In the damaged square, Beacon grew paler, and sweat stood out on his forehead. Pandora frowned up at him. "Is it really so bad, the way they work on you?"

"There's an easy cure," Beacon answered, neatly sidestepping the question. "I'll be back to rights once they're safely turned to ash."

Renewed suspicion bit at Pandora, sharp and caustic as her nascent spellfire. Perhaps she ought to use her power to sift Beacon's words for truth, after all. She glanced around the square, searching for a glint of silver buckles or the hint of a crimson uniform. The boy at least looked benign, in trousers and braces, waistcoat and shirtsleeves. Whether he truly was remained to be seen.

"This isn't all a ruse, is it?" Pan asked bluntly. "A ploy to have me spend my spellfire, making it safer for the Guard to take me into custody? Because I'm not sure what your magesense can pick up, but obliterating a few hellions won't even take the edge off my power."

She said the last not as a boast, but as a statement of unfortunate and inconvenient fact. Beacon, whose eyes had gone wide at her suggestion of an ambush, gave an adamant shake of his head. "No. It would have been clever, catching you out like that, I'm sure, but I'm not . . . I've never been one for plans, or any sort of deception. I like rules. I like order. If I'm honest, I just like being told what to do."

He said it in a half-embarrassed, self-deprecating way that left

Pandora inclined to believe him. Accordingly, she gave him a quick nod and pulled something from one of her gown's capacious pockets. An aura of blue spellfire surrounded the object as Pan worked a piece of parlor magic so familiar it barely touched the pain at her center.

"Here," she said, holding the carved trinket out to Beacon. "Take this. And wind it up once I give you the word."

He stretched out his bandaged hand, a potent reminder to Pandora that she'd have to be careful with her magic in a new and complicated way. Before this moment, she'd always either hidden or tempered her spellfire in company and given violent private release to it. Now she'd need to spend it while safeguarding Beacon, ensuring she didn't scorch him with the force of her power. The sensible part of her said, *Turn back, don't do this, don't let him see any more of who you are.* It was madness to show him what she was capable of—he may have been inclined to shield her from the mage laws when he thought her only a slightly more gifted Ingenue, but if he saw the true breadth of her power, he'd never let her remain as she was. He'd set the Guard on her and count on sheer numbers to do what a steel box could not.

But if she did not humor this boy, there was every chance he'd turn her in anyway. Pandora was entirely dependent on his goodwill. And perversely, rather than finding the idea daunting, Pan found she relished the challenge. Hadn't she spent five years learning to charm and dazzle? To bewitch and enchant? To render potential patrons helpless before the sheer magical allure of her? An Ingenue was meant to seduce via her spellfire. Pan was faced with just that task now—even the stakes were no different. Succeed, or face mortal punishment.

Picking her way across the square, now an ankle-turning labyrinth of cobblestones that had buckled into potholes or veered up to form jagged teeth, Pandora headed for the remains of the mill, a lonely, gossamer figure against a backdrop of ruin. As she did so, she let the tight coil of spellfire unspool inside her. It thrummed restively, suffusing her limbs with a near intolerable, aching burn. However Beacon's magesense worked on him, it could not possibly be a match for the pain Pandora carried every moment of her life. Waking or sleeping, she fought her power, never able to give way for a moment lest she lose control.

Like an outer manifestation of her rising magic, a hideous trio materialized before her. Three Weres emerged from where they'd lain in wait, disguised in the shadows that draped the wreckage of the mill. They were bestial, vicious things, wolflike in form and bearlike in size, and among the cleverest of hellions, possessed of a feral cunning. Immediately the Weres began moving as a pack, one of them stalking slowly toward Pan, fixing her with its predatory, lambent eyes. Its companions moved off to each side, bent on flanking her.

"Turn the key on the box," Pandora called back to Beacon, who she'd left safely at the square's far end.

"Three Weres is a lot to handle," he said, uncertainty in his voice. "We'd have a dozen guards to deal with an infestation like this. Are you sure—"

"Turn the key," Pandora repeated as the largest, dominant Were snarled, its jaws dripping spellfire that pooled in electric-blue patches on the cobbles.

From behind her, amplified by magic, the strains of a waltz began.

The little treasure she'd handed to Beacon was no tinker's music box, a tinny thing that could plink and plank a simple melody. Winifred had given it to Pandora on her sixteenth birthday, and it was fine craftsmanship, with the strains of a full orchestra captured on the inner ceramic disc. The sound wasn't perfect—it still crackled and grew a bit hollow in places, but it was as good as you could get, short of dragging a string quartet to the Fuller's Quarter with you. Sweet, mellow strings rang out, playing the opening notes of "Golden Apples, Golden Fleece."

With an inviting smile, Pandora dropped a curtsy to the oncoming Weres. Perhaps modesty was not an Ingenue virtue, but they'd elevated vanity to one in its place. Even without trusting the guard waiting and watching her, Pan could still do what an Ingenue did best—mask the brutality of the magic she carried behind a gleaming veneer of elegance.

For once Pandora was in her element, rather than fighting against it.

The first of the Weres sprang at her head-on and was met with a kaleidoscope of dazzling colors as Pan's magic flashed, a sudden barrier of power between them. A glinting hail of brilliant sparks fell, cast off by the Were's collision, and she was already spinning, dropping a rain of flowers on the leftmost Were, which tangled in its fur and sent out vines fast as quicksilver, trapping the creature in a net of spellfire. Pan's feet moved to the steps of the Golden Waltz, back and forth, as practiced in the art of dance as the rest of her was in the discipline of magecraft. The third Were let out a spine-tingling sound, something between a growl and scream, and made for the far side of the square, where it had scented Beacon. But Pandora was too fast. Turning on her heel and dipping into the waltz's lower form, she sent out the makings of an iron-solid ward, directing it with her outstretched hands. It settled around Beacon with a faint sizzle and puff of smoke, and Pan caught a glimpse of his shocked expression. She knew what he felt—knew what she'd put into that ward. Not only an impenetrable protection against the oncoming Were but a cessation of the pain the hellions' presence bred in him. A barrier to the scorching heat of Pan's own spellfire. A waft of lily of the valley. A frisson of pleasure, added to beguile.

It was parlor magic, subtle, refined, and lovely. It was unbound magic, wild, raw, and untamed. It was Pandora's magic—a potent, intoxicating blend of the two, the one tempered by the other, both bred and brought forth from a place of constant pain and self-denial, alchemized into something that could entrance or kill as she desired.

A rill of flutes from the music box. Pandora slipped neatly aside as the first and fiercest of the Weres broke through her barrier, rabid with fury. Her spellfire was a torch set to her insides, an agony and a joy, the best and the abject worst of her. She was dying for surfeit of it; it would tear her apart any moment now.

Without faltering, Pan turned the quick-footed, flirtatious forward-and-retreat motions of the Golden Waltz's middle steps. The Were mirrored her every move, snarling its hatred, bent on destruction, hungry for her blood and the rampant life it sensed within her. It crouched, ready to spring and devour, and Pandora took hold of her spellfire. With all the prodigious control she'd honed throughout the years, she seized its wildness and shaped it into a piece of magework. A deceptive thing, a little thing, seemingly harmless but seething with latent power to destroy. Pressing her fingers to her lips, she blew the scrap of magecraft to the Were as a kiss.

It glittered on the air between them, first a mote of light, then an incandescent butterfly, then a golden dove, then a mere mote again. It drifted to the Were and settled upon the beast's blunt, vicious nose. For a moment, the instruments stilled. Utter silence fell in the abandoned square. Then, a triumphant swell of strings. A flash of killing magic, as the mote burst into devouring flames of spellfire and the Were burned away in an instant, reduced to blue ash.

Next came the most technically challenging segment of the Golden Waltz—the latter steps, a complex set of figures and feints and dips. Pandora released her hold on the second Were's prison of glowing vines, and it shook itself free, scattering petals in every direction. It lunged at Pan, and she feinted as the dance required, the oncoming Were as fit a partner as any she'd taken to the floor with. She led the beast on a merry dance, checking it with tripping vines or glowing blue shackles when its onslaught threatened to mar the perfection of her steps. At last, when the creature was frothing with unvented rage and the grueling tempo of the latter steps began to slow, Pandora allowed the vines she'd wrought to trap the creature once more. Swift as serpents, they ran up its limbs, growing barbs and plunging under the Were's shadow-and-spellfire skin. The beast let out a tortured howl, and its pelt roiled as Pan's vines took over, engulfing its inner workings and finally bursting from its eyes, its ears, its mouth, its nose. A profusion of blossoms unfurled and fell to the ground as the creature they'd grown from disintegrated into ash.

Across the square, where Beacon waited, the music box fell silent. But there was still one more Were to deal with, and the Golden Waltz was not yet done. It was a peculiarity of the dance that the couples who carried it out completed the final steps in perfect silence, ghosting across the floor like spirits, or memories.

The last Were had not shifted its attention from Beacon and still stalked patiently along the boundary of Pandora's ward. She took hold of her power a final time, crafting it into a thin chain of blue spellfire, which drifted across the square to the waiting Were. Featherlight, her chain of magic looped around the creature's neck and drew it back to her, step by slow step. Unlike its companions, this beast came willingly, hackles smoothed back, jaw and eyes soft.

And unlike its companions, Pandora faltered before it. Perhaps it was the way the creature moved toward her, as if approaching one of its own monstrous kin. Perhaps it was the sight of herself reflected in the depths of its burning eyes. Perhaps it was only that she was worn out, still suffused with eager power that she must everlastingly push back. Whatever the case, she took a single wrong step backward, which was not a part of the magic or the dance. An upthrown cobblestone, mute victim to the last outburst of Pandora's power, caught at her heel. For a moment she hung suspended, floating between balance and chaos.

The Were's gentleness vanished in the blink of an eye. Pan heard its snarl as if from a great distance, while gravity bore her back and down. But all her energy, all her focus, was drawn inward, warring with the sudden surge of spellfire that roared up at her core. It was only human, to cling to life. To act in one's own defense. But no other human was able to react as Pandora could. The panic of a fall coupled with her fatigue had her control at its fraying edge. Rather than risk a killing outburst that might damage the boy waiting for her at the square's end, Pandora dragged her power back with everything in her, its unspent force splintering at her bones as she hit the cobblestones with a jolt.

The Were was on her, looming above, and Pan was beyond any capacity for precision. She could not risk letting slip a single spark of spellfire, for fear all the rest would follow. Instead, she wrapped herself around the fire and the pain and shut her eyes, waiting for the Were's teeth to meet in her throat, its claws to rend open her chest.

The earsplitting retort of a pistol shot rang through the square. Pandora's eyes flew open, and she found herself surrounded by a halo of falling ash. In another moment, she had mastered her spellfire entirely, forcing it down and down, not just beneath her skin but into her deepest, most secret parts.

Beacon appeared above her, where the Were had been. Without hesitation, he held out his hand just as he'd done that morning, seeming not to care if she burned him again. But Pandora had learned her lesson. Never again would she rely solely on the web of her skin as a barrier for the magic that raged within her. When she touched him, her fingers were cool.

Helping Pan to her feet, Beacon let go of her at once and turned aside to holster his pistol. It seemed to give him some trouble, and Pandora watched in puzzlement until she caught him swiping surreptitiously at his eyes with the back of one hand.

"Are you . . . are you *crying?*" she asked in utter disbelief. Self-loathing followed immediately. She'd meant to enthrall him, but of course her power was too monstrous to engender anything but revulsion. She hadn't thought it horrifying enough to reduce a strapping guardsman to tears, though.

"A little," Beacon said, owning to it without embarrassment. "Sometimes things take me like that. A sunset, or a piece of music, or a work of art."

For a moment, Pandora's jangling wits could not make sense of what he'd said. At last the fog lifted, and she gaped at him, forgetting all her pretty, hard-learned manners.

"You thought what I did was . . . beautiful? Killing Weres with spellfire? You thought it was so beautiful it made you *cry?*"

Truthfully, she hadn't held out much hope of succeeding in her efforts. Much as she'd tried to enchant with her power, Pandora knew the spellfire within her was too violent and forceful to ever pass for the far lesser, desirable magic she'd been taught.

Beacon shrugged, flushing beneath her scrutiny and disbelief. Gods above, if he was a sight in uniform, seeing him red-faced and bashful because of her made Pandora weak in the knees.

"None of us have really seen a mage reach their full potential since the wellspring opened up," Beacon said. "At first they died for want of control, and after that, their power was kept in check by bindings. I had no idea what you were capable of. And yes, I found it beautiful. Not the power, precisely. Not the spellfire. Hellions are spellfire, and they're nothing but ugly, ravening beasts. It's your control that moved me. The way you hold all that magic back, dole it out, keep it in check, shape it into something biddable. Even now"—he took a step closer to her, and Pandora swallowed back a sudden surge not of spellfire, but of butterflies' wings—"I can't feel a single hint of your heat. I'd never know you were a mage if I were only passing you by. It's remarkable."

"Remarkably difficult," Pan said drily. "I am exhausted all of the time. I can't let go, even in sleep."

"That," Beacon answered with sudden fervor, "is precisely what I find beautiful. It can't be anything but a torment, keeping so much magic bound up within you. Keeping everyone around you safe. Yet here you are. Here *I* am, standing before you, untouched."

Pandora let out an involuntary sigh, swaying slightly where she stood. No one had ever seen her so clearly before. Against her better judgment, she felt her suspicions begin to melt away.

"It has been very hard," Pan whispered, her dark eyes locked on Beacon's gray gaze.

When he reached out and took her chin in his hands, Pandora couldn't breathe. *You're a fool,* she berated herself internally. *You can't afford a complication or a distraction. You're meant to be bewitching him. He cannot get in the way.*

"Next time," Beacon said sternly, though his touch was soft, "you don't put me behind a ward. You don't make a hard life harder. You let me stand beside you and with you, and we face Hesperid's demons together."

"Next time?" Pan managed to ask, dropping her gaze to the

cobblestones because she could no longer bear the things her heart was doing.

"Tomorrow night."

"I've a ball tomorrow night."

"Afterward. Leave early and leave them wanting. Whatever gentlemen you're trying to entangle will think more of you if you're gone by midnight than if you dance till dawn."

Pandora pondered Beacon's words. He was right—gentlemen, she had been taught, relished the uncertainty of pursuit. Guards, she suspected, were no different.

"I'm not sure." Pan feigned a reluctance she did not feel. "This is such a risk to both of us. Tomorrow night is out of the question."

"The next night?"

Pandora looked up. She saw something in Beacon that frightened her—something she'd never expected to find. Not only had he witnessed a display of her power and potential, he was hungry for more of her. Not just of the charming, inconsequential self she presented to the world, but of her true nature. Her hidden fire. Beacon had seen her worst, and he'd liked what he had seen. Never in her most impassioned dreams had Pan imagined such a response to her secret.

Leave early and leave them wanting, was it?

"The next night is the queen's opera. I'm not sure when I'll be free again," Pan said, taking care to look a little crestfallen. As if the missed opportunity irked her, but she was a victim of circumstance. "What if you wait, and I'll come to you when I'm able?"

Beacon nodded eagerly, as if he'd wait till the foundations of the world crumbled. Pandora fell silent, her head and heart in a quandary as she allowed him to lead her out of the ruined square and back toward the palace. What she did not say, what she would not give voice to even for a moment, was how it had felt to have Beacon come between her and danger twice now. It was entirely alien to her, this sensation of being cared for and protected, whether she needed it or not.

It felt like safety. Warmth. Comfort. And Pandora would, she suspected, risk anything just to feel it again.

6

BEES!

Beacon knew himself to be a fool about a great many things.
He had no head for figures. He was no great speaker nor reader, either, and had twice been forced to repeat standards in the Townsend school. He'd been the largest, dullest, and most awkward student by far. The Guard was a reprieve from all that—here, he could shine, even if it was as a decorative object or a blunt instrument to be used against hellions.

But fool though he was in many ways, Beacon did not think he was playing the fool over Pandora Small by keeping her secrets. He *was* a decent judge of character, and he sensed something in her. Not necessarily honesty, but earnestness. A desire to be known, at war with years of enforced subterfuge. There was, too, the deeply distracting fact that every time he closed his eyes, he could still see the dazzle of her magic. Tendrils of power. Veils of light. Pandora dancing in the middle of it. She had been beautiful. She had been brutal. She had been perfect. Even now an occasional wash of remembered warmth flushed Beacon's skin, and he could all but smell lilies of the valley.

He pondered this in the commissary, over an enormous cup of bitter kantha and a still larger plate of eggs. In fact, Beacon was so preoccupied with what he'd seen that he failed to notice Captain Tanner approaching.

"Beacon. *Beacon*," Captain Tanner said from where she stood over him.

Beacon startled and shot to his feet, nearly upending his kantha in the process. He was embarrassed at having been caught unawares and guilty over what he'd been preoccupied with. A decent guard would turn Pandora in immediately. But Beacon couldn't shake the conviction that a decent *person* would shield her.

"Yes, ma'am," he said briskly. "I'm sorry, ma'am. Can I be of service?"

Captain Tanner sighed. "You can loosen up a little, Beacon, you aren't on duty at the moment. I don't own your time outside of scheduled hours. I only wanted to tell you that once again, you're not to report to your usual post this morning—the Guard chief has asked to see you, so you'll meet him on the parade grounds first thing."

Beacon frowned. The prince consort oversaw the Guard and, aside from taking a keen interest in magefinders, did so mostly as a figurehead. "Begging your pardon, ma'am, but what does a member of the royal family want with *me*?"

"I don't know," Captain Tanner said. "Frankly, I didn't ask. Are you concerned? You know you're permitted to have your direct superior present at a meeting of this sort. I can be there as well, if you prefer."

"I wouldn't want to put you out, ma'am," Beacon said, giving her a look of consternation. Captain Tanner only tilted her head to one side, staring thoughtfully up at him.

"Be that as it may," she replied after a moment, "I'll make a point of being there."

"You needn't—" Beacon began, but Captain Tanner cut him off with a raised hand.

"No. I needn't. But I will."

An hour later, Beacon stepped out into a brilliant flood of summer sunshine on the gravel parade ground before the soaring and ornate main entrance to the Guard wing. There was scaffolding and the sound of builders everywhere, as the Guard quarters were one of the palace's most ambitious expansions. The number of guards had swelled so dramatically following the wellspring, they needed accommodations for four times the number that had formerly been posted to the Hill. Beacon's compatriots were tucked into every spare corner of the palace at present—his own quarters had formerly been a broom closet. He ducked under platforms and sidestepped great mounds of masonry, making his way to the far end of the parade ground, where a small group of people stood waiting.

Beyond them, the Hill sloped downward, and a sullen bank of dark clouds brooded over the lower city, riven by occasional flashes of lightning. The flares of light were reflected in the numerous tributaries that snaked through the city to join the Hesper River, which cut through Valora's heart. It would be pouring down there on the riverbanks and breathlessly humid. But on the Hill, the mage corps had done their work. The air was temperate and stirred by a gentle breeze, and rain only fell to water the gardens while the palace's occupants were still abed.

"You must be Beacon," the prince consort said evenly as Beacon made his bow. "Your former captain in the lower city has told me a great deal about you."

Immediately Beacon grew wary. He much preferred to carry out his duties and go unnoticed, and the attention of the prince consort was far from desirable to him. As Beacon took in the prince consort's companions, his confusion only grew. With the consort were several mages, easily identifiable thanks both to their navy corps uniforms and the response of Beacon's magesense.

Shoving aside the jangling, discordant alerts from his sense, Beacon focused on the consort. He'd never been so close to a member of the royal family before. The consort was tall and slender, with graying dark hair that had begun to thin at the top. He bore himself with an air of quiet self-possession, as if he was accustomed to being the master of any situation he entered, and to unquestioning obedience. Beacon found that confidence privately off-putting, as all of Hesperid knew the degree to which the consort served as a puppet master, manipulating his mild queen. Maud had been merely a figurehead prior to the wellspring, and while she was publicly lauded as the creator of the mage laws, it was common knowledge that she'd only parroted her more forceful spouse's ideas.

Beyond the consort, his waiting mages stood in a huddled group, their latent power assaulting Beacon with dizziness, pins and needles, and a dry mouth all at once.

"Apologies," Captain Tanner said, hurrying across the gravel from parts unknown. "There was a mix-up with the garden exhibition patrols. May I ask what this is all about?"

The consort gestured to Beacon, his eyes sharp. "It's come to my attention that you failed to test the breadth of this guard's magesense before bringing him to the palace. Captain, you know the importance I place on protocol within this organization. Any skill brought about through spellfire is a resource to be used for the public good. We cannot afford to allow such gifts to go untapped."

Beacon's stomach dropped out of him. Though the consort never raised his voice, Beacon could see from Captain Tanner's posture that this was, to her, a severe dressing-down. The captain lowered her head and spoke no word in her own defense, instead capitulating at once. "Yes, sir. My mistake, sir. The boy's magesense is minor, so I didn't believe it necessary."

The end of the line, then. Beacon cursed his luck internally with all the viciousness he did not show, his face a stoic mask. He'd thought himself so clever, down in the city, failing to report the scope of his magesense and only ever letting it show when lives were on the line.

Not clever enough, and now he'd be forced to turn magefinder or leave the Guard in disgrace. Hellfire and damnation.

"Is that what he's told you?" the consort asked Captain Tanner. "That his ability is nothing to speak of? And you simply . . . believed him? Do you realize how often a mage or someone with the sense has attempted to use that excuse before? When it comes to spellfire, either the casting or the sensing of it, it is this government's policy to trust no one and leave no stone unturned. Are you aware that the boy has a reputation in the lower city for being particularly adept at tracking hellions? How could that be, unless his magesense is greater than he claims?"

"If I may speak, it's all exaggeration, sir," Beacon cut in with feigned assurance. "Hearsay. The ranks in the lower city are prone to talking in their cups. Stories down there grow far wilder than their origins in the span of a night or two."

The consort shot a scathing look at Beacon. "You may not speak, in fact. And I expect you to remain silent unless ordered otherwise."

Beacon fell quiet and seethed. He'd never been much of a respecter of titles or roles, unless they'd been earned, and his time on Palace Hill had only solidified that disdain for unmerited rank. Now he'd happily have knocked the consort's teeth in, if the man were only an ordinary guard calling both Captain Tanner's competence and Beacon's honesty into question.

You aren't honest, though, Beacon's perpetually guilt-ridden inner voice pointed out. *You lie about your magesense. You're shielding Pandora. Who knows what other treachery you might be capable of?*

"Go stand opposite the mages," the consort said with a dismissive wave of his hand. "Keep quiet until you've had enough, then you may tell us so."

The "us" put Beacon on alert. For the first time he took in the seemingly unassuming pair of guards standing on either side of the consort. They were quiet. Inconspicuous. Nearly invisible, they drew so little attention to themselves.

Of course. Magefinders, eager to swell their limited ranks. Just what Beacon was determined never to become. Inwardly, he let out a string of foul words. But there was nothing to be done. He crossed the parade ground and took up his place, a dozen feet or so distant from the group of waiting mages.

Being turned out of the Guard and returning home would be humiliating and troublesome, as there was little left for Beacon there. Becoming a magefinder, however, would be intolerable. At least he'd leave knowing he'd spared Pandora a steel box by keeping her secrets.

But as he thought the last, a realization struck him like a thunderbolt.

If the Guard learned he'd kept his magesense hidden by failing to report it, it was possible they'd question Beacon's judgment and truthfulness in other respects. They might declare the results of Pandora's parlor exam invalid and test her again, no doubt with genuine magefinders.

She'd slipped and shown her dazzling power to Beacon, who was not trained to ferret out and prosecute such things. How would she fare with guards whose entire role was the apprehension and execution of rogue mages such as herself?

The mere thought made Beacon sick. He would simply have to be impervious to whatever effects the coming demonstrations of magecraft worked on him. He would have to give no sign that his magesense registered them in any meaningful way, let alone troubled him. If it were only his own future at stake, he doubted he'd have the fortitude for what was coming. But for Pandora and her shining magic, which had moved him to tears with its wild elegance? He would make himself a stone.

The first member of the mage corps, elderly and grizzled, approached Beacon. The man could not possibly hold much power—most mages who'd reached adulthood before the wellspring were limited in their capabilities. It was the younger ones who were the greatest cause for concern, who'd still been growing in their bodies and their craft when spellfire flooded Hesperid in general and Valora in particular. Shutting his eyes, the old mage focused. Beacon felt a rush of power go out of the mage, manifesting in Beacon's body as thirst. He began to think longingly of cool water, of iced haxberry cordial, of cold kantha with cream. But he knew the source of that desire, and the thirst he felt was not even enough to make him clear his throat. After a few moments, the mage raised his head, and Beacon could feel from the sudden slackening of his thirst that this portion of the test had finished. The old man nodded to the consort and stepped aside.

"Hm." The consort sniffed. "Next."

A prickle of anxiety ran through Beacon as he saw the quiet magefinders, in tandem, retrieve odd metal devices from their uniform jackets. A set of steel ear cuffs. And a steel band to go around the eyes. Clearly they expected a great deal of discomfort.

Beacon's colorful internal dialogue grew more impassioned, but his resolve did too. Whatever was coming, he'd weather it without flinching for the sake of a mouselike Ingenue in ivory silk. He would not fail her as he'd failed Everly.

The next mage was a woman, a little younger than middle-aged. For whatever reason, a mage's talents seemed to manifest most strongly and frequently in women and girls, perhaps because they were more often in a physical state of flux than their male counterparts. Spellfire took advantage of any change or growth to root itself in and expand.

Sorry, the woman mouthed, pushing a strand of dark hair back from her face.

Vertigo assaulted Beacon at once, a violent sensation of dizziness and disorientation that he strenuously resisted. Dimly he was aware of the magefinders putting on their steel guards. For his part, Beacon stayed firmly at attention, his eyes fixed on the mage in front of him, taking slow breaths in and out to quell the nausea dizziness bred. He would not be sick. He would not falter. He would give the waiting magefinders and the consort no reason to doubt his claims to a poor and limited magesense.

His own future and Pandora's safety both depended on it.

At last, the dark-haired mage nodded and stepped away. Immediately the world righted itself, though Beacon's nausea did not entirely fade. Being around more than one or two hellions was similar—though the abominable headaches they bred lessened once they'd been put down, it took a day or so for an aftereffect of lingering discomfort to leave.

The only time Beacon had ever returned to himself completely and immediately after a hellion's destruction had been the previous night, in the presence of Pandora Small's magic. Her ward had wrapped around him, vivid with her presence, and driven out any vestige of other, hostile power.

The third and final mage took her place before Beacon. She was young, only a year or two older than he, and grinned at him wolfishly. Clearly there was no love lost between this woman and the Guard, despite her position in the mage corps. With a dull sense of resignation, Beacon braced himself.

At first, the stinging he felt was bearable, as if a pair of bees had got into his uniform. Unpleasant, but not maddening. However, the young mage's feral grin widened, and the feeling grew exponentially worse. Now it was the entire hive descending upon him, crawling and stinging under his clothes. Everything in Beacon screamed at him to move, to drop to the ground and roll, to tear indoors or across the lawns to throw himself into the nearest fountain. If Beacon hadn't known better, he'd have cast wildly about for the nest the creatures savaging him were emerging from. Instead, he remained rigidly at attention, falling back on the unassailable composure that so often served him well. He fixed his mind on one thing: the fact that it had been hell watching Everly bound. It would break Beacon to watch Pandora killed for her power.

So he stood and breathed, in and out, in and out, a solid rock for magic to shatter on. Invisible bees were covering and stinging every inch of his face. Any moment they'd be in his nose, his ears, attempting to crawl into his mouth and eyes.

At last, a sharp, strained voice cut across the parade ground.

"Eris. Enough."

It was a magefinder who'd spoken. With a last curl of her lip, the mage before Beacon withdrew her power and retreated to her companions. Beacon glanced over to the magefinders, and one of them was in a heap on the ground—even steel had not been an adequate check to his magesense.

Slowly Beacon stretched his hands. His entire body felt inflamed and inflexible, taut with swelling and poison, but when he looked down, the skin was unmarred. However other power manifested, only Pandora's had ever been great enough to leave a mark.

"Very well," the prince consort said in a dissatisfied tone. "I suppose your instincts were right, Captain. The boy's no magefinder, just another piece of grist for the Guard's mill."

Relief flooded Beacon. Careful to keep his steps measured and firm, he moved to Captain Tanner's side. The prince consort dismissed his cadre of mages with a word and stalked in through the ostentatious Guard's Entrance as the standing magefinder helped his companion to his feet and followed in the consort's wake.

"All right, Beacon?" Captain Tanner asked in a low voice, once they were alone in the summer sun.

Beacon cleared his throat and swallowed past a wave of nausea. It still felt as if he'd been attacked by a swarm of something venomous, albeit a day ago. He was feverish and sore, and doubted the discomfort would fade any time soon.

"All right, Captain," he said.

"I'd dismiss you for the rest of the day, but the consort is sure to notice if I do, and realize what that means," Captain Tanner told him, glancing up and fixing him with an inscrutable stare. Somehow she saw what the consort and his magefinders and mages could not, and yet no worry sparked in Beacon. Captain Tanner's interests did not lie with one set of Valora's populace over another, whether the divide rested between those of fortune and the poor, or those with magic and those without it. In his time on the Hill, Beacon had found her very fair, both in her opinions and her administration of the Guard.

Beacon began to nod in agreement and immediately thought better of it as his stomach churned and pain flared across his skin. "Thank you, Captain. I appreciate your understanding."

"Good. We'll say no more about it, then. You're on duty in the south gardens, where they're preparing for this afternoon's exhibition."

"Yes, Captain. Thank you again, Captain."

And Beacon limped off, feeling like death warmed over but also easier in himself than he'd been since joining the Guard. He would not be made a magefinder. Pandora's secret was still safe with him.

7

DREAMERS

Pandora could always tell when she dreamed of her patron and her childhood. There was no sense of confusion or disorientation as with most dreams, no blurring of the lines of reality and subconscious. Still, she knew. She knew when she dreamed, because in the world of sleep, she was terrified. Truthfully, it had not been like that. Throughout her younger years, Pan had often been exhausted and in pain, anxious and on edge. But she had not been afraid until the very end. Even then, it hadn't reached the pitch of terror. Because back then, Pandora had had nothing to lose. She'd known nothing besides her patron and the life they'd proscribed for her. Now she knew better. Now she stood to lose the world.

And in every dream of the past, Pandora was deathly afraid.

This time, the dream was of her nursery. For twelve years, she'd never left that single, spacious room. It had taken her years to realize that the walls behind the tapestries and the floor beneath the plush carpets were all steel, inches thick. The single door through which nursemaids and guards and her patron entered and exited was also steel. Even the chimney was a sham, blocked off with steel near the top. There was no need for smoke to escape from it—Pandora's patron kept flames of spellfire going on the hearth at all times, so that the nursery was an even and comfortable temperature. It was a shock to Pan, the first time she saw orange and red flames after escaping. She'd always been accustomed to blue.

In sleep, Pandora sat near the hearth, watching the blue flames. She was small, her feet tucked beneath her in the plush embrace of a wingback armchair. A book lay open on her lap, which was as much of the outside world as she was ever allowed. Many of the words were strange and meaningless. "Flower." "Tree." "Sky." "Mother." "Father." "Family."

Pan traced her favorite picture with one finger. It showed a man and a woman standing together outside a cottage, two towheaded children playing in the garden nearby. There was a creature gamboling about with them, which Pandora gathered from the story was something called a dog. Overhead, there was a stretch of blue, but nothing like the blue of spellfire. It looked serene, and fluffy white shapes moved across it. The whole image filled her with an odd sense of longing. What she loved most was the way the man and the woman looked at each other, with kindness in their eyes.

The steel door swung open behind her, heavy on its hinges. Boots sounded on the floor—her patron had brought a guard this time, as they occasionally did. Turning, Pandora took in the shapeless figure, obscured in black fabric from head to toe. Even in the dream, she knew this was wrong. She hadn't been afraid, but now her palms began to sweat, and her heart hammered in her chest.

"We're going to try something new," her patron announced without preamble. They always spoke so, assigning tasks bluntly, then leaving without another word after Pandora had succeeded or failed. "You've been working on wards for months now. Time to test their strength in earnest."

A black-gloved hand motioned to the guard standing by the door. He stepped forward with a dutiful nod. Broad shoulders. Strong jaw. Gray eyes. Pandora had only met him twice, but she'd already recognize Beacon anywhere.

"Shoot her," Pandora's patron ordered.

Pan watched uneasily as Beacon removed his pistol without hesitation, priming and loading it, then leveling the muzzle at her.

"But I—" she began to say, and a shot rang out.

Quick as a pistol ball could be, Pandora's magic was faster. She'd been shot at before—it was only her patron's words and Beacon's presence that had given her pause. Every time, her flawless wards had melted the lead balls as they passed through, rendering them harmless puddles of molten metal.

This time was different. Pan felt something tear through her shield and almost in the same instant, tear through her flesh, as well. She crumpled to the floor, blood spurting from her shoulder and pain exploding across her senses. She'd known many hurts by this point, and the constant dull ache of too much spellfire, but this was worse. It wasn't just the wound, either—as Pandora lay on the floor in shock, the steel pistol ball remained lodged inside her, and she was so much a creature of spellfire that it felt as though lightning surged through her over and over again, emanating from the steel.

Opening her mouth, Pandora screamed.

And woke.

For a moment, as she slipped into muddleheaded wakefulness, her spellfire surged. She had no idea where she was, a sensation she'd felt far too many times before. But it did not matter, because the steel shot had been only a dream. Oh, it was memory, too, still borne with her as a small white scar on her shoulder, but it hadn't been Beacon who'd leveled a pistol at her all those years ago. At least it hadn't been him.

Pan's surroundings swam into focus, and the power in her veins cooled to a dull warmth. Around her was the suite she and Winifred had moved into on Palace Hill only the day before. Their matching lace-canopied beds stood side by side, while an explosion of gowns and underthings and furbelows lay strewn over every available surface.

Neither Pan nor Winnie had ever been the tidiest, and in the excitement of the day before, they'd mutually agreed to delay proper unpacking.

"Where did you go last night?" Winifred asked curiously from where she sat at a small breakfast table, happily eating buttered toast and poached eggs with sunlight pooling around her. Though she didn't have Imogen's flawless beauty, Winifred was lovely in the morning sun, her mop of red curls like a blaze of fire and her eyes very green. "You know the Bellwether sisters held a private salon for all of us after the concert yesterday evening. *An exclusive event for select gentlemen,* they called it. But you were gone. No one could find a trace of you. Miss Elvira was *extremely* put out. Even Miss Alice seemed a little miffed."

Winifred took another bite of toast and fixed Pan with a searching look. Sitting up with a groan, Pandora scrubbed a hand across her face. Her arm where the Grim had raked her skin the morning before stung and smarted, and she could feel bruises on her back, courtesy of the fall she'd taken while tangling with Weres last night.

All in all, an interesting if somewhat unorthodox start to her time as an Ingenue. Pan tumbled out of bed, went to the washbasin and splashed cold water on her face and wrists before pulling on a dressing gown and joining Winifred at the table.

"Are you really not going to tell me anything?" Winnie said, sounding disgruntled. "I know Palace Hill changes some girls, but I didn't expect it to alter you."

"I was out," Pan said. She reached for a piece of toast and slathered it with haxberry jam before eating half of it in one bite. Spending a great deal of spellfire always left her ravenous, though it barely dented her prodigious inner reserves of power. "With a gentleman."

Winifred squealed and clapped her hands. "Oh, clever you! Of course you've got a potential patron on the hook already. Won't Imogen be furious? She wanted Theo at last night's salon and he never came. Who's your beau, then? A merchant or a lord? Oh, or a dignitary from elsewhere! Pan, you've got to tell me."

Pandora glanced across at Winnie from beneath the veil of her dark lashes. She'd never confided in the other girl about her magic—to do so would be dangerous not only to herself but to Winifred, too. Beyond that, they had no secrets. And Winnie, unlike any of the other Ingenues, would be delighted over Pandora dallying with a guard. She wouldn't think it scandalous or a step down on Pandora's part. Winifred, after all, had conducted her own clandestine and torrid romances over the years, with the butcher's son and a boy mage bound and apprenticed to a merchant. Pan had been Winnie's confidante through them both.

"Do you remember that guard from yesterday?" Pan asked, keeping her tone light and easy. "The one who did my parlor exam?"

"The crusty one or the beautiful one?" Winifred poured herself a cup of jessamine-petal tea and sipped the fragrant brew.

"The . . . the second one," Pan said. "You know I had some difficulty with the exam."

"Yes!" Winifred wrinkled her nose in horror. "That Grim could have killed you—I was beside myself when I heard about it. Are you sure you're all right?"

Pandora nodded. "Yes. Thanks to the guard in question. He more or less threw himself between me and the Grim."

"Oh, how romantic." Winnie let out a dreamy sigh. "He's so satisfyingly large, too. A boy that size you could climb like a tree. I'd wager he knows how to toss a girl around in all the right ways, if you're looking to be tossed. I certainly would be, if he was the one doing it."

"Winifred!" Pandora blurted out, scandalized not for the first time by her friend's breadth of knowledge in all things related to romance. "I'm not a lawn dart, or a cricket ball. Anyway, the guard injured himself while he was helping me during the exam, so I brought him salve last night, as a way of saying thank you."

Winnie leaned forward and rested her chin on one hand, grinning impishly. "And did you stay to rub it on him yourself?"

"Certainly not, you shameless trollop! But he asked me if I'd like to take a walk in the lower city, and I went. It was . . . nothing like I expected. He was nothing like I expected. He saw me—understood things about me—like no one else ever has."

And he held her fate in his hands.

Winifred's face grew suddenly and uncharacteristically solemn. "Pan, it's all well and good you having some fun with the boy. But you can't fall for him, you know that. You've got to find yourself a proper patron. How else am I going to survive Palace Hill summer after summer, and life in the first set? We need each other, as allies."

"Of course." Pandora fixed her eyes on the tablecloth, guilt tying her stomach up in knots. Even if she *were* unbound, she'd never be able to find herself a normal patron like the rest of the Ingenues. The moment anyone took her binding, they'd know how much power she hid—that she was an abomination who ought to be killed for the sake of Valora's safety. Pan was under no illusions. The sort of person who'd keep her secret was the sort who'd also use her cruelly and bend her inferno of spellfire to their own advantage, while any good and upstanding citizen would turn her in at once.

Unless . . . but no. Pan had devoted quite enough time to a certain broad-shouldered guard already. Never mind that he'd witnessed her magic with total equanimity, asking nothing of her in exchange for keeping her secret. It would be a great scandal if an Ingenue bound herself to a lowly guardsman, and Pandora already had a binding she chafed under. The last thing she needed was another.

A decisive knock sounded at their door, and Winifred frowned. "Are you expecting someone? Your new friend, perhaps?"

Pan shook her head, and Winnie went to the door, peeking through a tiny slot designed to allow Ingenues to see out and make themselves appropriately charming while calling out apologies, should a suitor arrive unexpectedly.

"Ugh, it's *Imogen*," Winifred said in disgust. "Whatever did we do to deserve a visit from her?"

"I can hear you, Winifred Harper," a cool voice said from the other side of the door. "And I'm coming in, whether you like it or not."

Rolling her eyes, Winnie opened the door to the suite's small receiving area.

"Imogen," Winnie said, with forced politeness. "To what do we owe the pleasure?"

"To Pandora's truancy," Imogen answered, forever blunt when chastising her fellow Ingenues. "She damaged her own reputation and that of the Bellwether School by failing to turn up at the salon last night. Which means by extension, she's harmed your reputation, Winifred, and mine, and I won't stand for that. So I've come to ensure she makes a good impression at the queen's exhibition today."

"I'll be fine," Pan muttered around a mouthful of toast. "Don't fuss over me. You know I can have anyone falling at my feet the moment I show my parlor magic."

"She's angry about being slighted by the prince and taking it out on you," Winifred said in a loud stage whisper, very much meant for Imogen to hear. "Let's both ignore her, and perhaps she'll leave."

Heaving a gusty and dramatic sigh, Imogen swept across the room and chivvied Pan onto her feet. "Being an Ingenue is more than parlor magic, as you're well aware, Pandora Small. To begin with, you've got to be ready to show yourself off to the greatest advantage anytime, anywhere. Annabelle!" Imogen clapped smartly, and a beribboned lady's maid with half a dozen under-maids in tow swept into the room. "Please set this ridiculous mess to rights. The young ladies must be prepared to receive company at a moment's notice."

Though Winifred looked rather pleased to have an army of maids doing the tidying for them, it was Pandora's turn to bridle.

"I don't want a stranger touching my unmentionables!" she sputtered at Imogen as the room erupted into a whir of activity.

Imogen fixed her with an impatient look. "Pandora, you're here specifically to find a stranger to touch both your spellfire and your unmentionables. Please stop being so precious. Now sit down at the dressing table and let me do something about your hair."

"What about mine?" Winifred asked cheerily, entirely reconciled to Imogen's presence now that it brought a material advantage. Imogen waved over the maid, Annabelle.

Against her will, Pan was steered to her dressing table and forced to sit by Imogen's implacable hands.

"As I mentioned," Imogen said around a mouthful of hairpins, "all the Ingenues are meant to be viewing an exhibition of exotic plants and animals and curiosities in the gardens this afternoon, and it's nearly luncheon already. If the pair of you are going to be a credit to the Bellwethers—and to me, by extension—you'll need at least an extra hour to make yourselves presentable. Two hours, if I'm honest."

The last addendum was accompanied by a dubious look at Pan and Winnie. Pandora twisted in her seat and glared. "How is it we've been at school together for five years and you've never realized what terrible manners you've got?"

Imogen blinked. Unlike Winifred and Pandora, who were still in their nightclothes, she was already immaculately fitted out for the exhibition in an afternoon gown of rose silk, with a sheen of gold Ilaran powder glinting on her cheek and collarbones. "What on earth do you mean? I have the prettiest manners of all the Bellwether Ingenues."

"Like hell you do," Pan snorted. "You make everything a backhanded insult. You've being doing it since I met you. Any time you say something to another Ingenue that even approaches complimentary, you've got to temper it with some sort of jibe."

"I do not!" Imogen protested.

Pandora fixed her with a scathing look. "It'll take two hours to get me and Winnie ready? Really?"

"I'm only being honest," Imogen said, all wounded innocence. "I make it a personal practice to tell the truth whenever possible."

Pan glowered. "There's a difference between honesty and using the truth as an excuse to be a complete cat to anyone you're speaking with."

A strangled yelp of laughter sounded from Winifred's dressing table, and Imogen shot Pandora a reproachful look in the mirror.

"Well, if I'm so abrasive, I'll simply have to try to do better. Though I'm sure no one else finds my manners deficient."

"Theo might," Winifred said, the words disguised as a cough. But Imogen took the high road and made no reply.

Silence fell, aside from the low voices of the maids discussing where to place various feminine trappings and accessories. Annabelle was busy with Winifred, and Imogen stood behind Pandora, capably plying a brush, hot tongs, and scented hair oils.

"You know," she said presently, "I don't mean to be insulting. It's just that you could *try* to make yourself a little less plain, Pandora. I understand your position at the Bellwethers' doesn't allow for a wardrobe like mine, but you could do a bit more with your scholarship funds, or whatever it is that pays your way. You could borrow things from the rest of us girls too, if need be. It's an Ingenue's job to draw attention to herself, and you're always so . . . understated."

Pandora could not say what she was thinking. That if she truly wanted to draw attention to herself, she could have every eye on Palace Hill riveted to her. A single display of the true scope of her power, and no one would dare look away. Of course, such a performance would engender revulsion, rather than desire, but she'd certainly compel a greater reaction than any Ingenue had ever managed before.

"My hair looks very pretty," Pandora offered instead, extending an olive branch to her haughty classmate, and it was the truth. In keeping with Pan's desire to remain plainer than her fellows, Imogen had done no more than crown her with a little coronet of narrow braids, the rest of her curls piled up in a sweetly unstudied mass. Tiny white silk rosettes dotted the sleek coronet, while a silver Hesperidian star rested like a gem at their center.

"I suppose I can't convince you to borrow one of my gowns." Imogen stepped back and surveyed Pandora, transparently pleased with her handiwork. "I've got this gorgeous thing in pewter silk, with an overlay of midnight-blue gauze. You'd look divine in it with your coloring."

"And trip over the skirts every other minute because you're so much taller than me," Pandora said. "No, I'm much better off in something of my own."

"It'll be ivory, as always." Imogen gave Pan a hopeless shake of her head. "That's such a trying shade, with your complexion. I don't know what you've got against anything darker or brighter. Did you have some nightmare of a nursemaid as a child who wore only black?"

Pandora bit her tongue as Imogen's incessant needling struck too close to home. Her patron had always been clothed in black from head to toe, their form hidden by a voluminous cloak and gloves, their face by a mask, and their voice disguised by magic. She hadn't even the first glimmer of a clue who they might be. All she knew was that they'd evidently had money—a fortune's worth, to be able to keep Pandora as they'd done—and been accustomed to power.

An hour later, the girls stepped out into a flood of warm sun and cool wind, the light and the breeze a perfect counterpoint to each other. Members of the mage corps were tucked discreetly around the gardens, ensuring the ideal weather remained. Vast iron cages rested here and there, housing bizarre animals Pan had never seen the like of before, while others grazed at the ends of pickets or were led about by attendants dressed in harlequin garb. Living statues stood on pedestals, and displays of incomprehensible machinery or strange statuary and other works of art sat atop tables or cleared patches of flagstone tile.

Pandora frowned at the dazzling array of curiosities.

"What's the theme?" she asked Imogen as the beautiful Ingenue linked arms with her and Winifred. Winnie was charming, sweet in a frock of apple green, with sky-blue ribbons in her fiery hair. Already, a little ripple was beginning among the milling nobles, as gentlemen headed toward the three of them like arrows loosed from a string.

"Theme?" Imogen raised an eyebrow in amusement. "Novelty, I suppose, if there is one at all. You are *funny*, Pandora."

Pan shook her head, annoyed.

"There ought to be a proper theme," she insisted. "It's just a lot of junk and pageantry, otherwise."

A not unpleasant-looking man, perhaps fifteen years Pandora and her companions' senior, was the first to reach the girls. Imogen smiled graciously as he bowed to them both in turn, while Pandora only managed to look disgruntled as the gentleman turned his attention to her.

"Miss Hollen," the stranger said to Imogen, with his eyes fixed on Pan. "Last night you promised to introduce me to your friend. The one you were telling me so much about."

Pandora shot Imogen a horrified look.

"Of course," Imogen answered smoothly. "Baron Hax, this is Pandora Small. She's by far the cleverest Ingenue I've ever seen when it comes to parlor magic. Pan, this is Hax—he owns most of the manufacturing town of Whistley, and a great deal of the countryside surrounding it."

"Hax like the berries?" Pandora asked.

"Yes," the baron said with a sly smile. "Just so. We grow a great deal of them on my lands."

"Hax is terribly eligible," Winifred breathed at Pandora, behind the cover of her painted silk fan. "Rich even by the first set's standards. And bent on making himself richer by any means possible. You'd be an asset to him, and I think he'd be a good patron—he'd know your worth, and you'd never be bored."

Pandora did not whisper back, knowing it would seem appallingly rude. Instead she pasted on a smile and took Hax's proffered arm. The moment he drew her away from Imogen and Winifred, the pair like gold and flame, half a dozen young men descended on the other girls. But Winnie extricated herself briefly, hurrying after Pandora and Baron Hax.

"Can I have just a moment before you both wander off?" Winnie asked, offering Hax one of her darling smiles. The gentleman nodded, and Winifred drew Pandora away, her eyes bright with excitement.

"I didn't get a chance to tell you earlier, because I don't want Imogen tagging along," Winnie said. "But later, between the exhibition and tonight's dance, a few of the Grace College Ingenues and I are going to do a bit of exploring. We want to poke about the palace and see if we can find any clues as to the wellspring's whereabouts. Just imagine if we could find it, Pan. Everyone in Hesperid would know our names!"

Pandora raised a dubious eyebrow. "Are any of the other Bellwether girls going?"

"No." Winifred pulled a face. "I didn't bother asking Leslie, because she's Imogen's underling, and I don't want Gin. But Eleanor and Mamie both told me they wouldn't come."

"I can't believe you asked Eleanor," Pan chided. "Of course she wouldn't want to come, the wellspring all but ruined her family. Besides which, looking for it's a wild-goose chase. You're better off finding a symphonium and practicing your scales, or picking oranges in the conservatory. Either would be more useful."

Winifred's eyes went wide as saucers. "Those are the queen's oranges, Pan, no one's allowed to pick them!"

"You know what I meant."

"Of course I did." Winnie grinned wickedly. "But where's the fun in that? And where's the fun in staying cooped up between events or sticking strictly to our social calendar? Depending on who my patron is, this might be my last chance at a bit of unruliness. Do come along. Don't be a spoilsport."

Pandora humored Winifred with an indulgent pat on the arm. It didn't hurt to dream, she supposed, or for the Ingenues to have a harmless distraction from the worrisome task of securing a patron.

"I'll be there," Pan said to Winnie. "You can count on me."

It would, she supposed, be as good an opportunity as any to canvas the palace, attempting to see if a particular location tugged at her latent binding. If she pleaded a headache, the other girls would overlook her being quiet and distracted. They were welcome to search for the wellspring, if doing so served as a convenient cover for Pandora to hunt down her patron.

For now, though, Pan would have to play an Ingenue's game. With a quick goodbye to Winnie, she took Baron Hax's arm once more and let him lead her on. The last thing Pan saw as Hax ushered her through the maze of curiosities was a flash and sparkle of parlor magic—Imogen and Winifred indulging the gentlemen in their desire to see an Ingenue's skills.

Similar flares of magic-wrought color or rills of unearthly music snagged at Pandora's attention as she and Hax drifted toward a tall boxwood labyrinth at the heart of this particular garden. And Pan realized that she'd been wrong—there *was* a theme to the exhibition, only it was one that had nothing to do with the oddments on display. Those were all merely sleight of hand, a distraction from what was truly being exhibited.

Power. Both that which the Ingenues possessed, and that which they could win by indulging a particular suitor.

"Shall we try our luck?" Hax said courteously as he gestured to the shadowed entrance of the labyrinth.

Pandora glanced over one shoulder for the dozenth time since coming out of the garden and realized, with a guilty shock, that she'd been looking for a tall boy in the Guard's crimson uniform.

Foolish, she chastised herself. *You don't need the distraction. You have quite enough to manage without any of that.*

"Oh, very well," Pan answered, her acquiescence inelegant to the point of unpleasantness. She didn't like to be on display, for the most part—a grave failing in an Ingenue. But her patron had demanded constant tests and exhibitions of Pandora's skill, until her childhood had felt like a single drawn out and harrowing performance. Whatever feats she achieved, there were always more challenging tasks waiting to be mastered.

Without a doubt Hax would expect some show once he'd neatly hidden her away and would have the spectacle all to himself. The better to ensure he had no rivals for Pandora's patronage. Pan gritted her teeth and forced a thin smile, but by the time they reached the center of the labyrinth, she was out of sorts in both body and spirits. She did not want to show off for this perfectly courteous but ultimately grasping noble. She did not like being alone with him. She wanted to be anywhere but here.

An alleyway in the lower city, perhaps, with hellions closing in and a certain guard at her back.

"Miss Small," Hax began, as they emerged at the labyrinth's center.

"Yes?" Pandora half snapped as she took in the grotesque follies ringing the room of boxwood and grass at the maze's heart. They were a trio of vast ogres' faces, cut from moss-greened stone, each one of them sporting a yawning mouth through which a labyrinth-goer would have to proceed.

Palace Hill was determined to eat its occupants alive.

"I've been warned that you don't share your fellow Ingenues' enthusiasm for the game of patrons and pawns we're all engaged in," Hax said, seeming not to notice Pandora's rudeness. He settled himself on a stone bench at the center of the boxwood room, and in taking a few steps toward him, Pandora realized with a shiver that they'd entered by stepping through the mouth of a fourth ogre. The stone archway had been concealed from behind by swags of ivy—only at the labyrinth's center could its hidden monsters be recognized for what they were.

"I respect your reluctance to be bartered off," Hax continued, motioning to the place on the bench beside him. Pandora shook her head in refusal, retreating to stand beside the maw of the least intimidating ogre instead. "And I want you to know that what I have to offer you is a different proposition entirely than what you might receive from other quarters. I'm not looking for an Ingenue bride. I don't especially want your hand, in addition to your binding."

Pandora blinked twice in surprise. "I beg your pardon?"

"I understand the arrangement I'm looking for is outside the norm," Hax said, removing the ornate pocket watch from his fob and polishing it meticulously with a handkerchief. "But I already have a more than satisfactory lover, one suitable to my age and temperament. You would be my wife in regards to name and privilege, but the more . . . personal aspects . . . of the marital union are not what I'm seeking from you. I've been told by Alice Bellwether that your parlor magic is unsurpassed. 'Beyond true comprehension or description' were her exact words. She cautioned me to complete secrecy in that regard, of course, and said you hadn't expressly made her privy to the extent of your power. But she saw you once, facing down a hellion."

Pandora stood stock-still, watching him warily. Bad enough that Beacon had learned her secret. Worse by far, finding that Miss Alice and a grasping noble were party to it as well.

"I want you primarily as a business partner," Hax said, and his straightforwardness drew grudging admiration from Pan. At least she'd know what to expect from him. "You may have heard I'm well-to-do—I'd like to make myself vastly more secure before the end. An Ingenue with powers like those Alice swears you possess would be a great ally. With your skill, you could suss out the truth of every bargain, and discern the most advantageous tactics to be used in any new business arrangement."

Pandora remained in the shadows. "Break the second mage law, you mean? Repeatedly, and for the sake of your enrichment?"

"Come now," Hax scoffed. "Don't be coy. You know Ingenues are already an exception to the first mage law and the age requirements it lays out for patronage. After binding, you're all considered an exception to the second law as well. No member of the Guard has ever enforced the restriction against exercising magic on another if an Ingenue is involved. Some men want you for pleasure, others for prestige. I merely want you to determine the motivations of those I pit myself against in business, for our mutual benefit."

"And just how are you connected to Miss Alice?" Pan asked coolly, even as she guessed at the answer.

"A gentleman doesn't kiss and tell," Hax said, and Pandora slumped in the shadows.

His lover, then. All these years, Miss Alice had been feigning kindness while honing Pandora's skills, helping to teach her the artfulness and civility and control Hax's ideal lackey would possess. Though the Bellwethers' tutelage had been less cruel than that of her patron, Pandora had still been a puppet in their hands. It seemed that she was destined to manipulation and would never be free.

And just like that, a horrific thought struck her. It had always seemed like the greatest stroke of good fortune, managing to escape her patron at all. What if she never had? Hax had no magic—as a potential patron, he'd have been even more strictly vetted than an Ingenue. It was unthinkable for one mage to be bound to another, for such a connection would only amplify both their power, rather than taming and controlling it. Nevertheless, Pandora's patron had been a mage, and their bond had grown Pan's power exponentially, inflaming and enhancing the spellfire she carried.

What if her patron was Alice Bellwether, set on carefully raising and tending the perfect Ingenue companion for her paramour? Amplifying Pandora's magic and first schooling her in brute force, then in the art of elegant concealment?

"I want you to show me something," Hax said. "Something no other Ingenue can do."

Pan was filled with a sudden and fierce longing for rescue from any quarter. But such a desire was as much a fantasy as Winifred's dream of finding the wellspring. All her life she'd been alone in her struggle against a faceless tormentor, and her efforts to hide her power. None of that would ever change, so long as her patron lived.

"I daren't," Pandora murmured. "Not on Palace Hill. The Guard will know."

"I'll lie for you if you indulge me," Hax answered quickly. "But if you don't, you'll never make it out of this labyrinth. I'll leave you here and go straight to the nearest guard, and when I find them, I'll report you. Tell them the abomination everyone has feared is currently residing at the heart of Palace Hill. So you see, you're better off giving me what I want."

Pan's spellfire burned so hot, fueled by her anxiety and anger, that she limped a little as she stepped out from the shadows, racked by the pain of it.

Parlor magic, she thought. *Make it parlor magic, or as close to that as possible. Don't let him see what you can really do.*

Fixing her eyes on the grassy center of the labyrinth, Pandora envisioned a tall silver tree, and even as she did so, a sapling sprouted and grew at preternatural speed. The magic-wrought tree glittered so brightly, it hurt to look at. Putting out branches and leaves and petals, it grew and spread, setting a canopy above them and painting the ground with shimmering light.

No Ingenue could make something so vast, so real, so beautiful. And yet Baron Hax only shook his head in disapproval.

"No. Alice assured me you can do more than that. Show me."

The whispers were rising up, amplifying Pandora's pain and chipping away at her control.

Let it go, they taunted. *Be a flame. Set loose the power we gave you.*

With a twist of her mouth, Pan ignored the words and pictured a vine. A snaking, thorn-studded thing wrought of spellfire and shadow, as like to a hellion as she could make it. The vine burst from the ground and slithered up the trunk of her newly crafted tree, engulfing its branches and leaves. It constricted like a serpent, until limbs and wood and bark caved in on themselves with a sound of shattering glass. The tree and the vine both collapsed to the ground, melting into a pool of blue spellfire that glowed for a moment on the grass and then dissipated.

"Not good enough," Hax goaded. "That's all illusion. I want something real."

Pandora cast about herself, expecting to see guards appear at every entrance to the labyrinth's heart. Surely she'd worked enough magic to catch their attention, and yet there was no one. It was just possible that all the parlor magic being done at the exhibition was confusing enough to mask her richer, deeper skill—a fireworks display disguising distant cannon shots.

Come back to me, the whispers said enticingly. *You will not be a pretty object, but a force to reckon with, a weapon in human form.*

The stone ogres at each end of the boxwood chamber leered at Pan, as if promising that at any moment they might divulge the contingent of guards she feared. An unreasoning hatred of them swept over her, and without allowing a second thought, she sent out power. An explosion of earth and grass burst in front of each ogre, as vines dark as pitch and veined with pulsing blue spellfire shot up, entangling the vast statues, probing every crack and cranny and weakness with inexorable fingers of magic. A tearing, grinding whine of collapsing stone filled the silence of the boxwood room, and for a moment, clouds of dust and flurries of spellfire sparks rose, obscuring what was happening around Pandora and Baron Hax.

When the air cleared, nothing remained of the ogres but piles of tumbled stone.

There, Pandora thought dully. *I've done it. The Guard's sure to come for me now.*

But a part of her was perversely glad, too. She'd spent so long hiding who she was and what she was capable of. It would be a relief, in the end, to be seen and known, and to finally face the steel box and self-immolation that had always haunted her.

You were always meant to burn, the whispers hissed. *You could have burned so brightly for me.*

"Yes," Hax said hungrily. "You're just what Alice promised. Just what I need. I will keep your secrets, child, and allow you greater freedom than any other patron would, if you only give me your binding."

Once again, Pandora felt her expression twist. She'd spent years in one gilded cage, subject to a moneyed and privileged captor. She would not bind herself to a second tyrant, for any price.

"I think you mistake your position," Pan said, taking a slow step toward Hax and then another. Instinctively he backed away, and she thought of Beacon, who'd been burned by her power yet still held out his hand without hesitation. "You will keep my secrets, to be sure. But it won't be because I bind myself to you. It will be because if you breathe a word of what or who I am, I will tear your insides out through your throat by magic and strangle you with them. Do we have an understanding?"

All the while, she spoke in the soft, perfectly modulated tone of an Ingenue. There was nothing fearful about Pandora's person—she was, as ever, a demure and unremarkable creature, small and unassuming in her ivory and rosettes.

But Hax had seen her fire, and his throat worked convulsively at the threat. He was about to speak when Pandora raised a hand to silence him. She'd heard something—an odd, muffled sound from just beyond the labyrinth's heart. Pan's pulse quickened. She'd listened in on others often enough to know they weren't alone, and the thought of an unknown party learning her secrets sent a chill down Pandora's spine.

She picked her way across the grassy room to the settling rubble at one end, her gaze fixed on a scrap of apple green. Gathering up her skirts and moving meticulously among the rocks, Pan stopped short.

Once beautiful in bright silk, Winifred Harper lay just beyond the rubble. Her limbs were contorted, her fingers and mouth and eyes stained spellfire blue. As Pan stared down at her in numb disbelief, Winnie's mouth worked soundlessly, trying to voice some unknowable last word. But while Pandora watched, she fell still, and the light died in her eyes.

It felt, to Pandora, as if something had died in her, as well. She'd watched a score of people succumb to her patron's tender mercies during childhood. Seen dead bodies aplenty on Valora's troubled streets. But this was different. This cut her so deep, she could not fully fathom the pain. No one had ever been as kind to her as Winifred. No one had ever known her so well, aside from her worst secrets.

Be numb, she thought desperately, as her spellfire roared in response to the desolation of standing over Winifred's body. *Don't let it touch you. Don't let it make you lose control.*

Behind her, Pan heard Hax's sharp intake of breath. She turned, but too slowly—he was already disappearing into the maze by the time she fixed her fraying attention on him. It was all she could do to keep hold of her spellfire, and she stood over Winnie's body with her hands balled into fists, striving to master her power. But it rose inexorably, in response to her fear and grief.

Worse yet, the whispers were all Pandora could hear, enticing her with their siren song.

Come back. Come back to me, to safety, to security.

Lies. Pan knew all too well that the bodies she found in the lower city, and poor darling Winifred, were victims of her mortal enemy. There was no safety with her patron, no security. Only endless pain and confusion, as they dangled her like a puppet on a string. Pan clapped her hands over her ears and let out a small, helpless sound, but the whispers could not be silenced. They emanated from within, not without, and there was no escaping them.

There was no escaping her patron. She'd been a fool to think she could even find them, let alone sever the loathsome bond that tied her to such a person. Any moment now, the Guard would appear and accuse Pandora not only of the magework that had destroyed the labyrinth's center, but of Winifred's murder. She would be boxed—a failure in the end, unable to master whatever devious test this was— and die in flames of her own making. Worse yet, she would die with the world believing she'd killed Winnie.

A flash of crimson. Beacon appeared, striding over the rubble at one of the entryways, his face a mask of perfect composure. He did not stop until he reached Pan and seized her by the arm.

"Faint, Pandora," Beacon said, the words fraught with urgency. "You have to faint."

Pandora fixed her eyes on the guard, pleading with her gaze.

"It wasn't me," she said. "Beacon, whatever you felt of my magic, whatever you think, it wasn't—"

"I know," Beacon said firmly. "I believe you. Which is why you have to faint."

Already, voices were ringing through the labyrinth—the loud cries of other guards and higher-pitched, more hysterical sounds of nobles and Ingenues.

Nodding, Pandora let herself sink inward and down, into the place where her spellfire and the whispers that haunted her rested. She let the pain and the clamor of them rise up, instead of forcing them aside, until she could not breathe or hear anything but the licking of flames, and tears burned at her eyes and throat. The world spun, and the last thing Pan saw before she lost hold of consciousness was Beacon's solid, reassuring shape, bending at Winifred's side.

8

PANDORA'S PATRONAGE

It hurt Beacon to watch Pandora crumple so easily, not because it spoke to any weakness in her, but because he instinctively understood what it meant, that she could lose her grasp on consciousness with such swiftness. The pain she felt and the effort she expended in holding back her spellfire must be very great indeed.

"Beacon," Captain Tanner said breathlessly, arriving at his side and looking down at the stricken Ingenues with shock written across her face. "What's happened?"

"I don't know," Beacon said, and he meant it. He'd been watching when Hax led Pandora into the labyrinth and positioned himself outside its single entrance. Beacon had heard rumors about Hax coercing serving girls back home on his estate, and while the guard misdoubted Hax would try such a thing with an Ingenue, his conscience would not rest easy until he stationed himself as if he were Pandora's personal guard. Laughable, really, to think he might need to protect *her*.

At first, he'd felt warmth emanating from within the hedge-lined maze, like sun coming out from behind a bank of clouds. It had carried on for several minutes, and then . . . nothing. Not even a hint of magic, until a sudden blast of heat like air from an oven had burst from the labyrinth's entrance and sent him running for Pandora. The heat had carried with it a sensation of panic, and Beacon had not needed to be told that the little Ingenue was in distress. That wasn't what puzzled him—it was the nothing in between. It wasn't so much that Pandora's warmth had been absent, as it was that Beacon's magesense had *stopped*. He'd need time to think that over and sort out what it meant.

"One of them's dead," Beacon informed Captain Tanner. "This one's only swooning. There was a noble in here who ran off—I'm going after him, to make sure he doesn't leave Palace Hill, and to ask some questions. Someone should see to the girl. The smaller one, in ivory."

Before Captain Tanner could do more than nod, Beacon tore himself away. It was a wrench to leave Pandora as she was, lying in a fragile heap on the ground. It reminded him too much of the night before, of how she'd looked when she'd fallen and the Were had been about to end her.

Calm. Despairing. Resigned to her fate. As if she'd known for years that death would come sooner for her than for others and that she would not answer with a gout of defensive spellfire. It had wakened fury and a protective instinct in Beacon like he'd never felt before, knowing how much power she hid and that she would willingly die to protect others from it.

Witnessing that moment was why he would not and could not believe the dead Ingenue had anything to do with Pandora Small. Yes, he'd felt her magic from beyond the labyrinth. Yes, he'd seen the

STEEL & SPELLFIRE

body, twisted and stripped of spellfire. But having watched Pandora work in the lower city the night before, Beacon could not help believing that her magic and murder were anathema to each other. The girl could no more maliciously take a life than she could add a foot to her diminutive height.

Emerging from the labyrinth, Beacon cast about himself, scanning the crowds for the noble he'd seen beating a hasty retreat. Hax, the man was called—Beacon recognized him from the dossier incoming palace guards were required to memorize. Baron Hax had neither magic nor the magesense, but enough of a fortune that he could purchase the services of a dozen lackeys possessed of either.

Standing a head above the crowd served Beacon well. He spotted Hax at a distance, entering the palace through a side door. Striding after the man, Beacon cursed the consort and the magefinders who'd tested him that morning. He still felt feverish and sore but tamped the discomfort down as he hurried into the palace, where the interior felt odd and deserted with most of its occupants in the gardens. There were still servants moving about here and there, but the halls echoed, and Beacon caught a glimpse of Hax headed into a gentlemen's lounge.

Excellent.

Following, Beacon slipped through the door just as Hax seated himself at a tall counter, the liveried barman behind it asking for the noble's preference in a smooth, servile voice.

"Indiran spirits," Hax said. "With a twist of Hecate spice."

Beacon settled himself onto the stool beside Baron Hax and placed his hands on the countertop, a subtle gesture he'd used many times in the lower city to breed trust in the person he was questioning. No weapons, nothing to hide. His skin still felt swollen and taut, but nothing looked amiss.

"You were there just now, when that Ingenue was killed," Beacon said, a statement rather than an inquiry. The barman set a cut crystal tumbler down in front of Hax, who drained half the spirits in a single swallow.

"I was there when a dead Ingenue was found," Hax corrected. "When she was killed, I don't know."

"And the other girl," Beacon pressed. "Miss Small. She'd been demonstrating her spellfire for you, I believe. Was she involved with the death in some way? What exactly happened?"

Hax scoffed and threw back the rest of his spirits. "She's an Ingenue. How could she possibly have been involved? She doesn't have the power for it. We went to the labyrinth so I could see her skills in private. While we were there, a tremor occurred. You know they're common enough in Valora and Hesperid's south. This one was minor, very localized, but enough to shake the ground and tear those stone figures down. Miss Small and I were fortunate not to be harmed. As for the dead girl, I've no idea how she got there or what happened to her. Miss Small and I were not involved."

It was all music to Beacon's ears. Hax must have had reasons of his own for choosing to lie on Pandora's behalf, as did Beacon. And suddenly it struck him—perhaps Hax's motivation to protect Pandora stemmed from the fact that she'd promised her patronage to him. She'd only just arrived on Palace Hill, and they'd only had a few minutes together. But desperate Ingenues had committed themselves after briefer acquaintances. Needing to hide her prodigious power, Pandora might just have been willing to hastily accept the first patron who came her way. Better yet, Hax was known to be unscrupulous—someone who was likely to keep Pan's secret so long as he could use it to his own advantage.

Beacon's stomach turned over, and his blood ran hot just thinking of the girl under Hax's influence. A vile, half-corrupt lordling should have nothing to do with that shining magic or with the strong-minded mouse who wielded it.

"You'd swear that Miss Small had nothing to do with the other girl's death?" Beacon pressed Baron Hax. "Before the Guard, and before the queen, if necessary?"

"Certainly," Hax said with perfect conviction. "It's the truth."

"And are you willing to have me record all of this and register your statement with the Guard?"

"Yes. I've nothing to hide."

There was one more point Beacon felt obligated to press, to ensure this slippery-tongued noble would truly prove an unimpeachable alibi for Pandora, if necessary. "If that's the case, I do wonder why you left immediately, rather than staying to ensure Miss Small's safety and that the Guard were on their way."

Hax shrugged. "Of course you were on your way. I could hear a racket coming toward us through the labyrinth. And I make it a habit not to be seen in unsavory circumstances. It's one thing for potential business acquaintances to hear I was tangentially involved in this unfortunate affair, but another entirely for them to come across me with two stricken Ingenues at my feet. Whatever the truth of the matter, that image isn't one a person can shake easily. I have a reputation to maintain, and take great care to see it's preserved."

Cowardly. And self-serving besides, Beacon thought. A totally unworthy patron for Pandora Small.

He rose with a last polite nod. "Thank you, sir. If the Guard requires anything more, we'll be in touch."

Hax lifted his empty glass. "I'm at your service."

Beacon retreated, perhaps more quickly than was courteous. Hurrying through the corridors back toward the garden exhibition, he stopped short upon glimpsing Captain Tanner down one of the hallways lined with guest quarters for the Ingenues.

"Captain," Beacon called out. "I've spoken to Baron Hax, the noble who was in the labyrinth. He claims what happened there was a small earthquake of some sort, and that he and the girl with him had nothing to do with the other Ingenue's death. For all they know, she might have been lying there for hours."

Captain Tanner nodded. "That's reassuring. Hax has no magic, and you conducted Miss Small's parlor exam yourself. However, *something* killed that other girl. Winifred Harper, her name was. For now we're operating on the assumption that it was some manner of hellion. They don't spawn on Palace Hill often, but every now and then one takes shape and has to be dealt with. The Guard's on high alert, and no one is to go anywhere we don't routinely patrol."

Uncertainty gnawed at Beacon, and he shifted his weight from one foot to the other. "Not that it isn't a good theory, Captain, but . . . we dealt with far more hellions down in the lower city than Palace Hill ever does. I never saw one leave a body looking the way that girl did. Never heard of one that does either."

Captain Tanner shrugged. "Well, they have their common forms, but aberrations still appear now and then. It's the best lead we've got for now."

"Yes, ma'am. About Miss Small, ma'am. Would it be all right if I looked in on her? She's been through a great deal in two days, and I feel partially responsible for it, given how her parlor exam ended."

"Of course." Captain Tanner gestured to a nearby door. "That's the Bellwether sisters' suite of rooms. They have her in there. The dead girl was apparently a close friend of Miss Small's. Unfortunate, that her time on Palace Hill has been so fraught."

Beacon was nearly lightheaded with worry as he knocked at the door, and a uniformed maid ushered him through a little antechamber and into a bedroom that could have fit seven of Beacon's own quarters within it. There were two canopied beds, and all was in perfect order. It was not a girl's living space, but very clearly the abode of women—everything about the furnishings spoke of exquisite, understated taste.

Near an interior door, an immaculately dressed older matron waited, still and perfectly upright in an upholstered chair, as if on guard.

"Is Miss Small through here?" Beacon asked evenly. "I have a few questions for her."

"She is," the older woman said with a stern nod of her head. "But don't upset her any more. She's had a difficult day already, and I need her in good spirits by evening—Miss Small has a ball to attend tonight."

Resisting the urge to scowl at the woman's cool response, Beacon entered what proved to be a small sitting room. A single long window, flanked by lush velvet drapes, looked out onto the gardens, and a settee and two armchairs surrounded an ornately carved tea table.

On the overstuffed couch, in a flood of tears, sat Pandora. Another woman was at her side, this one less severe in aspect. She had an arm around Pan's shoulders and was murmuring comforting words, though Pandora's face was entirely hidden by an enormous lace handkerchief.

"I need a word with her," Beacon said quietly. "In private."

The woman gave Pandora an encouraging squeeze. "There's a guard here to see you, love. He wants to ask some questions. Will you be all right?"

Pandora peeked over the handkerchief, her eyes red-rimmed and brimming.

"Oh, Miss Alice," she said in an effusion of watery, well-brought-up gratitude. "You've been so kind already. Don't trouble yourself about me any longer, I'll manage."

Her breath caught on sobs between the words, and Beacon would have been happy had the earth opened up to swallow him whole. This Pandora, a delicate and wilting flower, was exactly the sort of girl who set him on edge. She was just another Ingenue, fit for parading around a ballroom and simpering in the courtyards. Gone was the brilliant creature of grace and flame he'd witnessed the night before. Her, he couldn't look away from. This girl, he'd rather *get* away from.

Miss Alice left them, with a heartening backward glance in Pandora's direction. But the moment she was gone, Pan straightened, smoothing her skirts and casting the damp handkerchief aside. Her face was still blotchy and tearstained, but her breath came steadily, and she fixed Beacon with a flinty stare.

"Winifred Harper was my *best friend*," Pan said, restrained fury crackling through the words. "She was one of a very, very few people I actually care for in this world. I won't go so far as to say she was family—she had plenty of that, and didn't see me in such a way. But I have nothing, and no one. I can't afford to lose people. The Guard needs to find who did this and make them pay."

The sudden shift from helpless child to implacable young woman startled Beacon. She accomplished it without any seeming effort, just as she restrained her vast quantities of spellfire. It struck Beacon suddenly that even when she seemed to be falling apart, Pandora Small was never, not for a single moment, out of control. Any lapses she allowed herself were carefully chosen outlets, rather than true breakdowns.

Settling into an armchair across from her, Beacon gave Pandora an undaunted look. "*Who* did this? The Guard currently believes your friend was killed by a hellion. Do you have information indicating this was murder?"

Pandora fixed her eyes on the floor. "It was a mage. A mage . . . like me."

"How do you know this?"

"I've seen a death like Winifred's before."

"Were you the one who brought it about?" He had to ask. It was his duty as a guard, whatever he believed as a private individual.

Pan's gaze flashed back up to his, bright and ferociously defiant. "No! I told you, it wasn't me. It was a mage *like* me."

"Until yesterday, I wasn't aware a mage like you existed anywhere in Hesperid." Beacon was caught in a mire of conflicting emotions. He knew what he ought to be doing as a guard—keeping this girl at arm's length, until he'd proven her innocence. But he could sense a maelstrom of darker feeling beneath her brassy defiance. There was loneliness under the surface. Grief. Fear. It made him want to fix things for her. To repair all the ways in which the world had gone wrong since the wellspring, so that life might be easier for Miss Small.

"Well, there's at least one other mage as able as I am," Pandora said. "And I've seen them do something just like this."

"Who are they?" Beacon asked.

Quick as a cloud moving before a swift summer breeze, Pandora's bluster became uncertainty. "I don't—I don't know. I never have. I couldn't see their face, or their form, or even make out their real voice. They always came to me entirely disguised. But they were wealthy, I can tell you that much. A noble, in all likelihood. Certainly one of the first set, with constant access to Palace Hill."

"Miss Small. Pandora." Beacon leaned forward, resting his elbows on his knees. "I want to help you, and to ensure justice for your friend. But I can't tell the Guard I believe Winifred Harper was killed by a mage without having anything but the word of an anonymous accuser to back up my suspicions. I need more to go on."

"Don't you think I know that?" Pandora's frustration flared again. "I tried reporting them half a dozen times, years ago in the lower city. The guards only laughed at me, and I didn't dare do more than hint at vague suspicions. If I'd shown them bodies, with my power . . ." Her voice trailed off. They both knew very well such an effort would have led Pandora to a steel box. Though whether or not she could be killed by one, Beacon wasn't sure.

Drawing in a breath, she calmed herself. "I became an Ingenue and gained access to Palace Hill with the express intention of tracking this mage down. You don't understand what they were and are to me—the things they've done."

She was afraid, Beacon realized with a dull shock. Petrified. The idea of a rogue mage who could strike fear in *Pandora Small*, who danced with hellions and held enough spellfire to destroy a city, set ice in Beacon's own veins.

"Who are they?" he asked, his voice low. "What have they done? Here I am, speaking for the Guard. And I'm not laughing."

Pandora glanced up at him, tears glimmering in her eyes and anguish written across her face. This time, she seemed genuine. None of this was artifice, like she'd displayed to Miss Alice.

"I shouldn't tell you," Pandora whispered. "You'll end up like all the rest of them, over the years. Like Winifred."

Ignoring the rapid drumbeat of his heart, Beacon leaned forward, resting his elbows on his knees and returning her gaze without flinching. "I won't. I promise. Tell me who it is that's frightened you."

She tore her eyes from his, fixing her attention on the floor. "The thing is, I'm not here to look for a patron. Not a new one, anyway. I'm already bound, Beacon. *I'm trying to find the patron I've already got.*

For a moment, Beacon couldn't fully comprehend what she was saying, the idea was so unthinkable. He opened and shut his mouth, then straightened.

"A mage. Your patron is another mage?"

Pandora nodded, looking ill. "Yes. I've been bound to them for as long as I can remember."

"Gods above." Beacon scrubbed a hand across his face. His mind felt slow and syrupy, and his head ached with the aftereffects of the magic he'd withstood that morning. "No wonder you are the way you are. Mages are never bound together—any time anyone's tried it, they died. Usually left a crater in their wake and took a dozen people along with them, as well. It's too much power tied up between them."

"Oh, believe me," Pandora said flatly. "I know."

"I can't feel it on you." Beacon was bewildered by that. It put him in mind of what he'd experienced outside the labyrinth—a total absence of anything his magesense might detect. "I've always been able to sense a binding in the past. It changes a mage's spellfire—gives it a feeling of stifling, or constriction. There's none of that with you. Why?"

"I don't know," Pandora said. "I didn't create the binding, my patron did. Does it matter?"

"Maybe. I'm not sure yet. But I . . . gods, Pandora, I'm so sorry."

"So am I." She looked at her hands now, rather than the floor, and a single tear tracked down one of her rose-petal cheeks. Beacon fought back the urge to reach out and brush it away. *You don't know her like that,* he told himself sternly. *Don't take liberties. Wear the uniform well.*

"It would almost be easier," Pandora said, "if I knew I was only a mistake. That an accident of nature made me this way. But I was shaped into what I am with forethought and intention. Someone did this on purpose."

Rage flooded Beacon. He thought of Pandora in the lower city, on her back and waiting to die, for fear of harming someone if she loosed her power. He thought of how quickly she'd slipped into a swoon, overcome by the pain she carried forever at her center.

"I will find them," he said in a voice like steel, his jaw set in an implacable and outraged line. "I will bring every ounce of force the Guard possesses to bear against them. And I'll see to it you stay untouched in the process—none of this was your doing, and you can't be punished for it."

"Oh, Beacon." Pandora shook her head sadly. "You know exceptions aren't made for mages like me, no matter how good their reasons for circumventing the mage laws. No one but you will care that my power wasn't something I chose. I'm still a threat, and an abomination, and they will never see past that."

He couldn't look at her, he was so angry. To look at Pandora now would be fatal. He would burst out of the room and subject every noble on this wretched hill to a grueling test of powerlessness on her behalf. He would drag every last one of them off in chains, guilt or innocence be damned. Just suspicion would be enough, and no one on Palace Hill was untouched by it.

But no. Beacon balled his hands into fists and counted back from ten to calm himself. Now, as always, justice must be done. He must be cool. Collected. Measured in his actions and judgments.

"How did you get away?" he asked when he could trust himself to speak. "A patron can give incontrovertible orders to their mage. How did you escape, if your patron could command you to complete obedience?"

"The wellspring was my saving grace. Before it, I could never have left, orders or no orders. I'd have died for want of spellfire—it was so hard to come by then, and so dear, and I needed so much of it just to survive. All throughout childhood I was stretched and prodded—my patron subjected me to tests, and eventually siphoned spellfire out of me, wanting to see how far I could be pushed before falling into caster's fatigue. Then they'd inject more into me. A fortune's worth of it, until I felt I'd incinerate, it burned so terribly. All that only made things worse. It grew my capacity for magic, until I was insatiable. Except for the rare times when they filled my veins with so much spellfire I could hardly hold it, I was always starving for more. I'd have been dead of caster's fatigue within a day or two if I left them.

"But when the wellspring opened, I had what I needed. I could both live on my own, and I'd become powerful enough to block my binding. Not to sever it, but to keep it from acting upon me or allowing my patron to find me by it. What was a nightmare for every other mage in Hesperid was freedom for me. While other mages were dying for lack of control over their new spellfire, I got away and vanished. I spent a year on the streets, terrified that they'd come after me, but they never did."

"Why didn't you stay hiding?" Beacon asked. She looked so small to him, so deceptively frail. He wanted to take her away and tuck her into some remote cottage where not a soul on Palace Hill could touch her. "Surely it was a risk to join the Bellwethers, and to come here. In the lower city you could hope to stay unnoticed. Here, you're under far more scrutiny. It's a danger to you."

Pandora turned to the window, taking in the green lawns and clever topiaries beyond. Her face in profile was nearly elfin in its fineness. Beacon could not believe that only a day ago, he'd found her plain and unexceptional.

"My patron has always been . . . unique, in their requirements,"

Pandora said. "Before the wellspring, they would kill other mages in front of me, siphoning off their spellfire. I thought it was just that they needed so much of it, which led them to acquire it in such a way. But they've kept on killing people, even now the wellspring's open and no mage wants for power. Ever since I escaped them, I've found bodies in the lower city, stripped of their spellfire. My patron is still taking it that way, and I don't know why. I do know this—someone ought to stop them, and I'm the only person who might be fit for it. I don't want to. The idea of seeing them again, this time unmasked, makes me sick with fear. But just like you, I don't know of anyone else in Hesperid who's like us. Who could stand against us. So I've come to Palace Hill to find them and try to put an end to their murderous appetites."

"Winifred's death?" Beacon asked. Unspoken in the question was a thing they both knew—it could not be a coincidence that Pandora's dearest friend had been killed within two days of her arrival on Palace Hill.

"A message. A warning, perhaps," Pandora said. "With the binding between us blocked, my patron can't control me directly. And I think, as much as I'm afraid of a confrontation, they might be too. Otherwise they'd have put an end to me during my first night on the Hill. Instead, they're trying to run me off. But I won't go. I'm done hiding, and done running. I'm already terrified—what happened to poor Winnie doesn't make it any worse."

"I will find them for you," Beacon swore. All his time in the city, he'd been looking for a worthy cause. Since losing Everly, he'd been searching for a chance at redemption. Here it was, diminutive and prim, in the long-suffering person of Pandora Small. "Maybe the rest of the Guard won't act on your word alone, but I will. So you've got one of us, at least. We *will* track down your patron. And when we've unmasked them, I will be at your back while you put an end to all this."

"Beacon?" Pan said in a quiet, broken voice, as if she hadn't heard his offer. "Everything is very hard. It's been that way for as long as I can remember. And I feel so awful about Winifred—if I hadn't come here, if we hadn't been friends—"

"Stop," he said swiftly, and moved from his chair to kneel before her. It was an instinctive act—Beacon could no more keep away from her in that moment than he could work magic or extinguish his magesense. Taking both Pandora's hands in his own, Beacon looked up at her. "You didn't hurt anyone. You aren't responsible for your patron's choices, or for the actions of others. Every day, you safeguard the people around you just by being who you are and keeping your power under control. Let me be the one who safeguards you."

Pandora shut her eyes for a moment, and when she opened them again, her gaze was soft with longing. Something wild and intemperate rose in Beacon at the sight. Since the moment he first saw a Grim spring at her, all he'd desired was to protect this little mage. Perhaps it was foolish, given her power. Certainly, she did not need him. But if she only wanted his service, as he wanted to give it to her—

"Beacon, I can't," Pandora said softly, and the refusal hit him like a gallon of cold water. "Even if I'd like you by my side, it isn't fair. I'll take your help to find my patron, but after that, I face them alone. It has to be that way. As much as they made me, I made them. They couldn't have become who and what they are without me."

Beacon scowled. "They chose that binding. You didn't."

"No. But I'm choosing this. To face them on my own, and ensure no one else is harmed."

"If you'd only ask me—" Beacon began, but Pandora shook her head and stopped him with a raised hand.

"No, I won't. And I won't thank you for pressing me to."

Obedient, Beacon said nothing. He only took one of Pandora's small white hands, still held in his own, and pressed it to his lips, like a champion of old saluting his queen.

9

SMOKE AND ASH

The palace chapel was unlike any Pandora had ever seen before. At the Bellwethers', the sisters and their pupils walked in an orderly line to the chapel at the head of their prosperous tree-lined lane. It was a small place, with a painted wooden triptych suspended above an altar to represent the Higher Gods, and a portrait of the Lower Gods painted onto the flagstones before the altar. The Lower Gods were constantly having to be repainted, as worshipers approached to make their offerings and stepped upon the Lower pantheon.

The chapel on Palace Hill was a separate and gracious stone building, newly completed and built on a modern circular plan to represent the world. Older chapels were oval, from before the Canarite Theory had been proved and the worlds found to be spherical. At the center of the chapel's perfectly symmetrical space, a shrine to the Higher Gods hung suspended from the ceiling by thick lengths of gold-coated chain. All seven of the Higher Gods were represented there, sculpted into a vast, twisting wreath of ironwork and painted the glowing colors of the Upper Reaches they inhabited. Jewels studded the clothing and ornaments they wore, donated by wealthy and devout worshipers, and several hundred sweetly scented beeswax candles glowed from brackets in the Wheel of the Gods.

Beneath the Wheel lay Winifred.

They'd placed her on a raised platform draped in red silk, to represent the bright and unrealized potential of a life lost too young, and Pandora felt a twinge of devastation coupled with annoyance. Winnie had hated red. She'd always complained about how florid any shade of it made her, and she would have been mortified to find herself displayed on a bed of it now.

Her gown, at least, was emerald green, Winnie's color of choice. She did not look like herself, however. Someone had taken great care to attempt to rearrange her features into a semblance of peace, but there was still a hint of horror at the edge of her mouth and in the muscles around her eyes. Oils and powders were meant to hide the spellfire-blue stains on her face and fingers but only made the body unnatural and ghastly, while hints of blue still showed.

Besides the Bellwethers, their students, and a small knot of Winifred's family members brought up in a hurry from the lower city, the chapel was empty of mourners. An officiant ghosted about the perimeter of the single open room, tending to smaller, individual shrines and ensuring he was available for any special offerings or prayers. It shouldn't have surprised Pan that Palace Hill hadn't turned out en masse for the immolation rites of a single insignificant Ingenue, but she still found herself quietly furious. None of them cared. They were too caught up in their own world of frivolity and drama to mind that one unremarkable would-be courtier had died attempting to join their ranks.

"Pandora," Imogen hissed, and Pan started. Lost in contemplation, she'd failed to notice it was her turn to approach Winifred's state bed and lay down her offertory garland.

As she approached, the wreath of jessamine flowers in her hands smelled sickly sweet, coated with their own highly flammable sap. Pandora was careful to grasp the wreath only by the bare handholds left for that purpose, lest she daub herself with sap and meet with some stray spark that would send her up in flames.

At the state bed, Pan couldn't bring herself to look straight at Winnie. It hurt too much, knowing that she'd been at least indirectly responsible for her friend's death. Without Pandora invading their territory, her patron would likely never have selected Winifred as a target and a warning. Instead of fixing her eyes on Winnie, Pan looked down, to the circle of iron grating that interrupted the marble floor, mirroring the Wheel of the Gods.

Far beneath the ground, an equal distance below worshipers as the Wheel of the Gods above, a ponderous stone ring of statues stood. There was a Lower God for each of the Higher seven, their shapes monstrous, while the Higher Gods were sublime. Tiny lamps, each fueled by a few drops of volatile liquid spellfire, dotted the spaces between the Lower Gods, casting lurid blue light and shadows across them.

With a shudder, Pandora set her jessamine wreath among the others ringing Winifred and returned to the Bellwether girls. To her surprise, Eleanor Wellesley, usually silent and withdrawn, moved to Pan and put one arm around her shoulders. From the other side, Mamie Hawthorne did the same. Neither of them had ever been close to Pan, but they'd been good friends to Winifred. Aside from Imogen, who Winifred snubbed for Pandora's sake, everyone Winnie met had ended as a friend of hers.

"She loved you, Pan," Eleanor said firmly. "She was good to everyone, but she loved you most. Every time any of us spoke about becoming Ingenues and finding our patrons, she always said how she hoped you'd be by her side."

Pandora couldn't speak. She only nodded as Mamie laid her head on Pan's shoulder and Eleanor pressed a kiss to her hair.

"We won't forget her." Mamie's voice was soft. "And we'll look after each other while we're remembering, won't we?"

"Yes," Pandora managed to get out. "We'll look after each other."

What she meant was *I will look after you all. I will find a way to ensure this does not happen again.*

"Girls," Miss Elvira whispered in her sternest voice. "Look your best. Her Majesty is here."

As one, the Bellwether Ingenues turned and dropped into deep curtsies. From beneath her eyelashes, Pandora saw that not only the queen had arrived, but the prince consort and Prince Theo as well. The queen and consort went to Winifred's family first, but Theo made his way to the Ingenues, his eyes fixed on Imogen.

"Gin, a word?"

Imogen glanced at Miss Elvira, who nodded her approval at once. The prince drew Imogen a little aside, tucking her hand through one arm with a proprietary air. Pandora, who Winnie had always called prudish, flushed just looking at them. Not so much because of the familiarity between Imogen and the prince, but because seeing them so made her think immediately of Beacon.

Beacon coming to her in the labyrinth, saving her from suspicion. Beacon across from her in Miss Alice's study, somehow eliciting a confession she'd never spoken aloud before. Not a soul knew about her patron—she'd guarded the secret as jealously as she did her wildfire magic. Beacon on his knees, with her hands in his.

STEEL & SPELLFIRE

Bereft of Imogen, Leslie moved to join the rest of the Bellwether girls.

"Are they promised to each other yet?" Mamie asked, gesturing in the direction of Theo and Imogen, who stood very close, speaking in low voices. Gin had her eyes fixed on the prince as if he was a lifeline, and something electric seemed to pass between them, as if they were joined together not by a binding, but by something subtler and more essential.

Leslie shrugged. "If they are, I haven't heard anything about it. And Imogen's not exactly humble, she'd say if she'd won him over. I don't know that he'll ever offer—he likes her a great deal, and they've known each other since childhood, but he dallies with other girls too, from what I've been told."

"Gin's never struck me as the type who'd have patience for that," Pandora said, frowning in the direction of Imogen and the prince. "Odd she doesn't mind it."

Leslie smiled wisely. "Which one of us wouldn't overlook a great deal more for a crown someday?"

Me, Pandora thought. *I'd like nothing less than to be bound to a throne and an entire country's worth of expectations.* But she only nodded in reply.

Across the chapel, the queen finished speaking to Winifred's family and swept over to the Bellwether girls. She smiled sympathetically as they all dropped into curtsies once more.

"I'm so sorry for what's happened to your friend," Maud said. "A shocking lapse of security. But I promise you, the Guard will be doubled, and whatever hellion got hold of Winifred will be tracked down and extinguished."

"Thank you, Your Majesty," several of the girls murmured.

Pandora said nothing. Maud was polite and almost plain, and

everyone knew her reputation. She'd been superfluous to Hesperid before her marriage to the consort, and before the wellspring. It was the consort who Pandora looked to.

He stood waiting alone near the shrine of Orryx, god of the skies. He had a tense, impatient air about him, as if this was an unnecessary interruption in a schedule full of urgencies. Perhaps that was true—the consort *was* head of the Guard and sat on every council Maud convened, where he always spoke freely. He was generally considered to be competent, levelheaded, and the real power behind the throne. Beyond that, Pan knew little about him.

While she stood watching the consort, he turned as if aware of her attention. A brief, charged look passed between them, lasting only an instant before the consort strode across the chapel and out through its single door. Pandora only needed a moment, though, to see his eyes glow spellfire blue.

There were certain things that might cause such an afterglow. In the wake of a successful binding, both mage and patron had it for an hour or two. A particularly difficult piece of magework might cause a spellfire glow. And it could appear in both mage and subject when the mage laws were flouted and magic done directly on another soul.

But where Pandora had seen such eyes most often and most vividly was during childhood, in the confines of her steel-walled nursery. The one glimpse she'd ever caught of her patron was the glitter of a spellfire-blue gaze, emanating now and then from the depths of their hood and mask.

It's nothing, she attempted to reassure herself, while unreasoning fear still slicked her palms with sweat. *He's likely just taken a binding from some member of the mage corps.*

But the deeper, less certain parts of her whispered of suspicion instead. *What if it is him? How would you ever stand against someone so highly placed?*

Just the idea sat in Pandora's belly like a ball of ice as she half listened to the final pleasantries that passed between her schoolmates and the queen. She watched the royal family leave and the chapel officiant step forward to Winifred's state bed. The officiant struck a match and set it to the nearest jessamine wreath.

A gout of flame roared to life, engulfing the girl, the flowers, the bed of state. Plumes of smoke rose up through the Wheel of the Gods, toward a small round opening in the chapel roof. Ash began to fall, through the grate the funeral pyre stood on and down to the waiting Lower Gods.

"We live and die at the gods' pleasure," the officiant intoned. "By their will we fall as ash or rise as smoke. May this soul be a pleasing aroma in the Upper Reaches, and be drawn like smoke to the Higher Gods."

"So it is spoken, so it will be," the Bellwether girls chorused, knowing their part.

And that was the sad end of Winifred Harper, the first friend Pandora had ever known.

Miss Elvira would not allow grief to derail the proceedings of her elaborate social calendar. Within eight hours Winifred had died and been sent to the gods, and the rest of the Bellwether girls were back on display, ornamenting a palace ballroom. Pandora felt emotionless and remote, as if the swirl of music and dancers was a dream that could not truly touch her.

Over and over in her mind, she heard her patron's voice, echoing a warning from the troubled labyrinth of her past. *Every time you attempt to escape my influence, people will die. Their lives no lon-*

ger belong to the gods, but rest in your hands. Over and over she saw flashes of Winifred's body—the girl once vivid and passionate and dearly loved, rendered an empty husk. Stripped of spellfire, of vitality, of life.

The familiar strains of the Golden Waltz struck up like a mockery of Pandora and all she'd ever tried to achieve. What did it matter if she could spin brute force into precision and power, and that a boy found her talents beautiful? The reasonable part of Pandora knew that her patron would continue to take lives with or without her. But the softer, grieving side of her felt that she would never be more than a motive for murder as long as her patron continued to punish her through others.

Murmuring an excuse to the faceless partner spinning her across the dance floor, Pan retreated to the edges of the room, the province of matrons, wallflowers, and the silent Queen's Guard. She scanned the room desperately for Beacon, wanting just to stand near him without words and to feel bolstered by his solid presence, but he was off duty, or perhaps stationed elsewhere tonight.

Pan squinted up at the flock of immense cut-glass chandeliers hovering over the dance floor, feigning awe in order to let tears drain unseen from the corners of her eyes. Only hours since Winnie's death and Palace Hill carried on as if she'd never lived. People laughed and frolicked everywhere, swanning about in a rainbow of colored silks and glinting gemstones and waving feathers. In an adjoining room, tables groaned with refreshments—nothing satisfying, but delicate little morsels and tiny glasses of rum punch, meant to keep the dancers giddy and light on their feet.

For once, Pandora wished she could indulge and soften the edges of awareness as they did. But giddiness was not a state she understood. The spellfire in her ran so hot, it burned off alcohol the moment it hit her blood, and she was too wary to ever let her guard down fully. On a raised platform at the front of the room, the chamber orchestra shifted tempos, moving from the elegant strains of "Golden Apples, Golden Fleece" to the riotous melody of "All Awhirl," while the couples on the floor stamped and leaped as the dance required.

"Pandora," Miss Elvira said in her perpetually disapproving voice as she materialized from among the watchers along the wall. "You're not dancing."

"I need a few moments." Winnie's death cut too deep for the frivolous displays of emotion she'd be required to put on, and fear was stifling her as well. Somewhere, her patron was watching and waiting, biding their time as they attempted to suss out Pan's aims on Palace Hill. But they could not resist reminding her of their presence and power. Her recent suspicions regarding Miss Alice and the consort had her on edge, startling at shadows. "I'm a little out of sorts, Miss Elvira."

The older woman pursed her lips in dissatisfaction and shook her iron-gray head. "I understand Winifred's death was a blow to you. It was to all of us. But I must remind you, Pandora, that you have two months to forge your own destiny here, or be relegated to a forced binding. You cannot afford to waste time. You've made no impression whatsoever—Eleanor has already caught the eye of Lord Wattley, and Imogen had a veritable queue of suitors waiting to squire her around the gardens this afternoon. Two of the Grace College girls have secured offers of patronage already, and promised themselves, as have several of the Ingenues from smaller schools or private tutors. You must make your presence known."

A sour taste filled Pandora's mouth. She had no interest in a wealthy suitor and patron to counteract her older, more malevolent binding—that was *not* why she'd endured an Ingenue's training and come to Palace Hill. Nor did she enjoy the game of social climbing the way so many other Ingenues did. With the image of Winnie's lifeless body seared into her mind, the last thing Pan wanted to do was simper and flatter and charm. She wanted to kill something. Wanted to find an army of hellions and tear them to shreds with her spellfire, giving way to the violence locked within her core.

But five years at the Bellwether School had helped with that. She'd already learned a vast measure of control before coming to them, and the school had honed her other, equally useful skills: patience, circumspection, strategy.

"Ah, Baron Hax," Miss Elvira said suddenly, and Pandora's heart sank. "I believe you've already experienced the particular charms of our protégé, Miss Small. Miss Small has an exceptional talent for parlor magic, which I know is an interest of yours."

Hax turned and raised one ironic brow. "Yes, I was electrified by Miss Small's skills earlier today in the gardens. Truly, she is a devastating creature."

A flare of anger burned past Pandora's grief and guilt. Stupid, self-aggrandizing, grasping man. He held a glass of brandy in one hand and acted as if Pan could not flay the flesh from his bones with a single thought.

"Miss Small?" Hax prodded. "I should dearly love to be treated to another sampling of your power."

He knew all too well how the game was played and stood expectantly, waiting for Pandora to demonstrate her skill. Mindful of Miss Elvira's warning, she let off a shimmer of parlor magic—only the barest spark from Pandora produced a dazzling aurora above the dancers that stretched the length and width of the entire ballroom. It glowed and danced in every shade of green Pan had seen Winifred wear. Throughout the room, several would-be patrons glanced up with sharp interest, abandoning their conversations or their wooing to make inquiries as to whose parlor magic had created such a vision. But before anyone else could approach her, Pan let the aurora fade and die.

"I'm so sorry," she said, eyes downcast. "I'm afraid I'm not myself at the moment. You must understand, Baron Hax—the Ingenue who was killed was a particular friend of mine."

"Ah yes," Hax said smoothly. "In a city rampant with hellions, very few of us are ever truly safe. What a thing it would be, to feel secure and unassailable while also profiting from the wellspring. If a mage could grant a patron that, their binding would be priceless—a treasure beyond compare."

He might as well have said it aloud. *Whatever horrors you're capable of, whatever sins you may have committed, whatever stain of suspicion may occasionally blight your path, I still want you by my side. I still desire your patronage and will play whatever hand necessary to obtain it.*

"Perhaps a few dances tonight," Hax said with mellow warmth, "and tomorrow will see you in a better frame of mind. Then we might take tea in the conservatory, and you can continue the demonstration of skill that was so tragically interrupted this morning."

"For shame, Elvira," a welcome voice cut in, chiding Pan's overseer gently. "Keeping this child up when she's suffered such a blow. What on earth can you be thinking?"

Miss Elvira and Baron Hax immediately dropped into a deep bow and curtsy, and Pandora turned before following suit. Queen Maud and the royal retinue stood before her, the queen's curious gaze fixing on Pan as it had not that afternoon in the chapel. She was a thoughtful-looking woman, with streaks of silver in her chestnut hair. The queen wore few ornaments besides a single silver Hesperidian star hanging from a velvet ribbon around her throat, but her gown was a lush abundance of midnight-hued Kandoran silk. She looked regal enough, even if it was other, perhaps more sinister forces, that ultimately moved her.

"Your Majesty," Pandora murmured. "I believe you're right, and I'd best excuse myself."

"Of course I'm right," Maud said. "Elvira, you must let the girl rest, at least until tomorrow."

Miss Elvira made a flurry of apologies, all while furtively glaring daggers at Pandora. Pan didn't care—she'd never been in Miss Elvira's good graces.

"Run along, then," the queen said, giving Pandora's arm a sympathetic and perfunctory pat. "Tomorrow is a new day, full of opportunities of its own. A single evening won't deprive you of your chances. Will it, Hax?"

Even the baron hurried to agree with the queen, and Pandora seized the chance to say her good-nights and flee the ballroom.

Away from the crush of revelers, it felt as if she could breathe again. Pan found herself in a long, dimly lit corridor. Aside from an occasional guard, there seemed to be no one about, although warm lamplight and raucous men's laughter spilled from the open doorway of a nearby lounge. None of that mattered to Pandora, and she'd already bypassed the lounge when a well-known golden voice stopped her in her tracks. Just inside the lit doorway, Imogen had spoken in low, earnest tones.

"—wish you'd reconsider and leave the Hill. At least for a month or two, until the Guard sorts out what happened with that Ingenue." It was a male voice speaking now, taking up after Imogen had fallen silent. Imogen herself replied, and Pandora could hear frosty disdain in her rival's words.

"You know this is my last chance to find a decent patron, Theo. If you'd only man up and do the job yourself—"

"I can't. Gin, we've been wrangling over this for years. I can't be your patron, much as I'd like to."

Imogen let out an unladylike snort, which startled Pan. In her experience, Imogen Hollen was never anything but the picture of decorum while among her elders or social betters. "'Much as I'd like to.' You make it sound about as appealing a prospect as having a tooth out. If you don't want to, I'd rather you come right out and say it."

The other speaker, who Pandora could only assume was Prince Theo, groaned. "It isn't not wanting. I've told you that a thousand times. Don't dredge this up. Not now. I only took you aside to try to get you to leave the city for the rest of the summer. Even if you won't do it for your own sake, think of your father. They're trying to pin that girl's death on a hellion, but it won't be long before they decide it might have been someone associated with sliphouses, too. No one else knows so well how to draw spellfire from a mage. The Guard will come knocking on Ander's door, and I don't want you involved in some unsavory investigation just because you're his daughter."

Imogen's disdain grew lethal. "Well, that's the difference between us, isn't it? I'm loyal to those I love. I'd never leave them alone, in dire straits. If the Guard comes for Papa, they'll get to him through me."

Pandora ducked behind an immense potted palm and shrank into the shadows as Imogen appeared in the doorway of the lounge, imperious and impossibly lovely in a gown of beaded gold silk.

"Don't be like this," Theo pleaded, following her into the corridor. He was tall and slender, with dark hair, and had a plaintive, winning way about him. Truly, he and Imogen would make a beautiful pair. "I'm only looking out for you, you know that."

"If you were looking out for me," Imogen said, whirling and delivering a fatal blow, "you'd take my binding. Don't pretend to care for me when you won't. We'll do as you so brilliantly decided. Go our separate ways this summer, and find unobjectionable partners. I fancy Lord Myers—he's near eighty, so I'll only have to wait a few years before he dies and the binding kills me along with him. As for you, you can take whatever pretty, useless girl turns your head and make her a sparkling little queen."

Gathering her skirts and her air of wounded pride, Imogen strode away, only to stop after a few steps and turn to Theo, who stood forlornly watching her go.

"Any girl," she said, correcting herself, "except Pandora Small. She's one of the Bellwether Ingenues. As you love me, Theo, stay away from her, or somehow, someday, I will make you pay for it."

Pan stayed behind the palm as Imogen carried on into the labyrinth of the palace and Theo retreated into the gentlemen's lounge nearby. For all she and Imogen had sparred with one another over the years, Pan hadn't realized the other girl truly disliked her. It irked her, even as Prince Theo's words raised suspicion. Succumbing to temptation, Pan squared her shoulders and drifted lightly into the lounge.

She hadn't been in a mood for dancing, but with Winifred's death resting heavy on her, she felt a sudden and dangerous urge to gamble.

Though the dull clamor of male voices lowered perceptibly as Pandora entered the room, and several gentlemen reached for their frock coats, no one seemed unduly scandalized. Imogen had of course, just been in, and it was not unheard of for Ingenues to make brazen plays for attention. Nodding to all and sundry, Pandora made her way through a warren of furniture and tables and young men to a long bar at the end of the room, where Prince Theo sat with his back to the door.

Sliding onto the seat beside him, Pan held out a hand.

"I'm Leslie Moran," she lied, assuming the identity of the Bellwether girl who was closest to Imogen. Leslie had the added advantage of being practically promised to a Mr. Woolsley, heir to a vast southern estate and an even vaster fortune—as such, she was content to keep herself quieter than most Ingenues. Theo and Imogen hadn't been together much, and Pandora was betting on the fact that Imogen hadn't pointed Leslie out to him.

"I'm a friend of Imogen's," Pan went on. The prince stared gloomily into a glass of Occipitan whiskey, swirling its amber contents with one hand. "She asked me to introduce myself to you before we even arrived on the Hill. Said to tell you I'd make a reasonable queen, and one she wouldn't object to. I think you ought to be able to make up your mind for yourself on that score, but you know what Gin's like—loves to have a spoon in everyone's teacup."

"Yes, I do know what she's like. Pleased to make your acquaintance, although I'm in a foul mood," Theo said, and drained his glass with a single, decisive movement. He tapped on the bar, and a liveried servant appeared immediately. "Another, please. And get the young lady whatever she wishes for."

"I'll have what he's having," Pandora said. "But make mine a double."

For the first time, Theo turned to look at her, disbelief in his eyes.

"Are you certain?" he asked, taking in her diminutive size and her slightness. "The Occipitan's an '84, it packs a hell of a punch."

Pandora beamed at him, the smile feeling false and unlovely on her face. "Certain as sunrise. Is it true you're expected to choose an Ingenue bride before the end of this summer?"

Theo heaved a bleak sigh as the attendant set glasses down before them. "No. And yes. I'm expected to choose an Ingenue with no time limit on the requirement, but we're all of an age with each other this year. So I'll have to find someone sooner rather than later. If I let it drag on too long, I'll end up a cradle robber, and I don't fancy that. Too much risk for the girl—I'm not dragging a mage into the grave with me before her time."

Pandora let out a gale of silvery laughter, calculated to charm. Theo was easier to read than Beacon—she'd only needed to overhear a single exchange between him and Imogen to realize he appreciated forthrightness and cleverness. Imogen was, after all, both of those things, albeit in a sharp-tongued, shrewish way. "No taste for younger girls? It seems you're a rarity on Palace Hill. Most of the gentlemen I've met or heard of thus far have no such compunctions."

Taking up her whiskey glass, Pan swallowed a mouthful, fighting the urge to pull a face. She wasn't partial to the taste, but her capacity to imbibe quantities of spirits with no ill effect always seemed to win either respect or awe. Theo blinked as her smile never slipped.

"You said your name's Leslie Moran?" he asked. "Imogen's never mentioned you. She's never spoken of any of the other Ingenues at the Bellwethers', besides someone called Pandora. That name I've heard more than once over the years."

"Oh, *Pan*," Pandora said dismissively. "Of course she'd bring her up, we all talk about Pan. How that horrible little guttersnipe ended up at a fine establishment like the Bellwethers' is beyond me."

Theo drained his whiskey and gestured for another, as Pandora followed suit. She could see the prince's eyes beginning to glaze over and his mannerisms growing more pronounced. Likely, he'd been sipping rum punch all the fore-evening and was half in his cups by the time he and Imogen had quarreled. Pan meant to get him all the way there, and he was proving a terribly easy mark.

"Can I be honest with you for a moment?" Theo asked, and Pan nodded solemnly. "I was rather surprised when Imogen said she'd chosen to study under the Bellwethers. It isn't that such places aren't respectable, or a fine chance for many girls. But when you're like Imogen—from a family that already has access to the Hill—it's expected you'll have a private tutor and learn at home. I'm in company often, and I've heard unflattering talk about Gin being there. The girls in the first circle . . . well, they say she's slumming it."

Pandora let out a genteel gasp, and none of her surprise was feigned. What an interesting piece of information. "Do they? How absolutely catty. Imogen never does anything without reason, so I'd imagine there's a very compelling one for her being at the Bellwethers'. Hasn't she ever hinted at it?"

"No." Theo peered at her owlishly. "I've tried to pry, but you know what she's like. A closed book when she wants to be."

"Hm," Pandora said, nodding her understanding and then swallowing the dregs of her second double. Theo stared at her in frank admiration, and she smiled brightly, as if it was nothing out of the ordinary for a dainty Ingenue to be able to drink any gentleman on Palace Hill under the table. "I do know what she's like. And you know, I . . . I'm worried about her."

Pan lowered her voice, leaning in toward Theo with a conciliatory air. "This business with Winifred, the girl who was killed. It's a ghastly thing. And I do wonder about Imogen's family connection to sliphouses. Mightn't her father end up under some sort of suspicion or scandal?"

Now they were coming to the point, and to Pandora's reason for approaching the prince. What he'd said about sliphouses had sparked her interest. Though she hadn't thought of it before, it made good sense that her patron might have been connected to sliphouses, at least before the wellspring. They were an outdated institution now and had never been strictly legal. Prior to the flood of power the wellspring unleashed, spellfire had been a scarce commodity and outrageously valuable. Mages who harbored a decent share of it would sometimes sell it right out of their blood, visiting sliphouses where it was siphoned from them in exchange for a modest payment, then resold for an eye-watering sum. Pan had never been to a sliphouse herself, given the shape of her childhood. But access to sliphouses would account for the abundance of spellfire Pandora's patron had been able to provide her. Yes, her patron had killed people to draw out their sparks, but they'd have had to commit a dozen murders a week to keep Pandora in spellfire. Surely someone would have noticed. It made far more sense that they'd have preyed on the desperation of poorer mages, who could return to a sliphouse every few days and sell their power time after time.

Learning Imogen Hollen had entered the Bellwether School for unknown reasons and had a connection to sliphouses, as well, seemed more than a coincidence. And with Winifred's death on her conscience, Pandora meant to leave no stone unturned in the search for her patron.

Theo's eyes widened as Pandora mentioned that Imogen would be wise to exercise caution as Winnie's death was investigated.

"That's *exactly* what I've been trying to tell Gin," he slurred. "Not many people know what it looks like when a mage's spellfire's been dragged out of them, instead of pushed out by their own magic. But the way that girl's fingers and face were still stained blue? That wasn't caster's fatigue. She didn't spend her own power. Someone ripped it out of her, right down to the last ember. I've made an academic study of hellions and never heard of one that kills like that before. Which means it was either a mage with monstrous power who killed that girl, or someone who knew their way around a sliphouse's mechanical devilry, or a person who's a bit of both."

"How awful," Pandora said with a solemn shake of her head. "I'll do my best to try to convince Imogen that discretion is the better part of valor. But it's hard to change her mind once it's made up."

"Isn't it?" Theo agreed fervently. He had his chin resting on one hand now and gazed up at Pan with bleary eyes. He wasn't at all like she'd imagined—the dailies painted him as an absolute rake in the making, but he gave off the air of a forlorn puppy. Under other circumstances, Pandora could envision herself liking him immensely. Being friends, even. But he'd find out her deception soon enough, and that would forestall any warmth or trust. She'd gotten the information she wanted, at least, and learned something new about Imogen, so the encounter wasn't a total loss.

"Leslie Moran," Theo said indistinctly. "Do you suppose I'll see you tomorrow? Or the next day?"

Pan slipped from her seat. "I'm sure our paths will cross again. But I'd best be going—I prefer to keep earlier hours than most. Good for the complexion, you know."

Like an arrow from a string, Pandora left the lounge and made straight for the Guard quarters. On the threshold of Beacon's door, she knocked. When he opened it, Pan could not deny the way something anxious and expectant came to life in her as his eyes brightened at the sight of his unexpected guest.

"I've learned a number of unsettling things today," Pandora said. "I'd like to hear your thoughts on them, if you meant it when you offered to help me track down my patron."

He nodded eagerly, as if there could be no more desirable task than to assist her, and it warmed Pandora to the core in a way spellfire had never done.

10

STILL LESLIE

Pandora was embarrassed.

It was impulse that had induced her to eavesdrop on Imogen the evening before, to pry information from Prince Theo, and to appear once more on Beacon's doorstep. The last was more than embarrassing—though Beacon had been infinitely helpful in talking over Pandora's suspicions regarding Miss Alice, the consort, and anyone connected to sliphouses, Pan felt a twinge of humiliation over how she'd begun to rely on him. He'd promised to question Ander Hollen in his official capacity as a guard, in order to carefully gauge whether Ander, whose family fortune had been built on sliphouses, might be Pan's enigmatic patron. It would have to be done discreetly and during Beacon's off hours, as the Guard still officially considered a hellion to be behind Winifred's death. But Pandora had no doubt Beacon would see it done.

As for her, today she would be independent. She would not turn to a certain broad-shouldered guard for assistance in investigating the pasts of those she considered suspect. Pan would manage it on her own, although she *did* require one favor to begin the process.

The royal family's wing of the castle was elegant in the extreme. The corridors were carpeted with lush Indiran rugs that muted footfalls, while potted palms, chattering fountains, and cages of bright songbirds stood like sentinels along the halls. The constant activity that marked the rest of the palace was absent here, so that the entire wing seemed a place of serenity and repose. Arriving at the fifth doorway in the westmost hall, Pandora knocked smartly.

Minutes passed. No answer. Pandora frowned, raising her fist and knocking harder.

"I'm coming, I'm coming!" an indistinct voice called from somewhere within. After another minute, the door was thrown open precipitously, revealing Prince Theo on the threshold.

Theo looked as exhausted and disheveled as Pandora perpetually felt. The only difference being she was an Ingenue and couldn't show it. While he was in yesterday's wrinkled clothes with his coat over one arm and dark shadows under his eyes, Pan was already dressed in spotless ivory muslin, with silver embroidery stars glinting at her neck and hems. Rose water and tinted face cream gave the impression of freshness and radiance, even when she felt worn to a raveling. Within her, the constant pain of containing her spellfire ground endlessly on and on.

"Good morning," Pan said sweetly to Theo, feigning confidence she didn't feel. "I trust you slept well?"

"Or not at all," the prince grumbled, "thanks to you. You see, I made a special point of remembering your face. It isn't often that an Ingenue manages to drink me under the table. I feel like a flaming pile of rubbish this morning, and I can't understand how you look so fresh."

"Parlor magic," Pandora said with an easy wave of her hand, though it was cosmetics and an unholy amount of kantha that had done it. But Ingenues learned that it worked in their favor to allow others to believe any pleasing attribute was a product of their power.

"How did you get down here?" Theo asked.

Pandora gambled once more. If there was one thing she knew about Imogen, it was that her fellow Ingenue loved to scold. So if Theo tolerated any degree of intimacy with Gin, there must be a part of him that loved to *be* scolded.

"The guards let me in as soon as I said you'd invited me," she told the prince entirely truthfully. "They didn't seem to find anything peculiar about a strange girl waltzing down to your rooms at an irregular hour. Are you aware of the reputation you've earned for yourself?"

But Pandora had misjudged. Theo grew morose and frowned darkly as he answered.

"Yes, thank you. Although I don't appreciate being reminded of it."

Fortunately, the Bellwethers offered a comprehensive education. Not only were their girls taught to woo and to please, they were also taught how to placate. When Pandora dropped her eyes and caught her lower lip between her teeth in an obvious agony of regret, it was only the gesture that was calculated and not the sentiment.

"I'm sorry," she said softly. "I was presumptuous, Your Highness."

Theo let out a weary sigh. "If I'm a bear, it's only because my head is splitting, so you really have yourself to blame for that. I apologize for being sharp with you, Miss—"

He didn't remember her ruse of the night before. Given how far in his cups he'd been, Pandora was surprised he'd remembered her at all.

"I'm P—" she began, and immediately thought better of it. She wanted a favor, and while Theo might grant one to Leslie, Imogen's confidante, he would certainly not be inclined to assist Pandora Small, the thorn in Imogen's flesh. "Leslie," she finished. "Leslie Moran."

Theo raised an amused eyebrow. "Well then, Miss Pleslie Moran. How can I be of service? I'd assume that's why I find you on my doorstep at this wretched hour."

"It's past second bell," Pandora pointed out, unable to be anyone but herself even as she attempted to curry favor.

"Second bell? I wasn't aware there was such a thing. I thought they started with five chimes," Theo said, his sense of humor returning.

"I would like to look through the palace archives." Pandora had finally come to the point. She wanted to go over the palace chronicles and the social columns from twenty years back and onward, in hopes of finding some piece of gossip inferring that a particular mage might be possessed of unusual talents. If that mage was someone on whom her suspicions already rested, so much the better.

"I've an interest in family history," Pan lied neatly. "I was hoping to find references to my mother and grandmother during their time as Ingenues. But the archives are off limits to us girls. I thought perhaps if I had an escort?"

"The archives before third bell." Theo let out a pathetic groan. "What a gruesome prospect. Give me a minute to make myself presentable."

In less time than Pandora would have thought possible, the prince joined her in the corridor, shaved, brushed, and dressed in clean clothes. He held an enormous porcelain mug of kantha in one hand and watched Pan over the rim as he took a long, indulgent sip.

"Want some?" Theo asked, proffering the mug.

"No." Pandora declined with a genteel shake of the head. "I've had mine already."

For all his apparent exhaustion, Theo set a swift pace as he led the way through the tangle of corridors that comprised the palace proper. Surprise and pleasure unfolded in Pandora as they entered an unfamiliar wing, and one of the guards flanking the archives resolved into a stolid, broad-shouldered form. Pan flashed a meaningful look at Beacon, who only looked stoic.

"We have some fascinating family history to research, which is apparently so urgent it can't wait," Theo said with an impatient gesture to Beacon. "Please show us in."

Swiftly locks were dispensed with, and they were ushered into a massive, shelf-lined room full of benches and study tables and the smells of dust and old glue. Dutifully Beacon returned to his partner and his post outside the door, but not without an unreadable glance in Pandora's direction.

"Ugh." Theo shivered, speaking under his breath. "I hate it in here. Whatever you do, don't get on Lady Pomfrey's bad side. She runs the archives, and she's terrifying."

Pandora glanced around. The place seemed lifeless, save for a tiny, gray-haired clerk soundlessly pushing a cart of documents down an aisle.

"You mean that little woman who looks old enough to be a great-grandmother?" Pan asked.

"*Yes,*" Theo said. "Don't let her fool you, she's a monster deep down!"

Pandora had already gathered up her skirts and started toward Lady Pomfrey, leaving Theo with no choice but to follow in her wake.

"Excuse me," Pan called, in the clear, musical tone Ingenues were taught. "Your Ladyship? I have a question for you."

Lady Pomfrey turned, revealing a wizened, clever face, dark eyes, and a crooked nose. "And who might you be?"

Lies upon lies. It was going to be hard to keep track of them if she kept this up. "Leslie Moran. I'm one of this year's Ingenues. I wanted to look at some family history, and I was wondering if the archive keeps genealogies and society columns?"

"Of course we do," Lady Pomfrey said. "You've got pretty manners, child, and I'm sure you'll take care with any documents, won't you? Some people"—she cast a withering glance at Theo—"used to make a habit of coming in and gluing pages together with their jammy fingers."

"I haven't had jammy fingers in years," Theo muttered.

"Some people," Lady Pomfrey said again, "are as likely to spill spirits on my records now as they were to smear them with jam years ago. And I'd prefer the jam."

Pandora waved one of her hands, clad in perfectly fitted white gloves. "I won't leave so much as a mark."

With a pleased smile, Lady Pomfrey started off along the room's perimeter, beckoning to Pan to follow. The elderly clerk moved at a surprisingly brisk pace, wending her way past shelf after shelf of histories, novels, volumes of poetry, and foreign texts.

"Here we are," Lady Pomfrey called breezily from ahead of them. "Genealogies to your left, society papers to the right. Is there a particular year or decade you're interested in, child?"

"Oh, no. Just general gossip."

"Very well. I'll be back in the political treatises section if you need anything."

Lady Pomfrey moved off, and Theo, rather than taking his leave and returning to his bed as Pandora had expected, indolently ran a hand along the nearest shelf.

"Why don't you tell me what you're looking for?" he offered. "Maybe I could be of help."

Having enlisted the prince's assistance, Pandora now faced the unanticipated task of having to get rid of him.

"You've already been of help," she said with a sweet smile, gesturing to their surroundings. "This was all I needed. You're dismissed."

Theo opened and shut his mouth soundlessly. "I'm *dismissed*? Like a scullion? You little harridan, see if I ever do you a favor again!"

And yet he looked half-pleased. Pandora's smile grew brighter and sharper. "You and I both know you can't have been friends with Imogen for years without liking it a little when a girl runs you down. You'd never tolerate her otherwise. I thought I'd follow her lead."

"I'm a beaten man," Theo said fervently. "All I've ever wanted is to please her, but year after year she grinds me to dust under the heel of her dancing slipper."

The prince's eyes glinted as he spoke, as if he relished the process of being ground to dust by Imogen. Watching him, Pandora came to a sudden realization. However much Theo had protested in Imogen's company, refusing to take her binding or her hand, he craved the particular notice of the Bellwethers' golden girl. Any attention from Imogen Hollen, was, to this privileged boy, a good thing.

"Then you're used to following orders," Pan said. "And I'll thank you later if you run along now."

Mumbling something dramatic under his breath, Theo strode off with a doleful set to his shoulders. Pan couldn't help but bite back a smile as she watched him go. After a moment, she turned her attention to the daunting, ceiling-high rows of shelves before her. There had to be over a hundred volumes of genealogies alone, and stacks upon stacks of yellowing society columns, extracted from the Valoran dailies.

Pandora let out a despairing sigh. Where to even begin? A good twenty years back, but how much further beyond that, she couldn't say. It could be the work of a lifetime just combing through these records, looking for some offhanded mention of a noble who might have more magic than was considered proper. It wouldn't have been such a dangerous thing before the wellspring's opening—to have more than a smattering of magic then was a great rarity, and though still considered scandalous, it wasn't a capital offense.

With no real hope of success, Pan drew out a society column and began to read, the chronicles of a careless time before the wellspring seeming alien and unfamiliar. No hellions. No mage laws. It had been a different world. She looked particularly for any mention of Miss Alice and found nothing. Baron Hax's family was mentioned on occasion, but their ancestral holdings were far outside Valora, and none of them seemed possessed of magic. The prince consort came up often, but nothing indicated he might be able to work spellfire.

Lady Pomfrey's and Prince Theo's voices wrangled back and forth at a distance, little more than a dull murmur. At one point, the door opened and shut softly behind them, and Pandora glanced up to find herself alone, save for the books and dust and sunlight.

On and on she read, each breathless recounting of balls and concerts and social mishaps much like the last. A hundred stories of some mésalliance or another, but nothing about magic. Not a single rumor that someone moving in Valora's first circles might be able to harbor more spellfire than was proper. Only rarely was a mage with great talent mentioned, and every time, they were boxed immediately upon discovery, well before becoming entrenched in the social life of Palace Hill.

Frustrated, Pandora skipped backward a decade. More of the same. And back again. Nothing. Lavish picnics on the Hill, parties at summer estates, and a great festival month when Queen Maud was born. Shoving documents aside, Pan buried her face in her hands. She should have known better than to hope.

From somewhere among the freestanding shelves that cluttered the archive's center, a muffled sound drifted. Straightening, Pandora scanned the room. It seemed empty, abandoned by Lady Pomfrey and Theo. But something prickled across the back of her neck—not spellfire, not magesense, but a warning of danger. She'd learned to anticipate any risk to herself over the course of childhood and honed the skill while hunting hellions. Now that instinct for self-preservation was setting off a chorus of alarm bells.

Light poured in through the archive windows. All seemed at peace. But once more, that odd muffled, scratching noise came from the island of shelves at the room's heart. With spellfire surging beneath her skin, Pandora rose and crept forward, through shafts of sunshine thick with dust motes, the warmth of it not enough to drive the chill from her skin.

She rounded one shelf. Nothing.

A second shelf. Nothing again.

A third. And Pandora shut her eyes, balling her hands into fists as she drew in a trembling breath.

Splayed on the floor, drenched in sunshine, lay a pointed reproach to her. Leslie Moran, dark hair pooling around her face. The Ingenue's fingers, her lips, the whites of her eyes were all stained spellfire blue. Her expression was the same look of horror that had marked Winifred when Pandora found her. But she had not died as quickly—Leslie still clutched a pin in her hand, and with it, she had etched the figure of a four-pointed star into the base of the nearest bookshelf before she died.

Hesperid's beloved public emblem. And surely the making of it was the sound Pandora had heard.

Pan opened her eyes. Still there. Not some hellish nightmare, as she'd hoped. Her mind raced, considering what could be done. Lady Pomfrey and Theo were gone. The guards posted at the door had seen Pandora go in and not come out—if they were still in their places, there was no hope of keeping herself clear of association with yet another unprecedented and violent tragedy. Beacon might cover for her. The other guard almost certainly would not.

Ghosting to the archive doors, Pan cracked one open and peered out.

For once, luck was with her. Theo and Lady Pomfrey must have required the presence of a guard for something—only Beacon was left at his post.

"Ellis," Pandora breathed. "Help."

In an instant, he was through the doors, locking them behind him. And Pandora was overcome by a sudden, irrational sense that everything would be fine now. Here he was, stolid, immovable, a wall for her troubles to break on.

Perhaps it was panic. Perhaps it was grief. But for the briefest instant, she flirted with the idea of what it would be like to have this boy as her anchor. As her patron—not a successor to the one she'd always known, but a rival. A bond to Beacon would surely be strong as steel, a match for the old, insidious binding Pandora already carried.

"What can I do?" Beacon asked. There was a world of staunchness and loyalty in those simple words, and all Pan wanted was to break down at the sound of them. To cry as she'd never done before, because she'd never felt safe enough to do so. Stupid, really. She didn't know him well enough to be so dependent, and life had not fitted Pandora out to trust other people. But time after time since coming to Palace Hill, she'd been *forced* to trust Beacon, and he'd never once come up short.

Pan fought to keep calm, despite the knowledge that her presence on the Hill had proved deadly yet again. She reminded herself of the countless bodies she'd found over the years, stripped of their spellfire and their life by her patron's malevolent magic. This was no worse, and yet it felt like Pandora's responsibility. She had known these girls, and if they hadn't been unlucky enough to cross paths with Pandora Small, undoubtedly they'd never have drawn the attention of her patron.

"I thought I was in here alone," Pan told Beacon. "I could have sworn I was. Lady Pomfrey and Prince Theo left, and I'd been reading, until I heard a noise. When I went to look, I found Leslie here. Killed the same way Winifred was. I have no idea how it could have happened, in the same room as me. But I know how it looks. That other guard saw me come into the archives, and Theo and Lady Pomfrey. One dead Ingenue tied to me is a coincidence. Two is a pattern. Once the Guard finds out, they're going to put me through tests even I can't bluff through. I'm going to be boxed, Beacon. And a steel box can't hold or kill me, but I can do the job myself. I will, before I let anyone see how much I am, and everything I can do."

Her voice broke on the last words, and she pressed a hand to her mouth to force composure. This was no carefully chosen outlet for her emotions. Pandora felt perilously close to a true loss of composure, which she could not afford. Not with spellfire searing the underside of her skin.

Beacon simply stood for what felt like an eternity, with a disconcerted, thinking look on his face. Pandora had never seen him so before, worrying away at an internal problem like a persistent dog with a bone.

"I didn't feel anything," he said at last. "When you first came into the archive and passed me, I could feel your warmth. I always do, if you're within earshot now, because I know what it's like. It's easy to overlook a mage if you don't know them, but once you've learned them, they're impossible to ignore. But if this girl was killed while you were in here, and I was just outside, that would've taken a great deal of magic. And I didn't feel anything. I ought to have—I can feel you now, you're upset and burning hotter than usual. But how could someone be killed by magic under my nose, and I didn't even notice?"

"Can you sort it out later?" Pandora asked, still fighting to keep panic at bay. "What if someone comes back? What are we going to do?"

Beacon looked at her, and it was as if he was seeing the depth of her fear for the first time. When he reached out and settled a hand on Pandora's shoulder, it took everything in her not to move a few steps forward and press against him, so that she might feel his arms enfold her and be anchored to hope by his embrace. It wasn't even Beacon in particular who she craved—just someone, anyone, who could hold her and promise that everything would be all right.

"That door leads to a servants' corridor, and along it there's a storage room," Beacon said, pointing across the archives to a small doorway with his free hand. "Every guard is made to memorize a blueprint of the palace, and that's probably where both the Ingenue and your patron came in. We'll put the body in there."

Pandora flinched, hearing Leslie referred to as a body. But that's all she was now, thanks to Pandora drawing her into a lethal web of lies. Poor Leslie hadn't even known.

Pan cursed herself internally, with every ounce of viciousness she could summon. It was just like her patron to send pointed messages like this, to chastise her for any perceived misstep or character flaw. She'd been a fool to think she'd ever find them, used as they were to hiding in the shadows. It was evident they were following Pan's every move and that she was not proceeding even close to carefully enough.

Beacon gathered Leslie up like a broken doll, and the constant pain in Pandora's middle twisted. Had Leslie been eager to wed her promised patron and husband? Had she dreamed of just this—being taken into someone's arms and carried over the threshold of a new home and a new life? Instead, thanks to Pandora, she'd been ushered into a pointless and ignominious death.

Within moments, they'd reached the storage room and its jumble of oddments. Beacon set Leslie down gently, as if she could still feel his touch, and then they were out again, a door shut between them and another Ingenue's remains.

Pandora did not feel better with Leslie safely hidden. She did not feel relieved. She felt only regret and a sickening sense of inadequacy and obligation, as Beacon continued his steadfast management of her crisis.

"This way," he said firmly, leading her back to the archives. He sat her down in the place where she'd been reading. "Do whatever you were doing before, and wait until someone else comes in. You have to be seen."

Pan nodded, wide-eyed and suddenly cold despite her inner fire. She began to shiver, and Beacon took her chin in one hand, so that she had no choice but to look up at him.

"I am not going to let anything happen to you," he promised. "I will not allow you to be boxed. I will not let your former patron touch you. No one is going to hurt you again."

A foolish promise, particularly when Pandora already sat aching at the thought of the deaths stacked against her. Yet somehow, when Beacon spoke the words, she believed him. She could see how he was an asset to the Guard, and down in the city, people would have pulled themselves together at Beacon's request, calming themselves and rising to the occasion as was necessary. No wonder he felt frustrated and wasted on Palace Hill. The boy was made to be bedrock in the face of disaster.

Nodding, Pandora fixed her gaze unseeingly on the stack of society columns before her. She'd been looking for something, though what escaped her mind just now. All she could see was Winifred in the moonlight and Leslie in a pool of sunshine, both of them dead and stripped of their power.

After what seemed an interminably long time, Lady Pomfrey bustled back in, and Pandora could hear low voices from outside as Beacon spoke to his fellow guard. With great care, Pan got up and put her reading material away. Nothing had been of help—she hadn't found a single cast-away reference to a mage with an improper degree of power in Valora's first set.

"Thank you, Lady Pomfrey," Pandora said, forcing a smile as she passed by the elderly archivist. "This was very helpful. I may be back to do some reading again."

"Of course, pet," Lady Pomfrey said with an indulgent smile. "Any time you like. You needn't have that rapscallion prince along to give you access, either—just have a guard tell me you're the one wanting to come in, and I'll see to it they let you past."

Pan nodded her thanks and drifted into the corridor. Beacon stood straight-backed and unyielding at his post as she passed by, and Pandora wondered if he'd still be inclined to help if he could feel the full extent of the pain that plagued her, understand how constantly she toyed with the idea of breaking down and letting her power go, and hear the whispers rising in her even now.

Haven't you done worse than this? her patron's voice murmured, emanating from the binding that tied Pan to them even yet. *What are these few deaths compared to your greater sins? But I would overlook them. I would cherish you and raise you up in power, if only you allowed it.*

Come back.

Come back to me.

11

DEADLY CREATURES

Beacon knew, perhaps better than Pandora knew herself, that the little mage with an inferno of power required a means to let off steam. He was beginning to sense that she spent so much time struggling for control, it wasn't always clear to her when she came closer to a breakdown than usual.

Now, in the wake of two deaths that could be directly tied to Pan, she needed an outlet. Beacon could feel her prodigious power, not at a distance, but when he was near her. If he stood within two steps of the girl, the air went from its ordinary palace coolness to the humid, stifling heat of lowland midsummer. Gods forbid anyone else with the magesense get within an arm's length of Pandora before she'd calmed down.

Which was how Beacon found himself once more wandering the lower city with an Ingenue after dark. He'd had to slink to Pandora's rooms covertly, like some rake courting scandal. Pan had let him in without a hint of surprise, only excusing herself to don a pair of trousers and braces. She could pass for a kitchen boy now, with her hair tucked up into a soft cap. Beacon wondered if he'd ever come to an end of the different people Pandora Small could be, and which was the real and truest version.

Tension hung between them all the way down to the lower city. Pandora had hardly spoken since agreeing to Beacon's illicit invitation, and it bothered him that after all his help, she was pulling away. He had his neck on the line for the girl, and while he'd never call in favors or hold it over her head, it still stung to have her put up a wall between them. He wanted to know her better—so far, it was her magic and her control and her tragic history that had him captivated, as well as her studied Ingenue's way of catching and holding attention. But Beacon wanted to see past all that, beyond the glamor of parlor magic and the polish of good manners, and through the burn of rampant spellfire, even. Who was beneath it all?

"This way," he finally said to the silent girl at his side, setting his jaw at the sick headache that came with sensing a hellion. "I'll take the lead this time."

Pandora nodded mutely and continued to keep pace as he led her through dingy and thickly shadowed streets to a boarded-up shop. It was a ramshackle, single-story building, the sort of place that housed a store in front and living quarters in the back. Beacon tried the door, and it swung open easily beneath his hand, forced in years ago by looters, no doubt.

As he unholstered his pistol and held it at the ready, Pandora reached for her spellfire. Though it had run hot and ready since Winifred's death, Beacon felt it flare up behind him. It was both deeply troubling and strangely reassuring, knowing that even when his awareness of Pandora's power dimmed, the force of her magic never did.

Ahead of Pan, Beacon picked his way through a jumble of shelves and antiques, all cobweb-strewn and rimed with dust. There was little of value here, even for looters. As the room grew oppressively dark within feet of the doorway, Pandora worked parlor magic, setting a series of soft lights to glowing near the ceiling. Silver bathed the shop's interior like moonlight, lending an air of forlornness to the scene of abandonment and banishing the more sinister shadows.

"Thank you," Beacon offered, and Pan made no reply. Though it was foolhardy and a risk to do so, he glanced over one shoulder and found her trailing along behind him, transparently downcast and preoccupied.

The storefront was empty, with no sign of a hellion lying in wait. A narrow, dank corridor led to the living quarters in back, and Beacon felt the brief, initial shimmer and retreat of pain as Pandora began a ward around him. But she let it die unfinished—he had asked to take the lead, after all.

The squalid kitchen they emerged into was a puzzle. It was still lifeless but seemed to have been lived in far more recently than the shop. Fetid dishwater pooled in the washbasin, and a plate with decaying food sat at the table, smelling of rot and crawling with maggots. Pandora pulled a lace-fringed handkerchief from her pocket and pressed it to her nose, and for one tantalizing moment lily of the valley scent drowned out the vile air.

Beacon pushed open a nearby door and froze on its threshold.

"Why don't you go back out to the alley and wait for me?" he said gently. "I can manage this on my own."

"I'm not leaving you," Pan answered with a frown, the first words she'd spoken since they'd left the palace grounds. "What did you—oh."

The soft, unhappy sound died between them as Pandora reached Beacon's side.

If there was one breed of hellion the residents of Valora feared most, it was Gaunts. Shadowy, barely corporeal creatures, they did not prey on their victims outright as most hellion did. Rather, Gaunts stalked their victims silently and slowly, insinuating themselves into one's dreams by night and weaving a web of thick, inescapable slumber.

Before Pandora and Beacon, an elderly man lay on his narrow, moth-eaten bed. He appeared to be sleeping peacefully, but the set of his mouth spoke of troubled dreams, and at his head, a Gaunt floated. A column of dark shadow, the only thing recognizable about it was a pair of vast, luminous eyes. Skeins of the shadow it was made of ran out to the sleeper, permeating his skin and running through his veins as the Gaunt slowly siphoned off his life force.

To be Gaunt-ridden was to face a slow and certain death. From the moment they cast their web of dreams and sank their tendrils into a person, there was no rescue. A Gaunt never let go its death grip, and the creature's end brought about the sleeper's death as well, no matter how precise the pistol shot, or how surgical the flare of spellfire. Both Pandora and Beacon stood together, heavy in heart, burdened by that knowledge.

"I'll do it," Beacon said at last, his words thick with regret. The sick headache plaguing him was worse than usual, and his hands shook a little, though he was sure his pistol shot would still fly true.

"No." Pandora stopped him with a touch to his arm. "Don't. Not yet. I can—"

Frustration choked her, and she turned aside.

"If I could work *on* him," Pandora whispered, "instead of around him, I think everything would be all right. If I could use my own spellfire, I'd go through and banish the Gaunt from him. Vein by vein and sinew by sinew, if necessary. I'd force it to loosen its grip.

And once it let go, he'd be safe. It wouldn't kill him, when the Gaunt dies."

Beacon said nothing. They both knew the laws. And while Ingenues were allowed exceptions, they were never permitted to do anything of real utility. They could not help, nor save, nor heal. All they could do was please and pointlessly dazzle.

"I'll do it," Beacon repeated heavily, but oh, he did not want to. He wished they'd found anything in the world other than a Gaunt.

Pandora's eyes were on him, fixing Beacon with a sharp, searching look—the first real interest she'd shown since they'd hidden Leslie's body together.

"No," she said, and the word was an order. "You won't. I'll take care of this."

And he let her. He shouldn't have—all his better instincts told him not to allow Pandora to assign herself responsibility for one more death. But he stood by as a silent witness while Pan stepped forward. Power seethed within her, bringing tears to Beacon's eyes again. At least he told himself it was that. With none of the fanfare or frills or beauty she'd brought to bear in her last exhibition of power, Pandora let go of a precise and killing bolt of spellfire. The instant it struck the Gaunt, only falling ash remained.

This was Pandora's magic without ornament or artifice. Sudden. Complete. Brutal in its efficiency and simplicity.

On the bed, the sleeper's eyes flew open, rheumy white and unseeing. His breath came in juddering gasps as froth formed on his lips. He seized, skeletal hands clutching the threadbare covers. A high, keening whine escaped the man, halfway between a moan and a sob.

Beacon knew what he should do. He knew it would be a mercy to give the Gaunt's victim a quicker death, but he could not force himself to move.

"Give me your pistol," Pandora said, and her voice was steel.

Beacon felt her take it from him. Without flinching, Pan leveled the weapon and compressed the trigger. The sharp retort of a gunshot rang out, accompanied instantaneously by a spray of blood and bone.

The sleeper fell utterly still. Silence closed around them in the wake of the pistol shot.

Habit took over. Beacon reclaimed his weapon. He meticulously cleaned, primed, and reloaded the pistol, the dutiful guardsman ever at the ready. Then he led them back out into the moonlit alley.

"Do you mind telling me why that rattled you?" Pandora asked after a few moments. The sound of their footsteps rang loud on the night air, Pan's quick and light, Beacon's firm and measured as he slowed his natural stride for her comfort. "I've never seen anything get you off balance before."

"I'll do better next time," Beacon said, squaring his shoulders.

"I'm not scolding you. You didn't underperform. You were bothered, and I want to know why."

Beacon was silent, and Pandora let out a wistful sigh. "Very well. I don't suppose I deserve a confidence. Just because I keep burdening you with my secrets, doesn't mean I'm entitled to any of yours."

Moonlight. Cobblestones. Sad Pandora. Beacon tried to focus on the present, rather than being dragged back into the past.

"My father was killed by a Gaunt," he managed at last, dredging the memory up for her like a dark gift. "Or rather, he fell prey to a Gaunt and was killed . . . by me. Our village had an uncommonly strong vein of spellfire under it, after the wellspring, and we were plagued by hellions now and then."

"I'm so sorry," Pandora breathed, and it was not the hollow condolence others offered. She sounded as if she was apologizing for his father's death and the wellspring and the way the world had turned out, all at once.

"After my father died, it was only my sister and me," Beacon went on. Now he'd begun, he might as well tell her all of it. It had only been a matter of time before she learned of his past failures. "She'd never had any magic before the wellspring, but she was very small, and spellfire hit her hard afterward. She nearly died when her magic first came. One of the mages in our village did die just after the wellspring. But Everly learned to manage, and I tried to take her binding when she was the right age for it. We didn't know anyone else who'd be willing to serve as her patron, and who'd do it kindly. Or rather, we did, but it was an old woman who'd taken us under her wing. If she'd served as Ev's patron, Ev would have been dead in ten years, along with Mistress Haskell.

"The binding failed for me, and so our village council chose a patron for Everly. They sold her to the highest bidder—minor gentry, a local lord who needed mages to clear his land and light fires and do a drudge's work. Ev didn't want it and knew she'd be miserable. She begged me to leave after she was bound, so I wouldn't have to see her unhappy, and because I'm a coward, I did. I left the same afternoon she was bound to Lord Rockford, and I came to Valora to join the Guard. Fighting hellions feels like doing something, you know? Something worthwhile."

"I do know," Pan said fervently, and tucked her arm through Beacon's. It was a confiding, elegant, out of place gesture, as if they were moving across a ballroom rather than through one of Valora's worst neighborhoods. But Beacon liked it. Oh, he liked it a great deal. It cut through the fog of regret he felt mired in and brought him back to the present.

"Where are we going?" he asked, when it became apparent that he was no longer leading but that Pandora was directing him with soft pressure on his arm.

"Somewhere nearby," Pan said. "There's something I want to show you."

She led him through a series of run-down lanes and derelict alleys until they came to a lifeless-looking tenement building. Most of the windows were no more than jagged teeth of glass, and the door had been torn from its hinges—claw marks scored the old wood, and Beacon could picture the Were that must have done it. Without hesitation, Pandora stepped through the empty doorway and into the gloom of the near-ruined tenement.

With a halo of silver magelights ringing them, she escorted Beacon up the stairs. On the second story, one door was in less disrepair than the others. Black mold still crawled across it, but the hinges were intact, and, to Beacon's surprise, Pan produced a small key and turned it in the lock.

As she opened the door and ushered him in, Beacon found himself made welcome in a shabby but homely retreat.

Pandora had furnished the tenement flat with castoffs. A threadbare rag rug that had once been bright and cheerful, now torn in several places. A dented copper kettle. Several mismatched pieces of chipped or mended crockery. She'd even managed to drag a pair of stained and moth-eaten wingback chairs up from gods only knew where—people left Valora precipitately these days, often dumping whatever goods they could not convey on street corners.

"Why don't you sit?" Pandora said, flushing a little with self-consciousness as she offered. Beacon did and watched her set a spark of spellfire to the fuel sitting ready on the hearth. It all caught within seconds, glowing with snapping blue flames that produced the same warmth and smoke and noise of an ordinary fire.

Moving to the corner that served her flat for a kitchen, Pandora lit a small cookstove as well and started the copper kettle boiling. A place like this shouldn't have running water, but Beacon suspected the pipes had been kept working by magic.

While the kettle heated, Pandora bustled about with an air of happy importance, opening cupboards and drawers and fussing over her dishes. Beacon had seen her as a devastatingly powerful mage; he'd seen her as a clever and poised Ingenue; now Pan was as contented and domestic as any village housewife. Yet another piece to add to the puzzle he was attempting to assemble.

At last the kettle sang out. Pan poured hot water over two cups of hylan root and joined Beacon, carrying a tray with only one handle. On it, she'd set little plates of things to eat—bits of dried meat, a few slices of strong cheese, store-bought biscuits in both sweet and savory varieties. The hylan root smelled fresh and astringent. Coupled with the scent of woodsmoke and the soft silver-blue glow of Pan's fire and her magelights, Beacon couldn't think when he'd last been somewhere nicer.

Pandora settled in the chair opposite him. At some point, she'd donned a large, frowsy linen apron. Rather than finding it ridiculous, coupled as it was with trousers and braces instead of a gingham work dress, Beacon thought it heart-stoppingly endearing.

"I'm sorry there's no kantha," Pan said, sounding a little shy and self-consciousness. "I only keep hylan here, though I can't think why."

"This is better. Perfect, actually," Beacon said with such force that she glanced up at him with a puzzled look.

"Help yourself," she offered.

For several minutes they were quiet, sipping their root tea and eating their late supper, neither wanting to speak first.

Go on then, Beacon prodded. *Be a man. Say something to her. You've never had trouble before. Half an hour ago you spilled your guts to the poor girl, which she certainly never asked for.*

"Pandora?" he began seriously. She nodded, licking icing from her fingers after delicately consuming a pastry stuffed with haxberry jam. "Where are we?"

"Leadbetter Road. The north end, I believe. I'm not terribly good at directions."

"You know what I mean."

Folding her hands in her lap like the prim schoolgirl she'd been only days ago, Pandora transfixed Beacon with her dark eyes.

"This is where I came after my patron," she said, her voice quiet. "I lived here alone until I joined the Bellwethers. Even after I had a place with them, I kept coming back. Once or twice a week, after hunting hellions. I've never shown this to anyone before."

It was as if she'd read his thoughts. Beacon had wanted a glimpse of the truest Pandora, and here she'd laid bare to him her private self—the Pandora Small who existed when no one else was watching. He felt a swell of gratitude, but also a twinge of suspicion, that she had so adeptly anticipated what he desired from her. When Beacon met Pandora's eyes, though, her gaze was clear. She'd done no magic to read his longing, not even parlor magic. If she'd used her skills as an Ingenue to ferret out his precise state of mind, she'd only done it in the more ordinary ways. Through attention to detail, empathy, and understanding.

"Why did you leave if you were happy here?" Beacon asked. He had his feet up on the fender, a steaming cup in one hand, and his eyes on Pandora. He felt immensely comfortable, as if the world had tipped upside down the day his father died and suddenly, in this moment, turned upright again.

Pan shrugged and got to her feet, turning her back to Beacon.

"Will you untie my apron strings? I always forget not to fasten them with spellfire—it saves time but makes terrible knots."

Obligingly Beacon began to work at the tangle of her apron ties, trying very hard not to think of Pandora's warmth and her nearness, and the curve of her waist beneath his hands.

"I went to the Bellwethers' because all through the year I was away from my patron, I found bodies here in the lower city," Pan said at last, as if she was free to speak now she no longer had to look Beacon in the eye. "People stripped of their spellfire like the girls on Palace Hill. There's only one person I know who can kill like that—well, two. I suppose I could do it, but I never have. I've never broken the mage laws."

"Is that why you joined the Bellwethers, rather than using your magic to gain access to Palace Hill?" Beacon asked, carefully loosening a particularly recalcitrant knot.

"Yes. I've counted a hundred bodies since I left my patron. It's a horrible number. But I'm too afraid to work magic on someone else, and I obey the mage laws to justify that fear—if I lost control, a hundred dead would be a paltry sum by comparison. So I had to find another way to get onto Palace Hill. Five years is a very long time, especially when people are dying, but becoming an Ingenue helped me become better and stronger. Less prone to breakdowns, which I had to ensure happened far from anyone else, and disguise as the work of hellions afterward."

"There." The last of the knots gave way beneath Beacon's fingers, and he let go, though not without reluctance. Pandora turned to face him, slowly folding her apron as she did so.

"Perhaps this is a foolish question," Beacon said, "but couldn't you find your patron instantly just by restoring the binding between you?"

A bitter expression flashed across Pan's face, half anguish, half fear. "I daren't. Before the wellspring, I was completely under their control. I didn't realize it for most of my childhood, but by the end I knew. And I knew they were making me into something terrible. I could tell by the tasks I was set. Warding against steel shot and steel blades. Tearing apart steel girders. I was being made into a weapon, who could be used against anyone who felt they were safe from a mage's power."

In spite of himself, Beacon's blood ran cold. He could think of nothing more frightening than Pandora's power bent toward evil.

"Why have you been helping me?" Pandora asked abruptly, leaning forward in her armchair, her eyes glittering blue by the light of the fire she'd made. "You know you shouldn't be. You're a guard. You should know that if a powerful mage has appeared on Palace Hill, told you a melodramatic story about shadowy patrons and childhood secrets, and people have started dying around her, logic dictates she's the most likely murderer. We do learn that much of philosophy at the Bellwethers'—that the simplest explanation for a thing is generally the correct one."

She was testing him. Seeing if coolness or a challenge could drive him away. But Beacon had always been mule-headed and strong-willed.

"I just believe you," he said stubbornly. "About Winifred and Leslie. About never having broken the mage laws. About your patron and your past. I believe you about everything."

Pandora let out a trembling breath, as if she'd hoped desperately for such an answer but never considered it truly possible. *"Why?"*

Beacon crossed his arms over his chest and gave her a quizzical look. "I don't know, exactly. Because you seem to be in a hellish position and still trying to make the best of it. Because you haven't killed me yet, when you could in an instant, and I'm the worst sort of loose end. Because if I were you, I'd have broken the second mage law just now and considered myself right. Because I'm used to relying on instinct, and when I stand beside you, nothing in me says *danger*."

Pandora turned away from him, staring into the light of her fire. "I don't deserve you."

"I think you're wrong," Beacon said. "I think you do, and that I might have been made for you. I think the Higher Gods themselves might have brought us together. Or the Lower. I don't much care—it only matters that someone did."

"I'm sorry about your family," Pandora said quietly, her face in profile made soft by some deep grief.

"It isn't your fault. The world is what it is. We can't make it otherwise."

All the softness drained from Pandora in an instant, leaving only weariness and resolution in its wake.

"I could," she murmured. "If I really wanted to."

"I believe you," Beacon repeated.

In that moment, watching Pandora by the light she cast herself, he thought he'd believe anything she told him. If Pandora Small said up was down and down was up, Beacon would take to walking on his hands. If she said he was a fish and could live beneath the sea, he'd fill his pockets with stones and cast himself into the waves. If she told him he could fly, he'd leap from the nearest cliff. Not because of her power, but because of the way she held it—like a steel door and a perpetual ward, keeping the world safe from her inner flames no matter the cost.

To him, she was power, she was goodness, she was perfect control. He'd have protected her because of that. But now, having seen the rest? The girl who'd made herself a life and a home and set herself on a long path to face the very foe she dreaded, and who did not expect trust or thanks from a single living soul? Beacon felt his whole heart moving toward her, and he did not care to stop its going.

12

ILLUMINATION

"Pan."

For a brief instant Pandora's power flared to an agonizing pitch, then subsided to a low burn as she sent magelights flying to every corner of her palace bedchamber. Eleanor and Mamie had startled her—a dangerous thing to do, though of course they didn't realize. They both sat on Pandora's bed in the dark, with their arms around each other and tears drying on their cheeks.

"What is it?" Pan asked in a panic, flying to them from where she'd just come in the door. She dropped to her knees, searching both of her classmates from head to toe for some sign of injury. "Who hurt you?"

"Not us," Eleanor said shakily. "Leslie. They found her dead an hour ago, killed the same way as Winifred. The queen's scheduled her immolation for dawn."

Eleanor looked pale but resolute, for Mamie's sake. She was like that—stoic thanks to her family's ordeal of watching Robert Wellesley publicly boxed for opening the wellspring. Eleanor had lived through a drastic decline of fortune and a thousand social cuts from the first set, but she persisted in her resolve to become a well-respected Ingenue, doing her bit to restore the family name. Though they'd never been close, Pandora thought the world of Eleanor, for her fortitude and good sense.

Mamie, by contrast, was a veritable puddle of tears, transparently heartbroken over Leslie. Mamie suffered heartbreak a dozen times a week, though—over a dead sparrow, a lost hair ribbon, a piece of trivial bad news. She was as sweet and soft as a kitten, sure to win an excellent patron not by virtue of her parlor magic, which was weak, but her irresistibly pleasing temperament.

"Oh no," Pandora said, rocking back on her heels and only half feigning shock. She'd hoped to have more time before the Guard found poor Leslie.

"Why *us*?" Mamie hiccupped. "Why would a hellion only be killing Bellwether girls? There are so many people on the Hill, and only six of us. Though I suppose now we're four."

She started crying again, her shoulders shaking as Eleanor gathered her close with a soothing sound.

"Don't be a little fool," Eleanor said, though not without affection. "Hellions are monsters. They've no more wit than animals, though some can be devilishly clever in that way. If we're being picked out specifically, whatever's hunting us isn't a beast, not even a spellfire one. It's human."

"I've never even seen a hellion," Mamie wailed. "How should I know what they can and can't do?"

Pandora knelt, keeping very still as Eleanor caught her gaze and held it. Pan returned the stare evenly, without quailing. If Eleanor had gathered that the Bellwether girls were being targeted, surely the Guard would alter their suspicions and their investigations as well. They'd be under Pandora's slippered feet as she tried to find her patron, and worse yet, possibly on her tail. She was as likely a suspect as anyone, the moment it was determined that a mage had killed the girls.

"Pan," Eleanor said carefully. "Your parlor magic has always been so lovely. So strong. I don't suppose you could stretch to a ward for Mamie, that could serve as some form of protection for her?"

It was like Eleanor, not to ask for herself. And it was like her too, to have been discreet all these years despite clearly having suspected that Pan's magic was more than it ought to be. Eleanor had lived through the scandal and ruination that accusations of improper magecraft brought. She was not the sort to ever wish that anguish on another soul.

"I can ward you both," Pandora said with a decided nod. "Get up and come away from the window, though. I don't want anyone to see."

Drawing the curtains, she ushered Eleanor and Mamie to the middle of the room, farthest from any doors or walls, through which someone with the magesense might detect her power. Directing Eleanor and Mamie to stand several feet apart, Pandora began her wards.

She ought to have worked them one by one—undertaking two pieces of magecraft at the same time was difficult and taxing, requiring far more spellfire than a single piece of work. But Pan was worried that someone would feel her power and wanted to spend as little time on the wards as possible. She didn't dare make the wards as strong as she could manage with her full power either—Pandora was best at wards and could have cast a net around her classmates that nothing would get through. But they'd have to dance and flirt and be in crowded rooms full of guards and the first set, so Pan did a far trickier piece of magic.

She warded them against ill intent.

Even then, Pandora held back, too afraid to strengthen the wards as far as she might. This was a tacit acknowledgment to Eleanor and Mamie that she was a living flame, empowered in ways that were unacceptable to the people of Hesperid. Eleanor would certainly notice and keep the secret safe. Mamie would understand only part of it but was so silly, she couldn't be relied on to hold a confidence. Pan was taking an awful risk, yet couldn't bear to deny the other girls.

Sending out her power in glowing tendrils of blue light, she wove her twin wards around Eleanor and Mamie and knew that they could feel what she put into the work. Security. Safety. Love. And a breath of lily of the valley. The tears dried on Mamie's face, and she smiled, beaming as the embrace of Pandora's magic closed around her. Eleanor's lips parted, and she looked through the spellfire, fixing Pan with a look of wonder.

The magic would hold for days. Pandora would strengthen it when it began to fade but would not need to for another week at least. And inside her, spellfire still burned and burned, barely a fraction spent. She winced at the feel of it and the knowledge that she'd barely touched her power. Never mind. She'd let Eleanor and Mamie take that wince for the first chills of caster's fatigue, thinking that she'd flirted with the edges of her ability to help them.

"Thank you, Pan," Eleanor said fervently, hurrying forward to take Pandora's hands in her own when the work was done. "That was beautiful."

Pan smiled wryly. The second time since coming to the Hill she'd heard her illicit magic described as beautiful. If she wasn't careful, soon she'd be believing it.

"Yes, thank you," Mamie chorused with her bright, guileless smile. "Eleanor and I knew you meant it when you said we'd look out for each other. I only wish Imogen would be a little less . . . well. You know. Imogen."

"We asked her to come with us," Eleanor said. "I told her we were certain you could manage a ward. But she was almost angry. Said that under no circumstances would she be asking you to work *that sort of magic*, and we shouldn't either."

"She's always been jealous of your parlor magic," Mamie said with a wide-eyed shake of her head. "But I'm sure even she would have thought those wards were pretty."

Bless Mamie. Silly enough to think Pan's wards had been parlor magic, even. No one else would be so naive, the moment the girl mentioned being given an imperceptible ward by a fellow Ingenue. Eleanor knew as much and took Mamie's arm in her own.

"Mims, you *can't* breathe a word about this," she said earnestly. "It's just between you and me and Pandora. Do you understand?"

"A secret," Mamie said with a smile of delight. "I'm glad we're all close enough for secrets now. I've only got brothers at home, and I've always wanted sisters."

Pandora sighed as Eleanor gave her an apologetic look. At some point, this would go badly for Pan. Unless, of course, she'd already found herself a powerful patron to bury the rumor whenever it got out. Hax would do the job credibly. He certainly seemed the type to have put many pieces of unsavory news to bed before, and Pandora had found no indication that her patron might be connected to him. But patron or not, Pan hated the idea of playing into Miss Alice's hands. She'd been maneuvering Pandora for years, and Pan had a monumental distaste for feeling her strings were being pulled. You couldn't spend your childhood as a pawn without developing such a dislike.

At the thought of being used and abused so many times, an unbidden image flashed across her mind.

The little flat she kept on Leadbetter Street. Her secret haven, made all the more welcoming by Beacon's solid presence, sitting comfortably in an armchair with his boots up on the fender. He looked at her so *kindly*, as if he'd never ask for anything, but only give whatever she needed. Pan was all at sea when it came to him. Her entire life, she'd been a resource—something for people to bend to their own ends. Even Eleanor and Mamie, in their distress, had come to Pandora for help. Beacon had required nothing from her, so far. When faced with the Gaunt and stricken by memories of his father's death, he'd still been willing to spare Pandora pain.

It made her, contrarily, want to protect him with every last spark she had. To set a ward around the boy that even the world's ending wouldn't shatter. To tie herself to him with a bond of magic death itself would be unable to sever.

If ever she gave her patronage to someone willingly, Pandora knew it would be him. But doing so would make him an accomplice to her inferno of power, and if she were boxed, he'd be sent to his death by her side. Nothing would induce her to risk that.

"Go to bed," Pan told Eleanor and Mamie, pressing a reassuring kiss to Mamie's cheek. "You'll both be fine tonight, I promise."

She could be assured of no such thing, and Mamie, a creature of emotion and instinct, seemed to sense it.

"Could—could we stay with you?" Mamie asked tremulously. "Just for tonight? Please, Pandora, let's all stay together."

As a very young child, Pandora had often wakened from bad dreams in the throes of caster's fatigue, with every stick of furniture in the nursery she inhabited burned to ash. She had to be brought back from such lapses with vial after vial of spellfire, injected into her small arm until she was black and blue from wrist to elbow. But she'd learned to control her power even in sleep, no matter how hideous the nightmares that haunted her. She, at least, would not be a risk to Eleanor and Mamie overnight.

"Of course," she said without hesitation. "You both go and fetch your things. Anything I have is yours."

Mamie slipped out into the hallway first, and Eleanor took the opportunity to glance over her shoulder.

"Pandora," she said. "Thank you. Really. I won't breathe a word."

Pan nodded. "I know. I never thought you would."

"We're in the dailies," Mamie said in an awestruck tone. "Not just one of them, all of them."

Pandora's heart ached within her at the sight of Mamie with her white-blond hair and cornflower eyes, sitting at the breakfast table just as Winifred had only days ago. The morning dailies had arrived, and Mamie was poring over a stack of them with a smudge of newsprint on her nose.

"What do they say?" Eleanor asked, moving over from where she'd been sitting at Winnie's dressing table, making her toilette.

"They say . . ." Mamie squinted at the front page of the *Clarion*. "They say Winifred and Leslie are dead, which is right, but they say no one up here cares about it. That's not right at all."

Eleanor shot Pandora a swift, meaningful look. Leslie's immolation had been held at dawn, an extremely private affair attended only by her closest family. No halt or pause to the palace's social calendar had been called. Neither of the dead Ingenues had been mentioned or commemorated publicly. It was as if they'd never been.

Scanning several front pages quickly, Eleanor shook her clever auburn head. "The *Clarion* says it's callousness, and that the first set doesn't care about a few dead girls. The *Tattler* agrees. The *Hornet* and the *Crier* disagree—they think things are being kept quiet because the queen or the consort are afraid of a panic, if people on the Hill begin to feel unsafe."

"I'm sure the Guard will sort everything out very soon, don't you think, Pandora?" Mamie asked hopefully. Eleanor hid a brief, anguished expression, but not before Pan caught sight of it. The Guard were no friends to her family. By all accounts the Wellesleys were a close-knit clan, with a sprawling ancestral home that housed several generations. Eleanor had been there the day her brother Robert, a favorite with everyone, was dragged off and boxed. Why he'd opened the wellspring was never made clear. Retribution for mages treated poorly. A grudge against some political adversary of his family. A desire to watch the world burn. No one could say, really.

"I'm sure they will," Pan said without any certainty.

Caught up in thoughts of the people they'd lost, all three girls startled when a loud banging started up in the hall. It was not their door being pounded on, but one nearby.

"Stay here," Pan told Eleanor and Mamie firmly, finding it easy to serve as their de facto leader when they stared at her wide-eyed, with perfect trust. "I'll go see what's happening."

Out in the corridor, she found an unexpected figure. Prince Theo, extremely disheveled and smelling like a distillery, stood outside the rooms Imogen and Leslie had shared, knocking as if he meant to batter the door down.

"Gin!" he called loudly. "Gin, you'd better be in there! Let me in so I can see if you're all right. Lower Gods take you, Imogen Hollen, I'll kill you myself if you're dead!"

The door flew open, revealing Imogen on the threshold. She radiated imperious fury, perfectly dressed and made-up as always, in a gown of bronze silk overlaid with gold-threaded lace.

"Are you *quite* finished with your outburst?" she asked, sharp as a knife's edge. "I've only just come back from poor Leslie's immolation—her family wanted me particularly—and now I've got to prepare for a private exhibition of parlor magic I'm putting on for a few select nobles. I don't have time for your theatrics."

"You're all right," Theo said, slumping in relief. "I had to be sure."

"You would know beyond the shadow of a doubt if you held my binding," Imogen said, and scowled at Pandora, who still stood watching. "Enjoying the show, Pan? You've always loved to eavesdrop. Though I suppose the corridor is a step up from your broom closet beside the Misses' office."

Theo turned in confusion, and the moment he caught sight of Pandora, his face went white as powder. He clutched Imogen's arm and pointed.

"That's—that's the dead girl, Gin. *Do you see her?*"

"Pandora?" Imogen turned her terrifying frown on Theo this time. "I wish I didn't. But she's never been dead, she's as alive as you or I."

Pan had been dead, or at least extremely close to it, more times than she cared to count. But Theo shook his head in confusion, keeping his finger trained on her.

"Not Pandora. Leslie. She's standing just there."

"Not. Funny. Theodore," Imogen hissed, and broke away from him, slamming the door to her quarters in her wake.

Theo was left blinking at Pan, his wits still muddled after a night of dissipation. For her part, Pandora felt awful. She'd forgotten about the lies of convenience she'd told the prince and hadn't meant to sow more chaos in what was already proving to be a tempestuous summer.

"Not Leslie," Pan admitted, without bothering to keep a note of true misery from creeping into her voice. "I'm awfully sorry about that. I'm Pandora Small. Imogen and I don't get on, and I didn't think you'd want to know me, if I gave my own name."

"You lied?" The truth was finally dawning in Theo's alcohol-sodden mind. "You lied to make me think better of you?"

"It doesn't matter why," Pandora said. "But I did, and I apologize."

Theo's mouth twisted, as if he tasted something sour. "I *liked* you. And Gin doesn't make up my mind for me—I do it myself. But I don't like liars, and I don't care to maintain an acquaintance with them."

He turned and stumbled away, muttering under his breath as he went. Pandora stood and watched him go, only to be caught still in the corridor when Imogen's door flew open again.

"The exhibition I've got in an hour?" she said, with fury still rolling off her in waves. "You're coming. We'll make it an Ingenues' duet."

Pandora let out a groan as Imogen slammed the door. A duet would certainly show them both off in a way no other display of magic could—it was a refined and elegant opportunity for two Ingenues to work in tandem, pushing themselves just to the edge of caster's fatigue, showing the extent of their power and what they could do with it. Neither Eleanor nor Mamie would be able to keep up with Imogen in a duet—only Pan had the necessary spellfire (and more) to equal her. Under other circumstances, Pandora might have knocked on Imogen's door and refused. But Pan had a healthy enough instinct for survival that she never chose to further irritate Imogen when the Bellwethers' golden girl was in a rage. Gin's fuse was very long, but once she lost her temper, woe betide the man or woman, beast or child, who fell afoul of her next.

So it was that Pandora found herself standing outside an

unfamiliar palace sitting room an hour later, which Miss Elvira had reserved especially for the occasion. None of the gentlemen had arrived yet, and Pan could hear Imogen and the Misses speaking in low tones on the other side of the door. Briefly she contemplated turning tail and vanishing. But before Pandora could pivot on one heel, the door swung open and Imogen reached out, dragging her in.

This particular parlor had been decorated in all of Imogen's favorite shades—golds and silvers and creams, along with buttery maple parquet floors. She stood out in stark contrast to the metallic hues, dressed now in deep emerald green accented with gold. Imogen looked a gem in a rich setting. Pan, in her usual muted ivory, all but faded into the background. She would certainly make Imogen seem a paragon of grace, beauty, and style.

Annoyance sparked in Pandora. She knew her life required exquisite caution, but playing second fiddle to any Ingenue when it came to parlor magic rubbed her very much the wrong way.

Just a little indulgence couldn't hurt. After all, she'd taken a risk on behalf of Eleanor and Mamie. The smallest possible risk for herself was in order, as a treat.

"Here she is," Imogen said with a dismissive wave of her hand, leaving Pandora standing before Miss Alice.

Pan regarded the younger Bellwether sister warily and clamped down on the burn of her binding even harder than usual, just in case. No whispers were rising up to taunt her inner resolve. She did not feel as if she was in the presence of the cruelest person she'd ever encountered. And Miss Alice's posture and mannerisms did not put her immediately in mind of the cloaked and masked figure that had haunted her childhood. But Pandora knew none of that signified anything. Her patron had been careful and devilishly clever. It was still possible that they stood before her now, having pulled her strings for the past five years in a defter and more covert way.

"Miss Alice," Pan said with a sweet smile, determined not to let a glimmer of her anxiety show. "Where would you like me?"

"I thought the interior table." Miss Alice's answering smile was apologetic. One tea table with two chairs set beside it stood in a pool of molten sunlight, near the windows. Imogen would glow like a gemstone in that setting. Pan's table, by contrast, was placed before the fire, in shadows. A careless smudge of ash marked the floor beside it.

"Perfect," Pandora beamed. "I always show to advantage against shadows."

Airily she took her seat as Imogen did the same. A swell of voices sounded from the corridor. Their audience had arrived.

Miss Elvira ushered two gentlemen in morning coats into the parlor. A dozen more waited outside, and a flock of chairs had been set up for them at the room's far end. Down the center of the cluster of chairs ran an open aisle—those who preferred Imogen's magic would sit to the window side, those who preferred Pandora to the other. The gentlemen would only take their final places once they'd had a chance to sample each Ingenue's power.

"Lord Merriweather and Lord Delacourt," Miss Elvira announced, gesturing to the gentlemen to take seats across from Imogen and Pan. "First choice goes to Miss Hollen."

"Pleasure," Imogen said immediately, and Pandora fought the urge to pull a face. It was an intentional effort to unsettle Pan, throwing her off balance. She'd always been more prudish than the rest of the Ingenues when it came to the provision of pleasure and had her own way of working that particular parlor magic. While the other Ingenues worked directly on their subjects, in contravention of the mage laws, Pan didn't dare. She worked *around* them instead.

Lord Delacourt looked like a cat with cream, seated across from Pandora and anticipating her magic. She stole a glance at Imogen and Merriweather. The ginger-haired lord already had his eyes shut, a beatific expression on his face.

"May I ask a question before we begin?" Pandora inquired. "Is there a particular moment in time when you were most happy, my lord?"

Delacourt's surprise was evident. He thought for a moment. "At the seaside, as a boy. We'd summer at the coast every year, and I'd run wild on the sand, renting donkeys for a trot and eating half a dozen ice creams a day."

"Lovely," Pandora said. She folded her hands in her lap and, without any effort at all, surrounded Delacourt with the perfect imprint of a summer's day at the sea. A briny breeze ruffled his hair, bright sun emanating from nowhere warmed his skin, and the lacework of watery reflections danced on the parlor ceiling. When Delacourt drew in a shocked breath, Pandora added the taste of haxberry ice cream to the air, coupled with the sound of waves and children's laughter.

In an instant, it was gone. But she saw from the light in Delacourt's eyes that she'd transported him back perfectly. Across the room, Merriweather let out a small, animal sound of pleasure, and Pan flushed to the roots of her mousy hair. Imogen looked triumphant, and Miss Elvira raised a hand.

"Switch."

The lords changed places, so that they could contrast the quality of the two Ingenues' power.

Merriweather's happiest moment was a triumphant night out with friends, after an unexpected pass on his collegiate exams. Pandora conjured the smell and taste of spilled jimson beer, the raucous celebratory sounds of male voices, the encompassing warmth of a roaring fire, and the languid touch of a woman's hand. Merriweather gave her a look of frank approval when she'd finished.

"I think you might have improved on the original."

When they took their places among the waiting flock of chairs, both men looked at Pandora with gratitude and appreciation. But they looked at Imogen with wanting—naked looks of unfettered desire. Gin tossed her head and shot Pandora a glare.

"Truth," Pandora called out, as the next two gentlemen were ushered in.

Here, Pan used her Ingenue's training rather than parlor magic, as Imogen did. It would be all too easy to slip imperceptibly while ferreting around someone else's mind, and doing so would certainly prove fatal to Pandora's subject. Instead, she watched the minute details of posture, expression, breath, and pulse, gathering truth not through magic but through observation during conversation.

"The Duke of Cassley has taken a new mistress," Imogen said archly. "He's given her a diamond bracelet and a fine mare."

"Baron Gaswick has the same mistress," Pandora answered, grinning like a goblin as she watched the baron's jealousy, written plain as printed words on his face. "She hasn't thrown him over yet, but never breathes a word about other men. He has, however, noticed the diamond bracelet and the fine mare."

A fight would have broken out if it wasn't for Miss Elvira's deft management of the suitors and redirection from their anger toward each other to appreciation for her protégés' skill.

Slowly the suitors' seats filled. Sometimes Pandora refrained from using parlor magic at all, giving the appearance of it instead. Other times, when she was unable to avoid working magic, she used her power deftly, without ever bringing it to bear directly on her partner.

By the end, she was surprised to see the gathered gentlemen evenly split, half seated in Imogen's chairs, the other half in hers. Baron Hax grinned wolfishly at her from the head of her designated suitors—his exhibition had been deception, and Pandora had, for a moment, genuinely induced him to believe that she was the princess royal, spirited away at birth and now returned to claim the throne that was her birthright. No doubt Hax was considering the implications of such a skill, and how many business partners he'd be able to cheat with impunity.

Imogen rose from her chair and curtsied, looking exhausted. Pandora had never seen her anything other than dewy and fresh before and felt a momentary pang of guilt. Gin had obviously expended a great deal of her power keeping pace with Pan, who ached with a surfeit of spellfire, as always.

Miss Elvira made a flowery speech about the charm and grace of her Ingenues, clearly leading up to the announcement of their final exhibit. Truly, the number of times she referred to light and brilliance was embarrassing. Pan, for her part, drew Miss Alice aside with a worried whisper.

"We ought to close things now," she breathed. "Gin's just about done in, she needs a rest so she can restore her spark."

Miss Alice shook her head. "Imogen told Elvira that under no circumstances were we to finish early. She requested the theme for this last exhibit as well. She'd be livid if we stopped now, and you know the school depends upon contributions from her father."

Pandora ground her teeth in frustration as Miss Elvira beckoned the girls to craft their best displays of illumination. Still elegant as a swan despite her weariness, Imogen glided forward, joined by a reluctant Pan.

The Misses Bellwether pulled heavy gold and silver curtains

over the windows, shutting out daylight and plunging the parlor into heavy gloom. At once, a halo of glittering magelights sprang up around Imogen, revolving slowly and casting her in a flattering golden glow. Impatiently Pandora matched her, but where Imogen's lights were the divine shade of the Upper Gods, Pan chose the ghoulish spellfire-blue glow of the Lower pantheon. The illumination cast on her was eerie and unfavorable, picking out flaws and rendering everything it touched unnatural and hair-raising.

Fixing Pandora with an incomprehensible and annoyed look, Imogen ramped up the glow of her magelights, until they were like a dozen small suns. She set them to spinning faster and faster, her chest heaving as she did, her breath coming in ragged fits and starts.

"Imogen, stop," Pandora warned, but she met the magelights' strength and speed. Gold and blue battled for dominance, like the Upper and Lower realms striving for supremacy over the world, their hinterland. Faster and faster Imogen's lights spun; brighter and brighter they glowed. No one could look directly at her, and the waiting suitors shielded their eyes. Grimly Pandora matched Imogen's magecraft. A musical, keening note began to emanate from Imogen's lights, though Pandora's remained silent. The note rose, higher and louder, until it was unbearable.

"Imogen!" Pandora shouted, but the magic carried on, and she had no choice but to match it. They were meant to keep perfect pace with each other—to break their accord would not show Imogen as a victor but reveal her as a poor mage, who could not gauge her own limits.

Gin was out of control now, and her eyes fixed on Pandora. Pan read fear there, as the magelights whirled, the light grew blinding, and a sudden burst of horrible brightness exploded through the room.

Pitch-darkness followed. It was not the natural gloom that had reigned in the room before—a little sun had still filtered through the cracks in the curtains, and some light had risen from the embers of the fire. This was an entire absence of light, so that no one could see even to the end of their noses.

"Get them out," Miss Elvira snapped, and shuffling broke out in the perfect dark. Miss Alice was silhouetted in the hallway door, ushering suitors out into the corridor. But not a bit of light penetrated the parlor. Not until the last of the suitors had left, and Pandora lifted her darkness.

Imogen sat on the floor at Pan's side, dazed, with one hand in Pandora's own.

"What happened?" Imogen asked blearily. Bruises were spreading across her skin—the first sign of caster's fatigue. They were a faint purplish green, though, and did not deepen to the terrible blue black that preceded a mage slipping their final spark.

Pandora shrugged. "You overspent."

What she did not say was that Imogen would be dead now, without Pan's touch. In the moment the light burst, Pandora grabbed for Imogen, held to her for dear life, and crafted a ward like nothing she'd ever made before. It was not an outer shield or an inner one, but rather a net of protective magic perfectly fit to Imogen Hollen's skin. The vital sparks of Gin's magic had not been able to escape her, having no recourse but to sink back into her body and reinhabit her blood and bones. Experience had prepared Pandora for just this moment—wasn't she used to making a ward of her own skin? To do so with Imogen's had only required a shift of focus.

Still, it had been strange and prodigious magic. Miss Alice would have no inkling of what Pandora had done. But Miss Elvira—Miss Elvira had once been courted by the Guard's magefinders, who offered her a great deal to add her sense to their ranks.

Pandora scrambled up and helped Imogen to her feet.

"I want to go home," Gin said in a small, frightened voice. Her father had a villa in the most fashionable part of the Hillside, and though many of the wealthiest Ingenues stayed at their family homes rather than the palace, Imogen had chosen to be with her schoolmates.

"I'll take her," Pandora offered. After that expenditure of power, it would be best for her to spend a bit of time out of the palace, so that any after-impression of magic clinging to her would fade. Pan scrupulously avoided meeting Miss Elvira's gaze until she was in the doorway with Imogen leaning on her.

Miss Elvira's hand dropped onto Pandora's shoulder, and Pan felt the breath leave her in a sudden rush. This was the end. Fearing for the reputation of her school, Miss Elvira would report her. Pan could see the steel door closing on her, feel the confines of the box as it hemmed her in.

"Pandora," Miss Elvira said with a nod. "That was well done."

Relief flooded Pan, and for the first time that she could remember, Miss Elvira met her eyes and smiled.

13

BEACON'S DUTY

Beacon had never been entirely sure how to spend his half days on Palace Hill—it wasn't enough time to do much more than travel down to the lower city and back, and there was nothing to occupy him at the palace. This particular half day, he knew exactly what to do. It was time to follow up on Pandora's interest in sliphouses. Such establishments had been dubious places even before the wellspring, and the only frequent visitor to Palace Hill with a direct connection to them was Ander Hollen, whose family had made a fortune trafficking in spellfire when it was still the rarest and most precious of commodities.

The Hollen villa, outside the palace compound but still in the opulent, elevated neighborhood of the Hillside, was by far the most luxurious place Beacon had ever been. The palace itself was awe-inspiring with its sprawling network of new buildings, its excessive finery, and its constant flow of occupants, both courtiers and servants. But it was a public building, made for display and state affairs and the proper representation of Hesperid. Beacon could understand, in a way, why the palace had to be as it was—glittering, ostentatious, and sharp-edged. It needed to speak of power, on behalf of a country relatively new to such things.

But there were older and softer forms of power. The Hollen villa, by contrast to the palace, was exquisitely private. Thick hedges, twice the height of a man, surrounded the entire estate, punctuated by a single massive gate. The drive curved just enough to hide the villa from view, enshrouded as it was in lush gardens rich with color and life. Beacon came upon the house quite suddenly after rounding the bend—an Excelsior-style mansion, three stories high and covered in intricate gingerbread-cut wood ornamentation. Syrupy morning light spilled over the vista as it unfolded, rendering the entire scene luxurious and inviting.

Beacon climbed the front steps, the air around him fragrant with scents of hydrangeas and roses and flowering similon trees. Knocking briskly on the front door, he waited the barest moment before a uniformed maid appeared.

"Officer Ellis Beacon," he informed her, falling back on his stone-faced, unreadable demeanor. "I'm here to speak with Ander Hollen."

"Do you have an appointment?" the maid asked.

Beacon allowed a moment's silence. Then: "Does a representative of the Queen's Guard require one, in order to secure your master's cooperation?"

The maid blinked and faltered. "Why not follow me into the library, Officer, and I'll go make inquiries for you?"

Beacon nodded his assent and fought back nerves. It was the first time he'd ever misrepresented the Guard—he was under no orders to come here, unless one considered a beseeching request from Pandora Small to be an order. Beacon was getting to the point where even a hint from her counted as such. He was led into a dizzying atrium, which rose the full height of the house with open galleries ringing each level. The floors were honey-gold parquet, and more flowering similons in enormous pots graced the foyer, filling the air with their complex aroma. Somewhere, some manner of fountain was working, adding the soft sound of falling water to the similons' fragrance.

"Just through here," the maid said, and ushered Beacon into a sun-soaked library at the house's front, which looked out onto the brilliant gardens.

Though there was an array of leather furniture scattered throughout the library, Beacon remained on his feet, waiting near the window until the whisper of the door opening alerted him to a new arrival. Turning, he found a tidy, pleasant-looking man of medium height walking toward him. Beacon had learned, since arriving on Palace Hill, to identify degrees of fortune via clothes, and Ander Hollen's gray morning suit was the finest cut and highest quality. Ander was fair, with ash-blond hair beginning to whiten, lightly tanned skin, and piercing blue eyes. He held out a hand without hesitation, greeting Beacon as an equal.

"A visit from the Guard?" Ander said as Beacon shook his proffered hand. "This is an unexpected honor."

Unsure how to respond to such a warm welcome when he'd come under false pretenses, Beacon chose duty as his disguise. "I'm afraid I'm here on unfortunate business, sir. By now I'm sure you've heard about the Ingenues who were killed on the Hill."

Ander nodded, his expressive face growing solemn. "Yes. A terrible thing, that. The girls were friends of my daughter, Imogen. Do you believe there's any danger to the rest of the Ingenues?"

A light rill of female voices sounded from the foyer, and over Ander's shoulder, Beacon saw the same maid escorting Imogen and

Pandora across the entryway. Imogen looked poorly, walking with short, pained steps, and the maid was fussing over her. Pandora seized the opportunity to catch Beacon's eye and gave him a quizzical, expectant look before she was swept away.

They had not arranged to be at the Hollen villa together, and Beacon immediately felt grounded and bolstered by Pandora's unexpected presence. This was why he'd come. This was why he was acting outside the Guard's purview, using his perceived authority and his uniform in a way that would get him flogged, if it was discovered.

Returning his attention to Ander, Beacon shook his head. "Impossible to say whether there's further risk to the Ingenues, sir. Publicly, the Guard believes the death to be the result of a hellion hiding somewhere on Palace Hill. Privately, we're leaving no stone unturned."

"Do you think it would be best if I removed Imogen from the court?" Ander asked. "She doesn't want to go—Ingenues take their summer there very seriously, but I'm certain I could arrange a suitable patronage for her in private, if it would be safer."

"I think it's too soon for alarm yet," Beacon lied with a twinge of guilt. Were he in Ander's position, with a daughter at the palace and two of her classmates dead, he'd be spiriting her away to the farthest end of Hesperid. Ander, however, seemed the picture of unconcern, sinking onto a vast leather couch and removing a pipe from his jacket pocket, which he lit with the strike of a sulfur match. "But the manner of the girls' deaths is peculiar and bears investigating. Their spellfire was torn out, you see. With your expertise in the removal of spellfire from a mage, you might be able to offer some insight as to how that was accomplished."

Ander took a long draw on his pipe, and Beacon made use of the brief lull to assess his surroundings for any hint of magic. Nothing that he could detect. If Ander was Pandora's patron—a mage with power approaching her own—he was at least as talented at hiding it. Beacon had learned to distinguish the small shift of temperature in Pan's vicinity and begun paying closer attention to all mages as a result. Pan was not as perfect in her masquerade as he'd believed, but practiced enough that he'd never have noticed the constant imprint of her power if he hadn't known to look. Now Beacon racked his brains and analyzed every sensation in his body for the slightest inkling of spellfire.

Still nothing.

"Did you check the girls' bodies for injection points?" Ander asked. "Spellfire can be taken out of a mage in three ways—involuntarily by another magic worker, voluntarily through their own magecraft, and mechanically in the sliphouses. Spellfire's drawn to blood and life, so if a little of a mage's blood is tapped into a vial, their spellfire will eventually begin to follow. It's a sensitive process, though. Every mage is different, so there's no telling when spellfire will follow blood until you've begun. Some mages who came to our sliphouses were what we called stingy with their spark—meaning they'd have to be nearly bled out before any spellfire followed. Those we turned away. Others lost spellfire more easily, but you still had to take great care to ensure they didn't slip too much of it. It was a risky business, which is why I shut all the Hollen sliphouses down after I inherited the family holdings from my father. That's a matter of public record—the last Hollen sliphouse closed its doors three years before the wellspring opened up."

"Wasn't that a financial loss?" Beacon asked. "Spellfire was worth more than gold, before the wellspring."

"It still is when sold outside Hesperid, though Queen Maud and the state take the lion's share of any profit made by export," Ander said, watching Beacon through a cloud of thin blue smoke. "And yes, closing the sliphouses was a financial blow, but one I was willing to weather, as it was the right thing to do. In the long run, it did us more good than harm. Without sliphouses in the family portfolio, I set myself to thinking how spellfire might be taken from the earth, rather than directly from mages. I was never able to get the catchment system I came up with to work before the wellspring—there was too little spellfire for it to be viable. But now the wellspring's opened, every catchment station scattered around Hesperid runs on my systems. This country is becoming astronomically wealthy because of me, and the business decisions I made."

Ander Hollen looked well pleased with himself, leaning into the leather sofa and extending one arm along its even back. Beacon fought the urge to roll his eyes. Closing sliphouses on a matter of principle, he could admire. Congratulating oneself over it, he could not.

"I'll be sure the dead Ingenues are thoroughly examined for injection points," Beacon said. "But I'd like to ensure you, at least, don't fall under suspicion if any are found. Would you mind giving me a look at your financial records, to confirm that you no longer own any equipment from your former sliphouses?"

It was the Guard in him taking control—though Pandora seemed convinced her mage patron had been responsible for Winifred's and Leslie's deaths, Beacon was expected to be thorough in everything he undertook. He could not shake the habit, and as he'd come to the Hollen villa, he'd at least be sure Ander was not engaged in *anything* untoward or unreported.

"Certainly," Ander said easily, rising and gesturing to Beacon to follow. "We'll need to visit my office for that, though. I keep all my ledgers there."

Beacon walked in Ander's wake, through the palatial lobby and down a corridor lined with green tapestry carpet, depicting a menagerie of fantastical creatures along the banks of a meandering stream. He was ushered into an office, darker and more masculine than the library, with smaller windows that looked out onto a cobbled stable yard. From behind another doorway, the sound of voices drifted, accompanied by the sounds of silver spoons against fine porcelain. As Beacon passed near the shut door, he felt a slight warming of the air that had grown impossible to confuse with any natural shift of temperature.

Though he had no idea what had brought her here, Beacon was glad Pandora had come. He hadn't even mentioned his plans to visit the Hollens this morning, hoping he'd be able to surprise Pan with a piece of new and useful information. He'd spent a pleasant night imagining how her eyes would light up when he came to her with something helpful—when she was grateful, her face softened and her voice went gentle in a way that Beacon found irresistible. But for her to see him here, gladly doing as he was bid—she'd be equally pleased with that, and Beacon looked forward to receiving her thanks. Not because he wanted her in his debt, but because it satisfied him to serve her, to ease the burden she was used to shouldering by herself.

You're a fool, the stubborn, sensible part of him warned. *What do you really know about that girl, besides the fact that she could destroy this city with a thought?*

Beacon took the moment of suspicion and redirected it deftly, channeling it toward Ander Hollen and his finances.

"Here you are," Ander said, pulling a ledger from a nearby shelf and placing it on a vast oak desk littered with papers. Outside, a clatter of horse hooves sounded on the cobblestones, and Ander glanced up, then frowned. "Do you mind if I leave you alone for a few minutes with that? There's something I need to attend to outside. You'll find all business records for the sliphouse closures and equipment auctions in there."

"Certainly," Beacon said, and watched with some relief as Ander left. He wasn't entirely sure what he was looking for—figures and business were outside his expertise, which ran strictly along the line of *find a hellion, turn it to ash*. But it seemed the right thing to do, to confirm both that Ander Hollen had no magic, and therefore could not be Pandora's patron, and that he no longer had access to sliphouse equipment, and so could not have killed the dead Ingenues by mechanical means either.

Paging through the ledger, Beacon saw neat accounts written out in a clear, easily legible hand. Inventories from each sliphouse, taken several weeks prior to their closing sales, and then auction records detailing items sold and profits earned.

Everything was accounted for. Nothing had been held back or left unsold, at least that Ander had documented. Which didn't mean the man might not have kept equipment off the books, but Beacon could not think why someone with so much wealth and access to nigh-unlimited spellfire would go to the trouble of siphoning power from marginally gifted Ingenues. Surely Ander Hollen, with his vaunted catchment stations and his fortune, would have no trouble acquiring quantities of spellfire elsewhere.

But there was still the question of Pandora's patronage. Was it possible that Ander could be hiding his power so effectively that Beacon could not detect a trace of it? He'd nearly judged Pandora to be harmless and useless, after all, and the failure still haunted Beacon. He ought to feel guiltier over it. Ought to feel more than an occasional minor prick of conscience, that he'd betrayed his duty and responsibility in sheltering Pan and keeping her secret.

Pushing the ledger aside, Beacon stared down in frustration at the jumble of papers littering the desk. The corner of a piece of stationery caught his eye, and he slid it out from a stack of other documents. It was the insignia printed on it that had captured his attention—a rising phoenix, the emblem of the Bellwether School.

The page was a receipt, for a donation in an eye-watering amount and for a list of expenses charged to a school account. The costs were for trinkets and gowns, and much lower than Beacon would have expected from Imogen Hollen, the petted only daughter of one of Hesperid's richest men. Beacon had glimpsed Imogen a few times over the past few days—it was hard not to notice her, as she was inevitably surrounded by a throng of admirers and clearly bored by them all. The girl had a penchant for fine dress in golds and silvers and jewel tones, which showcased her as the treasure she was clearly meant to be.

The receipt, by contrast, listed half a dozen plain gowns, done up with no more embellishment than embroidery, all in ivory and cream. At the bottom of the page, confirming Beacon's guess, was a small annotation: *all amounts charged on behalf of student P.S.*

Ander Hollen must have thought he had nothing to hide. In the normal run of things, a Queen's Guard would not care or especially notice evidence of a rich man's bastard child. Half the men on Palace Hill had some by-blow or other, spirited away to a school or a country estate with a tutor and kept from the public eye. But this was different.

This was Pandora.

And for the first time, Beacon realized that ever since Pan had recounted the shape of her childhood and role of her patron, he'd been furious. It was why he'd come here in the first place, haring off into the weeds, acting not on behalf of duty or state but on personal interest. He could not bear the thought of anyone misusing Pandora Small and her magic. Could not stomach the idea of another person holding power over her, not even if they held it lightly. It had become intolerable to Beacon, to think of Pandora bound to anyone with dark intentions.

No. If he was honest, it had become intolerable to think of Pandora bound to anyone but *him*. Personal interest in a diminutive Ingenue with an elfin face and a molten core of spellfire had blotted out his sense of duty and decorum like a thundercloud.

Outside the window, Ander spoke a few words to a groom, who held the lead rope of a fine blood-bay stallion. After hearing the groom's response, he turned back to the house.

Beacon did not need time to decide what must come next. His mind was made up, fueled by the seething anger wakened in him when he thought of someone—anyone—pulling Pandora's strings. Taking up a position beside the door he'd been led through, Beacon waited, just as he'd done for dozens of hellions while safeguarding the lower city.

His conscience smote him, and he ignored its warnings. Right now, Ander Hollen was not a wealthy and innocent man. With Beacon's heart going like a forge hammer in his ears and Pandora only a room away, Ander was a threat.

Footsteps sounded in the corridor. Ander entered the room and frowned in confusion, casting about himself when he saw Beacon was no longer at the desk. But his frown shifted to an expression of angry disapproval as he found Beacon already behind him, swinging the door shut with one hand while leveling a steel-loaded pistol at the merchant's throat.

Ander's gaze cut from side to side, clearly searching for some manner of escape, but he was trained for a world of figures and wit, whereas Beacon was a blunt instrument. One way or another, it was hardly a fair fight. If Ander wasn't Pandora's patron, Beacon was a half foot taller and three or four stones heavier, besides being trained for combat. If Ander *was* Pandora's patron, he'd be able to kill the boy in an instant, though Beacon would at least give Pan a warning with his death. With his blood up, Beacon didn't care if it took his life to unmask Pan's tormentor.

"Who are you to Pandora Small?" Beacon asked, his voice clear and wrathful. "Why have you been paying her way at the Bellwethers'? Answer me quick, or I'll see you regret it."

14

NEAR MISSES

Pandora fought to keep her composure as she watched Imogen open a velvet-lined case across the tea table. Inside rested a hypodermic syringe and three vials of wicked blue spellfire. With practiced hands, Imogen rolled up one sleeve and found a vein, sending the spellfire into her blood. For a moment, a blue glow picked out the tracery of her veins before fading and becoming part of her.

Pan shivered. How many times had she watched her patron or one of their lackeys do just the same to her? Hundreds. Perhaps thousands.

Imogen let out a sigh as the bruises vanished from her skin like magic. When the last had faded, she fixed Pandora with a flinty look.

"Why did you do that?" Imogen asked. "End our duet so abruptly? You ought to have let me finish."

Pan cursed herself for not dumping the girl on the Hollen villa's doorstep and leaving at once. But on their way down the hill, Imogen had been polite and stiff with gratitude, and Pandora, admittedly, had been curious about the Hollens' home. She'd let herself be asked in and then, after glimpsing Beacon in the library with Ander, gladly accepted an invitation to tea. Once an eavesdropper, always an eavesdropper, and Pan hoped to overhear a little of their conversation.

"You would have killed yourself," Pan said, attempting to sound matter-of-fact rather than prideful. "I did what was necessary."

Imogen tossed her golden head disdainfully. "I wouldn't have killed myself. I'd have ruined the duet, yes, but I'd have lived. You shouldn't have stopped things. It would've shown your skills off to advantage, finishing the duet after I fell apart."

"I don't need you to fail at something to be seen in a flattering light," Pan said drily. "You're far too concerned with the business of the other Bellwether girls. You ought to focus on finding yourself a patron, since the one you want isn't interested."

She meant that last to sting, and Imogen flushed. An awkward and bitter silence ensued.

Pan shifted in frustration, taking a sip of her overly sweet tea and casting about herself. She'd never become used to excess. Pandora spent the bare minimum each year at school, anxious lest she overstep the boundaries of her limited scholarship and anger her anonymous benefactor. There were, too, the pervasive memories of what life had been like during the year between her patron and the Bellwether School. Pan had made the best of it, but she'd still been one step shy of living on the streets, surviving on what she could beg or steal or scavenge.

None of the Bellwether girls besides Pandora knew what true want or deprivation was. They hadn't gone to bed at night with hunger eating holes inside them, or cold rattling at their bones. Pan had done all that and counted it a blessing, because at least she'd been free. What were hunger and cold compared to the torment of having her spellfire torn from her repeatedly to satisfy her patron's curiosity as to whether she'd live? Even worse had been the injections that followed, her arms going black and blue as she was given vial after vial of spellfire, until her blood burned so hot with it, she thought she'd burn from the inside out.

Before her, Imogen refilled Pandora's cup with practiced motions, an ornament in a lavish setting. Pan squirmed again, impatiently. She felt a pull toward Beacon, as if some invisible thread tied them together, but she'd have to content herself with mincing and simpering and prying what information she could from Imogen while Beacon interviewed the elder Hollen.

A clattering sounded outside, and Pandora glanced up as a groom led a massive horse across the stable yard and Ander Hollen appeared to join him. A sudden idea struck her—a way to get a moment's reprieve from Imogen and find out if Beacon had learned anything of use.

"I've heard when you aren't busy with school, you've been embroidering a tapestry which charts the history of Hesperid from its founding to present day," Pan said primly. Indeed, Imogen's prowess with a needle was legendary, whereas Pandora inevitably pricked her fingers and bled all over whatever handkerchief or bit of lace finery she meant to embellish. "I don't suppose I could take a look at it?"

Imogen shot her a dubious *I doubt you're really interested* sort of look, which wasn't unfair, given how little attention Pandora had paid to her needlework in the past. "It's upstairs in my rooms. Shall I fetch it for you?"

"Please." Pandora nodded. For once luck was on her side—Imogen could easily have rung for a maid to retrieve the tapestry but likely welcomed the idea of a short reprieve from Pan's company.

Watching as Imogen swept from the room, Pan hurried over to the window and let out a curse beneath her breath. Lucky in one aspect, unlucky in another. She'd temporarily rid herself of Imogen, but there was no sign of Ander in the stable yard any longer. Pandora didn't dare risk a quick word with Beacon when they might be interrupted.

Instead, she slipped to the pair of doors that led from the parlor to the room beyond. Pan peered through the crack between the doors and saw Beacon studying something at a paper-strewn desk. A stormy look wrote itself across the guard's face, and he got to his feet abruptly, moving to take up a position by the entrance to the hallway.

Pan stifled a gasp as Ander reentered the room and Beacon leveled a pistol at him. Fury was evident in every line of the boy's posture, and when he spoke, his voice carried clearly into the parlor.

"Who are you to Pandora Small? Why have you been paying her way at the Bellwethers'? Answer me quick, or I'll see you regret it."

Something snapped within Pandora. A searing wall of blue spellfire blotted out her vision, and all she could remember was the first death she ever saw.

Her opulent, windowless nursery with its steel walls. Her patron, hooded and cloaked as always, standing before Pan and looking like a giant when seen through the eyes of childhood. They gestured, and a uniformed guard stepped forward.

"Watch," Pandora's patron said simply.

And they began to tear spellfire from the guard.

The man was tall and weathered and stoic, but an expression of shock and anguish still crossed his face as Pan's patron began their work. If the guard could speak or move, he made no sign of it, standing in one place while sweat beaded on his forehead and his entire form began to shake. At last he dropped to the floor, seizing, and a helpless sound escaped his lips.

"Stop," Pandora whispered. She'd felt this torment before—by then her patron had subjected her to the same process a hundred times and never managed to extract the last of her spellfire. But Pandora had never seen this cruel magic done to anyone else. "Please, please stop."

Tears blurred her vision, but not the blue glow of spellfire. Back then, she had not been so much. Had not contained so much. Still, she had been a force to reckon with, even as a young child.

"If you wish me to stop, you must make me," her patron said, their voice perfectly even, distorted and disguised by magic. "What you desire in life, you must grasp by force or by subterfuge."

Pandora tried. She leveled her own power at her patron's magic, trying to force it back, and it was as if she'd done nothing. She tried to craft a ward, and ruthlessly her patron countered it, so that the protection fizzled and died. The man on the floor was rigid now, with bruises spreading across his skin. His eyes were wide, and Pandora could see he felt everything happening, and it was agony.

She knew firsthand. It. Was. Agony.

"You may not be able to stop my power," Pan's patron said. "But you can stop his suffering. Snuff him out. End this now, and he will thank you from the Upper or Lower realms, wherever his soul finds its resting place."

Pandora had understood something fundamental in that moment. One way or another, the guard would die. Her patron had no intention of letting him live. What they wanted was to draw Pan into their wickedness.

Pandora planted her small feet stubbornly and balled her hands into fists at her sides. She would not be drawn in.

The memory came and went in the span of a heartbeat. Before Beacon had finished speaking, Pandora burst through the parlor doors and clapped an impenetrable ward down around him. She was better now, and more, and would keep Beacon safe from her patron's dark magic if she died trying. But even as she did so, the veil of spellfire blue clouding her vision worked its way outward, limning Pandora like lightning, snapping and sparking as it swirled around her in a corona of deadly power.

A blur of emerald silk shot past as Imogen threw herself between Pandora and Ander.

"None of this is what you think," Imogen blurted out, all her careful composure cast aside for the moment. She was wide-eyed and desperate, her gaze fixed so intently on Pan, it was as if Imogen hoped to hold back a torrent of spellfire with a single look. "If you only give us a chance, we can explain. Pandora, stop. You have to stop. If you don't, I'll ward him, and even with all that spellfire I just had I'm nowhere near your equal. It will kill me if I try."

Whispers were flooding Pandora's hearing, so loud she could hardly make out Imogen's words. *Let go, give in, come back to me. Rise in power and live by fire.*

Yes. It would be such a relief, to finally loosen her iron control. Ander was wide-eyed with panic, Imogen ferocious in her defense of him, and Beacon looked aghast within Pandora's ward. The maelstrom of magic around Pan swirled and crackled and sang to her like a siren.

Two images surfaced and held her back, wavering on the threshold of a great and catastrophic breakdown. The first was Imogen, coming to on the palace floor with bruises on her skin. Gin was right—any attempt to ward against Pandora's magic would surely kill the girl. And the second was Beacon, sitting before the hearth with his feet up. He watched Pandora with perfect trust, as if he knew she could never do anything wrong or damaging.

A fool, the whispers inside Pandora goaded. *He doesn't know what protections life requires. You must burn to keep him safe. You must rise in power.*

Pan nodded. She'd flay her patron alive and make a crater of Valora before letting their magic touch this particular guard.

Stalking forward, Pan shoved Imogen aside brutally with a shock wave of magic and pinned Ander to the wall, her spellfire an invisible hand around his throat. It was the closest she'd ever come to breaking the second mage law—to working magic *on* someone, rather than around them. She'd scrupulously refused just this course during all her years in a steel-walled prison, and now not a shred of her cared.

"I've been looking for you," Pan snarled, so flush with spellfire that flames crackled in her voice. "You made my life a misery and my conscience a ruin, and now I will ensure that you never hurt me or Hesperid again."

"Pandora!" Beacon snapped, her name a warning.

"Pan, don't," Imogen pleaded, pulling herself to her feet as her voice caught on a sob. "Please, he isn't who you think. None of this is. Just let us explain."

Maintaining her implacable hold on Ander, Pandora turned her head to look at Imogen, the other girl swimming in a sea of brilliant blue.

Yes, the whispers sang. *You are a force, you are power made manifest, you will not falter for none can check you.*

"I'm no one's pawn anymore," Pandora gritted out. "Why would I wait the barest moment to be entangled again? It took me *years* to escape this filthy spider. I won't be caught a second time."

Take your place, seal your fate. Come back to me, the whispers urged.

"Pan, your binding," Imogen begged. "I know it's still there. I know you're only blocking it. *Feel* for it. A bound mage knows when her patron is speaking. You'll see it isn't him. I swear this to you."

Pandora's breath was coming in ragged gasps, and Imogen was no more than a mote of silver in a world of spellfire blue. Never since she'd been a small, half-feral child confined to a steel-lined cage had Pan been so close to losing all control and slipping her spark. She held desperately to the ward surrounding Beacon—it wasn't anyone else she was safeguarding him from now, but her own power. If the ward failed, even her unspent power, burning so close to the surface, would be enough to incinerate him.

Automatically Pandora groped for the place within her where her binding still rested. It sat at the center of her pervasive pain, white-hot and livid as a suppressed star, whispering for her to surrender.

"Order me to stop," Pan told Ander, spellfire burning behind the words. "Do it now, so I'll know for certain who and what you are."

Ander swallowed visibly, sweat beading on his forehead. His breath came in convulsive, ragged gasps, half-stifled by the force of Pandora's magic around his throat.

"Pandora Small," Ander managed to get out. "Stop what you're doing. At once."

No worsening of her pain. No eager response from her stifled binding. No compulsion to act. The shackle within her did not recognize him at all.

Dropping to her knees, Pandora crouched and twined her hands around the back of her neck. Something was happening in her chest—she was choking on her own magic, strangled by cords of spellfire and panic. Gasping for air, she set her jaw and bore down with everything in her, willing her power to stay caught, to remain within the all too fragile web of her own skin.

Dimly she felt a comforting hand on her back, tracing slow circles between her shoulder blades. It could not be Beacon—he was still trapped within the ward Pandora refused to let go of. Words filtered down through the mire of Pan's beleaguered consciousness, spoken in Imogen's golden voice.

"You're all right now. You can do this. I promise. I've believed it since before we ever met."

Imogen's words were another anchor, and Pan used the joint force of her ward and those words to draw herself back from the precipice, tamping her spellfire down spark by slow and agonizing spark.

At last, she raised her head. Sat upright. Let out a long, trembling breath. She dropped her ward, and the instant it was down, Beacon was on the floor at her other side, taking her chin in one hand with no regard for his own safety. He forced her to look at him, though tears of abject humiliation were burning in Pandora's eyes, replacing the spellfire that had suffused her.

She knew how she must appear to him. A blue-eyed, magic-touched monster.

"Are you all right?" he asked, his voice fraying on the question. "I mean *really* all right?"

Pan nodded, though she couldn't keep herself from trembling. Everything in her had gone wretchedly cold. Never before had she come back from such a lapse, or had it matter so much. Previously, she'd have slipped her spark and dispassionately been brought back from the debilitating throes of caster's fatigue with vial after vial of spellfire, until her arm was pockmarked with injection points and bore a six-inch patch of blue-black bruising. Afterward, there would have been no concern or help, her failure heralded by nothing more than a string of criticism.

"I'm fine," Pandora said unsteadily. The next moment she was engulfed in scratchy wool and the not unpleasant smells of kantha and shaving soap as Beacon pulled her into a rough, overwhelming hug. Everything in Pan relaxed, melting against him as she listened to the racing sound of the guard's heart in his chest, a testament to how badly he'd been worried. When at last he let her go, they both looked anywhere but at each other, faces flushed with twin embarrassment.

Imogen was at Ander's side, her father pale, the girl venting some manner of suppressed anger as they argued in low tones.

"—for *years* I've told you this was foolishness. We ought to have let her know from the beginning. It's been completely unfair, keeping her in the dark. And did I not say something like this would happen? Haven't I *always been right*?" Imogen shook a chiding finger at Ander, who wore a chastened expression.

"Yes of course," he said. "But I still don't think it would have been fair to you—"

"No!" Imogen scolded. "I don't signify. You've known from the beginning that I wanted to come clean. So don't make this about my good or my just deserts. You made that choice, not me. And we've got to tell her now, there's no getting around it."

"As I'm very obviously the person being discussed," Pandora said from where she still sat on the floor shoulder to shoulder with Beacon, "and as you clearly both have something to say, I think you'd better just come out with it."

Imogen cast a glance at her father, and when Ander remained silent, let out an impatient sigh.

"Pandora," Imogen said, smoothing her skirts self-consciously and setting her shoulders. "The reason the Hollen estate has been paying your way is this: my father is your father as well. You and I are half sisters. We're your family. I wanted you to be told your first day at the Bellwethers', but Papa wouldn't hear of it."

Briefly, Pandora sat motionless. Then she let out a hysterical laugh. "You can't be serious."

Nothing in Imogen's lovely face betrayed any sort of prank or jest. "I'm absolutely serious. When you and I were thirteen, Papa received an unsigned letter, saying his daughter was living in an old tenement building in the Fuller's Quarter, and detailing much of your history. Papa sent someone to you—an old woman, who was in fact a mage bound to the family's service. You'll recall that this same old woman advised you to visit the Bellwethers, if you wished to continue hiding your spellfire. She also ran a clandestine test on you, to determine whether or not you and Papa share blood. It's technically a contravention of the second mage law, to test a person in such a way, but the first set does it all the time. The Guard looks the other way for us, as usual."

"I wouldn't," Beacon growled from where he sat at Pandora's side. She pressed a little closer to him, wanting the solid, unshakeable reassurance of his presence, and he held firm.

Imogen raised an eyebrow. "No. I don't suppose you would. You and the rest of the Guard seem to have a rather different set of standards."

"I just . . . I can't . . . I don't believe you," Pandora said with sudden resolve. It was too ridiculous. "We've been at odds for five years. We don't even like each other."

Imogen rolled her eyes. "And whose fault is that? I tried to be friends when you first started at the Bellwethers', but you wouldn't give me the time of day. I only stooped to an Ingenues' school in the first place *because* of you."

"Oh, you stooped to it, did you?" Pan shot back, annoyance dripping from her tone. "How magnanimous, that you'd condescend to dragging your precious skirts through the mud on my behalf."

She caught a look flashing between Ander and Beacon—commiseration, long-suffering, understanding. And it occurred to Pandora with a sudden shock that if you looked at the enmity between her and Imogen in a slightly different light, it might read as the sniping and bickering that happened between sisters.

As she thought back, she found truth in what Imogen said. The other girl *had* tried to befriend her during their first weeks at the Bellwether School. She'd attempted to include Pandora in little tête-à-têtes in her quarters and offered the loan of various small sundries Pan's hastily assembled and scholarship-funded wardrobe did not include. Prickly and proud to a fault, Pandora had found it all offensively patronizing and quickly struck up a friendship with Winifred Harper instead.

"You just tried to get the better of me in an Ingenues' duet this morning," Pan said. "That's hardly the sort of thing a sister and an altruist would do."

Imogen gave Pandora a look. The sort every Bellwether girl was familiar with, which meant Imogen Hollen thought they were being absolutely and irredeemably thick.

"Pan. Do you really think that after five years at school with you, I'd be laboring under the delusion that I could best you at parlor magic? I already told you—I have been *trying* to get you noticed by a decent patron, who'll be willing to keep your power a secret. That was the entire point of the duet. Once you've dealt with your old patron, you'll need a new one who's both forgiving and discreet."

Once you've dealt with your old patron. Imogen said it with implicit faith, as if it was a forgone conclusion that Pandora would manage her nemesis neatly and come out of the encounter unscathed.

For the first time since Pan's near fatal outburst, Ander spoke.

"Pandora," he said, and there was a world of warmth and regret in his voice. "I owe you a thousand apologies. Gin wanted me to sit down and come clean with you from the start. But I was worried about scandal—my wife, Imogen's mother, is a woman with a great deal of influence, who has the ear of the queen. Ours is a marriage entered into for mutual advantage, rather than romance—she provides prestige and connection, I provide wealth. We've always had our difficulties, and I've been . . . faithless, over the years."

"It's hardly uncommon among the nobility," Imogen said defensively. She laid a protective hand on Ander's arm. "Many marriages are no more than business or political partnerships, with either party left to pursue their own romantic interests elsewhere."

"I wouldn't!" Pan was horrified by the idea of such an arrangement, and once again, Imogen seemed amused.

"Yes, well, just as Beacon's standards differ from those of the Guard, yours do from those of Valora's first set. Though I can't say I disagree with you. Papa and I have had many conversations about how he might have done better in the past."

"Do you know who my mother is?" Pan asked Ander abruptly. "Do you know who my *patron* is?"

"I'm afraid not, on both counts," he said with a rueful look. "At the time you would have come to be, I wasn't who I am now. The family fortune was still running on sliphouses, and I carried a great deal of guilt over that fact. I was in my cups more often than not, and I can't recall who your mother might have been. Oddly enough, it was finding out that I'd be a father—Imogen's father—which set me on a different path. And as for you, I hadn't an inkling you even existed until that letter was sent to me. I thought an Ingenues' school would be an ideal place for you—somewhere to hide in plain sight, and to learn the management of magic such girls are taught."

It was all too much for Pandora. She drew her knees to her chest, resting her forehead on them. A hand settled on her back, and she knew by its broadness and the weight of it that it was Beacon's this time, not Imogen's. At once, she wished fiercely to be alone with him. He was the only person who'd ever taken her just as she was, no blood ties required. And she'd never felt any sense of obligation toward him, as she did now to both Imogen and Ander. Gratitude, yes, but Beacon himself would be the first person to protest if she spoke of owing him anything for his loyalty and help.

He was *good*, Pan realized with a sudden pang. After only the briefest possible acquaintance, she suspected he was the best person she'd ever known, and that if he made a choice, she would always believe in its rightness.

"Beacon," Pandora whispered, her words barely audible so that Imogen and Ander would not overhear. "I don't know what to do about all this. It's very confusing, and . . . I want to go now. I need time to think."

At once Beacon was on his feet, helping Pandora up and positioning himself a step in front of her, a shield she could shelter behind if needed.

"Sir, I believe I've asked all the questions the Guard requires," he said to Ander. "It's safe to say you couldn't have been involved in the unfortunate deaths at the palace. I'll escort Miss Small back now, and if she wishes to hear anything further from you, I'm sure she'll be in touch."

"Pan," Imogen said pleadingly. "Can we at least talk tomorrow? We ought to get this settled."

Settled how? Pandora thought. *I've lived all my life without anyone to call my own. I don't know what you expect of me.*

"I'm sure we can arrange something," she said, the words coming out wooden and devoid of emotion. "Tomorrow, then."

Beacon led her out of the parlor, down a corridor, and through the foyer, and they were in the garden before Pandora realized the extent to which she was leaning on him. Any near loss of control left her exhausted beyond reckoning, and this lapse had been the worst in a decade. Coupled with the shock of Imogen and Ander's revelation, it had Pandora at the end of herself, her knees weak and her vision going gray at the edges.

Flagging a hansom that stood waiting at the end of the quiet lane, Beacon got Pandora inside and settled into a corner.

"Where would you like to go?" he asked quietly as he took the place at her side.

"Not the palace," Pan said with a shake of her head. "I don't know, really. You decide."

"I have somewhere." Beacon reached up and handed the driver a banknote. "Take us to the crossing of Hartshorn and Fawkes, down in the Flats."

15

OPPOSITES

Beacon hated to wake Pandora. She'd fallen asleep within minutes of the hansom beginning its journey across the city and lay with her head pillowed on his lap. It was a marvel to him that in sleep, her control never slipped. He could feel only the faintest wisps of heat emanating from her skin, giving no hint of the devastating power she kept locked away. Even behind the ward she'd raised at the Hollen villa, he'd been able to feel what she kept hidden. It had been like standing behind a shield of ice in a room burning to ash.

"Pandora," Beacon murmured as the hansom driver cleared his throat from the raised platform he stood on. "We're here."

She stirred and let out a small, unconscious sound. Half her hair had escaped its simple styling and lay in loose curls over her shoulders. Her face was flushed with sleep and perhaps, too, with the raging heat of the spellfire she held prisoner at her core. A shock ran through Beacon—a ferocious desire to keep her safe, come what may. He'd battle any enemy on her behalf—the shadowy patron who haunted her, the rogue power she contained, the Guard itself, if need be.

And yet, as she opened her eyes and sat up with a jolt, misgivings flooded Beacon too. Sparks of brilliant blue spellfire still swam in her dark eyes, though they vanished as she blinked and shook her head to clear it. Two truths existed within Beacon, at war with each other: Pandora was dangerous, and he wanted to be with her. Her power was anathema, yet he craved the sight and feel of it. There was nothing about Pandora Small he did not desire at this point, from the crown of her tidy head to the tips of her little feet; from the immaculately presented Ingenue exterior to the brutal magic burning at her heart.

But she could have killed Ander Hollen. The slightest twist of fate and the entire Hollen villa could now be a ruin of ashes. The realization rested in Beacon like a cold, hard stone. In dallying with Pandora, in keeping her secrets, he was quite literally playing with fire.

She fixed her eyes on him, patient, weary beyond belief, and clearly waiting for Beacon to take the lead. Holding out his hand, he shook off any lingering misgivings. He'd rather die than let the girl see his doubts.

"Where are we?" Pan asked with a faint spark of curiosity as he helped her from the hansom. The building before them was small and unprepossessing—a single-story shopfront, with no sign to indicate what it might offer and windows too small and grimy to afford a glimpse of what lay inside. The Hesper River slipped by behind it, and a barge was passing loaded with bales of wool and crates of dry goods.

"You showed me what's come closest to home for you in Valora," Beacon said. "Now it's my turn."

He opened the door to usher Pandora inside, and smells of bitter kantha root and good food enveloped them at once.

"Oh, I'm *starving*," Pan said under her breath, and Beacon smiled. He'd thought she might be.

The interior of the building was mostly given over to a single large room, crammed with tables and booths and dimly lit with the help of smoky oil lamps. At midafternoon, there were few people about, and Beacon led Pandora to a quiet booth against one of the walls. Having safely installed her on one side of the table, he hesitated a moment, deliberating. But his dilemma was solved by Pan's small hand slipping into his own and pulling him down beside her.

"Here," she said a little self-consciously. "Sit by me."

He did, and gladly. Whatever power she possessed, Beacon felt most at ease when he could place himself between her and the world, a ward made from sinew and life's blood and woolen uniform.

"Do you want to choose something yourself?" Beacon asked, gesturing to a small card on the table. "Or would you prefer for me to?"

"I can't think," Pan said. She let out a ragged sigh. "You decide."

A frowsy, aproned woman appeared before them and beamed at Beacon. "Hello, Ellis! Haven't seen you for a month or two. And now here you are with a young lady, no less. Keeping well, it seems."

She winked broadly, and Beacon grew red-faced, not sure how to respond. He settled on ordering bowls of summer stew, cups of kantha, and haxberry pastries to follow.

"What is this? I've never had it before," Pan asked when their stew arrived, fragrant and golden and smelling enticingly of root vegetables and fowl. She poked at it with her spoon, inspecting each piece of vegetable and meat before skeptically trying an infinitesimal bite. "Oh!" Her eyes widened. "It's delicious!"

"It's summer stew," Beacon said with a smile. "Country food. There are only a few places you can get it in Valora. But I'm not city bred, so this is the sort of thing I like."

The vast bowls of stew had come with a wooden board and an enormous round loaf of loose-milled bread, which Beacon cut into thick slices. He sopped up stew with a crust and bit into it as Pandora watched him out of the corner of her eyes. Delicately she reached for a piece of bread, tore a small square from it, and dabbed at the contents of her bowl. After putting the bread in her mouth, she made a happy sound and wiggled in her seat.

"This is the best thing I've ever eaten. I've never been allowed to touch food with my hands before."

"Never?" Beacon was taken aback. "Not to eat a sen'night roast? Or bread and wickets? Or nicks and scuttle?"

Pandora stared at him blankly. "I don't know what any of those are. When I was with my patron, I'd be punished if I didn't use silverware just right, and the food was much the same as what we got as Ingenues, and have at the palace. When I was on my own, I ate scraps, but old habits die hard. Even then, I found someone's tossed-out plate and knife and fork and did things the way I'd been taught."

A heart-wrenching vision flashed across Beacon's mind, of a much younger Pandora, clad in rags and seated in the corner of the flat she'd taken him to, eating scraps with the same refined precision she demonstrated as an Ingenue. Unconsciously he shifted closer to her, and she leaned into him.

Not until their bowls were cleared, the loaf of bread reduced to crumbs, and the table set with kantha and pastries did Beacon clear his throat and raise the subject that had been hanging on the air between them.

"The Hollens," he said. "I suppose we should talk about them."

Pandora leaned her head against the back of the booth and shut her eyes. "Do we have to? I'd rather pretend all of that never happened."

"It won't go away," Beacon pointed out.

STEEL & SPELLFIRE

Opening one eye, Pan squinted at him. "You're right, of course. I just . . . I don't know if I believe them. Imogen and Ander. They seem to know more about me than anyone else ever has, but . . . I can't get any of it to sit right."

Beacon nodded. "If they found out about you in some way—what you're capable of—it could be a ruse. Some sort of plan to make use of you, and your spellfire. Keeping it secret all these years hasn't just ensured you're safe from the Guard. It's prevented anyone from taking advantage of you. I'm sure there are any number of bad actors in Hesperid who'd love to get their hands on a mage with nigh unlimited power."

"I know," Pandora said flintily. "I spent the first decade of my life under the control of just such a person. I will send myself and half the city up in flames before I let that happen again."

Beacon took a long swallow of kantha, bitter as sin, before turning a little in his seat to face her. "About your patron, Pandora. You nearly killed Ander, when you thought it might be him. What do you plan to do if and when you find them?"

Pandora was silent, her lips a thin, tight line, her expression rebellious.

"They should be dealt with by the law," Beacon pointed out. "And by the Guard. You can't just take justice into your own hands."

"Why can't I?" Pan shot back. "I was born already outside the law, as far as I can tell. And with a mage like that—a mage like *me*—the Guard hasn't a hope of apprehending them without a hundred lives lost. Possibly more. If I'm strong enough, I'll do it far better, and more tidily."

"Will you?" Beacon asked. "Do you really think you can clash with someone like yourself and avoid collateral damage? Lives lost, property ruined?"

"I'll do better than the Guard," Pandora said, defiant.

"Perhaps. But if the Guard dealt with and dispatched such a mage, they would be seen as upholding the law and performing their duty. If you did the same, you'd be viewed as out of control, a threat beyond compare. Most people would not care why you'd done it. They'd only care about the fallout, and the extent of your power."

"It isn't fair." Pandora hunched her shoulders and glowered, a spectacle that Beacon found distractingly endearing. All he did, however, was to set one of his hands firmly over her own.

"I want you to promise me," he said, "that when we find your patron, you'll be circumspect. Don't give away that you know who they are. Come to me, and we'll find a way to handle it that does not reflect back on you."

Pandora thought for a moment. Beacon could see her turning over what he'd asked, examining the request from all angles with her quick and ready mind.

"No," she said finally, then took a decisive bite of her haxberry pastry. "I won't promise. But I appreciate that you want me to. And I'd like to have you with me when I speak to Imogen. I don't know that I trust her, but I do trust you."

"Of course," Beacon answered, glad just to be needed by Pandora. "I've been thinking about that. Imogen said Valora's first set have a way of testing someone by magic to see if they're a blood relation, and that the Guard looks elsewhere when it happens. You could do the same—put Imogen to the test, and see if there's any truth to the Hollens' story."

Pandora scrunched up her nose doubtfully. "I thought you said you wouldn't be like the Guard and overlook an infringement of the mage laws."

"I would for you."

The small bell at the café's entrance rang. Focused on her kantha and her pastry, Pandora did not look up, but Beacon, accustomed to taking careful notice of his surroundings, glanced at the door.

His heart clenched in his chest. A pair of guards was coming in, but though they wore ordinary uniforms, Beacon would recognize them anywhere. Magefinders. The same pair who'd put him to the test under the prince consort's direction. One of them stood by the entrance as the other crossed the room and exchanged a few low words with the café's proprietress.

It's a coincidence, Beacon tried to reassure himself. *It has to be. They're here for a cup of kantha to get them through the last few hours of a duty shift. Nothing more, nothing less.*

But the man at the door was searching the room, scanning it with covert looks. When his eyes lit on Beacon, something tense and electric flashed between them. Beacon turned to Pandora easily, as if he'd met the other guard's eyes by chance and hadn't recognized him. At the counter, the second magefinder took two cups of kantha and rejoined her companion at the door. The two of them spoke briefly, one of them nodding surreptitiously in Beacon and Pandora's direction.

"Pandora," Beacon said, keeping his voice very low. "We need to—"

But the magefinders did not approach. With a last look at Beacon, they left the café.

"Need to what?" Pandora asked. "Come here again? I absolutely agree."

"To leave," Beacon said firmly. Whatever the magefinders had been doing here, he'd rest easier with Pandora back on Palace Hill. There, she was an Ingenue, well respected and with the limits to her power widely known. He did not want her in the lower city any longer, where magefinders with a sense for magic as acute as his own might detect a stray spark of Pandora's consuming power. "I have some explaining to do to Captain Tanner—she expected me on watch in the Council Chambers this afternoon, and I'm here instead."

"Oh no." Pandora looked crestfallen. "Will you be in trouble on my account?"

"It'll be all right. Captain Tanner's fair, and easy to work for. If I say a friend needed me, she'll overlook things this once. I don't make a habit of missing shifts."

"I'm sure you don't," Pandora said with an amused smile.

Before Beacon could say anything more, the café's proprietress appeared at the table.

"The hansom you wanted is stopped at the door," she announced. "Shall I tell the driver to take another few turns around the block?"

Beacon frowned. "I didn't ask for a hansom—let me go see to it. I'll settle the bill as well, Minna. Perhaps you could bring a saucer of Hesperidian sweet whip for the young lady while she waits?"

Pandora stayed curled up in the corner of the booth, transparently happy to be looked after. Beacon paid at the front of the café and stepped into the street, where an enclosed hansom waited at the curb. The driver was nowhere to be seen, and Beacon cast about himself in confusion. At last, uncertain what else to do, he opened the door to glance inside.

And recoiled at once. Slumped against each other on the bench, were the magefinders who'd put him to the test. Their dead eyes were wide and unseeing, stained blue by the spellfire that had been torn from them. Fingers, mouths, and nostrils all bore the same taint. In one hand, the female magefinder clutched a scrap of paper.

Beacon drew it from the woman's still-warm fingers. Smoothing the scrap, he found a clipping from one of the dailies. It was old news, from half a year back—just a routine report of goings on in the lower city Guard. Underlined severely was a single line of text.

Two hellions were put down near the south wharfs, found and extinguished by Officer Ellis Beacon, newly out of training.

The shadowy figure of Pandora's faceless patron seemed to loom large behind Beacon. A chill passed over him, at being the subject of their communication. The message they'd sent was plain as day. If Beacon chose to throw his lot in with Pandora Small, her patron would grant him all the same consideration they gave the girl. Her troubles would be his. Her sins. The blood debts nailed to her door.

Beacon felt a great and mulish stubbornness rise up in him. He would not be threatened or badgered or terrorized. What was right in his eyes was right, no matter the cost.

Pocketing the scrap of paper, Beacon sent the hansom's horse bolting off into the city with a sharp slap to the rump. It would be apprehended by the Guard soon enough, all without further connection to Pandora or himself.

"Beacon?" Pan's voice said from the café door as the hansom careened away. "Is anything the matter?"

A note of worry colored her words, and he turned to her with a brisk shake of his head as he offered his arm. "Nothing. It was only a mistake. We'll find another hansom, down at the corner."

He hadn't felt a thing.

That was the thought that continued to plague Beacon as he hurried to an emergency briefing of the Guard late that evening. Music swelled from one of the palace's expansive ballrooms, and Beacon caught a glimpse of gaudy dancers whirling across the floor as he strode past.

The Queen's Council Chambers were far enough from the evening's festivities that none of the gaiety reached them. Housed in the government wing, the Council Chambers were where the laws and policies of Hesperid were decided upon. Though they were the queen's in name, in practice the prince consort presided more often. This evening, neither were present. Instead, Captain Tanner addressed a crowd of nearly all the Guard, with Prince Theo at her side to represent the royal family's interests. Beacon slipped in and took a seat near the back of the room, nerves prickling when he saw how many of his fellows were present. Surely it left the rest of Palace Hill poorly watched?

But it was not his place to question such decisions.

"I have unsettling news," Captain Tanner said, stepping up behind a podium where Beacon was accustomed to seeing dignitaries ramble about taxes and trade and infrastructure. "It seemed most efficient to convey it to you all in a body. Two magefinders have been found dead in the lower city, killed in the same way as the Ingenues. The Guard's official stance on the deaths has changed—we are no longer pursuing a rogue hellion, believed to have spawned on Palace Hill. The beasts don't range so widely, and the condition of the bodies found in the city was such that the killing could only have been done by human hands."

A visceral image flashed across Beacon's mind—the magefinders' dead bodies slumped together in the back of a hansom cab. He'd been a fool to leave them there. If he'd really wanted to keep suspicion away from Pandora, he'd have hidden the bodies in some back alley in the lower city, where they could pass for hellion prey. Damn his lack of wit.

"Any information pertaining to the magefinders or the two Ingenues who passed is of interest," Captain Tanner went on. "If you made the slightest observation which could be of use, I'd like to hear it. For now, do your duty, and stay on your guard."

"Was it a mage that did this?" an anonymous voice called out from the crowd.

Captain Tanner sighed. "I'm afraid it looks that way. As I said, we will proceed normally, but with an extra measure of caution. Meantime, understand that the matter is being handled by your superiors, and considered an issue of the utmost urgency and importance."

Muttering broke out across the chambers. A rogue mage was the Guard's worst fear—they dealt enough with magic, even on Palace Hill, to understand how destructive it might be if used for evil purposes.

"Is it someone in the mage corps?" another voice blurted out.

"Or an Ingenue?"

"Is it one of the nobles?"

Captain Tanner raised a hand, and silence fell at once.

"What we will not do," she said sharply, "is turn this into an inquisition. I thought you all should be informed—the consort was reluctant to have the entire Guard made party to this new development, but I fought for you all to hear the news. So you *will* go about your business, and you will treat everyone you encounter on the Hill and elsewhere with the usual courtesy. Have I made myself clear?"

A chorus of reluctant murmurs gave their assent.

"Good," Captain Tanner said, her voice still terse. "You're all dismissed."

Guilt slowed Beacon, making him linger on his way out of the chambers. And so Captain Tanner had no difficulty catching him in the corridor beyond.

"Beacon," she said. "You're the only person on the Hill who had dealings with those magefinders besides myself and the consort. You don't recall anything out of the ordinary from the morning you were examined, do you? I've been piecing things together and can't remember anything myself."

Beacon thought of himself and Pandora hiding Leslie Moran's body. Of how he'd taken his name from the magefinders and sent the hansom on its way.

"I'm afraid not," he lied, while a bad conscience soured his stomach. "I wish I could be of help."

He fought the urge to shift his weight from one foot to another. Captain Tanner, he often thought, saw and intuited more than even a magefinder could. But it was the truth, at least, that he could not recall anything that had piqued suspicion from the day his magesense had been tested.

Most of the guards had dissipated, only a few hanging back to talk seriously here and there. Prince Theo emerged from the Council Chambers and made his way to the end of the corridor, where he was met by a girl with a calm way about her and a wealth of nut-brown hair. Beacon watched distractedly as the prince and the girl walked off together.

"Do you . . . think I ought to have noticed something about those magefinders?" he pressed. "Does the Guard have someone in their sights?"

Beacon was wound tense as a steel spring, worrying Captain Tanner would mention a certain Ingenue.

"No," she said with a firm shake of her head. "And I won't breathe a word of any specific suspicion until I'm certain who's behind this. The general feeling toward mages has been fraught these last few years, and I won't give Valora a scapegoat."

For a moment, Beacon considered coming clean and telling the captain everything. About his chance discovery of Pandora, the growing connection between them, Pan's certainty that her patron was behind all this. The two of them could use an ally like Captain Tanner, and Beacon felt raw and bruised over keeping his superior in the dark. But what else could be done? He'd never forgive himself if he told Pandora's secrets only to have the girl apprehended by the Guard.

That night, Beacon paced his small, spartan room, racking his brains and trying to think what he might have overlooked. He certainly had more information than the Guard when it came to the deaths they were investigating. Winifred Harper had been killed in the labyrinth, only feet away from Pandora Small. Leslie Moran had been killed in the archives with her. And Pan was there, too, when the magefinders were sent to Beacon as a dire warning.

There was Pandora.

There was a mage killing with impunity.

And somehow, where both had been present, neither could be detected.

Letting out a frustrated growl, Beacon threw himself onto the bed, one arm behind his head as he continued mulling over the problem. He'd shed his uniform and wore only shirtsleeves, trousers, and braces, but he regretted the lack of a wool jacket now. Curse the mage corps and their weather magic, keeping it forever a few degrees below comfortable on Palace Hill.

A waft of warmth from beyond the door and Beacon was on his feet and face-to-face with Pandora before she had a chance to knock. She had on a flimsy rose-colored dressing gown frothing with lace, which did little to hide demure glimpses of a soft yellow nightdress beneath. It was the first time Beacon had seen Pandora in any color besides ivory. He no longer thought her a mouse—more a small and perfect hedgerow flower.

"Aren't you cold?" he asked, voicing the first question that came to mind in order to hide his sentimental train of thought.

Pan gave him a bewildered look. "Cold? It's been roasting on the Hill since teatime. Half the mage corps are off duty to be questioned and examined by whatever magefinder your Guard's brought in. The weather's nearly as bad up here as it is down in the lower city."

"You mean you don't feel a chill? At all?"

"If anything I'm stifling."

Beacon fell entirely still. Since first arriving on Palace Hill, he'd attributed the coolness of its peak to the work of the mage corps. But if Pandora could not feel it, it was not the tangible product of their magic. Neither could it be the combined impression of their power—Beacon had passed members of the corps on many occasions and could always feel odd, disparate jolts of magic as he did so. A strong wind. A wash of dizziness. A sudden numbing of his hands. They weren't unified enough to create a collective pull on his magesense.

Yet he felt cold, while Pandora was heat.

The truth seared through Beacon like electricity, and he cursed himself for a fool. Pulling Pandora inside, he shut the door behind them, and the two stood facing each other in the center of his room.

"I know why I can't sense magic when someone's been killed," Beacon said, his normally sedate mind racing. "I know why no one else can either. You and whoever's been murdering people here—your patron, in all likelihood. You're each other's perfect opposite. Your power cancels each other's out. I feel heat from you. Cold from them. So if you've both been giving off a strong impression of magic in the same place, it manifests as . . . nothing. Pandora, they've been using you as a mask."

Pan's face twisted, growing furious and bitter, and her power burned hot, until sweat beaded on Beacon's temples and at the back of his neck.

"They have been using me for as long as I can remember," she said, her voice dripping venom. "I hate it. I hate it more than words can tell. I have always been a tool for others to further their own aims. Just a *thing*, a means to an end. Unless I hide, no one sees me as anything but spellfire."

"I see you," Beacon said, and though her heat was beginning to prickle at his skin like the start of sunburn, he wanted more of it. Not to use, but to bask in. Because it was Pandora's power and a part of her truest self.

"I know." Pan drew closer to him, until they stood with no more than an inch of space between them. She reached out and took one of his braces between her forefinger and thumb, toying with the thin, supple leather they were worked from. "And you've never asked for anything from me, have you? You're the only person who hasn't. Even Imogen wants me to be a sister to her, but it's all strange and uncomfortable, and I don't know if I have it in me to be family, after all these years. Only you've never wanted anything."

She glanced up at him through her fringe of dark lashes, and the scorching heat of her power banked itself, subsiding to delicious warmth. With the two of them so near, Beacon was drowning in her lily of the valley scent, her small perfection, her hidden depths, fathomless as the heart of the sea.

Instinctively Beacon bent a little, bowing his head to be closer. He raised one hand to the curve of her neck, his thumb tracing the line of her jaw, and it did not matter to him if he'd once been burned by her skin. Any pain would be worth the suffering, to touch Pandora Small.

"It's not true," he said, his voice low, "that I've never wanted anything from you. I can think of a number of things I want, though they've little to do with your power."

Pandora's eyes drifted shut, and her breath caught.

"Why don't you start with one request?" she whispered. "I've never given a piece of myself willingly before, but I could make you the exception. Ask me for something, and whatever it is, I'll offer it up."

Beacon could already imagine the taste of her on his lips. There'd been dalliances back home with village girls—passing things of no meaning, where they chased after him until he allowed himself to be caught and kissed and petted, so that the girls could go back to their friends and giggle over how they'd toppled their village's beautiful giant. It had all been a meaningless distraction to Beacon, an idle amusement to take his mind off his family's troubles.

Pandora was different. She would taste of ashes and honey and lightning, and Beacon wasn't sure if he'd be able to stop himself once he had her on his tongue. With the village girls, he'd been careful, restrained, a gentleman. He did not want to be a gentleman with Pandora. Not while knowing she could kill him in an instant, and that for all his size and strength, she'd never be within his power. He would always, *always* be within hers.

Just the thought set him aching so badly, he thought he'd fall apart.

"What I want from you is this," Beacon said, his voice coming out deep and ragged. "For you to—"

A soft, erratic knock sounded at his door.

"Pandora," a girl's frightened voice called. "Pan, are you in there? It's Mamie."

"Gods high and low," Pandora breathed. "How did she find me here?"

But she went to the door and wrenched it open. Another girl in a nightdress, this one a strawberry-blond waif, blinked once at Pan and Beacon and dissolved into a flood of tears.

"Get in here, you little fool," Pandora said, though not urgently. She pulled the girl inside and shut the door while Beacon stood by overcome with awkwardness, suddenly unsure what to do with his hands and feet.

"Don't just stand there," Pandora chided him. "Make poor Mamie a cup of kantha. What is it, darling? Was someone unkind to you? Or did you find a mousetrap again?"

The girl's distress was no cause for concern, then. She was evidently a bleeding heart. Beacon relaxed a little as he began to fix a pot of kantha.

"Breathe," Pandora said, her voice low and soothing. "That's right. In and out. Good girl."

"Eleanor's *missing*," Mamie managed to get out. "She's been gone for two hour*s*."

Pandora shot Beacon a covert look of alarm. But to Mamie all she said was "You always think people are missing, and they always turn up. Eleanor will too. When did you see her last?"

"At the dessert table outside the blue ballroom," Mamie sniffed. "She said she was going to meet a possible patron, but that she wanted to keep it quiet because it would make Imogen angry."

"Imogen?" Pandora frowned. "Why should Imogen care . . . oh. It was the prince. She was going to meet with Prince Theo."

Beacon's ears pricked at that, and he turned to face the girls.

"What does she look like?"

"Why does it matter?" Mamie asked at the same time that Pandora spoke.

"Brown hair. Quiet bearing. Dresses in good taste, but not flashily."

"I saw her," Beacon said. "With the prince, a little over an hour ago."

"Oh, thank the gods." Mamie visibly melted in relief. "She's all right, then."

Is she? Pandora mouthed to Beacon. He shrugged. Under current circumstances, he wouldn't consider anyone safe unless he was absolutely sure of their whereabouts.

Pan got to her feet and took a fresh cup of kantha from Beacon's hands. She gave it to Mamie and smiled encouragingly at the girl.

"Drink that up and we'll take you back to my room," Pandora said. "You can stay with me tonight, if you'd like."

"No," Mamie answered bravely. "I'll go to my own room. Eleanor will worry if she gets back and I'm not there."

Mamie drank her kantha to oblige Pandora, and Beacon fell in with them at a gesture from Pan that he ought to escort the girls back to the Ingenues' wing. With Mamie safely tucked into bed, Pan turned to Beacon.

"We're going to find Eleanor. I don't trust anyone on this godsforsaken hill."

Beacon nodded. "I'd have gone alone if you'd thought she was all right. I wouldn't have been able to sleep otherwise."

16

CATACOMBS

Theo's rooms were empty. Beacon's uniform and the implication that his errand was urgent secured them entry, and Pandora stood in the middle of the prince's chaotic bedchamber with fear rising in her like fire.

"It's all right," Beacon said, keeping his voice low. It had not escaped Pandora that he could read most of her emotions now through the state of her spellfire alone. Being known so instinctively was an odd and not unpleasant experience. "They could be anywhere. Dancing still, or walking in the conservatory. We'll keep searching."

Pandora shook her head. "No. He's supposed to be such a rake—even the guards will tell you Theo's always bringing girls back to his rooms. But I haven't seen him spend much time with any of us since coming to the Hill. Except for Imogen."

"Then we look there."

Pan was silent all the way to Imogen's room, and shifted her weight anxiously from one foot to the other as they waited for an answer to her knock at the door. Beacon reached out ever so gently, putting one hand to Pandora's elbow, and that steadied her. At last, the door opened. Imogen appeared on the threshold, looking more perfect and golden than ever in a pure-white nightgown, with her hair a tumble of flawless honey-blond curls.

But Pandora did not even allow her to speak. Beyond Imogen, sprawled across a sofa, she could see Theo. An empty bottle of Indiran spirits lay on the floor beside him, and he snored faintly as Pan stormed past Imogen and over to the prince.

"Where is she?" Pandora snapped, shaking Theo awake. "Where is Eleanor Wellesley?"

Theo groaned, smelling like a distillery and fighting to focus on Pandora. "Who?"

But there was something in his eyes, behind the haze of alcohol and confusion. A desperate look, like an animal caught in a trap.

"You'll tell me where she is now," Pandora warned, her spellfire rising, "or by the Higher Gods, I'll—"

"Haven't you threatened enough people today?" Imogen asked coolly, sweeping over to settle herself on the floor at Theo's side. The prince took one of Imogen's hands in his own and kissed it fervently. "He doesn't know where Eleanor is, and couldn't tell you even if he wanted to."

"Ellis saw him with her," Pandora protested. "Don't try to defend him, Imogen, I've got an unimpeachable witness."

Imogen raised an eyebrow in a scathing look of patronizing disbelief. "Do you really think I, of all people, would ever dally with someone who stepped out on me? I've a far better sense of my own worth. Girls may visit Theo's rooms, but they aren't going there for him."

Pandora scowled back, prickly and bad-tempered where Imogen

was collected and condescending. "Then why do they? What brings them there?"

"I don't know. He can't say." Imogen shook her head. "I've asked, but he's never been able to talk about it. It's not that he's unwilling, mind you, I meant what I said. He's *unable*. Because of course I asked, once rumors started flying about Theo and his conquests. In fact, I was furious for half a year and didn't speak to him at all. Then I followed several of the girls, and realized he left them alone in his rooms. By the time he returns, they're gone. Until this year it's been serving girls and entertainers—no one who'd be missed. This is the first year he's sought out Ingenues. Neither of us know what happens to the girls after he invites them for a tryst."

Imogen flushed, going such a deep crimson that Pan knew at once she was only lying to spare the prince's feelings.

"You know what happens," Pandora pushed. "Maybe you didn't before, but you've found out this summer."

"It's all right," Theo said groggily, though he hadn't sat up yet. From the way he smelled, Pandora was surprised he hadn't poisoned himself with everything he drank. "Just tell her."

"Winnie and Leslie both went to Theo's rooms the night before they died," Imogen said. "So I don't *know* what happens to his girls, but I can guess."

"Then just stop!" Pan blurted out. "Stop taking them there!"

A look of anguish crossed Theo's face, and he pressed his eyes shut.

"I've tried," he said, abject despair ringing in the words. "I've left the palace altogether, determined to abdicate my place and never return, if that's what it took. I was perfectly resolved. And in three days, I'd come back. I couldn't help it. The only thing that helps is being completely off my head—I can't ensnare anyone if I can't think."

The girls made sense. The bottles made sense. *Poor Theo,* Pandora thought.

"It's a binding," she said, shooting a look at Imogen, who nodded assent.

"Yes. I've thought so for years. But he's not a mage, so he can't block it the way you can."

"That's why you won't take Imogen's binding," Pan said to Theo. "Because you're already bound, and because you're afraid you'd harm her in some way."

The prince looked wretched. "I'm already in hell. But if anything happened to Gin . . ."

Impulsively Pandora knelt at Imogen's side and took Theo's other hand in her own.

"I know what it's like being bound to a monster," she said. "And I'd stake my life that our monsters are one and the same. I know how the things they force you to do eat away at your spirit. But you can't help it—none of this is your fault, it's theirs."

"It doesn't feel that way," Theo whispered, his eyes fixed on Pandora as if she was a lifeline.

"I know," Pandora said, and she had never spoken truer words. "Believe me. With every fiber of my being, I know. But we're going to fix things. We're going to find whoever's behind all this. The four of us, together."

Beacon's hand settled on Pandora's shoulder in a gesture of approval.

"Imogen," Pan said tersely. "A private word?"

She drew the other Ingenue aside, to the opposite end of the spacious sitting room. Back by the settee, Beacon moved to a side table bearing a kanthivar service. Pan could overhear him speaking to the prince in reassuring tones.

"I'll fix you something to sober you up a little, Your Highness. It'll keep your head from splitting too badly in the morning, as well."

"Good luck," Theo said with a bitterness that bordered on despair. "I've kept myself in my cups the better part of three years, trying to stop myself from acting as a lure. If you put a torch to my blood at this point, it'd go up in flames."

Pandora returned her full attention to Imogen. "If Theo's been bound by my patron, it has to be someone with intimate access to the Hill and the royal family. I'd thought for a short while that it might be Miss Alice, but I don't think she'd have the wherewithal to get at Theo like that."

"Miss Alice?" Imogen asked in surprise. "Whatever made you think it might be her?"

"She knows about my spellfire," Pandora answered. "Has known for quite some time, apparently. And because of it, she's been grooming me as a bride for Baron Hax, who is her lover."

Imogen pulled a disgusted face. "Miss Alice and Hax? What an unpleasant image."

"Even more unpleasant when they want to draw you into it," Pandora said drily. "But I don't think she's my patron after all. Nor a member of Hax's family—they're hardly at court. Your father's in the clear too. Beacon couldn't sense a single spark of magic on him."

"Because he doesn't have any," Imogen said. "And he's not my father, he's our father."

Pandora stole a glance across the room. Beacon had propped Theo up against a mound of pillows and was holding a mug to the prince's lips with a stern expression on his face. Clearly, the guard did not trust the prince not to make a mess in his current state. In spite of everything, a smile tugged at the corners of Pandora's mouth as she watched

Beacon treating the heir to Hesperid's throne like a nursery child.

"I don't know if I believe you about our connection," Pandora told Imogen, choosing to be frank. "It's a lot to take in."

"Use your spellfire," Imogen offered immediately, holding out her hands like an invitation. "Divine the truth of the matter when I say that I'm your sister."

Pan shook her head. "No. I don't do that."

"Of course you do." Imogen wrinkled her nose in confusion. "I've seen you, in our parlor magic lessons."

"You thought you saw me work parlor magic on someone else. But I was always either partners with Winnie, who I knew very well, or used some secret I'd discovered about another Ingenue. I don't eavesdrop for pleasure, Gin, I do it to avoid ever using my spellfire on another person. Even the smallest magic of that sort could break my control and cause a death. I'd never be able to live with myself if that happened."

Imogen frowned prettily, thinking hard.

"What about truth and lies?" she asked after a moment. "The game we all played when we were younger. You wouldn't be working the magic then, not really. We'd be working it together."

Pan looked at her alleged sister with appreciation. "That's very clever. All right. Here you are."

Pandora conjured a magelight. The silvery orb glowed between her and Imogen, levitating waist high. But it was not just a magelight—Pan imbued it with a sense of both suspicion and honesty before separating it from herself. It pulsed between her and Imogen. Smiling, Gin set her hands on the spellfire orb.

"My name is Imogen Hollen," she said. The orb continued to glow silver.

"I'm an Ingenue from the Bellwether School." Silver still.

"My favorite animals are cats." The surface of the magelight roiled, turning electric blue.

"My favorite animals are pigs." Back to silver.

"Pigs?" Pandora asked with a snort.

"Mm. I do love pork belly. Needlepoint is a talent of mine." Silver.

"Pandora Small is my sister."

Pan stared at the orb so fixedly, she might have been trying to bore a hole through it with her gaze. But it stayed serenely silver. Letting out a slow breath, Pandora shifted her focus from the magelight, and it began to fade.

"Wait," Imogen said quickly. "Someday, I'll be bound and wed to Prince Theo."

The magelight shone like pewter, and Imogen gave it a small, contented smile. "Just so. There, Pandora. Are you satisfied?"

With a dainty shrug, Pandora accepted her fate. Imogen Hollen, her sister. What a world.

"I suppose I am."

There was nothing to be done that night. Beacon did not know the precise feel of Eleanor's magic, and so he could not search for it. The pervasive chill of the palace would surely mask any magecraft carried out by Pandora's patron. They were forced to wait.

Just before dawn, Pan pulled on her dressing gown and slipped out of her room and down the corridor. She knew there was no reason to hope, and yet a tiny spark of it still burned in her. Perhaps this was all a dreadful nightmare. When she knocked on Mamie's door, Eleanor would be safely inside, the two of them tousle-haired and sleepy and bemused by Pandora's early rising. Or perhaps Pan's ward had held. Perhaps it had been enough to ensure her friend's safety, and Eleanor had reappeared during the night, with a spine-tingling tale of near death at the hands of a masked figure.

But luck and hope were not things that characterized Pandora's life. Mamie came to the door with red-rimmed eyes, having obviously spent as sleepless a night as Pandora herself. She shook her head and melted into Pan's arms. Pandora did her best to hold up the other girl, but Mamie had fainted dead away. A flurried half hour followed—the Misses Bellwether were called, a nurse came to revive the girl, and it was some time before Pan found herself alone with her schoolmate. Mamie stared out her bedroom window while tears slowly tracked down her cheeks and Pandora held her hand. By now it would be all over the palace that yet another Bellwether girl was missing.

"Did she say anything to you?" Pandora asked in despair. "Anything that might indicate she expected to see someone besides the prince, or knew where she was going?"

Mamie shook her head miserably. "Not a word. I wish we'd gone away together. She said we would, if things got worse. I should've insisted on leaving at once. Our families would have been livid, but she knew a way out of the palace, and off the Hill. We could have been shopgirls, or ladies' maids. We could have found patrons who were poor but respectable. If she's . . . if anything happened to her, I'll blame myself forever."

It was a silly fantasy. The moment an Ingenue ran from Palace Hill, they'd be apprehended by the Guard and subjected to a forced binding or boxed. There was no alternative of a small but satisfying life beyond the clutches of family and fortune for them. And yet . . .

"Eleanor knew a way off the Hill?" Pandora asked. "Did she tell you what it was? If she met some sort of trouble, perhaps she tried to get away."

"Do you think?" Mamie asked breathlessly. "Do you think she's all right, down in the lower city, and waiting for me? Oh I do hope so!"

The silly girl's eyes were shining now, with an abundance of the hope Pandora had known was foolish.

"Tell me where she would have gone," Pan pressed.

"The catacombs," Mamie said at once. "Under the palace. It's where the royal family keeps memorials for their forebears. They aren't like us, you know—they bury their dead, instead of immolating them."

Pandora blinked. "I've never heard that."

"Yes, well," Mamie said gently, "you never paid attention when Miss Elvira taught us rank and etiquette."

"Thank you, Mamie," Pandora said, pressing a kiss to the other girl's cheek. "This was very helpful, I'm going to the Guard first thing to see if we can find Eleanor."

Pandora's mind was awhirl with plans to fetch Imogen, Theo, and especially Beacon, and to foray into the catacombs in case Eleanor had managed to hide herself there. She was so caught up in her planning that upon exiting Mamie's room, she nearly ran into two unfamiliar members of the Guard.

"Miss," one of them said, his face stern and unreadable. "You're to come with us."

Immediately Pandora's heart set to hammering in her ears, her palms going slick with the heat of unspent spellfire. *No, no, no,* she warned it, forcing herself into preternatural calm lest one of them had the magesense. But deep down, she knew what was coming. They'd found her out. The steel box she'd dodged for so long was waiting.

"Where to?" she managed to ask easily.

"Your rooms," the second guard, an older woman, said. "The

queen's been attacked. Everyone's being confined to quarters for the time being."

Pandora gaped in surprise. This was a gross aberration from the pattern, but perhaps her patron had grown desperate in their attempts to warn off Pan, or to draw her out. "The queen? Is she all right? What happened?"

"I can disclose that she's well, although shaken," the female guard said. "Anything beyond that, I'm not at liberty to discuss. Follow along, please."

Pan did as she was told. Inside her rooms, she stared hopelessly at the door. What could be done now? She didn't trust the Guard to go looking for one missing Ingenue when the queen's safety was in jeopardy. Neither could she leave to go find Eleanor herself.

Deep down, a leaden fear was growing too. With Theo bound, the queen injured, and what she'd seen at Winifred's immolation, it seemed increasingly likely that Pan's patron was the prince consort. How she would stand up to such a highly placed enemy, Pandora couldn't imagine. The mere idea chilled her to the bone.

A rustling creak sounded in the bedchamber. Turning on her heel, Pan was just in time to see a hidden door opening in the expanse of Dahlia Scroll wallpaper that covered the interior wall.

"How awful about the queen," Imogen said briskly, stepping through the door. "Any news about Eleanor?"

Pandora quickly recounted what she'd learned from Mamie, while glancing from Imogen to the doorway and back again.

"How did you know that was there?" she asked. "Is the palace full of secret passages? Maybe there's one we could take to the catacombs to find Eleanor."

Imogen rolled her eyes. "It's not a secret passage, you ninny. It's a servants' door. Every room has one. You'd know, if you ever called servants. But the corridor they join to is no use. It only goes a little way, and comes out at the next public hallway."

Pandora flopped down onto the settee in frustration and began gnawing at one thumbnail. "What are we going to do, then? We've got to get out of here and find Eleanor."

"We wait." Imogen settled serenely at Pandora's dressing table and tucked a stray curl back into her flawless coiffure. True to form, though it was several hours earlier than most Ingenues rose, Imogen was dressed and made-up. It was as if she had some alternate form of magic, which ensured she was always master of herself before any obligation or disturbance arose.

"Come here," Imogen commanded, and set about to dressing and styling Pandora as if she were a doll. Though Pandora chafed under the confinement and under Imogen's ministrations, there was nothing else to be done. She let herself be toyed with, until a brisk knock sounded at the door.

"You see?" Imogen smiled. "I told you. All that was required was to wait."

When the girls answered the knock, Theo and Beacon strode in.

"I came as soon as I could," Theo said. "Are you all right?"

Imogen raised a hand and cupped the side of his face. "Don't ask about me. Are you? Is your mother?"

Theo covered Imogen's hand with his own. "She's fine. Someone attacked her—a mage, though she didn't get a clear look at them. There are a dozen guards looking after her, as well as my father. Any news about your friend?"

The idea of the consort looking after Queen Maud chilled Pandora, but with Theo bound and still a thrall to her patron, she was unwilling to voice her suspicions. Her reservation proved wise—Theo was oddly resistant to the idea of searching the catacombs, and

Imogen shot Pandora a swift look. Neither could tell if his resistance was grounded in some fear or superstition, or was the outworking of the binding he bore.

"Gin," the prince pleaded. "I really don't think this is a good idea. I know we'd go down there when we were children, but things are different now—"

A sudden dark and pained look flashed across Theo's face. Shaking his head, he pasted on a thin smile. "Of course you know best, though. If you insist we go, we shall."

"I do insist," Imogen said, but she reached out and rested one hand on Theo's arm, as if to reassure him.

At Pandora's side, Beacon was tense with wariness, and he did not have to speak for Pan to know he worried her patron was leading them into some trap. They were all anxious, but Pandora felt something besides simple anxiety. The fear she'd been stricken with at the thought of the prince consort had given way to an odd, ebullient confidence. In company with her friends, she felt for the first time that she might be a match for her patron. With Hesperid's prince, Valora's brightest Ingenue, and the most stalwart of guards at her side, how could one shadowy tormentor possibly prevail?

So it was that the four of them ghosted through the palace corridors together, every guard giving way before Theo. The prince led them past empty and eerily quiet ballrooms and receiving rooms, echoing portrait galleries and airy cloisters, and finally to a section of the compound that seemed more or less abandoned. Thin gray dust grimed everything, the walls were unornamented, and even the omnipresent Guard did not have a foothold here. This was no new and glittering palace complex—this was what remained of the old hill fort, which was older than the city of Valora itself.

Imogen snapped her fingers, and a spellfire-blue magelight

appeared before her—one of the first bits of parlor magic any Ingenue learned. Old habits died hard, and Pandora wrought her own parlor magic reflexively, outdoing Imogen by setting a constellation of winking lights like glowworms to sparkling on the ceiling above.

But Imogen, at least, felt no need to compete any longer. She turned to Pan with one of her radiant smiles.

"You know, I've always loved your parlor magic. You're a wonder at it compared to the rest of us."

Pandora couldn't help it. Inside, she grew warm and soft in response to the praise and returned Imogen's smile shyly.

They flitted on, past shadowy room after shadowy room, the doors yawning open to reveal unfurnished and unused interiors. Finally, after what seemed a mile, the corridor abruptly ended, terminating at a solid and immensely thick oak door.

Theo sorted through his keys as Imogen lowered her magelight to give him a better view. At last, he found the right key and inserted it into the enormous padlock sealing the oak door. Removing the lock, Theo let it fall with a metallic clang and pushed the thick sliding latch out of its housing. With obvious effort, he pulled the door open, and Beacon reached out to help.

"It's only an oak veneer," Beacon said in surprise. "Underneath, the door's steel."

Beyond, there lay nothing but darkness. A dank smell of stone wafted from the opening, and Pan watched as Beacon's hand automatically went to his weapons belt, loosening the pistol in its leather holster and drawing his short sword a half inch from the scabbard. He hesitated a moment, then shook his head.

"I go first," Beacon said in a voice that did not allow for argument. "The rest of you follow behind. Yes, even you, Pandora, though you can be at my back if you like. I wouldn't mind you there—you're faster with your magecraft than any mage or hellion I've ever seen."

Meekly Pan did as she was told, taking up a place directly behind Beacon. He had his pistol in one hand now, cocked and ready to fire if necessary. It was the steel that was troubling him, Pan knew. Certainly it might defend against other things, but primarily it was used against hellions and wild spellfire. Pan's own magic burned viciously as they passed through the door and into the darkness.

She and Imogen twined their magelights together and sent them on ahead, so that a glowing orb like a lamp illuminated the stone tunnel for a dozen paces before them. At intervals of a hundred yards or so, niches were carved into the walls, each holding a stone chest no larger than a hatbox. A name was etched into the stone above every niche, some of the letters so worn, they could no longer be read.

"What are they?" Pandora murmured.

"Ossuaries," Theo said from the back of their procession. "The remains of retainers who showed special loyalty to the royal house."

Pan shuddered. This place was a relic of an older and fiercer Hesperid—a place with less magic, but no veneer of civility, either. No Higher and Lower Gods, no Guard and no mage laws, no council to check the ruling family.

"Do you feel anything?" she asked Beacon beneath her breath, so Imogen and Theo would not overhear. "Should we turn back?"

The guard was a towering silhouette before her, rendered shadow by the joined magelights that proceeded before him.

"There's only you so far," Beacon answered, keeping his voice low to match Pandora's. "But I'm not taking any chances."

Pan was suddenly and intensely grateful for him—for his misguided desire to place himself between her and danger, for his caution, his carefulness, his finely honed instincts to defend and protect. She wanted, more than anything, to reach out in the gloom and touch him—either his hand or the plane of his shoulder beneath his uniform jacket. But he was all watchful intent, and she wouldn't be a distraction, not for anything.

On and on they went, through the endless niche-marked stone tunnel. The ground sloped steadily downward, and morbid imagination began to weigh on Pan, as if Palace Hill itself must be bearing down on her. Surely they must be near its hidden heart.

"Stop. Stay where you are," Beacon said from his place at the lead, raising a hand to force a halt. Pan did so, but she sent her magelight on with him as he stepped out of the tunnel and into a vast open chamber hewn into the roots of the hill. Strengthening her magelight, she grew it into intolerable brilliance and cast it up to the soaring roof of the cavern, where it hung as a small and fiery sun. Imogen's lesser light stayed where it was and slowly winked out, unable to match the force of Pan's lantern.

For the first time in all its unknown centuries, the cavern at the heart of the hill was bright as day. The stone floor had been smoothed by craftsmen and by innumerable footsteps, and the walls were unmarked by the niches that had dotted the tunnels. Instead, stone coffins ringed the space, each of them bearing the carved likeness of their occupant. Beacon methodically walked the perimeter, inspecting the narrow space between each coffin and the wall. Only when he'd reassured himself that there was nothing untoward lurking in the burial ground did he motion to the others to enter.

"Hello, Aunt Rivelian," Theo said ruefully as he emerged into the tomb and placed a hand upon the feet of the nearest supine statue. "Here we are again."

"More like great-great-great-aunt," Imogen said, picking her way forward. She and the prince, at least, did not seem intimidated by the solemn, eerie place they'd arrived at. "It's odd seeing everything so brightly. We only ever had a torch or a dark lantern when we'd hide down here as children. It all looks different. Smaller. Shabbier."

Pandora didn't know about small and shabby—the burial chamber was easily twice the size of the palace's most imposing ballroom. An aura of immense age hung over everything, along with layers of grime and swags of cobwebs as thick as rope.

"Well, well, Imogen," Theo said, reaching behind a particular statue and coming up with a half-full bottle of dark amber liquor. "Do you remember this? You smuggled it down here in your petticoats. Your first and last taste of Cyrillian mead."

Imogen pulled a face. "Don't remind me. Just thinking of it still makes me sick. Let me have your keys, Theo."

Theo fell still, the bottle of liquor halfway to his mouth. "What do you want them for?"

"We're going on," Imogen said firmly. "You told me when we were children that the far door over there leads to a tunnel that will take you out to the lower city. That's where we're headed, in case Eleanor managed to get through."

As she spoke, Theo pulled back into a series of shadows cast by stalactites hanging from the cavern wall. His eyes glittered in the twilit gloom, and he shook his head. "I don't advise that."

"I don't care," Imogen said, never afraid of speaking her mind where the prince was concerned. "We're going on. Please give me your keys."

Reluctantly Theo reached into his pocket and withdrew the heavy set of ancient keys. Imogen went to him, brisk and businesslike, and for a moment he held fast and did not let the iron ring go.

"I can't . . . I can't go with you. But you should leave me the guard," Theo said. "You and Pandora can go on alone."

"Unacceptable," Beacon growled. "I stay with them."

STEEL & SPELLFIRE

"Come with us. Please. Just try." Imogen's tone was coaxing, her eyes on the prince soft and winsome. An agonized look crossed Theo's face, and Pan watched closely as he shook his head. He seemed at war within himself, in some way, and unhappy with the outcome.

"No, I can't. I'll see you when you get back. Kiss me for luck before you go, won't you?"

Imogen leaned forward and pressed a quick kiss to his cheek.

"Like you used to?" Theo asked, and after a brief hesitation, the beautiful girl drew closer to him. She put her hands on the prince's waist and kissed him full on the mouth, long and lingering, in a way Pandora had never been kissed and never expected to be. Reflexively Pan gazed at the ground, not wanting to intrude on a private moment.

"I'm sure there's nothing down there but old bones and spiders. And hopefully Eleanor, alive and well." Imogen reached out and teasingly ruffled Theo's perpetually mussed hair after she'd drawn away from him. "We'll be back before you know it."

But Pandora could hear an odd note in Imogen's voice. Imogen thought they were heading into danger and that the prince was abandoning them on the cusp of it, helpless as he was to withstand his binding. Theo clearly heard it too, for with a miserable look, he shoved his hands into his pockets and slouched away, off into the pitch-black of the tunnel leading upward into the castle. He had no lantern and no magelight to guide him, and Pan felt a sharp sting of concern despite knowing the tunnel only went one way, and that the floors were smooth and free of hazards.

"Follow me, then." Imogen smiled brightly and opened a twin to the door they'd come through, the sole other access point to the burial chamber. "More tunnel I'm afraid, and I haven't been down this one before, so I can't tell you what to expect. Beacon, you—oh yes, I assumed you'd prefer to be first."

Wordlessly Beacon strode through this next doorway, Pandora sending her magelight ahead of him and falling into place at his back. Within moments, she could tell something was wrong. Beacon slowed considerably, and she could see in silhouette that he reached up to wipe a hand across his forehead.

"Steady on, Pan," the guard said, his voice low and even. "You'll scorch me."

Pandora frowned. She wasn't particularly nervous—when she took a gauge of herself and her power internally, nothing seemed amiss. Her spellfire was no more restless or painful than usual, though nerves did begin to prickle at her as she watched Beacon mop his forehead again, then stumble.

Fortunately, this tunnel proved far shorter than the last. Already, they were at a final door, beyond which must lie the exit to the lower city. It couldn't have come soon enough. Beacon let out a slow, ragged breath and leaned against the tunnel wall as Imogen edged forward and unlocked the ponderous door, shoving at it with one shoulder.

Pan needed no more than a glimpse of what lay beyond, and magic burst out from her instinctively in a shimmering, protective ward that stretched around Beacon, herself, and Imogen.

Too late. A heavy, bone-jarring thud sounded beside her as Beacon collapsed despite Pandora's ward. Imogen, unfettered by the mage-sense, pushed the door open the rest of the way, lips parting at the sight of what lay beyond.

"No, don't!" Pan choked out as Imogen stepped forward.

17

PANDORA'S SECRET

Pandora's face swam before Beacon, ghost pale with worry. He could feel something—an aftershock or a memory of pain, coupled with the delicious, easy warmth and floral scent of one of her wards. When he struggled to sit up, a vicious throbbing started at the back of his head, and he put a hand to the place, which came away sticky with blood.

Anxiously Pan helped him upright and leaned him against the stone wall of the tunnel.

"Did I burn you?" she asked, the words urgent as she reached out and touched his face, his neck, his hands.

Beacon shook his head slowly. "N-no? I'm all right. But there was something before your ward. Heat, though not enough to burn, and something else. It felt as if I was going to fly apart."

His fractured attention began to cohere again, enough that he realized they were just outside another ponderous steel door, which was wide open. Beyond lay a space entirely unlike the burial chamber they'd been in earlier.

The rocks of this new cavern had been blasted bone white and marble smooth by some prodigious force. At the center of the cave lay a ruin of steel—vast pieces splintered and twisted into shards of half-melted metal, as if they'd been subjected to a forge fire with the force of a volcano. In among the steel lay incongruous odds and ends—pieces of wood and fabric and tapestry, which might once have been furnishings. Halfway between Beacon and the steel ruins lay an odd, poignant object—a porcelain doll, with half its face shattered.

But all of that he only recalled afterward, for down the center of the steel ruins, a fissure in the earth had been torn open. Imogen stood at its brink already, peering down into the depths, and brilliant blue light played across her face.

The same light, although more diffuse, lit the entire cavern, and it took Beacon a moment to realize that it came from wide seams of electric blue seeping out from the chasm and running in every direction. He'd thought at first that the veins of spellfire were only an effect of Pandora's ward. But no. They were beyond it, of a piece with the rock itself.

"It's the wellspring," Imogen said in a hushed voice, her tone all at once awestruck and a little frightened. "All this time the stories were true. It's been at the heart of Palace Hill, right under our noses."

Beacon got to his feet with a groan, his head aching fiercely where he'd hit it against the tunnel wall. Moving gingerly forward, he crossed the cavern and stood beside Imogen, safe behind the impenetrable shield of Pandora's ward. Pan herself hung back, near the tunnel door, and worried at her nails with an anguished look on her face. Beacon carried on, determined to see what lay ahead.

Below his feet stretched a fathomless subterranean sea of spellfire, once held captive by rock and now unleashed upon the country surrounding it. Staring down into the abyss that had broken the old

Hesperid and rebuilt it as something new, he felt a storm front of emotions. A sense of shocked reverence, for the wellspring's awesome power. Revulsion, knowing that it most often bred monsters when left unchecked. Rage, at what it had done to so many mages, forced into childhood bindings to check their growing power.

"Pandora," Beacon said. "Drop your ward."

"I don't want to," she answered softly. "It will hurt you."

"I can manage."

Little by little, her ward dissipated. She removed it so gently and gradually that Beacon was able to acclimate to the monumental force of the wellspring.

It was like nothing his magesense had ever detected before. It didn't wake sickness or headache in him, the way the presence of a hellion did. But it suffused his bones and sinew with overwhelming, unspent energy, until he felt he might burst out of his own skin. He wouldn't be able to bear it for long—if subjected to that feeling for a prolonged period of time, Beacon suspected he'd go mad. Just for now, though—for a moment—he could tolerate it and keep his wits together.

Though it required all his focus to stay upright and to walk over to the nearest cavern wall, he managed. Beacon half expected his hand to be seamed with spellfire like the rock itself when he lifted it and pressed it to the cave wall. But his skin showed no sign of the bizarre power it sensed.

Touching a vein of spellfire was like a static shock, magnified a hundredfold. The force of it surged through Beacon, accompanied by something else.

Phantom warmth, familiar as his own heartbeat.

Returning to the central chasm, Beacon knelt and pressed his hand to its edge. Again, the shock, enough this time to jolt him backward, followed by a whisper of remembered power.

Pandora's power.

He'd recognize it anywhere.

Slowly Beacon stood. Slowly he turned to face her. Pan was standing beside the tunnel door, looking small and lost and heartbroken.

"I warned you," she whispered. "I said it would hurt you."

"It was you," Beacon said, disbelief lacing his words. "You opened the wellspring."

To her credit, she did not deny it. She only nodded miserably, her gaze fixed on his.

"You tore Hesperid apart," Beacon went on. "Consigned thousands of mages to forced bindings. Bred monsters that still stalk the city. I couldn't begin to guess how many people are dead because of what you did. You let someone else take the blame, too. The Wellesley girl we're looking for—her family's paid for this in spades."

Tears welled in Pandora's eyes and traced a path down her pale cheeks. "Do you think I don't know all that? I've lived with knowing it for years."

"Did your patron force you?" Beacon asked, a lance of hope stabbing through him. "Did they use your binding to compel you to do this?"

Pandora let out a small, bitter laugh, even as she wept. "Wouldn't it be convenient for you if they had? But no. I'm afraid there's no way out for your conscience or mine. All my patron did was make me into an empty vessel, capable of holding more spellfire than anyone else who's ever lived. This was my own doing. I was young and afraid and desperate to be free. I'd seen them kill, and knew that's what they were shaping me into. A creature of violence. I'd been a dog on a leash all my life, and the idea of finally getting away was more temptation than I could withstand. Every time they set me a task, I kept back a few sparks for myself. I waited and hoarded power, and when I finally had the strength to reach beyond the steel box that had been my lifelong prison, I tore my way out. I did not care that I was tearing open Hesperid in the process. So here you are, and here I am. Here all of us are, still paying for my great escape. In the end, it was a poor and partial thing. I couldn't break my binding, only block it. I have my fill of spellfire, and it is as great a torment as the lack of it ever was. But I wasn't made to do this, Beacon. I chose it. Every forced binding, every mage who dies in a cage of steel, every hellion who takes a life, is because of me. In a city of monsters, I am by far the most wicked thing."

Imogen's eyes were fixed on Pandora now, rather than the wellspring. She took a step toward Pan, who stopped her with a raised hand.

Beacon looked at Pandora too. With everything in him, he tried to see past her words. He focused on her smallness, the lines of pain permanently etched at the corners of her mouth from restraining her violent spellfire. He thought of the softness of her dark eyes, of the way she'd come to him for help before anyone else, ever since he learned her secret. He remembered how she'd danced in her power, a fey creature fit for destroying Valora's monsters. Mostly, he recalled the Pandora he'd seen but once, safe and quiet in a shabby home of her own making, wishing for nothing but peace and a few scant comforts.

It was no good. To think of the lower city only reminded him of hellions, which brought every corpse he'd ever seen flashing across his inner vision. People torn limb from limb, or drained of their blood, or plastered across cobblestones after leaping from heights. Children with their throats ripped out, mothers lying in a pool of their own viscera, old men Gaunt-ridden and whittled down to nothing more than skin and bone. Valora's mortuary houses were full of hapless folk who'd fallen afoul of hellions and paid for it with their lives.

Beacon could still hear the pistol shot, ringing through his family's mill as he ended his father's suffering. He could still see his sister and the look of despair on her face as she was bound.

All of them collateral damage in Pandora Small's quest for freedom.

Looking at Pandora, trying desperately to convince himself of her innocence, Beacon felt the weight of her wrongdoings and her secrets like a ton of unyielding rock. Within him, his magesense continued to jangle, sending a crawling restlessness through his limbs and his mind until he could be still no longer.

Refusing to look again at Pandora's tearstained face, Beacon brushed past her, striding into the enveloping darkness of the tunnel. He toiled upward for what felt like hours, sightless in the pitch-black, and it felt like no more than a reflection of his inner turmoil. When at last he emerged into the abandoned wing the tunnel descended from, the sky beyond the grimed and cracking windows was a pitiless blue, caring nothing for the utter bleakness of Beacon's spirits.

Methodically he moved through the palace and returned to his room. He drew a clean uniform from the wardrobe and put it on. He shaved and smoothed down his hair. He cleaned his teeth and brewed a pot of kantha and drank it seated on the edge of his bed.

Then he got to his feet. Like an automaton, Beacon strode down the halls to Captain Tanner's office. He was a guard, fit for one thing—doing his duty in service of Hesperid's safety.

But the captain was not there. When Beacon claimed urgency, he was directed to the royal family's wing and the queen's own chambers. Still numb, he found his way. Raised his hand. Knocked. Was summoned in. In a luxurious, tastefully decorated parlor, Captain Tanner stood across from the prince consort at a worktable, both of them deep in some conversation related to the organization of the Guard and its protection of the royal family.

Queen Maud sat by the hearth, silent, with her eyes fixed on a small fire. She looked wan and shaken in the wake of the attack upon her. Maud's hands in her lap were freshly bandaged, and at the edges of one bandage, Beacon could see angrily burned skin. He shut his eyes as a wave of dizziness washed over him.

The burn on his own palm hadn't fully healed yet. What did he know about Pandora Small? What had he ever known about her, really? In his utter foolishness, Beacon had let a wolf in among the sheep on Palace Hill.

"Captain Tanner," Beacon said with his heart like a stone in his chest. "I have something to report."

18

STEEL WALLS

"It wasn't a choice," Imogen said with all the stubbornness that had characterized her rivalry with Pandora over the years. "I don't believe you, when you say that it was."

Pan stood beside the tunnel entrance, still in the bone-white cavern that she'd blasted with her reckless power years ago. She had her eyes shut, trying to erase the sight of Beacon's face as he'd left. She'd seen it in him—what her patron always warned of.

No one decent will tolerate you, child, once they understand your nature. I am the only one who will cherish and protect you for who you are. Do as I bid, and take your place at my side.

"A dog bred to fight will bite the hand that feeds it," Imogen said firmly. "But that isn't the fault of the dog. It's the fault of the master who brought it up to know nothing but cruelty."

Pandora opened her eyes. Imogen still stood before the chasm that was Pan's worst sin, backlit by brilliant spellfire blue.

"A vicious dog is deemed a danger to the public and put down,"

Pan answered. "Just like a rogue mage. I shouldn't be alive. Not the way I am. Not after what I've done. It's only cowardice that's kept me going all these years. The day I escaped, and every day since."

"No," Imogen said. She walked to Pandora and raised one hand, fitting it to the side of her face. "You don't get to speak about yourself that way. What you were made into is not your fault. The blame for what you did lies at your patron's feet, not yours. You were a child. You had been tormented by them for years. Do you think I haven't seen it in you, during all our time at the Bellwethers'? You weren't just a dog bred to fight, Pandora. You were a dog that had been kicked every day of its life before breaking free. You have lived with pain—are still living with pain—that I cannot imagine. So I won't hear you disparage yourself. Besides, you're my sister. No one gets to run you down but me."

Imogen said the last with a hint of an ironic smile, and it was so like her that Pan couldn't help smiling back, even through her tears. Impulsively she reached forward and pulled the other girl into a tight embrace.

"Imogen," she said. "You're the best enemy I've ever had."

"Given that your other enemy is a heartless mass murderer, I don't feel that's much of an accolade. Look, I have a thought. Can't you just *close* the wellspring, now that we're here? The same way you opened it?"

Pandora pulled away and shook her head. "I'm afraid not. I only had to start the opening, and the spellfire down there did the rest. It wanted to be unleashed, and it got away from me. Trying to seal it back up would take more power than I've got—even trying would kill me."

"Oh dear," Imogen said. "Well, we'll simply have to find some other way."

"Some other way to do what?" Pandora asked in confusion.

"A lot of things." Imogen shrugged. "To close the wellspring. To ensure you can live without it, once it's shut. To help you tolerate your power. To see your patron brought to justice. We've got a lot to do. Fortunately for you, I've always been goal oriented."

Imogen slipped her arm through Pandora's and steered her toward the tunnel, her own small magelight illuminating the path before them with soft golden rays. She kept up an equally bright and cheering stream of chatter as they went, about a tantalizing and (to Pandora's mind) impossible future, in which the wellspring was closed, Pan's patron gone, and her spellfire safely muzzled. The two of them, according to Imogen, would then have nothing to do but amuse themselves and entertain suitors from dawn till dusk, not as potential patrons, but as possible lovers and as goads to Theo and Beacon. Pandora could think of few things she'd less like to do than spend her time on flirting and mindless frivolity, but she appreciated the clear effort Imogen was making to raise her spirits.

The latter half of the tunnel left no room to travel side by side, so Imogen took the lead with Pandora behind. She was still chattering away at the final heavy door that led up into the palace, but as Imogen stepped out into the abandoned wing, the sound of her voice died away.

"Gin?" Pandora said, a little out of breath. "What's wrong, what are—"

Emerging herself, she found Imogen standing before what seemed a sea of guards. A black-haired woman in captain's uniform stood at their head.

"Miss Small," the woman said sternly. "It is the duty of the Queen's Guard to place you under arrest for contravention of the mage laws, for opening the wellspring, and under suspicion of having caused the deaths of your fellow Ingenues and two magefinders, as well as assaulting Her Majesty. It would be in the best interest of everyone if you came with us quietly, instead of trying to resist. No one wants this to lead to more deaths, but the Guard is prepared to take you into custody by force if necessary."

"Pandora," Imogen breathed in a panic, clutching at Pan's arm as she passed by. But Pan would not be stopped. She stepped forward and stood before the Guard captain, holding out both hands in a mute gesture of assent.

With an expression of acute relief, the captain fitted steel shackles around Pandora's wrists, and the guards fell in around her as she was led away.

She was still on the palace grounds, of that much Pandora was sure. They'd blindfolded her and taken her somewhere. Through long indoor corridors, across graveled courtyards, and finally indoors again. There were no windows and no light in the place she'd been left. Only a sense of spaciousness but not emptiness.

Pan conjured a magelight and found she was in a large, finely furnished room, with a single oak-paneled door. Thick tapestries hung from the walls, and lush carpeting swathed the floors. It was all so very familiar. Sickeningly so, right down to the stuffed bear resting on an armchair by the ashless hearth and the shelves of children's storybooks.

There were additions, though. Accommodations made not for the child Pandora had been, but for the young woman she'd become. The desk no longer held paintboxes and pastel crayons, but papers, quills, and ink. Alongside the children's books were volumes of natural history, of poetry, of statecraft, of popular fiction. A tall, commodious wardrobe stood in one corner, and when Pan pulled the doors open, she was startled to find an entire season's worth of clothing in what looked to be her precise size. Underpinnings, trimmings, and gowns themselves, all far more expensive than anything she'd owned before.

When Pan pushed aside the tapestry covering a wall, it did not surprise her to find the dull sheen of steel beneath. Once again, she was shut up in a steel box of her patron's devising. A sumptuous one, to be sure, but a steel box was a steel box, no matter its size and furnishings. It was just possible Pandora had never been free of her patron's boxes. Even with the binding between them blocked, she'd been drawn back into their clutches. Perhaps they had always been pulling her strings. Perhaps they always would.

The steel walls did not come as a surprise. The four-poster bed did. When Pandora pulled back the richly decorated bed curtains, she gasped sharply, spellfire roiling inside her. Laid out on the counterpane was Eleanor Wellesley.

Her hair had been curled and her face made up, though cosmetics could not hide the stain of spellfire blue around her mouth and nose and eyes. Hands at her sides, she'd been dressed in a frock that matched the one worn by Pandora's childhood doll. But while Pan's doll had eyes that closed, Eleanor's had been left open, so that they stared lifelessly up at the steel ceiling, the whites gone blue. Poor Eleanor, whose family had been dragged down by Pandora's deadliest sin. Pan herself had only found out about the Wellesleys' downfall via a scavenged daily—she'd been living on the streets of the lower city already by that point, and all she'd felt when she saw the report of Robert Wellesley's execution was relief. It had felt like a step closer to safety. But meeting Eleanor had showed her what that error in judgment truly meant—death for one party, and shame and suffering for all those he loved.

Something broke in Pan. She fell to her knees and pressed her fists to her eyes, until she saw stars in the darkness of her own making. She was a torch, burning, burning beneath her skin. She would tear this prison to pieces just as she had done with the first. She would harrow the palace, dragging the truth from nobles and merchants and servants alike—*are you or are you not my patron?*—until she found that despised childhood ghost and flayed the flesh from their bones.

Yes, the whispers within her exulted. *Yes, small one. Join us just so. Cast off your restraint and rise in power.*

With flames of spellfire licking at her insides, Pan splayed her hands against the soft carpeting, feeling the thrum of steel beneath. What was an impenetrable barrier to others, mages and hellions alike, would shred like paper for Pandora Small. She was ready, she was alight, she was power unquenchable—

An odd, incongruous thought struck Pandora as she prepared to rend the walls of her latest prison. During her time at the Bellwethers', she'd hated and admired and fought against Imogen's perpetual poise. Now, knowing they were tied together by blood, she wondered. What, in such a situation, would Imogen do?

And the thought gave her pause.

Pan knew what she herself would do. Her patron knew that as well. All her life, she'd been their pawn and plaything. But Imogen had grown up moved by her own free will, not stunted by the malevolent influence of a wicked patron. Even her parents appeared to have little power to prevent Imogen from following the dictates of her heart and conscience—she had chosen to serve as an unrecognized help to Pandora for years, despite their disapproval, and despite the fact that Imogen might have spent that time in more pleasurable pursuits.

And Imogen, if she were here now, would say, *Waste not, want not.* Imogen would say, *Don't show your hand until the final play.* Imogen would say, *Wait and see—why put yourself out when you could simply sit back and allow the gods to reveal destiny to you?*

Spark by slow spark, Pandora pulled her power back. She moved to the wardrobe and picked through its contents. Most of the gowns wouldn't do for day wear or were lovely but not to Pandora's taste. Near the back, she found one that suited. Not ivory, but pure white, overlaid with a net of seed pearls and gleaming diamond chips. Setting it out along with a frothy armful of new underthings, Pandora turned to the deep, cast-iron tub sitting in one corner. It was full of fresh, tepid water, with scented soaps and crisp linens waiting on a stand at its side. Skinning out of her clothes, Pan touched one fingertip to the water's surface and set it steaming.

Then she slipped in with a sigh. She would not think of the corpse on the bed, placed there to bait her. Pandora's patron expected her to rail against captivity as she'd done before. To attempt escape. To fight against the ties that bound her. To either unwittingly carry out some great evil like the wellspring, or to exhaust her spellfire, until she was desperate and helpless.

So rather than act, she would wait, with an Ingenue's composure and serenity, for whatever came next. She would spend no more than the slightest ember of her power at a time, safeguarding it for as long as possible. Given the inferno of spellfire Pandora contained, she would be able to hold out for a very long time. Long enough, she hoped, to wear her patron down. To provoke some sort of interview or confrontation, at which she would be ready with all the force of her prodigious power. Perhaps they believed her to be caught in their web, but Pan was no longer a mere gnat to be preyed upon. She'd become a spider in her own right and would not easily be trussed up and subjugated again.

After finishing in the bath, Pandora dressed. She shut the bed curtains and took a volume from the bookshelf, on obscure aspects of Hesperidian history, and read, taking notes as she encountered unfamiliar events. When she was tired, she undressed and lay down before the hearth.

Upon waking, she found a tray of food waiting for her and Eleanor's body gone from the bed.

So it went. Eating, bathing, dressing, and occupying herself, all in lonesome silence, with no conception of how much time was passing in the outside world. She did not mark how often she slept, knowing it would only unsettle her if she did. Whenever fear and anxiety rose up to claw at Pandora's throat, she did what she'd been taught by the Bellwethers as an Ingenue. Sat and grounded herself, centering on her breath until nothing else mattered. She was just the in-and-out rhythm of her own lungs, until the worry passed. Until she could master her spellfire once more. For the first time since the wellspring, Pan counted her power as she had in the days before, storing it up as a miser, cherishing every fiery spark.

She had damaged the very fabric of the world in the old days, to secure her own freedom. But she'd learned patience since then, and control. She could watch and she could wait, making what was meant for a prison into a trap.

What Pandora could not do, try as she might, was banish the memory of how Beacon had looked, pale and sick, upon discovering who she truly was. Every moment the recollection plagued her, worse than spellfire had ever done. All the Ingenue's training in the world would not cast that one image out of her mind. She must simply sit and bear it, alone in the prison she could escape but chose to tolerate.

"I'd have bound myself to you," she whispered once, when the time moved especially slow. "If you'd only asked, I'd have put my power and my heart in your hands."

19

REGRETS

Beacon had tried to give his notice.

After he laid everything bare to Captain Tanner and the prince consort and the queen—the location of the wellspring, Pandora's role in its opening, his awareness of her power since her arrival on Palace Hill—he tendered his resignation on the spot. Captain Tanner had refused, instead transferring him back to the lower city's division of the Guard.

But while he'd been happy and useful there before, the barracks were no longer a place of camaraderie. Putting down hellions each night no longer filled him with a sense of purpose. All he could think of was what he'd been told in the queen's chambers, by Captain Tanner and the consort. That a mage of Pandora Small's caliber could easily have altered his judgment, flouting the mage laws by toying with his ability to choose wisely in her regard. Though Beacon protested that he never felt such a magic being worked on him, Captain Tanner and the consort insisted that it was the likeliest turn of events.

All along, Pandora had been tampering with him. Clouding his perceptions. Ensuring he would not betray her confidence.

Beacon felt like he was drowning. He didn't know what he believed. He'd been so sure of Pandora, yet it was true he'd stubbornly ignored the obvious. Her story of another powerful mage on Palace Hill and her constant dependence on him had been tantalizing, and yet she was the only mage with such power he'd ever encountered. It *was* possible she'd used her power to twist and cloud his judgment, lending credence to her tale of a wicked patron and a tormented childhood. The queen's burned hands were a reproach to Beacon, a spark on the pyre of his belief in Pandora. Whether they were the spark that kindled a conflagration, he didn't know. What he did know was that he felt as if his conscience and his heart would be torn in two, because he knew duty and knew what was right, yet it still cut him to the core to betray Pandora Small. Even the thought of his sister's binding and his father's death did not take the edge off what he'd done.

Imogen came down to the lower city barracks to harangue Beacon. It caused a monumental stir among the guards there, seeing a radiant and brilliantly dressed Ingenue sweep through their domain as if she was crossing a palace ballroom. Her confidence in Pandora was unshaken. She wanted him to retract his condemnation—Imogen had known the little mage for five years, after all, and claimed she'd needled and annoyed Pandora so mercilessly that Pan would have killed her a hundred times over if she was truly as monstrous as Beacon and the royal family now claimed.

Beacon said nothing to her. He retreated into silence as if it was a shield, and finally Imogen left, giving him up as a lost cause. She would undoubtedly campaign on Pandora's behalf until her half sister's name was cleared, or Pan had been subjected to a steel box. Not that such a thing could kill Pandora, if she chose to escape. Beacon knew that all too well now.

Every night, he went out with his wounded conscience, his bruised heart, and his tattered pride and hunted hellions. He sought out the run-down and seedier districts of Valora and walked the streets as the moon rose high overhead, waiting for the telltale signs of a neighborhood plagued by monsters. Wary glances. Skittish folk hurrying from place to place. Cries in the night.

A week after his great betrayal, Beacon wandered the lower city, keeping company not so much with his regrets as with a nagging and relentless anxiety. There'd been nothing in the dailies about Pandora. Nothing at all to indicate that palace life had been interrupted in any way. Beacon felt he'd go mad for lack of news when, just after midnight, he found what he was looking for. Half a dozen people seated outside a run-down tenement, looking forlorn. There was a mother with a small child clinging to her skirts and a nursling in arms. An elderly couple, looking anxious. And a girl just shy of binding age, who kept glancing defiantly back at the tenement door. Her spellfire felt like a thick blanket settling over Beacon's shoulders as he approached—whatever had happened inside, she was clearly riled by it, though no match for any sort of monster.

"What seems to be the trouble here?" Beacon asked, stopping before the small group. They took him in—his confident posture, his uniform, the weapons at his waist—and an immediate, palpable relief washed over them.

Yes. That was what Beacon had been made for. To help when no one else could. Surely here he'd find a way to numb the guilt dogging him each time he remembered Pandora's stricken face.

"There's a Grim inside," the mage girl said. "It's killed Great-Aunt Effie's cat and broken down two walls already. We all went out a back window it couldn't fit through, after blocking off the doors."

"That was quick thinking." Beacon nodded to the girl as a sign of respect, and she flushed. "Trapping it inside will make things easier for certain. I'll go in directly."

"Wait." The mother with babe in arms shook her head. "We can't pay you. I know any guard come to this part of the city wants a bribe, and we'd never stretch to it."

"No money," Beacon said, raising a hand. It had always rankled him, that certain parts of the city were ignored by all but the more unscrupulous guards. "I'm not here for pay. I'm here to help."

The mother gave him a dubious look. "No one does something for nothing."

"I do," Beacon lied, because he needed this. He wasn't getting nothing in return. He was getting a chance at redemption, and at driving out the memory of Pandora's eyes on him as she confessed to opening the wellspring.

If she was a villain, why had she told him the truth? Why hadn't she laid the blame for that worst of all sins on her phantom patron and magicked him into believing it when she did?

The mother shrugged, still obviously skeptical. "Suit yourself, then. Seems like a waste of effort for no return, but that's your affair."

Beacon left them, skirting the building to the back, where the window the mage girl had spoken of still stood open. The frame had been torn away, and deep, vicious claw marks scored the wood around the opening. The walls had held, though, and distantly Beacon could hear the Grim rampaging inside.

Pulling himself through the window, he had one sinking moment of doubt where it seemed he might not fit. But then he was through and into the dim shambles of the tenement. In the way of such places, the back room was an entire family's living space—beds and sleeping mats pushed together on one side of the room, a cookstove, table, and chairs occupying the other. Everything was turned over or askew or ruined, musty straw spilling out of the grass-tick mattresses and broken crockery littering the floor. It crunched beneath Beacon's boots like gravel, and from the depths of the tenement, the Grim fell silent.

The creature knew Beacon was coming.

For a moment, Beacon's hand hovered over his pistol. Then he reached for his short sword instead—he didn't want a quick or clean finish, not this time. He wanted a scuffle, and to put himself at risk. He wanted to be only a body and instincts, not a thinking mind or a conscience-stricken soul.

Prowling forward through another wreckage-strewn flat, Beacon did not let his eyes linger on the smear of blood and sparse tufts of fur that were all that remained of Great-Aunt Effie's hapless cat. The Grim was still silent—though they were not known for their cunning, this one appeared at least intelligent enough to realize it had the element of surprise.

Cautiously Beacon carried on. He was spoiling for a fight, but not foolish enough to let his guard down completely. A narrow central hallway ran between the tenement flats, and when he came to a third gaping doorway, Beacon stopped.

In among the ruins of another family's worldly goods, the Grim was waiting. But it was not waiting for Beacon. All its attention was fixed on a man—older, late sixties, perhaps, with lank, thinning hair and a sallow face—who looked at the creature evenly. The man did not appear afraid or angry in any way. He simply stood and met the Grim's fiery gaze. No spellfire emanated from him to trigger Beacon's magesense, and he was unarmed.

Yet beneath the man's stare, the Grim faltered and turned aside.

It seemed confused and disoriented until its spellfire eyes fixed on Beacon. Then vicious purpose ran through the creature like lightning once again. If it had been a Fell or a Were, it would have hesitated a few moments longer, planning an angle of attack, assessing Beacon for signs of weakness or inattention. But the Grim thundered forward immediately, enormous jaws spread wide while a sharp howl and a smell of brimstone emanated from its throat.

Beacon sidestepped neatly with a sigh. This wasn't what he'd hoped for. Fighting a Grim was no challenge—he could do it in his sleep, or with one hand tied behind his back. Even as the creature collided with a wall and shook itself free in a hailstorm of plaster dust, Beacon could see *her*. Pandora, tangling with hellions as if it was a dance. Exterminating the very monsters she'd brought into the world not just with efficiency, but with a ruthless sort of beauty. She had no love of the beasts. And, if Beacon was fair, there was no possible way she could have known they'd be birthed along with the tidal wave of spellfire she'd unleashed. Before the wellspring—before Pandora—there had simply not been enough magic in Hesperid for such things to exist.

She had remade the world, and not for the better. In her own image, perhaps—tormented by spellfire all her life, Pandora had brought about a Hesperid that shared her struggles, both steeped in power and haunted by it.

The Grim charged Beacon again. It was like breathing, to turn aside just so, to drive his left shoulder into its unprotected flank, to thrust his short sword into the creature's half-corporeal belly. A crackling death wail filled the tenement flat as the creature writhed, bleeding ash and sparks from a vast wound. Beacon stepped back, wiped the ash from the flat of his sword, and waited. There was no need to close with the beast again. In a moment, it had dwindled to a mere silhouette of powder and cinders and collapsed in a rain of blue dust.

Beacon stood and looked at the place where the Grim had been. Another inescapable reminder of Pandora and her power. When he raised his head, the man at the doorway was staring at him.

"Do you want another?" the man asked with something odd and hungry in his voice. He jerked his head in the direction of a closed door. "There's one in the cellar no one's been able to get rid of—not sell-swords nor guards, we've had both try."

"Really?" Beacon was desperate enough to overlook the strange way in which the man stared at him. "I could try my hand at it for you."

"I thought you'd say so." The man grinned, revealing stained and missing teeth. "Follow me, then."

He removed a key from his pocket and unlocked the door, revealing a rickety wooden staircase descending into darkness. The man took a lamp from a hook at the head of the stairs, lit it with a sulfur match, and led the way down, surrounded by a ring of pallid light. Beacon followed at his heels, short sword still in hand.

The moment his feet hit the cellar floor, *something*, some instinct, some alarm system, went off in Beacon. Not his magesense—his head had been aching and his stomach turning over since he first came face-to-face with the Grim. It was more than that. There was a hellion here, to be sure, but he felt a wrongness about the place. A creeping sensation of dread and an animal sort of fear he hadn't experienced since childhood.

As the man before him grinned again and lifted the lantern, Beacon realized why. The dank, windowless cellar was ringed with moldy beds. Each one housed a body, all of them carved down to bone and leathery skin, clothes hanging off them in rags. Their emaciation and state of half-preservation could only mean one thing, and Beacon fumbled with his short sword, sheathing it in favor of his pistol.

No one toyed with a Gaunt. No one was willing to risk that long and lingering death.

"We haven't had a hellion trouble this building in years," the man with the lantern said. "Only reason that Grim turned up is it was too stupid to realize there's a Gaunt in residence. Even other hellions don't infringe on a Gaunt's hunting grounds. If you don't want risk and can't afford defenses, it's one way to keep your place and your people safe—ensure a dream feeder is present and satisfied."

"The Guard calls that murder," Beacon said hotly. "Once I've killed the beast, I'll put you in irons, and that will be the end of your nasty little killing field. You'll answer for every death you were a part of."

"Will I?" the man asked, raising an eyebrow. "I don't think so."

Beacon turned, a moment too late. He had a confused impression of a tangle of shadows. Felt a bitter sensation of cold flooding his veins. And a sudden vision of Pandora filled his mind, sweet enough that he slipped into it willingly. He saw her in a green field, happy and dressed in one of her simple ivory frocks. She wore a crown of daisies in her dark hair, and her eyes were bright and glad when they fixed on him. There was no reproach in her, no specter of pain, and Beacon could only sense the slightest breath of warmth. This was Pandora as she might have been—free and unfettered by shackles of internal spellfire. She smiled and held out her hands, and Beacon went to her without hesitation, even as he felt his body fall to the floor and be dragged to the nearest empty bed while skeins of insidious magic ran through his veins.

What did it matter, after all, when the waking world was so fraught with troubles, and the dream world was so sweet?

"Ellis," Pandora said, taking his hands in hers and rising on her toes to kiss his cheek. "I'm so very glad to see you."

"In spite of everything?" Beacon asked, even as the agonizing memories of what she'd done and how he'd betrayed her began to slip away.

"Don't worry about all that," Pandora said, smoothing the frown from his forehead. "It doesn't matter anymore. Nothing matters so long as you stay here, and now."

Beacon nodded and let himself be led away, further into the green fields, further into dream, further from the wearying weight of his own overburdened conscience.

20

A SPIDER AND A FLY

Pandora sat quietly, a spider at the center of a web it had not made.

A book rested on her lap, though her eyes stared past it, unseeing. A gossamer gown of moonlight silver hung from her shoulders, with little froths of white lace at the neck and wrists. She was caught up in a waking dream—an imagining of herself free, wandering through green fields. There was someone else there too, a familiar and welcome presence that put her at ease, but every time she turned to look at her companion, she saw nothing. Just the same green fields, stretching to the horizon.

The grating scrape of a key in a lock sounded from outside. It was the first time anyone had come to the steel-walled prison while Pandora was awake. When she slept, dishes were cleared away, bathwater changed, and new meals left. How long she'd gone on like that, she did not know.

Now it was time to meet her fate.

Latent power swirled around Pan, so potent it shrouded her in a column of restless blue sparks. Whoever appeared, she was ready to kill or be killed, to gain her freedom and end her patron or die in the attempt. She was fire, and she would not be easily tamed. But she was also a tempered flame—whatever happened, she would maintain her hard-won control. There would be no collateral damage this time, only a single searing dart of magic, enough to kill a hundred but concentrated on a single soul.

The consort, she thought. She was sure it would be him.

The door swung open. Blinding daylight streamed in, dazzling Pandora for the briefest instant, but at the same moment a familiar whisper hissed at her.

"Pan, hurry, we only have a moment."

Pandora wrenched her power back. Her vision cleared, and she found Imogen and Theo on the threshold, both of them looking nervous and furtive.

"We didn't know where you were, at first," Imogen said in a rush. "It took ages for Theo to track you down, and to do it in a way where he wouldn't be ordered not to speak of what he'd learned, or to interfere with you. Come with us, we've got to get you off Palace Hill."

When Pandora spoke, the question that came first to her lips took her by surprise. It was not *Who did this?* or *Where should I go?* or *What have they said about me?*

"Where's Beacon?" she asked instead, urgency burning in her words. She could still see him, his bowed shoulders and anguished face a mute reproach.

Imogen frowned. "I don't know. It doesn't matter. He's the one who turned you in to the Guard."

"Is he still with them?" Pandora pressed.

Imogen shook her head. "Not here. They sent him back to the lower city. He's been sulking down there ever since."

"I have to find him. He'll be sick over what he did, turning me in."

"Serves him right." Imogen glanced uneasily over her shoulder. "If you want to worry about him, do it once you're off the Hill. Come along now."

"Who did this?" Pandora asked finally, as Imogen seized her hand and dragged her along, through an overgrown area of palace gardens Pan had never seen before. Theo followed in their wake, keeping close watch over the way they'd come to ensure they weren't being followed. "That room was tailor-made for me, and I spent my entire childhood in one just like it. Who commissioned it? If we find who built that prison, we find my patron."

"No one was involved with your arrest besides the Guard, as far as we can tell," Imogen said. "And no one particular within it. They apprehended you, and locked you up. It wasn't a prison, anyway—you tore your way out of one steel box already, I don't see why you didn't just break out this time, as well. We went to an awful lot of trouble to find you. Or rather, Theo did."

"They knew I could leave if I wanted," Pandora said. "My patron. They were counting on it. They *want* me to show myself. They've been urging me to ever since I blocked our binding. So I won't do it. But that box—it wasn't just the Guard preparing to hold a powerful mage. Look what I'm wearing." Pan gestured to the glistening silver gown she had on, which fit her like a glove. A snarl of frustration rose in the back of her throat, and she swallowed it back. "That cell was made for *me*. Pandora Small. Who put it there? I'll tell you who I think it was—who has the Guard in his pocket. Theo's father. The prince consort."

She glanced backward and found Theo's face a mask of agony.

"You know for certain, don't you?" Pan asked the prince, stopping dead in her tracks and pinning him with a ferocious stare. "They haven't kept you in the dark, like they did with me. You've seen their face. You've known all along."

Slowly, miserably he nodded.

"*Who?*"

With equal anguish, he shook his head.

"I can't—" Theo choked, half strangling on the words. "I can't say. I swear by anything, I would if I could. I'm doing everything I can to help, but it's difficult when—"

He let out a sharp, pained sound and fell silent.

"Theo," Imogen said with heartbreak in her voice. She went to him at once, cupping his face in her hands. "It's all right. You're doing wonderfully. We'd be lost without your help, but just now we've got to carry on."

Again, Theo nodded, and they continued, fleeing through the old ruins of outbuildings and parade grounds from the palace's former life as a hill fort. Much of what it had been was overgrown with saplings and rampant weeds, slowly becoming a tangled woodland. Ahead of them, an impenetrable box hedge loomed, shaggy and unkempt, unlike the hedges surrounding the Hill's newer buildings and gardens.

"To the left," Theo called, and the trio swerved, finding themselves at a small, rust-covered gate.

"I haven't got a key," Theo apologized. "Pan, you'll have to take care of it yourself."

As she'd done with the bath, Pandora pressed a finger to the ancient lock. A puff of smoke rose, and the gate opened with a loud, grating protest.

"Go," Imogen said, enveloping Pan in a swift, sweet-smelling hug.

"Keep yourself clear of the Guard. Don't draw any attention to your whereabouts down in the city. We'll stay here, and take your case right to the queen. If we can find your patron and turn them in and Maud issues you a pardon, no one will hold your past against you any longer. Even if it is the consort, Her Majesty holds the final say in Hesperid. All we've got to do is get her on our side."

"I don't want you going anywhere near my patron, no matter who it turns out to be." Pan shuddered at the mere thought. "If you find them while I'm gone, send word and wait for me. I'll think of some way to let you know where I am."

She did not dare form a more specific plan, when Theo could hear and might be forced to give a report to her patron.

Another quick embrace, and there was nothing for it. Pandora carried on alone, hurrying down a winding, empty laneway that led downhill from the narrow gate. Within minutes she was in the city. Flagging a hansom in her elegant gown was the work of a moment, though Pan was briefly perplexed as to how she'd pay for it. Inspiration struck, and she smiled up at the driver.

"Send a bill to the Hollen manor. Have them tell Ander the charge is for his *other* daughter."

With the hansom connected to her, Pandora got off at the edges of the Fuller's Quarter, to be safe. She wouldn't want the driver to be able to inform the Guard precisely where she'd gone. Though anyone would be able to give an account of her progress through the Fuller's District, given the finery she wore. Ducking down a back alley, Pan pulled off the dress, albeit with a little reluctance. It was lovely, but her underthings were plenty more than some of the district's less savory residents wore. Scooping up handfuls of dry earth from between gaps in the cobblestones, Pan dirtied herself to a satisfactory degree, until her corset and chemise were no longer snowy white, but more a grubby beige. She tore delicately tatted lace from the hems and left it in a heap along with her gown, mussing her hair as she strode off.

Better to pass for a tart in the Fuller's Quarter than a highborn and wealthy lady. No one would look twice at a girl her age soliciting a little bedpost business.

For the most part people glanced through or past Pandora as she walked to the nearest marketplace. A few times, she could feel the lingering stares of men following her, as they considered offering her temporary patronage of a decidedly nonmagical sort. But by the time they'd decided, Pan was long past. She did not stop until she found herself surrounded by run-down shops and hawkers' stalls.

"I'm looking for someone," she began to ask of anyone who'd listen. "A young man. Tall—about this high—broad in the shoulders, would catch your eye if you saw him. Looks as if he knows his way about a pistol and blade, and carries himself like a guard. He might have been wearing their uniform, or he might not. Have you seen him?"

"We don't get any guards in these parts," an elderly woman laughed. "Try further toward the Hill. Though they won't take kindly to your sort in those neighborhoods—they want their whores to look like ladies, up there."

Pan let the nasty word slide, turning to another marketgoer.

"Please. A boy called Beacon. About this tall, looks as if he'd be next to the word 'reliable' in a lexicon?"

"He forget to pay your bill?" a middle-aged man jeered. "Trust you'll never be able to collect on it now, girl. You'd best be getting your payment before anyone's between your legs."

Pandora skewered him with a malevolent stare, and he wandered off, shaking his head. But a few moments later, she felt a tug at her sleeve.

"Miss?" It was a girl, close to binding age, with a worried expression on her thin face. "I know where your sweetheart is, only I'm not supposed to tell."

"He's not my—" Pandora began, before realizing there was no point in correcting the child. "Never mind. Where is he?"

"Come with me."

The younger girl took Pandora by the hand and led her away, through a maze of sparsely inhabited streets. At a tenement building, she stopped on the threshold and chewed at the inside of her cheek, clearly unsure whether to lead Pan any farther.

"The thing is," the girl said uncertainly, "I don't know for *certain* your sweetheart's here. I saw him go in, but never saw him come out. And if he *is* still here, well, I expect he's in the worst trouble a person can find."

Pandora frowned. "What do you mean by that?"

The girl shook her head, refusing to say any more. "Don't want to tell you. But if you go looking for him, I think it'll be the death of you."

Pan couldn't help herself. A short, dry laugh escaped her lips.

"Oh, darling," she said, a hint of the Ingenue escaping her, "do you know how many terrible things might have been the death of me by now? And none of them ever succeeded."

Perhaps it was the bitter light in Pandora's eyes that convinced the girl. At any rate, she nodded and led Pan into the tenement. It looked as if chaos had reigned there lately, but attempts had been made at tidying up. A door torn off its hinges stood between them and a squalid flat, and the child squeezed through the gap between door and crumbling wall.

There was no one beyond, only an empty and cheerless living space. But the girl gestured to another door on the far wall, this one intact and firmly shut.

"Down there," she said. "If you've got to go looking. But you shouldn't. You should leave now, and forget your sweetheart ever lived."

Pandora regarded the girl seriously. "I can't. It's not often someone like me finds kindness, and he's been kind to me in every way he could. He did his best. That's not something I can forget, or cast aside."

The girl shook her head, sadness in her wide, haunted eyes. "All right. But he's as good as dead, and you will be too if you walk through that door."

As if she could not bear to stay any longer, the child left. Pandora put her head to one side and glanced at the door critically. Just plain wood, not steel. And her patron would never condescend to enter a place like this. Whatever lay ahead, Pan was sure she'd prove more than a match for it.

She swung open the door and descended the narrow stairs beyond, taking in the cellar by the pallid glow of her magelight.

The squalor. The beds. The bodies.

The Gaunt hovering over a sleeper, slowly and languorously drawing the life from its victim's veins.

"Oh, Beacon," Pandora breathed.

21

PANDORA'S PATRONAGE, REDUX

After his first surrender, Beacon did not give up so easily. He had lucid moments, where he struggled into wakefulness and was aware of the Gaunt and its influence. He could feel himself weakening as the creature slowly siphoned off his life force and vital energy, but he could also feel the spellfire it sent trickling into him. By means of magic, the monster kept him from needing the usual requirements of the body—food, drink, a place to relieve himself. It turned him into a sort of automaton, a source of sustenance that would last as long as possible.

The Gaunt, Beacon realized, was enjoying the process. It was savoring his long, slow end, and the dim realization made him struggle harder for consciousness. Reality swam in and out of focus, interspersed with irresistible dreams.

Pandora dancing through a sea of hellions, rendering each of them ash with a single touch.

Pandora dancing with him, the two of them alone in one of Palace

Hill's glittering ballrooms, kept company by nothing but ghostly music. He held her close, and whether she led or he did, Beacon couldn't be certain. He did not care—all that mattered was that he had Pandora within his arms, and that when he lowered his head, her lips met his, the moment of contact like lightning before he himself fell apart into ashes.

Pandora in green fields.

Pandora in autumn forests.

Pandora rising from the sea, swathed in veils of blue spellfire, like a goddess from a painting.

She was the sum total of his imagining and his desires, and he had betrayed her. She would be sent to a steel box, had perhaps entered it already, and by the time Beacon's withered body lay lifeless, no more than bones and leathery skin and regret, Pandora Small would be dead, killed by his treacherous sense of duty and her refusal to use her power wrongly.

The worst dreams were of her coming to him here, in this squalid cellar. She stood over him glistening like a star and said not a word. With her implacable dark eyes, she took in the Gaunt, the bed, his predicament, and turned and walked away. Those were nightmares to Beacon. He could not bear the weight of her abandonment and called out and writhed on the narrow bed.

So it was that the Gaunt began to subdue Beacon, because he would always turn from a dream of Pandora leaving. He'd drag himself further into sleep and further under its influence to escape such fantasies, replacing them with dreams in which he'd never played the traitor, caught between the bonds of loyalty and the shackles of duty. After a week, he could barely struggle into wakefulness any longer. His lucid moments were few and far between, and fraught with pain and misery. He'd forced himself into one such moment when yet another nightmare of Pandora in the cellar seized him.

He saw her descend the stairs, a magelight aloft in front of her. His gaze followed her as she crossed the damp, packed earth floor and knelt at his side.

"Oh, Beacon."

The whisper was a knife to his heart, and he pressed his eyes shut, willing himself toward other imaginings.

Pan in a ballroom.

Pan in his quarters on Palace Hill.

Pan in his bed back home, at the mill that belonged to some other family now.

But then, searing through the web of sleep he'd become entangled in, came the burn of her touch. Her hand took his, and the scorching shock of it dragged him back into life and consciousness.

In his dreams, he could never feel Pandora's power. She was only ever a specter of herself, pallid and incomplete without the constant heat that burned at her core.

"Pandora," Beacon rasped, and she nodded.

"I'm here now. I'm going to save you."

She grasped his other hand, and all he wanted was to burn, so that he might remember he was still alive. With the fire came implicit faith—Beacon knew, beyond the shadow of a doubt, that if Pandora said she could save him, she would see it done. No matter that he'd never heard of a sleeper surviving being Gaunt-ridden before. What Pan purposed, she would accomplish. Hadn't she remade the world already?

It no longer mattered to Beacon that she'd inadvertently made it worse. All that mattered was that she'd *done* it.

Dimly, he felt her climb onto the bed and straddle him, kneeling with her legs on either side of his waist, her hips against his, her hands spread against his chest.

"I need to be close," Pan whispered apologetically, but it was what Beacon wanted. Reality and his tortured dreams were converging, and he was burning not just with Pandora's heat but with his own yearning to be close and closer still.

"Beacon." Pan's sharp voice summoned him back into wakefulness as his eyes began to roll back, the Gaunt dragging him into a sea of dreams more tempting than any he'd had yet. "I'm going to break the mage laws. I'm going to work magic on you. But I can't do it unless you tell me it's all right. I'd never do it unless you told me it was all right."

He fought for consciousness harder than he'd ever fought before, tearing himself away from sleep and the clinging images it brought—Pandora in her palace room, in her nightdress, in nothing but silver moonlight.

"Do it," Beacon managed to get out. "You can do . . . anything to me . . . that you wish."

Pan nodded, but here, in the waking world, her eyes were wide and frightened and sad. Beacon couldn't help himself. He fell back into sleep, where her gaze on him was not anxious and pitying, but soft and heavy with desire.

He could feel her hands on his chest, both waking and dreaming, the brush of her long, dark hair come undone. A scent of lily of the valleys washed over him and then . . .

A jolt of the purest, most exquisite pain and power Beacon had ever felt. It surged through him like quicksilver, like lightning, like the most unbearable of pleasures, and with Pandora's power *in* him, Beacon realized how cautious she was being. How terribly restrained and gentle. She was an inferno, and all she'd given him was the slightest spark.

Even that was enough to tear the veil of fevered dreams and render him intensely, agonizingly awake. He could sense every tendril of the Gaunt's malevolent influence, tangled in his veins. He could feel the small bright places within, where Pan's power had touched him and the Gaunt's darker magic had withdrawn, replaced by the afterglow of her perfect fire.

Struggling to sit upright, Beacon leaned against the splintering and mildew-stained wooden bedstead, keenly aware of two things—the Gaunt still hovering behind him, siphoning off his life, and Pandora on his lap. She'd shifted a little, and her hands had fallen to rest on her legs like small broken things. The curtain of her dark hair hid her face from him, and Beacon brushed it aside, glad that for this moment only he could be fully himself again.

"What's wrong?" he asked, his heart breaking at the sight of tears glimmering in her eyes. She would not meet his gaze, looking down at her cupped hands as the first tear fell.

"I can't do it," Pandora whispered. "Not because of the Gaunt, but because . . . I can't manage my spellfire. It's too hard to keep it back. I want to help so badly, I can't hold on to it. It'll get away from me, and then it won't be the Gaunt that kills you. It'll be me that did it, and Beacon, I'd rather die than live knowing I'd hurt you."

For the first time since her power had touched him, he felt a need to let sleep wash over him again. It came as a response to guilt, because she was better than him. Purer in what she offered, and in her feelings toward him.

Beacon hated himself for ever having doubted her.

"I hurt *you*," he said, shifting his weight a little and feeling the infinitely desirable answering shift of Pandora against him. "Pan, I'm so sorry. The wellspring, I—I didn't know what to do. Or rather, I did know what to do. I knew what my duty was, and I behaved as a guard instead of your friend. I'll never forgive myself for that. I was angry and off balance and out of line."

"I forgive you," Pan said without hesitation. At last she looked up, fixing her fathomless eyes on him, and all he saw there was a world of trust and devotion. No bitterness. No accusation. No new reserve or withdrawing of her beloved heart. "I know I've been hard to reconcile since the beginning. I'd give anything to be uncomplicated for you, Beacon, but that's not who I am. I can't be less or other to make your life simpler, much as I would love to."

"I'd never ask it." He placed his hands on her hips and drew her an inch closer, and she caught her breath with a small hitch. "But I don't want to be caught between duty and my heart ever again. Pan, there's something I want to tell you."

She nodded, and was so close to him now that if he leaned forward only a little, he'd be able to kiss the tears from her face. At the thought, a fresh wave of acute fatigue moved through Beacon, and he shook his head to banish it.

"Since I first met you," he forced out, struggling for full consciousness, "since the first time I felt your power, I've wanted to be your patron, Pandora. I know you have one already. I know they used you cruelly. I know the idea of a binding is hateful to you, and that all you want is your freedom. But I wouldn't be a patron who binds you to himself so that he might order and be obeyed. My wish is to allow you to use me not as a master, but as an anchor. Something to help you hold and temper your fire. I don't want to be served, Pan. I want to serve you. And I want a reason to hold my allegiance to you higher than any other loyalty, so that I'm never torn between conscience and my regard for you again."

Beacon felt himself to be weak as he spoke, and imperfect, and less than Pandora Small deserved. If he was good and strong and worthy of her, he'd be able to stand by her side without faltering regardless of their bond. He wouldn't need her patronage to justify overlooking anything she'd ever said and done. He'd be loyal, and that would be the end of it. But he was who he was, and needed a decisive coup to end this war within him. To make Pandora empress at last of his mind and heart, as he desired and as she deserved.

"Bind yourself to me," Beacon murmured, reaching forward and cupping the sweet curve of Pandora's neck with one hand. She closed the distance between them, leaning her forehead against his own until he was intoxicated by lily of the valley fragrance and by awareness of her presence. "Let me be a help to you, rather than a hindrance."

When Pandora answered, it was with her touch. Her fingers brushed the slick scar tissue at the hollow of Beacon's throat, and the warmth of her banished any thought of his previous failure. He could not even consider his past when the present, this moment, was the summation of all his longing. Pan touched him and shut her eyes, and if feeling her power before had been glory, the sense of Pandora binding herself to him—bringing them into alignment, orienting him to her power and her pain, casting ties that could not be broken or unmade and that would fix them together like the North Star to its pole—was transcendence.

The binding act stretched on and on, a sublime piece of magic, the only direct magework permitted by the law. When, at last, it was complete, Pandora drew away a little and looked at Beacon, her gaze tentative and solemn.

"I'm sorry," she said. "If I was better, I wouldn't have done it. But I wanted to. Oh, Beacon, I've wanted this so badly."

It was so like his own thoughts, his own heart, and Beacon knew what she meant and where the regret stemmed from. Because now, bound to Pandora as her patron, he felt her pain with every breath.

It was his pain as well, to share in and to carry along with her.

She hurt.

He hurt.

They hurt together.

Beacon would not have it any other way.

"Set me free," Beacon said, and she knew instantly what he meant, with the untarnished sympathy that would always exist between them now. It was not the pain of the new binding he referred to, but the evil cloud that still hung over them, its tendrils running through Beacon, the intimacy between him and Pandora observed and scrutinized by a Gaunt's insatiable gas-lamp eyes.

Once again, Pandora splayed her hands out across Beacon's chest. Once again, her power surged through him, until he was racked with ungovernable pleasure and pain. Her force in Beacon was so great, he shook with it, sweating and gasping, but every moment he endured was another in which the Gaunt's influence lost sway.

From a distance, he heard the dark creature keen as it was cast out from him utterly. He felt the outer blast of Pandora's magic, rendering it ash in an instant, even as her power within him remained. She turned back to him and withdrew her spellfire slowly, tenderly, bit by bit, so as not to shock or injure him with its sudden absence.

When it was gone, he was left whole and healed and oddly bereft, wanting nothing more than to someday feel Pan's power within him again. For a long moment, they simply regarded one another, a patron and his mage, a mage and her true guardian, the two of them joined by spellfire and by the subtler magic of the heart.

"Thank you," Beacon said presently, and Pandora nodded.

"Thank *you*."

He leaned forward again, knowing what came next. Having given him her power, Pan would allow him her lips as well. The thing that haunted his dreams—a night with Pandora Small—would now become reality, and it was everything Beacon had ever wanted. He could imagine the plush softness of her mouth beneath his already, taste the sweetness of her breath.

His eyes shut of their own accord. He felt her, warm and pliable before him, waiting to be taken. And then . . .

"Oh, Beacon," Pandora said, disgruntled. "Not here. You can't be serious! I don't want my first kiss to happen in some disgusting cellar surrounded by corpses, where you almost died. It's too gruesome. What will we tell our children someday?"

Beacon's eyes flew open. Pan, diminutive, adorable, and exasperated, sat staring at him, annoyance in every line of her features. She was half feckless urchin, half fastidious Ingenue, and entirely herself. No one was like Beacon's Pandora, and he knew he would never, ever betray her again. His loyalty and his binding to her were supreme now and trumped all else.

"Lead on then, Empress," he said with a good-natured grin. "Take me away and I'll follow you anywhere, as long as you promise me that kiss at the end."

"Well, of course I do," Pandora said, and tapped him lightly on the nose.

22

THE BELLWETHER SCHOOL FOR YOUNG LADIES

Everything felt different for Pandora.

She had flirted with the idea of being bound to Beacon. Had known he would make a staunch and undemanding patron, and one she could trust. What she hadn't realized was the monumental relief a binding to him would provide.

The magic sat within her, a shining and welcome fetter, a voluntary and permanent work of magecraft. She could feel the new connection to Beacon with every breath. Was reminded of it every time she looked at him and saw that the scar at the hollow of his throat was gone, replaced by unblemished skin. The binding between them had been a work of healing, not only for him but also for her. It tempered the tie to her old patron greatly. Within, Pandora could still feel that other bond. But it chafed and frustrated and called out for attention and power to a far lesser degree. She could not hear a single whisper from it.

Beacon's binding had tamed her guardian's tie in a way Pandora and her spellfire had never been able to do. If she'd known taking a new patron would distill the evil effects of the old one, she'd have done it years sooner, Pan thought as she glanced up at the guard by her side.

But no. Even had she known earlier, she'd never have been willing to connect herself to anyone else as she was willing to be tied to him.

"What is this place?" Beacon asked curiously. "I thought you'd take me to your little flat."

Pandora had his hand in hers and her heart in her throat. While she'd led him away from that nightmare tenement basement, night had fallen. They'd wandered through the city together under cover of darkness, both of them looking a sight. Pandora was still easily mistakable for some lower city doxy, and Beacon was filthy and disheveled after his time in a Gaunt's clutches. But there was a fineness about him that shone through, Pandora thought as she stole glances at him in the moonlight. Even the ash that streaked his face couldn't hide the perfect line of his jaw, the intent and devoted look in his eyes, the way he carried himself like the last soldier left standing in a war of honor.

She'd brought him by back ways to a significantly more well-heeled part of Valora and one she knew like her own reflection. Pan took Beacon through an expansive and silent garden to an elegant three-story building that sat dreaming in the shadows. Climbing the steps onto the welcoming front verandah, Pandora dropped Beacon's hand just long enough to bend and fish an iron key from beneath a potted rose. Then their fingers were knitted together again, and she unlocked the door, leading him into a quiet, spacious foyer.

"This was my first new beginning," Pan said with a smile, as Beacon took everything in. The floors of honey-colored hardwood, the soaring staircase, the walls lined with portraits of Ingenues from years gone by. "No one's here now because they're all on the Hill. But I wanted to show it to you. I thought it would be fitting if we began here too."

Beside her, Pan could see Beacon's beautiful face pull into a frown.

"I appreciate the sentiment, but it isn't safe," he said seriously. "If the Guard or your patron come after you, this is the first place they'd look."

Pandora shrugged. "I don't care. Let them look. They won't be able to get in."

"What do you—" Beacon's voice trailed off as Pan envisioned the Bellwether School, intimately familiar as it lay in the twilight. She saw her power envelop the building, encasing it in a shimmering ward. And as Pandora saw, so it was. What she could imagine, she could accomplish. Such was the scope and breadth of her power.

Newly bound to her, Beacon could now feel her magecraft in ways he never had before. But he was still his own self—cautious and circumspect and dutiful to a fault.

"You *are* my empress," he said. "But you've as good as painted a target on us. No one who walks by will fail to notice a piece of magic like that. And the Guard will know it's you immediately. They may not be able to get in, but they can wait."

"They're welcome to," Pandora said uncaringly. "When I was arrested after you told the Guard about the wellspring, I was put in a box. Not *that* sort of box," she hurried to assure Beacon as his face went stormy, "but the kind I grew up in. A beautiful room, full of everything I could possibly need, with walls and floors and a ceiling of steel. My patron is evidently able to move the Guard as they will, and wants me confined or pushed into some sort of catastrophic breakdown. Very well. Here I am, but I'm not a child any longer. I will not break, and I will at least choose the location and means of my confinement. I'll choose a companion to take into captivity with me too, if he agrees to stay."

Pandora moved to the stairs, rising onto the lowest step. "Besides, I've been an Ingenue for quite some time now, which means I'm not without my vanity. I've no intention of spending any more time traipsing around the city dressed like this."

She gestured disparagingly at her torn shift and ash-streaked stays. Beacon put his head to one side and took her in with a wicked half smile. "I think you look quite nice."

"Of course you do." Pan rolled her eyes. "I'm in my underthings. But I don't plan to be for long."

"Oh?" Beacon raised an eyebrow, and Pan thought he'd earn Theo's unwarranted reputation easily, should he decide to turn rake.

"I promised you a kiss," she said, her voice scathing. "Nothing less, and nothing more. Which is all you'll have from me for now."

Lightly she hurried back across the entry floor to him, rising on her toes and pressing the briefest and most demure of kisses to his mouth.

"Not so fast, minx," Beacon growled, seizing her by the wrist and pulling her to him as she coyly tried to turn away. But his touch was gentle and she wanted to be caught, and when he had her in his arms, Pandora gave herself up willingly. She turned her face to Beacon's and let him see the adoration in her eyes, a reflection of what shone in his own.

"I have wanted you," she breathed, "since you first learned and kept my secret. And I will want you every day until I die."

Then she kissed her guard. She did not kiss like a mere girl in love, either, but like an Ingenue—with parlor magic to sweeten her lips and soften her hands and send thrill after thrill of pleasure through the lucky party she'd chosen to bestow her favor on.

Beacon groaned and trembled, and Pandora smiled against his mouth before kissing him deeper still. She hadn't realized until now how badly she wanted this particular power—to have him fully in her sway, helpless before her, ready to do the terrible or the sublime should she only ask it.

When she pulled back, Beacon stood for a moment with his chest heaving before running a hand across his face. He fixed her with a look that was hunger and amusement and respect all at once.

"Just a kiss. Nothing less and nothing more, eh?" he asked.

"I'm an Ingenue," Pandora said primly. "We tend toward more."

Later, Pandora sat on the plush carpet of Miss Alice's office floor with Beacon. A small fire snapped in the grate before them, and the windows were thrown open to catch the cool night breeze. The view of the twilit street beyond was dimmed and slightly obscured by the shimmering veil of Pandora's ward, which she maintained with a slow and constant trickle of power.

In the school kitchen, Pan had watched with utter contentment as Beacon mixed batter for hotcakes and fried them with bits of salt pork. He'd brewed kantha at the same time and scrounged through the pantry for apples and sugar and spice nuts, which he'd baked together in the covered pan as they sat at the long kitchen table and ate their dinner. To see Beacon work so capably and come up with something delectable at the end was—well. Pandora wasn't sure which had been more delicious—what he'd made, or watching him undertake the making of it.

Now they sat side by side, eating their baked apples off tin plates and licking their sticky fingers afterward. When Pandora finally set her plate aside with a sigh, Beacon turned to her, a stern expression on his face.

"You know we can't stay here forever," he said. "We've got to come up with a better plan."

"I can stay here forever," Pan protested, shifting to lie on her back and stare up at the ornately decorated plaster ceiling. She was comfortable in one of her own nightgowns now, and a satin dressing gown and slippers. "That ward's no trouble at all. I could hold it for a thousand years, if need be."

"We'd be out of provisions in a fortnight," Beacon pointed out with annoying practicality. "The larder's not well-stocked, since all your teachers and classmates are gone for summer. And the moment the Guard finds we're here, they'll block the pipes leading out to the well, which means no fresh water. You didn't bother including the well in your ward—I saw it down at the end of the garden, when we were coming in."

"I'll make the ward bigger," Pan said, reaching for his hand.

Beacon lowered himself onto his side, propping himself up on one arm, and Pandora could feel him watching her. He had her hand caught securely in his own, and a bittersweet pang ran through Pan as she realized this was the happiest and safest she'd ever felt. On the run from both the Queen's Guard and her patron, holed up like a mouse in a cellar, and with no clear plan as to what she ought to do next.

"Pan," Beacon said. "I think it's time for you to stop hiding."

She let out one of Imogen's unladylike snorts, scowling up at the ceiling as she did so. "I'm not hiding. As you pointed out, I've advertised both my whereabouts and my power to the whole city with the ward we're sitting behind. The Guard knows about the wellspring. You know. Imogen and Theo know. This is the least hidden I've ever been."

Beacon shook his head. "You're still hiding where it really counts. You're hiding from your binding, and from your patron."

Pandora stared fixedly at the ceiling and its plaster scrollwork, unwilling to meet his eyes.

"I'm afraid," she confessed. "You don't—you *can't*—know what it was like being under their control. I am terrified of doing something monstrous again, either because they bid me to, or because I'm so desperate to escape, I stop caring about anyone and anything beyond myself. I've lived that already. I can't go back."

"Things will be different this time," Beacon promised, and his hand was warm around hers. She thought of their first meeting—of how she'd burned him, and he'd kept her secret anyway. "I'll be with you. I'll stay with you through everything. I'll be your anchor, in any way I can."

At that, Pandora did want to look at him. She pulled her hand from Beacon's and rolled over to face him, the two of them side by side, heads pillowed on their arms, alone and untouchable in the little world Pandora's ward had made.

"You're already my anchor," she said. "You have been since the moment we met. No one else had ever seen my power before and just accepted it. I needed that so badly, Beacon. I didn't know how badly until you'd already given it to me. And now—I've told you what it's like, constantly fighting off my patron. The binding between us has made it so much easier. I might sleep through the night for the first time I can remember. I don't know if this will last, or if as your binding settles in, theirs will grow stronger and harder to bear again. But for now, this is the best I've ever felt."

Beacon's steady gaze on her was sad. "I can feel what you feel now, you know. And if this is the best, I hate to think what the worst was like."

Pan couldn't help herself. She knew it discomfited him when a girl was brought to tears, but her vision blurred over and her throat tightened.

"I've told you before," she admitted in a bleak whisper. "It's been very hard. Harder than I could ever put into words. And no matter how I try, I can't be good, or powerless, or fully under control. I can't sever the bond to my patron. All I can do is stave off disaster, and survive."

Beacon, it seemed, had grown used to Pandora's occasional fits of weeping. Rather than frown or shift or seem uncomfortable, he reached out and brushed tears from her cheeks with the ball of one thumb.

"I wish you could see things as I do," he said. "You're harder on yourself than on anyone else, Pandora. No one else could have lived through what you have. Any other person would be a thrall to your patron now. And I know what I did when I learned about the wellspring—I know I betrayed your trust. I couldn't find a way to reconcile what I knew with the duty I'd sworn myself to as a guard. But I will never speak against you again. What you did to Hesperid—who's to say it wasn't necessary? Who's to say if you hadn't freed yourself from your patron, they wouldn't have used you for something more vicious still? The way they were raising you, that must have been the plan. Yes, you changed the world, and no one could argue for the better. But maybe if you hadn't, you'd have been forced to subjugate or end it, instead."

Pandora nodded. She could see Beacon clearly now, the fog of tears dissipated. Taking his hand once again, she pressed it to her lips.

"I have an idea," he said presently. "Something that might allow you to be rid of your patron's influence once and for all. But I'll have to leave this ward, and you'll have to trust me to do so. I know I don't deserve—"

His voice trailed off as he felt Pandora call back her magic. The ward dissipated at once, leaving a view of unobscured night sky outside the office windows.

"I trust you," Pan said. "I've always trusted you. I trusted you even when I told you about the wellspring and knew—yes, I knew—that you'd go to the Guard. You do what you believe is right, regardless of the cost. How could I not trust that?"

Beacon sat up decisively. He looked down at Pandora, who lay in the moonlight with her dark hair pooled about her. When he bent and kissed her, she did not respond with magic. She knew she didn't need to. Just her mouth against Beacon's and her heart bound to his was enough.

"Stay where I can find you," he said, after finally pulling away. "I'll be back as soon as I can. And then we'll see about your patron."

23

PANIC! AT THE BALLROOM

Pandora waited. She paced the halls of the Bellwether School until the small hours of morning, before finally curling up in a corner of Miss Alice's office settee to nap.

But she could not have been dozing for long when something dragged her from a dead sleep. A prickling sense of wrongness. A premonition of evils yet to come.

Rising, Pan pulled her dressing gown tighter about herself and shivered. She hadn't bothered to renew the ward with Beacon gone. What did she care if the Guard or anyone else found her in his absence? Her own being was protection enough—she did not require shields of any kind, should she choose to put up a fight.

Creeping through the shadowy corridors, Pandora peered out of window after window, searching for the source of her all too familiar sense of dread. She found nothing but the quiet midsummer gardens, until at last she dared to open the school's front door.

Splayed out on the verandah, her fingers and mouth and eyes and nose stained spellfire blue, was Mamie Hawthorne, the last of the Bellwether Ingenues on Palace Hill, save for Pandora and Imogen. Mamie's hands were torn and bloodied and her nails cracked, as if she'd tried to damage herself to prevent her spellfire's going. Just as with Eleanor, Pandora's ward had not been enough to save her. Set atop Mamie's chest was a small framed miniature, bearing a deftly painted portrait.

A perfect face gazed serenely out from the picture. Golden hair. Sea-green eyes. A scattering of freckles. Pandora's patron had never spoken so clearly. Imogen Hollen would be next, unless Pandora ended this game of cat and mouse. She was expected to slink back to captivity, tail between her legs, chastened by the murderous results of her brief stint of freedom.

When Pandora stood, it was not dread or resignation or fear that coursed through her. Bolstered by the strength of Beacon's bond, she felt only fury.

Enough. She had tolerated and permitted her patron's misdeeds for far too long. It was past time for Pandora to stand in her power and bring their baleful influence over both her and Valora to an end. It didn't matter who they were—whether the lowest scullion or the prince consort himself, Pandora would administer the justice they'd escaped for far too long.

An hour later, Pandora's hansom pulled up before the glittering central complex on Palace Hill. Lights and guards and glistening silk-and-gem-clad revelers were everywhere. The mood on the Hill was heady, ebullient, more celebratory even than usual.

As Pan stepped lightly from the carriage, a guard hurried to take her hand. For a moment, her heart leaped into her throat, but the boy was only an underling in uniform. He appeared to have no idea who

Pandora was, or that she'd been arrested and charged with Hesperid's worst crime, then escaped captivity.

"My, we're all in high spirits tonight," she said to the guard. "I've been away a few days due to family matters—has something happened?"

"The higher-ups in my ranks and on the queen's council caught a mage," the guard said with a grin. "The one who's been responsible for the deaths here on the Hill. It was an Ingenue, hiding in plain sight. What's more, they're saying that same mage opened the wellspring, years back. So we're safer now than we've been in years."

"Oh," Pandora said a trifle faintly. To hear the wellspring and herself tied together, even when her identity wasn't fully known, made her skin crawl and her stomach turn over. She'd spent so long hiding from what she'd done, having it spoken of before her acted like a toxin in her blood. "Have they said who it is?"

The guard shook his head. "No details for now, aside from letting all of us know there's no need to worry anymore."

A commotion sounded at the head of the palace drive. Pandora glanced over and saw a mounted guard from the lower city rein her horse to a halt, its flanks white-flecked and its eyes red-rimmed. The woman slid from the saddle immediately and ran to the nearest group of guards. She gestured wildly, and Pan caught a few words.

"Down in the city . . . a ward . . . like nothing any bound mage could make."

"You ought to go see to that," Pan said, her voice even and her face a pleasant blank as the attention of the young guardsman at her side pivoted to the uniformed group gathered on the drive. "It seems urgent."

With a polite excuse, the guard dismissed himself, and Pan slipped away, disappearing into the people milling about at the palace's soaring front entry.

Inside, music cascaded out from a distant ballroom. People laughed and chattered everywhere, their relief palpable as they flirted or gossiped or argued among themselves. Every room had its waiting attendants with trays of summer wine in crystal flutes, its tables loaded with dainties, its profusion of honey-scented flowers.

Standing on her toes, Pandora craned her neck, trying desperately to catch a glimpse of Imogen. She cursed her height and wished for Beacon—the binding between them told her he was somewhere on Palace Hill, and would alert her if they grew closer in proximity. You were never truly unaware of a patron you'd bound yourself to—Pan knew that all too well.

"Have you seen Imogen Hollen?" she began to ask anyone who looked even vaguely familiar.

"Imogen? The Ingenue with the golden hair?

"Ander Hollen's daughter. Is she here tonight?

"Yes, the one who's often with Prince Theo. Do you know where she is?"

Every query was fruitless. Systematically Pan went from room to room, scanning its occupants and asking after Imogen. As she went, her anxiety only grew. Horrible images flashed across her mind—Imogen being led away unsuspectingly by a shadowy figure, taken to some far-off, overlooked corner of the palace. Imogen in her death throes, at the feet of Pan's masked and cloaked patron, writhing as power was stripped from her blood and bones. Imogen lying dead on the floor, her face twisted in a rictus of fear, her hands and features stained spellfire blue.

By the time she reached the crowded corridor that led to the palace's sprawling central ballroom, Pan had bitten her nails down to the bloody quick. She stopped for a moment, pressing herself against the wall and drawing a few deep breaths in an unsuccessful attempt to quell her panic.

Deep within, Beacon's binding was the only thing keeping her from truly falling apart. It was a bulwark, as strong and reassuring as the guard himself. It buoyed her up, tempering her power, silencing the constant siren song of her other, earlier binding. The boy was everything Pandora's first patron had not been, and contemplating their connection lent her courage.

Perhaps too much of it.

As Pandora stood with her back to the wall, terrified for Imogen and strengthened by her tie to Beacon, she did something that she had not in many years. She reached for the binding between herself and her first patron.

There it was, a phantom pain, quiescent after long disuse. Pan prodded at it, feeling the pain intensify a little, the pull to restore the bond—to make herself *whole*—growing marginally stronger, but nowhere near overwhelming. The connection to Beacon was far more prevalent. She could feel him now, on the move somewhere in the palace, the sensation of his motion setting restlessness in her limbs. With him at the forefront and her patron's bond hardly stirring within her, Pandora allowed a temptation that had been niggling at the back of her mind to come to fruition.

She'd fought the restoration of her binding for so long, but if she could not find Imogen, she could find her patron. All Pan needed to do was let go of the yearslong choke hold she kept on their binding. As she thought it, Pandora felt her control slip a little.

Nothing.

She loosened her white-knuckled inner grip on the binding still more.

Nothing again.

And Pandora let go.

For so long, she'd feared this moment, anticipating a sudden influx of alien power as her patron regained control. They would seize her like the puppet she'd always been and make her dance, whether through direct commands or more insidious manipulation.

But none of that materialized. All Pandora felt was a sudden awareness of her patron's whereabouts.

Ahead. Very close. Somewhere in the giddy throng that packed the ballroom. It was a little like activating some strange, long-unused sixth sense, following the pull of her binding. Complicating matters was the constant tug Pandora felt toward Beacon, as well—he was not here, but somewhere else in the palace, no more than a thousand or so yards away.

Pan breached the ballroom. The lights and noise and swirl of colors and dancers and laughter were overwhelming. Keeping to the edges of the dance floor, she moved step by unsteady step, bent on a mission she'd never undertaken before—finding her patron, rather than escaping them.

Closer.

Closer still.

A break in the crowds, and Pandora caught a glimpse of something that flooded her with unspeakable relief. At the ballroom's far end, Imogen stood with a party of nobles, speaking earnestly to them all. She was more dazzlingly beautiful than ever, in a gown of brilliant spellfire blue, with diamonds glinting on her neck and wrist.

"Gin!" Pandora cried out above the swelling music. "Stay just where you are, I'm coming to you!"

Stares snagged on Pandora, and disgruntled outbursts followed in her wake as she pushed her way through to her sister. She did not care. At last she was standing before Imogen, who was whole and well, with a petrified look on her lovely face.

"Pan, what are you *doing* here?"

But Pandora could not reply. She was overcome with a sudden wash of dizziness and the overwhelming awareness that she stood, at last, in her patron's presence, the binding between them heating and throbbing until it seared at her core.

Dragging her gaze from Imogen, Pandora found herself face-to-face at last with an all too familiar figure, hooded and cloaked and unrecognizable. It could not be the consort—no, he stood to the side of the scourge of her childhood and bane of her youth—the ghost that haunted her every nightmare and the villain who had pushed her to flood Hesperid with a plague of monsters and power.

"Who are you?" Pandora breathed.

"Hello, darling," said a woman's voice. "I've been waiting for you to come and find me. You have made the task much harder than it needed to be."

Everything around them froze. The orchestra fell silent. The dancers grew still. A glittering rain of golden motes, recently set off by some Ingenue, hung suspended on the air. Nothing moved. No one breathed. The ballroom, or Palace Hill, or all the world perhaps, had been stopped in its tracks by Pandora's patron's magic. She and Pandora were the only creatures who still thought and acted.

Instinctively Pan reached for her tie to Beacon and cursed her own hubris, because just like everything else, it was frozen, caught fast in the magework that had settled over Palace Hill like a thick blanket.

"Show yourself to me, you coward," Pan gritted out, hiding the fear singing in her veins behind a facade of bravado.

"I can't," her patron said sympathetically. "Because I've never hidden from you. That, I am afraid, is your own doing. If you wish to see me, you must look past your own fear, your own magic."

Pandora felt as frozen as the remainder of Palace Hill.

"Don't be ridiculous," she managed to stammer. "It's not that simple."

"Oh, my dear. I'm afraid it is."

Shutting her eyes, Pandora fought for control over her fear the way she fought for mastery of her spellfire. It took what seemed like an intolerably long time. When she opened her eyes again, the dizziness she felt grew acute. For a moment, her patron's hooded form wavered in and out, finally resolving into its true shape.

Pan looked at Queen Maud. At the bandages on her hands and the silver star of Hesperid on her brow. And she felt unutterably foolish, knowing that whenever possible, her fellow Ingenues had tried to warn her as best they knew how. Leslie, scratching the four-pointed star into a shelf as she lay dying. Mamie, tearing at her hands. The weight of Pan's despair over missing their messages was near crushing. The fear she felt was still enough to choke on, and she knew beyond the shadow of a doubt that it had indeed been her own magic veiling Maud for all these years. To face down Hesperid's monarch had seemed impossible, and so she had hidden the truth from herself until such a time as she was ready for it. It hadn't been a conscious act, but that did not temper the force of the self-loathing rising in Pan. She was weak. So many people had died because of her desire to be free, and then after because of her inability to face the truth.

Carefully, intentionally Pandora set that despair and hatred aside. Instead of feeling its full weight, she reminded herself of other things. She was no longer who she'd been as a child. She'd remade Hesperid, held off her patron's insidious influence for five long years, and become an Ingenue in that time. She'd bound herself to another by choice, found at least a part of her family, and learned that her power could be more than a blunt instrument. It could be a thing of beauty, too. It could be tamped down into something graceful and desirable, or given free rein and vented with such passion and precision that it brought a boy named Ellis Beacon to tears.

Beneath the queen's gaze, Pandora drew herself up to her full, albeit inconsequential, height. She jutted her chin out defiantly, and rebellion sparked in her eyes. She would not be brought low again, whether it was by the queen's magic or the aftereffects of her own.

"I've come to unbind myself," Pan said with unspent spellfire crackling in her voice. "And to make sure you never harm someone with your power again."

Queen Maud laughed, a dark, melodious sound. "Late, as always. Less impressive than you ought to be, as ever. How does it feel to know half a dozen people died for you to find your courage?"

"Only half a dozen?" Pandora answered, finally putting words to the guilt that had plagued her for five long years. "Hundreds have died because of what I did, opening the wellspring. Thousands, possibly. If you don't lay the responsibility for those deaths at my feet, you're more generous than I."

"Little girl." Maud smiled and stepped forward, taking Pandora's chin gently in one hand. "How I've missed you. You oughtn't to have taken so long to come back to me. What a fire we could light together. All Hesperid would burn in its flames. All the world, perhaps. We could build an empire together."

Pan shook her head, pulling back from the queen's touch. "I intend to use my magic to mend, not mar."

"Of course you do," Maud purred, and Pandora could feel the binding between them strengthening, gaining power, her head becoming muddled and fuzzy as Maud spoke and flattered and cajoled. "Why else do you think I had you sent to the Bellwethers'?

You were a blunt instrument under my tutelage. A powder keg, ready to go off. You wanted refinement and control before you could be of full use, all skills I could not give you."

"You sent me?" Pandora asked. The words came out thick and slurred, and Maud frowned, easing her hold on the binding between them. Pan's head cleared a little.

"Yes, of course I did. Who else would know your full history, and just how to pull Ander Hollen's strings to ensure he secured a place at the Bellwethers' that could not be traced back to me? Who else would be able to so neatly erase his memory of your conception? I *made* you, Pandora, in every way. I gave you life. I gave you power. I gave you control. There is nothing you do not owe to me, no circumstance you lived through that I did not orchestrate. Even when you believed yourself rid of me and choked off the binding between us, I always knew where you were, how you were, what you were doing. You've never undertaken a single act unless I willed it. That, after all, is a mother's duty. And as a queen who requires a worthy successor, I've had to be far more conscientious in carrying out my duty than most."

Pan felt sick. Instinctively she reached for Beacon's binding and found it once more alive within her, although faint. It was no longer frozen like their surroundings—like the kaleidoscope of colors and partygoers that remained trapped in time. A bit of Beacon's soul and being rested within her, like a small and reassuring ember.

"I will never be your successor," she told Maud firmly. "And Hesperid would never accept me either. You've trained its people to hate mages too well."

"You're not a mage," Maud said, stepping forward and stroking Pandora's cheek fondly as Pan gave up ground yet again. "You're an Ingenue. And no one need ever know you're more than that. I'll see that they don't. There are few on this Hill who aren't under my sway."

"The consort is your thrall, isn't he?" Pandora asked. "That's why he pushed for the mage laws. That's why I've seen spellfire in his eyes. But I don't understand why." This time, she did not shy away from Maud's touch. She stood motionless and endured it, even as it dredged up dozens of memories of her tormented childhood. Now she could see clearly. She could recall the woman she'd known was her mother and her queen, but who never offered her even the slightest hint of kindness. "You could have revealed yourself to Hesperid. Instead of subjugating those like you, you could have been our advocate. Trained us up to channel our spellfire properly, so we would not be a threat to others. So that we were thought better of, and treated well. Every mage in Hesperid would have been devoted to you, had you chosen that path."

Maud gave Pandora a look of unbridled amusement. "And foster a generation of rivals to my throne? Create a nation wherein a battle between mages could cause untold damage at any point? No. It is best for Hesperid that we alone hold power and chart the course. I've set the example for you, in directing your childhood and your youth, in overseeing your upbringing with such care. At the same time, I have been caring for all Hesperid, as you will do after me. Only we have the strength to outlast one another, and the will and capacity to govern rightly. No one else is our match."

"And how exactly do you ensure that your word is carried out?" Pandora asked. "How is it that you maintain so many bindings, and override so many wills?"

Maud's smile widened. "I discovered young that the final spark of spellfire, upon leaving the body, possesses strange power. It allows you to craft a binding far more restrictive than any other. The sort where you can alter reality, and bend even the strongest mind. My gift has always lent itself more to subterfuge and the manipulation of others. But I required more than that—enough power to bind my court wholesale, and to enrich Hesperid with the spellfire that made us who we are. I've never had your raw power or your more destructive talents, which is why I needed you to open the wellspring. I've been able to accomplish more and further Hesperid's interests in ways I'd never dreamed of before you gave me access to so much spellfire. In the countryside beyond the city, most citizens are enjoying greater prosperity than they have in centuries. A few deaths in the capital, a few easily dispensed with monsters, is a small price to pay."

"Did you know about the hellions?" Pandora asked. "Did you know that if I opened the wellspring to escape you, they'd come to plague us?"

Maud shrugged. "It was a possibility I was aware of. A risk I was willing to take."

"That you were willing for *me* to take," Pan said, spellfire sparking in her voice once more. "When I never would have done it on my own."

"Wouldn't you?" Maud looked at her quizzically. "Perhaps not as you are now. I see you've learned more than poise during your time at the Bellwethers'. You think you've grown righteous. Better than I am. But I remember you as you were then—young and hungry, starving for spellfire, ready to do terrible things in the pursuit of freedom. Had I told you about the hellions, you would have opened the wellspring and unleashed them without a second thought, I've no doubts on that score."

Pandora could feel the little ember at her core growing warmer and nearer. Beacon was on his way to her, and the thought gave her courage. Not just to stand against Maud, but to grant herself the benefit of the doubt.

"Perhaps you're right. Perhaps regardless of what I'd known then, I'd have done the same. But I wouldn't now, and that's what matters. I am older and wiser, and I mean to atone for my past sins."

Maud tightened the bond between them, until Pandora could not help but hear truth in her words. "There's no atoning for creatures like us. Only power, and whether or not we have the fortitude to wield it. You cannot reconcile Hesperid to who you are, or what you've done, or ever earn forgiveness for the sin of being born an abomination. So why not revel in your true nature? Why not join me, and allow our foolish people to dream of safety as you and I chart their course? We could bind them all and reveal ourselves, as you wish, forging a dynasty of mage queens, wise and powerful, ushering in a golden era for Hesperid."

Her mind sluggish, Pan fought for clarity, pushing against Maud's binding and holding Beacon's close. But Maud pushed back, until she could hardly see through the blue veil of spellfire beginning to obscure her vision.

"I will have you at my side," the queen murmured. "Whether it comes by your will or not. Eventually, you will give in. Eventually, you will realize the futility of struggle. We will be as we were—a mother and her eager daughter, ready to obey and to do my bidding."

"Pan," an unsteady voice said from a few yards behind her. "Are you all right? What can I do?"

Pandora turned to look, and there was her guard. Beacon was in spotless uniform again, his face twisted with the effort of moving through Maud's magic, which still lay heavy over the ballroom.

"Ignore him," the queen snapped as a jolt of wakefulness and independence shot through Pandora at the sight of Beacon. "He's nothing to you compared to me. I will not share your attention or your affections. He ought not even to be waking."

She seemed oblivious to the fact that a binding existed between Pandora and Beacon now, new but growing more powerful by the hour, which would someday rival the old connection between Pandora and the queen.

"Be still," Maud ordered Beacon, and for the first time, Pan witnessed the full, visceral horror that was a mage exercising her magic and her will against another. To be compelled by her mother's magic was second nature to Pandora—she'd been accustomed to it from her earliest memories. But to hear the searing sound of Maud's voice, to witness skeins of her spellfire snaking out to Beacon in order to shackle him, was more than Pan could bear.

"Do not. Touch him," she snapped, and clapped an iron ward around the boy before Maud's power had even come close. "You will not *ever* touch him. Nor will you touch my sister. You keep your bloody hands and your filthy magic off those I love, or I will see to it you lose every spark of power that burns in your veins."

Maud laughed, amused by Pandora in the way an indulgent mother was entertained by a petulant child. "Oh really? You intend to best me? I was only burned by your sad little ward around the Wellesley girl because it took me by surprise. I won't be caught off guard again."

She reached out with her magic, and Pandora could feel it, slithering around the ward, searching for weaknesses, pushing at the chinks and tearing at the cracks. Pan bore down harder, and Maud smiled at her beatifically, redoubling her efforts. Sweat stood out on Pandora's forehead, and at last she knew she would not be able to hold out against the older, more experienced mage. But neither was she willing to surrender.

In the same instant, Pan dropped her ward and hurled a bolt of spellfire at Queen Maud—not enough to kill, but enough to pain and stun. Maud's smile grew wolfish as she anticipated Pandora's resistance and lifted the thick, numbing enchantment laid over the ballroom.

With a clangorous sound, the orchestra pealed back into life. Conversation erupted again. Dancers completed their figures. And all eyes flashed to the head of the ballroom, in time to see Pandora strike Queen Maud with her power.

A wave of crimson and silver built from the edges of the room, as every guard at the perimeter sprinted toward their seemingly stricken queen. And Maud's voice, pitched to carry, rang out in the sudden, horrified silence.

"This is the mage who tore open the earth and unleashed demons on our capital city—we've been deceived for years, thinking the wrongdoer was already brought to justice. This is the one who attacked my person, and who has been killing our beloved daughters. I call you to bring her to heel by any means possible—whoever wields weapons, let them be used against her. Whoever is capable of magecraft, I waive the laws in regards to this girl. Let her be taken, whether steel or spellfire."

Even as the queen spoke, Beacon had already seized Pandora and Imogen both by the hands.

"This is no place for a last stand," he warned. "Pan, we need a ward, and to run."

Instantly she did as he'd bidden her, surrounding the three of them with the protective cocoon of her magic. Maud's binding still seethed within, attempting to force Pandora to turn, to repent, to yield, but Beacon's tie was blazing now in response, and the queen's poison could not contend with his fire.

Sparks glistened around Pan, her guard, and her sister, and no one could stand against Pandora's shield. One by one, revelers and law enforcers fell away as her ward touched them. Harmless bits of parlor magic broke like fireworks against the ward, and pursuers dropped behind as Imogen cast illusions to distract or dismay or mislead those who followed.

Like a shooting star, they made their way through the palace, seeking its darkest places and its lowest ground. To attempt escape would be useless—a single glance out one of the many windows told them as much. The crown of Palace Hill was engulfed in magic, the mage corps's innocuous weather-working spells revealed for what they truly were—a net to ensnare and pollute and govern, cast by Queen Maud herself and maintained by the vast bulwark of the wellspring.

"This way," Beacon grated out, and Pan nodded, knowing exactly where he was headed.

To the source of Maud's dominance, a fount of spellfire she'd been unable to access without Pandora's help.

If they could not face the queen head-on, at least they could attempt to cut off her power. And this time, Pandora found she was willing to pay any price to right her prior wrong. Should closing the wellspring cost her life, so be it.

24

PANDORA'S PATRONS, PLURAL

Pandora followed Beacon through the heavy steel door that led to the wellspring chamber, with Imogen close behind. Once inside, she stopped short.

As always, the chamber she'd transformed was brilliantly lit by the glow of fathomless spellfire. In that preternatural light, a dozen people stood waiting. The Bellwether sisters and Baron Hax, Ander Hollen and several members of Winifred Harper's family, Prince Theo, and even a uniformed woman who Pandora recognized as Captain Tanner, Beacon's direct superior.

"What is this?" Pan asked, turning to Beacon.

"Patrons," he said. "It occurred to me that you couldn't manage your spellfire safely enough to deal with that Gaunt until we'd been bound to one another. And then I thought how you said your first patron could use a binding to control you, rather than the other way around. So clearly, the way you work the binding has bearing on how it plays out. I thought with enough other patrons to give you greater control, you might be able to close the wellspring safely. And that you could bind yourself to all of them for that purpose without giving them the ability to issue orders or commands. This is everyone I thought might be willing to serve as anchors for you. They all said yes, and this seemed like the logical place to gather them."

Hot tears pooled in Pandora's eyes. "But what if they end up tied to me forever? I couldn't break my patron's binding, and I'm not sure I'd be able to break ones I've made myself, either. Who'd want to be stuck with me all their lives?"

"I would," Beacon said staunchly, and put an arm around her. She nearly fell to pieces at that but pulled herself together at the sound of Miss Elvira's sharp voice.

"How many times have I told my girls that self-pity is one of the most unattractive qualities an Ingenue can display?" the headmistress said in acid tones. "Compose yourself, Pandora. We're all aware of what a binding with you would entail. And we're all entirely willing to undertake it, for your sake and for the greater good of Hesperid."

"Please, Pandora," Ander Hollen said, stepping forward. "Let us help you now. Some of us ought to have done more long ago."

Baron Hax smiled, a calculating, pleased expression. "I don't suppose I'll ever be your patron in any other capacity. So if this is all the chance I have to see the full extent of your power, I'm still awfully curious about it. And being one of the select few who helped mitigate the wellspring and save Hesperid can only elevate my business standing. Don't assume we're all self-sacrificing and altruistic, child. In the long run, it pays to be a hero."

Pan let out a trembling breath as Beacon's arm around her tightened.

"All right," she said finally. "I'll do it. But they all know how the wellspring came to be in the first place, yes?"

"I told them," Beacon said. "I told them that you were forced into it by your first patron, because that's the truth."

Pandora thought of Maud's assertion that every choice she'd ever made was shaped by the queen's own baleful influence. And it struck her that the only things she'd ever done that were truly outside Maud's purview were acts of reaching out. Trusting Beacon. Trusting Imogen. Perhaps, here and now, trusting these would-be fellow saviors of Hesperid. It was reaching out in faith that Maud did not condone or understand.

"Who's first?" Pandora asked, and immediately Imogen came forward, dropping to her knees before her sister. Pan smiled at Imogen, lovely as ever even in the glow of the wellspring, and at once she knew what this binding should be. A reflection of her feelings for her sister, golden with devotion and gratitude, with just the slightest hint of exasperation for spice. Pandora put her hands on either side of Imogen's face and bound them, with ties of blood and spellfire and loyalty, a bond that Imogen would immediately recognize.

And the beautiful girl did, beaming up at Pan through tears.

"I love you, too, Pandora," Imogen said, getting to her feet as the binding work finished and wrapping her arms around her sister. For a moment they stood together before Imogen moved off and was replaced by Ander.

Again, Pandora built her binding out of her feelings for the man. Reservation. Hesitation. Respect. But most of all, hope for what might someday grow between them.

Each of her new patrons was given some essential truth about how Pandora saw them and how she hoped to be seen by them. Even Baron Hax, who grinned at his binding wrought of suspicion and distaste and annoyance.

"Just as I thought," Hax said, having been last of the volunteer patrons. "But you mark my words, girl. Someday, we'll be friends."

Pandora tossed her head. "I wouldn't count on that if I were you."

Just when she'd thought she was finished, Beacon knelt before her.

"Beacon, what are you doing?" Pan asked in confusion. "We're already—"

"I know," he said, voice low so the others wouldn't overhear. They were all clustered around the wellspring, peering down into its mesmerizing depths, talking in hushed tones among themselves. "But I want more of you than anyone else has. Let me be selfish, Pandora, when it comes to you. I want to be your strongest binding, the anchor you reach for before all others. I want the ties between us to cut so close that even your first patron's hold is less than mine. Let me be your first, and last, and foremost."

In answer, Pandora reached for him. She put her hands around Beacon's beloved face and worked a magic like she'd never undertaken before. She bound them together so securely that their hearts slowed, and quickened, and began to beat in time. Her will was subject to him, and his to her, until they were both master and servant to the other. When Beacon rose to stand at Pandora's side, he was the north and she a compass, or perhaps it was the other way around. Regardless, they were oriented to each other in an unbreakable and imperishable fashion, and when Pandora glanced up at her guard, there was a look of quiet satisfaction on his face.

"Well," Pandora said, turning her gaze to the wellspring. "I suppose there's no time like the present. I'd like everyone to get back behind the door, please. I don't really know what I can manage, or how this will go, and I won't have anyone getting hurt."

Her patrons filed out, led by Baron Hax, but Beacon stayed rooted to the spot at her side.

"Beacon, I need you to go too."

The guard only shook his head. "I won't. And you don't need to worry on my account, or ward me. I can still feel your power, and the wellspring, but everything's different now with our binding. I don't think you could hurt me if you tried."

With a frown, Pandora let spellfire surge beneath her skin, a firestorm of trapped power. She reached out and brushed a fingertip against the back of Beacon's hand. Nothing. She took it in her own, blazing with suppressed magic as she did so. Not a burn, not a blister.

Reaching for Pandora's other hand, Beacon gazed down at her hungrily.

"I can still feel you," he said. "Clearer than before, even. But it doesn't hurt. Or it doesn't in a lasting way. I can't explain, really. It's like . . . it's like this."

He stooped and kissed Pandora, until her head spun and she rose up on her toes, running her fingers through the close-cropped and immaculately trimmed hair at the back of his neck. She was awash in the scents of kantha and peppermint shaving soap and open air, dizzy with the overwhelming nearness of Beacon and with how badly she wanted to be closer, always closer, to be given more, always more.

"Yes," Pandora said, blinking up at Beacon with wide eyes when he straightened. "I think I see what you mean."

Buoyed up by Beacon, by his nearness, by his bond, by his kiss, Pandora approached the wellspring for the first time since she'd opened it. She stood on the edge and gazed down into its tumultuous spellfire depths and felt . . . nothing. No great longing for its power. No hatred of what it had wrought in Hesperid. No fear of what it might do to her, should she try to close that monumental chasm. Not even guilt over her part in its opening. It was an inevitability, she supposed. As long as Queen Maud held sway over her, she had not been able to escape its opening. And now, having given other people her truths, she was no longer able to escape the wellspring's closure. It was her beginning, and if necessary, it would be her end.

Reaching deep into herself, Pandora dredged up her own spellfire. At the same time, she reached outward as well, to the force and fury of the wellspring. And binding the twin powers together, she began a work of magecraft like nothing seen in Hesperid before.

As Pandora worked, Beacon retreated, moving to the wellspring chamber's steel door. There was nothing much to see of the magic Pan was bringing into life—it wasn't a visible thing but something that could be *felt*, as a series of low, ominous tremors in the ground. Such tremors were common enough in Valora that Beacon was surprised to find Pan's new patrons still waiting in the stone passageway beyond the door—when the earth trembled, it was best to find open ground, or some safe spot to take cover. A tunnel at the heart of Palace Hill wasn't the place anyone would willingly choose for refuge from a quake.

"We're staying," Imogen said in response to Beacon's questioning look. "In case she needs anything."

It was then that Beacon noticed not all of Pandora's patrons had stayed. Captain Tanner and Theo were missing from among them, though he hadn't realized they were absent at first.

"Where's the prince?" Beacon asked Imogen. "Where's my captain?"

"They said they had to go," Imogen answered. "Theo looked very worried about something—I didn't like to make him stay. And your captain seemed like she was becoming ill. They went back up to the palace together."

"Damn." It had been a risk, including them among Pandora's new patrons. He'd known Theo was already bound to the queen and had his suspicions about Captain Tanner. But Beacon had wanted every soul he could get to bolster Pandora's strength. He'd hoped somehow the twin bindings within the prince and the captain would cancel each other out, as his own binding had mitigated the hold the queen had over Pandora. Not so, it seemed.

Even as he thought it, the ironclad binding between Beacon and Pan twinged. He was so close to her now that he could feel that other, older binding that rested at her center as well. Whispers rose at the edge of his hearing.

Foolish girl. I'm coming for you.

The temperature in the air dropped precipitously. A glaring white magelight blazed up the tunnel, and Beacon had no time to do more than shout to Pandora's friends to get through the steel door and slam it shut, before a violent blast of magic blew the door from its hinges.

Pandora, still at the edge of the wellspring, did not even bother to turn. Without so much as looking at them, she clapped an impenetrable ward around Beacon and her little band of patrons, all while continuing her work on the wellspring. Peering through the haze of magic her ward brought with it, Beacon thought he could see the wellspring's edges beginning to narrow, almost imperceptibly.

Maud strode into the chamber, and scarlet-uniformed guards poured in behind her, lining the white-blasted rock walls. Among them were Theo and Captain Tanner, both looking agonized and sick by the conflict between their warring bindings.

"Pandora," Maud said. "I should like you to stop what you're doing."

Pan said nothing, and Beacon felt her focus on the wellspring redouble.

"Someday, whether today or years from now, you *will* give way," Maud persisted. "I cannot for the life of me sort out where this stubborn streak comes from. All I've ever wanted from you is a dutiful and biddable daughter, fit to stand at her mother's side and to take my place when the time comes."

"Best look in the mirror if you're in search of the source of my disposition, Mother," Pandora answered grimly. "You'll never stop coming after me, and so long as I draw breath, I'll never stop trying to get clear of you."

"Always choosing the hard way." Maud shook her head in dismay. "When your life could be so easy, and so pleasant. Step away from the wellspring, Pandora."

"*No*. I made it, and I'll unmake it. The last thing you need is this sort of power."

Maud raised an eyebrow and stepped toward Pan. Beacon set to pacing like a caged animal—he hated to be trapped behind Pandora's ward, even as he knew it was the only way to ensure safety for himself and her patrons.

"Don't test me, child," Maud said. "You recall the price of disobedience."

Turning, the queen tilted her head in the direction of the guards ringing the perimeter of the wellspring cavern. One crumpled, convulsing as skeins of spellfire left him and entered Maud. A few moments later, another followed suit, and then another. It was like watching a Gaunt, but worse. No person should possess that capability, or the will to strip another of their life and spellfire so ruthlessly.

With a snarl of frustration, Pandora cast another ward. To encompass the guards dispersed along the cavern walls, she was forced to make the shield vast and narrow, a ring of power stretching like a halo around the open chasm and the two mages facing off along its edges.

"Can she hold both wards?" Imogen asked Beacon worriedly, and he shrugged, eyes fixed on the wellspring and Pandora's slight figure, silhouetted against it. The slight inward movement of the chasm's edges faltered and resumed again.

"Wayward," Maud chided. "You've always been wayward."

And Beacon let out a warning shout, because for the first time, Maud reached out with her power to strike at Pandora. The cavern shook as a lance of spellfire arrowed toward Pan, only to be met with a counterstrike and shattered in midair. This time, Pandora turned, tearing her attention from the wellspring and fixing it on Maud with a scowl.

"Why can't *you* be the one to give way?" she asked, flinging the words at the queen. "All I've ever wanted is to be left alone. You can have Hesperid if you just leave me be."

"Lies." Maud smiled in amusement. "If you'd wanted to be left alone, you'd never have come here. Don't you think I know what you've been after, posing as an Ingenue and infiltrating Palace Hill? You want this. You tell yourself you don't, but you've been spoiling for a fight with me since you were in leading strings. All your life you've wanted trouble. If you truly desired to be left alone, you'd obey when necessary and keep to yourself the rest of the time. You'd be a good girl. An exemplary daughter. Like your younger brother, who's always brought me whatever spellfire I need."

Beacon glanced to Prince Theo, whose face was a study in misery and guilt. Before the wellspring, Maud circled Pandora, her long, jet-fringed skirts sweeping the cavern's stone floor. Pan gave way, moving backward to keep distance between herself and the queen, and Beacon was so furious, it felt like he might choke.

"There is a great deal of weakness in you," Maud said patronizingly. "You hate me; you wish me dead. And yet you can never bring yourself to harm me. I had hoped for so much more when I was making you. I kept myself so filled with spellfire while you grew within me, I was certain the child I created would be a fearsome and indomitable creature. I raised you and trained you up with the same goal in mind. Anything that might have softened you—love, affection, stability—I held at bay for your sake. So that you might become a ruler fit for an empire. An empire we might forge together, by this power."

Maud gestured to the wellspring, behind her now, while Pandora stood uncertainly at the center of the white-walled cavern.

"You gave this to me," Maud went on. "The most precious gift I've received from you. And while I've been able to use it to secure and cement my uncontested control of Hesperid, I need you to make us more. To rise as a great power, rather than just a small and gifted nation. We are a curiosity on the world stage, but with you and me partnering together, we could be an unstoppable force."

When Pandora answered, she did not look at Maud. She looked at her patrons and, finally, at Beacon. She fixed her eyes on him, and her smile was sad.

"You mistake me," she said. "I've never craved power, even if I've been forced to unleash and to wield it. What I want is peace—to live my life unharassed, and to be as ordinary as possible."

Maud let out a dismissive, scoffing noise. "You could no more be ordinary than you could snuff out your spellfire. I created you to be exceptional. And though the weaker parts of you regret it now, you made Hesperid exceptional through your power as well."

"My mistake," Pandora said evenly. "And one I mean to rectify."

With a monumental effort Beacon could feel through their binding, Pan turned her attention away from the queen once more. She fixed it on the wellspring and resumed her work.

"I will kill you if need be," Maud warned. "Though it would be a setback, I can begin again with a new infant, a new, more suitable heir. Step away from the wellspring, Pandora."

Pan said nothing. Around them, the earth shook and trembled, and the chasm began to narrow faster than before, moved by Pandora Small's titanic power. But even as she pushed with everything in her, Beacon felt a blast of cold through the protective veil of Pan's ward. Maud was livid and gathering her own vicious magic.

25

PANDORA SHUTS THE LID

What happened in the wellspring chamber came as a blur to Pandora. The shock of relief provided by her new patronages. The intensity of her bond with Beacon. The agonizing, supernatural effort required to narrow the wellspring. The despair she felt upon Maud's arrival.

It was, Pandora thought, her lot in life to be bested by Maud. She stood with her back to the queen, all but pulled apart by her various wards and magic, the inferior daughter of a cruel and unmatched parent, constantly struggling to step out from her first patron's life-sapping shadow. But if Pan could only accomplish this—if she could just close the wellspring, or negate its damaging effects—she could die absolved. No longer marred by a legacy of monsters and killing magic.

With all her attention bent on the wellspring and the wards she still maintained, Pandora did not notice Maud drawing closer. Without the magesense, she couldn't detect the buildup of her mother's magic. Instead, she was taken entirely unawares when it struck her like a wall of spear-ice and howling snow, knocking her off her feet and away from the wellspring's edge. Pan's own magic faltered, her hold on the wellspring slipping, her wards flickering in and out of existence.

Wards first, she thought grimly. She could feel places that would bruise terribly where she'd slammed into the cavern's rocky floor, and the splintering pain in her wrist likely meant it had broken. No time for that now, though. Unhesitatingly she poured power back into her wards. They stabilized, but the effort of holding them now was tremendous. Where Pandora's body usually sang with heat and power, she had grown bitterly cold. Maud had set something in her—some slow and draining work of magic. Pan glanced down at her hands, and her teeth began to chatter as she saw her fingertips going first white, then ice blue. The chill crept up her fingers to her palms and then her wrists.

Turning inward, Pandora fanned her own spellfire into a raging flame. She banked it up with strength from her bindings, and most especially with heat that pulsed from her connection to Beacon. She shut her eyes, set her jaw, and *burned*. All her life, the fire within had been an unwelcome torment. Now she needed it, and it rose up eagerly at her summons. Life and color and power flooded back into her hands as she scrambled to her feet, shaking loose curls back from her face and turning to Maud with a snarl.

"I am not a dog to be confined to a cage anymore, or kept at the end of a leash," Pan said, fury lacing her words. "I will die before I bend to your will again. You've had your way with me long enough, and I will never, *never* do your bidding from this point on. Nor will I let you keep power that *I* dragged up from the earth. You couldn't open the wellspring without me, and you won't keep it without me either. We were both less before it opened, and I will whittle us back down to what we once were."

"I will kill you if you try," Maud warned, and it was the first true thing Pandora had ever heard the queen say to her. Throughout childhood and even now, her mother's words were always double-edged, dropping from a forked tongue, meant not for truth but for manipulation and domination. But this was honesty. This was Maud's heart unveiled—that she would do anything to retain power.

"Very well," Pandora said, turning her back to the queen one last time and facing the wellspring.

But Pandora Small hadn't spent all her life kicking against the goads to simply allow her treacherous patron a victory at the end. She started her magic anew, tying her power to the wellspring like seams at the edges of a torn cloth. And when Maud's ice struck her again, Pan seized hold of it despite the stinging cold and *pulled*.

She dragged at Maud's spellfire the way the queen had done to so many others, drawing the final spark from guards, from magefinders, from Pandora's fellow Ingenues. And though Maud was strong, she could not prevail against Pandora. Using the binding Maud had set on her before she'd even been born into the world, Pan anchored the queen's power to her own. Then, with Maud's spellfire tied to hers and her own fixed to the wellspring, Pandora did the one thing she'd avoided all her life.

She let go.

Power roared out of her like a tidal wave, dragged from her own reserves and from Maud. The cavern roared in answer, shaking until Pan could not keep to her feet and fell to her knees. Around her, the guards and her patrons were stumbling as well, no one able to keep upright as Pandora's power surged forward, a ceaseless gout driving into the wellspring, forcing its raw spellfire back, shifting immovable stone. Maud struggled against her, but she was nothing compared to the force Pan had been holding at bay her whole life, white-knuckling her way to control moment by moment, day by day, year by year. The queen's magic and Pandora's twined together in a torrent of fire and ice, and the wellspring groaned.

With a shudder and a great cascade of falling stone, it shut.

Darkness fell at the heart of Palace Hill.

Or nearly so. Because as Pandora pulled back from the seam, safeguarding the last essential spark she and her mother required for life, a narrow, intolerably bright fissure glowed at the heart of the wellspring cavern. Pan watched in horror as the single band of light grew wider, the chasm she'd once torn open beginning to expand again.

Behind her, Maud laughed, a sharp, merciless sound.

"Some wrongs," the queen said mockingly, "cannot be righted."

But Pandora never had it in her to fail. She scrambled forward and slapped both her hands over the small gap in the cavern floor. An inadvertent cry escaped her as the raw spellfire burned her skin, but Pan kept her hands where they were and dredged the very last sparks of power out from her. She stripped them from her blood, from her bones, from her heart and lungs and every vital part. And with that last magic, she pushed at the wellspring one final time.

A snap of rock meeting rock. The shock of sudden darkness. And Pandora felt the all too familiar sensation of her heart slowing. Her lungs losing the strength to expand and contract. How many times had she nearly died like this in childhood, only to be dragged back by her patron's ruthless will?

Not this time. A pair of hands wrapped around her neck in the black.

"You have never been anything but a disappointment," Maud whispered viciously. "And I won't give you the satisfaction of leaving the world on your own terms. I'll send you out of it, just as I brought you in."

There was nothing left in Pan to fight with. She couldn't so much as raise an arm to ward off Maud's throttling fingers. But all at once, blinding light flared in the darkness, and the crack of a pistol shot rang out. For an instant, Pandora saw Beacon's face, ashen in the glare of his own gunfire. Then Maud slumped to the stone floor at her side. Pan felt the hot, liquid touch of blood against her arm, and with her last breath smelled the iron scent of it on the air, undercut with the sharp odor of black powder.

Within her chest, her heart stopped. Her lungs stilled.

But the wellspring was closed, and Beacon's face was the last thing she'd seen. That was enough to take out of the world with her, into whatever lay beyond.

26

UNBINDINGS

Three weeks later, Beacon sat in a hansom jolting its way out of the city. The transition was abrupt—all at once the cobblestones ended, giving way to wider dirt roads and smoother travel. The low, ramshackle buildings of Valora's outskirts melted into green countryside, and the air grew suddenly sweet. Beacon lowered both the hansom's windows and let the breeze blow in, taking great breaths of the clear air.

"Churchill, you said your name was?" the hansom driver asked from above. It was just Beacon's luck that he'd ended up with someone chatty. "And you're headed to the Oaks? Got a position in the household there?"

Beacon said nothing, pretending the dull clatter of the wheels was drowning out the driver's voice. He did not feel inclined to make polite, false conversation. Worse yet, he felt odd and awkward out of uniform, without the familiar weight of short sword and pistol to balance him out.

Just for now, Beacon promised himself. He'd back in uniform and back where he belonged soon. He comforted himself with the knowledge that his kit was at least close at hand, stuffed into the rucksack at his side.

Not far outside the city, the hansom turned off the main road and onto a winding drive lined with ancient, looming oak trees. Shade and sunlight flashed through the windows intermittently, and they drove for what seemed ages before coming out before a vast stone manor house.

At the head of the drive, the hansom driver made to turn his cab toward the back of the house and the servants' entrances that would be there.

"No," Beacon said as he swung down from the hansom while it was still moving. "The front door's all right. They're expecting me."

The driver let out a low whistle, drawing his horse to a full halt. "Important, are you? Got business with the family?"

Again, Beacon was silent. He swung his rucksack out of the back of the hansom and fished a few coins out of it, handing them up to the driver. The man looked disappointed, but whatever he might think about Beacon's importance, the boy was a guard on a guard's salary, not some gilded noble.

As the hansom pulled away, Beacon knocked at the front door and was met not by a maid, but by Imogen Hollen.

"Hello, Ellis," she said, kissing his cheek with a sudden waft of fresh, orange blossom scent. "We've been waiting for you. Is everything ready?"

Beacon nodded. "Ready as it'll ever be. All well here?"

Imogen smiled, looking as self-satisfied as a cat with a dish of cream. "Of course it is. Come and look."

She led Beacon up a wide, carpeted staircase to the second floor of the Hollens' sprawling country home. He could not imagine having grown up in such a place—it was entirely foreign to what Beacon had known as a child, in the few small rooms behind his father's mill.

A long, sun-soaked gallery ran along the second floor, and Imogen took Beacon down to the far end. There, a uniformed maid was just emerging from a doorway with an exasperated look on her face.

"I can't do it, Miss Hollen," the girl said apologetically, nearly in tears. "I know you said to try to convince her, and I did, but—"

"Don't worry, Annabelle." Imogen raised a hand to calm the young maid. "I'll take care of it myself."

Gesturing to Beacon to wait, Imogen rapped on the door. She was elegant as one of the portraits hanging in the great hall on Palace Hill, Beacon thought. Imogen wore gold, as she so often did, and the fabric of her gown shimmered. A thin diadem of twining gold studded with sapphire chips sparkled in her hair.

"Are you decent?" Imogen called out, and received a muffled, disgruntled reply.

"We can go in," Imogen said, rolling her eyes. And she ushered Beacon in to an exquisite morning room, decorated all in shades of white and cool green.

Ander Hollen and his wife lounged on a settee together, and whatever troubles they'd had in the past seemed to have melted away. Euphemia Hollen was very much like her daughter, Imogen, and Ander kept a possessive hand resting atop hers.

"—well I think it's lovely," Euphemia finished saying, clearly having just delivered a bracing lecture of the sort Imogen favored. "You've got to stand out, you know. It wouldn't do for people to overlook you."

All of that—the Hollens, the room, the wide bank of sunny

windows—Beacon saw and dismissed in a moment. Because what consumed his attention was the girl standing in the sun.

Pandora looked weary and a little frail in the wake of her brush with caster's fatigue. There were still faint bruises beneath her eyes and spread across her flesh. Her right wrist was splinted and bandaged, but the physicians Ander Hollen hired had assured her it would heal well. Beacon had come close to losing her in the wellspring chamber—he'd felt the binding between them begin to fray and the first hints of something like madness clouding the edges of his mind. It was Ander Hollen who'd saved them both. With the wellspring shut, Maud dead, and everyone cast into confusion, only Ander had kept his head. He'd had spellfire on him—six vials in his jacket pocket, along with a syringe. Old habits from when his family owned sliphouses, Ander explained to Beacon in a voice that shook as he injected spellfire into Pandora one vial after another. He'd learned to be careful around mages, forever worried that someone would slip their spark.

Even with Ander's quick thinking and quick action, things had been precarious for a week. Pandora's life had hung in the balance, and she'd been spirited away to the Hollens' country house, for her protection as well as her healing. Ander had disappeared into his study, working night and day, until at week's end, he'd come out with a bizarre apparatus. A needle, rubber tubing, and a stand, by which a thin stream of spellfire could be kept constantly flowing into Pan's veins.

Another week after that had been needed to taper it off, until she could function without the additional sparks. Beacon would have stayed in the country and slept outside her door were it not for the fact that every guard was pulling double duty on Palace Hill. The nobles and the queen's council were in chaos, with Theo doing everything possible to manage them.

"Like herding cats," the prince had told Beacon morosely one evening. "Or something worse than cats. Weasels. Like herding weasels. I could use a drink."

Theo said the last woefully, with a longing glance at Beacon. For his part, Beacon stood stone-faced by the prince's bedchamber door. When Theo rose and made as if to leave, Beacon stepped in front of the door, barring his way out.

"Must you?" Theo complained.

"It was your own orders, sir," Beacon said stiffly. "Now you're no longer bound by magic, you said you'd not be bound by a bottle as well."

"You have a distressingly good memory, Ellis," Theo told him with a narrow look. "And I absolutely forbid you to call me *sir*. I think you might be older than I am—you're certainly taller."

"Yes, sir," Beacon said.

"Yes, Theo."

"Yes, Your Highness," Beacon said, allowing himself a rare moment of wickedness.

"Ugh, worse." Theo pulled a face. "Sir will do. But what are you going to call *her*?"

Beacon, as ever when faced with a question he did not want to answer, chose silence.

Now, standing before Pandora in the Hollens' morning room, he thought of a thousand things he could call her, some of them only fit for Pan's own ears. He went to her and took the little mage's hands in his own.

They'd dressed her up so that she shone and gleamed like a pearl. In that at least, Imogen had honored Pandora's own preference. Pan was in a gown somewhere between soft white and the palest possible gray. She wore gloves to her elbows and diamonds around her throat.

Beacon had never seen her look more like an Ingenue—no, more like his empress. He'd have been tempted to kneel before her, if not for the ridiculous white feathers rising from her curling hair and nodding a foot above her head.

"I look like a stork," Pandora said in annoyance. "Beacon, tell them I look like a stork."

"You do not look like a stork," Beacon answered as he reached around her to pluck the offending plumes from her hair. "But you don't need these to prevent being overlooked. No one will be able to take their eyes off you."

Beacon had never felt anything to be truer. Once, he would have realized that Imogen was the sun to Pandora's moon—a brilliant and stately creature that could not be outshone by a smaller, paler copy. But he'd lost all perspective. To him, there was only Pandora. When she was present, no one else shone as bright. Nothing else mattered.

"Feathers are the fashion," Imogen said in despair. "You'd have been perfect."

Ignoring her, Beacon drew Pandora aside. The Hollens began to talk among themselves, perhaps about Pandora's low taste in hair stylings, perhaps about the inscrutable concerns of the fabulously wealthy.

"How has it been?" Beacon asked Pan. "Are they treating you well? Because if not, I'll—"

"You'll what?" Pandora asked in amusement. "Spirit me away? Hide me in your village along the Hesper River? It can't be done. I'm afraid it's even more impossible for me to escape Valora or my own fate now."

"Pandora." Beacon was stern. "Are they being kind to you? I have to know."

Pan regarded the Hollens thoughtfully. "Yes. Yes, they are. Even

Euphemia. I was worried about coming here, after the wellspring. It was the only thing I could think of, oddly enough. I was so muddled, and it kept running round and around in my head. *Euphemia doesn't like you.* But I think we're managing all right. She's been polite. Helpful, even."

"Of course she has," Imogen called over. "I told her to."

Witch, Beacon thought. It was absurd, an Ingenue's capacity to listen to more than one conversation at a time.

"She's frightening," Beacon said to Pandora, and Pan smiled.

"No. I'm frightening. Imogen is terrifying."

The same little maid who'd nearly been brought to tears by Pandora's distaste for feathers appeared in the doorway.

"The carriages are ready," she said breathlessly.

Beacon was hurried into an antechamber by Imogen, where he was able to take the uniform out of his rucksack and change into it. Pandora's location had been a carefully kept secret for weeks now—though the time for secrecy was nearly over, no one had been willing to risk a scarlet-coated guard arriving at the Hollens' country home.

Back in the kit that felt like a second skin, Beacon strode out only to find the Hollens gone and Pandora waiting for him alone.

"Are you ready?" she asked softly.

Beacon blinked. "Pan, I ought to be asking you that."

She looked down at her long gloves, toying with a cuff of diamonds clasped over one of them. "It matters to you, too. I want to be sure you're all right. If you aren't, we'll just go away together, no matter how hard it is. I don't have to stay in Valora, or in Hesperid at all, for that matter. I only need to be with you."

Beacon stepped forward, encircling her with his arms. "But you *want* to be here. Don't pretend otherwise—I can feel it in you."

"I hadn't thought I would," Pandora said with a note of wonder in her voice. "But I've reconciled myself to everything, now that I know how to manage what's to come. But truly, Beacon, you don't mind?"

"I think you're a marvel." He bent to kiss her forehead, her eyelids, her nose, her mouth. "Since the moment I first met you, you've been magic to me."

"Not the first moment," Pandora pointed out tartly. "You thought I was a mouse."

"An adorable mouse." Beacon knew he'd never live that admission down, but he also knew that he loved to be chided for it. Even now, he watched her stare up at him sternly and wrinkle her nose, and knew he'd lie down and die for her.

"I am no mouse," Pandora said. "You'll pay for that, Ellis Beacon. You will pay, and pay, and pay."

Beacon grinned. "I'm counting on it."

In the carriages, there was no more opportunity for much talk. Ander insisted on riding with Pandora, as did Beacon, and the atmosphere was strained. Ander kept shooting measuring looks at the guard, and Beacon was certain he was doing the same to Pandora's father. They'd entered the city and were jouncing over cobblestones by the time Pan let out a weighty sigh.

"Honestly, the two of you are like tomcats yowling at each other in an alleyway. You both have my best interests at heart, and I'm quite capable of looking after myself around either of you. Does that make everyone feel better?"

"No," Beacon and Ander said in concert, then gave each other a look with a little more respect than suspicion.

The carriages climbed up and up, winding along the beautifully maintained roads that led to the Hill and its sparkling royal compound. Just before entering the palace grounds, the coachmen turned aside—the front drive where Beacon had once watched Ingenues arrive was packed with people who spilled out onto the roadway and even perched atop the palace's tall fence.

Skirting the crowd, they arrived in a servants' courtyard at the back of the palace and were quickly ushered inside by Captain Tanner and a contingent of guards. Theo was waiting in the palace's grand central foyer, pacing back and forth like a caged wildcat while nobles ringed the room, looking sullen. Many of them wore crimson mourning bands around their sleeves—nearly a hundred of the first set had died along with Maud, their lives snuffed out with hers thanks to the bindings they bore. Others had survived by virtue of being bound to someone else, rather than solely to the queen.

Outside, glimpses of the crowd could be seen, and their voices were a dull background noise, like the first rumblings of a quake. At the sight of the Hollens, Theo hurried over, though it was Pandora and not Imogen who he caught by the hands.

"Everyone with a title and a seat on the council is livid," he said. "And you've got more than you bargained for—there's an absolute sea of people out there. Can you manage?"

Pandora smiled. "Quite nicely. The Hill's still flush with spellfire—I expect it will be for some time."

Nodding, Theo drew Pandora into a quick, rough hug. "I'm glad we're doing this together."

It was odd to Beacon still, knowing that Pandora was not only half sister to Imogen, but to Theo as well. She was the indomitable small center around which they all orbited, and they followed in her wake as she floated to the palace's front doors and out onto the wide verandah beyond. The voice of the crowd escalated to a roar at the sight of her, though whether they cried out with excitement or disdain or approval, Beacon couldn't say. Automatically his hand went to the hilt of his short sword, and he stepped forward as Pandora's shadow, only a step behind her. Imogen and Theo were at her sides, and Beacon was glad of them.

After a few moments, the noise of the crowd subsided, and Theo spoke.

"As you know," he said, "we've had some trouble with the succession. Hesperid's laws dictate the throne and the crown pass to its ruler's eldest child. Which is no longer me—my sister, Pandora, is eldest by a year. But I've been informed by just about everyone on Palace Hill that they won't support another mage queen. Not after what happened with the last."

It was like Theo to speak so frankly—in the past fortnight, Beacon had come to know the prince better and liked the boy immensely. Whatever pain or guilt he felt over Queen Maud's death and her ill use of him Theo had subsumed in tireless work sorting out the succession.

"I do support a mage queen," Theo said, with a ring of assurance in his voice. "I saw firsthand what my sister did at the wellspring, both withstanding our mother and shutting off the spellfire she unleashed on this city. Pandora did all that at great risk to herself, and nearly died in the process. I don't believe Hesperid could ask for a better queen, and I won't take her birthright from her."

"Neither will I take the throne and the crown that were meant to be my brother's," Pandora said, and her voice was warm. Beacon had been so focused on gauging the mood of the crowd that he hadn't noticed at first how Pan's own magic was amplifying what she and Theo said, broadcasting it out to the gathered people on gentle waves of spellfire, so that all those present could hear each and every word.

"Theo and I have reached an agreement," Pan went on. "Rather than either one of us giving way to the other, we intend to take on the governance of Hesperid together. As family, and as joint rulers.

We'll be supported in that task soon by Theo's intended, Imogen Hollen."

"What'll the prince's wife be if we're to have a king and a queen already?" someone shouted.

Pandora smiled. "Queen as well. I have no concerns about sharing the title. In fact, I'd prefer it."

"And what exactly are you each to do as joint rulers? Will the little mage use her magecraft on anyone who opposes you?" The laconic voice emanating from the crowd was far too familiar, and in a moment Beacon had located Baron Hax, not standing with the nobles but within the mass of people. Hax shot the guard a wicked look, and Beacon's grip on his sword hilt tightened.

It was Theo who spoke. "Imogen and I will be handling most of the administrative tasks ruling requires. Pandora has a different role in mind."

Here it is, Beacon thought. *No turning back in a moment.*

But Pandora did not seem the least bit reluctant as she took a step forward, distancing herself from even Theo and Imogen.

"Hesperid, I would like to be your voice," she said with all of an Ingenue's winsomeness. "You've had a queen who used you wrongly and subjugated you to her will. I intend to subjugate myself to you in recompense. I offer to bind myself to any citizen who wishes it—to belong to all of you. If the majority of our people ever wish a thing from me, I will be required to accomplish it just as any bound mage who is subject to her patron would be. I ask for you to take me as your servant."

Absolute silence fell. No one in the crowd had expected this— Beacon hadn't either, when Pandora first suggested it. He'd protested and growled and stomped, and had not been able to alter her resolve in the least. Pan meant to travel the length and breadth of Hesperid in the weeks to come and bind herself to every last soul who desired it.

Somewhere in the palace gardens, an eranlark burst into liquid song, and a breeze sprang up, pulling at the flag above the drive. The fabric unfurled, sky-blue background punctuated by the four-pointed Hesperidian star.

And the crowd burst into absolute chaos.

The cheers and shouts and protests were deafening. Worse was the way people pushed forward, a living wall trying to get to Pandora. They *wanted* her—Imogen had done brilliant work, disseminating the story of her sister's brutal childhood and victory over Maud to the dailies down in the city, until every last soul knew of Pandora's past, Pandora's battle, and Pandora's frail state following her salvation of Valora. While the nobility and the council might be resistant to the idea of another mage queen, the people of Hesperid had no such compunctions.

For a quarter of an hour, the guard struggled to maintain order and reorganize the crowd. At last they managed to create some semblance of a queue, and Pandora moved to the very edge of the verandah, where people would be brought up the stairs to her, one by one. Beacon followed doggedly, worry biting at him as he watched his small beloved. She was still prone to weakness following the wellspring, and the task before her was monumental—she'd be working bindings till well after dark, given the look of the crowd and the queue.

He kept his eyes fixed on her, scanning for any sign of faintness or fatigue as the guards ushered a first patron forward for binding. As they did, Pandora's power stirred. She opened to it, dropping the inner walls she kept her spellfire hidden behind. And at once, Beacon's fear abated, because his Pandora burned as brightly as ever. The breeze was no match for the heat wrought by her power, which caused Beacon to flush and go a little giddy. There was an inferno within her—he could feel every spark of it and feel too how the spellfire still latent in Hesperid's soil and air converged now on Pandora. It was as if that most unpredictable of elements had learned to love Pandora Small and now sought her out as a perfect host, rather than running wild and breeding monsters.

Beacon shut his eyes and smiled, feeling the most exquisite relief at the sudden realization that Pandora would be all right. But his eyes flew open again as he heard the first of Pandora's new patrons speak.

"May I ask you something?" the girl before Pandora said, her voice pitched only for Pan and those nearest her to hear. "If there will be a king and two queens, what will my brother be to you?"

With his focus so entirely on Pan, Beacon hadn't looked at the girl being brought forward. Now that he did, he found something he never expected to see—Everly, his younger sister, standing before the mage queen he loved.

"Ev," Beacon said, hurrying forward and taking her hands. "What are you doing here?"

"Rockford came and needed waiting on," she answered. "I begged to come. So here I am. I want to speak to the queen. I can see how you look at her, and I mean to know her intentions toward you."

Heat that had nothing to do with Pandora crept up the back of Beacon's neck. He opened his mouth to speak, but Pan beat him to it.

"May I ask you something first?" Pandora said in reply, her voice lower than Everly's even, so that no one besides herself and Everly and Beacon could make out her words. "Do you wish to keep your binding?"

Everly glanced up sharply, clearly shocked. "I—what do you mean?"

"I don't just intend to bind myself to the people of Hesperid."

Pandora smiled, and there was something calculating and pleased in it. "I mean to unbind every mage who wants the connection to their patron broken as well. Instead of asking permission and waiting months or years for the council to wrangle over it, I'll do it as I go. Theo and Gin can sort out the laws for me later. I know I can manage it—the Hollens have several mages in their employ, who I unbound only yesterday."

Poor Theo, Beacon thought. *Poor Imogen.* But he had never loved Pandora more.

"Break it," Everly said with a flinty note in her voice.

Pandora reached out, and Beacon felt the work. The hot, sudden flare of Everly's binding shattering. The balmy warmth of the new connection to Pandora, as Pan willingly placed herself within Everly's power. When it was finished, there were tears glistening in Everly's eyes. But Beacon knew Ev and knew she wouldn't leave until she had an answer to her question.

"Well?" Everly asked expectantly, wiping at her eyes with the back of one hand. "What about my brother, then? Who will he be to you?"

It was Beacon who answered this time.

"I'm the Queen's Guard," he said firmly. "Now and forever, if she'll have me."

Pan turned to him, her smile radiant.

"You are, aren't you? And I'll have you forever, if you please."

ACKNOWLEDGMENTS

Pandora Small has been with me since my teens, and was the central character of the very first novel I ever queried (without success). During her long, long journey to bookshelves, she has brushed shoulders with a host of people, and I am grateful to everyone who assisted me with her development over the years. You would not be reading her story without the persistent advocacy and excellent creative insights of my editor, Nicole Fiorica. This is our fourth book together, which is hard to believe, and every time we approach a new project, Nicole brings enthusiasm, openness, and wonderful ideas to the work. Laura Crockett, my agent, first met Pandora when she made the rounds eons ago as the heroine of my first queried novel, and it is such a pleasure to have (finally) brought Pan to full life with Laura. Speaking of bringing Pandora to life, Fernanda Suarez created the gorgeous and vivid rendering of Pandora and Beacon you see on this book's jacket, and I'm indebted to her for capturing them so richly.

Debra Sfetsios-Conover is the creative genius behind the jacket layout of most of my books, and I'm always so pleased to see the harmonious designs she comes up with. Irene Metaxatos oversaw interior design for this book, which is one of my favorite first looks as an author—it's where the book part of the book really comes together, and I love the little details within *Steel & Spellfire*. Thanks also to managing editor Jen Strada, production manager Elizabeth Blake-Linn, and to copyeditor Brian Luster and proofreader Brooke Littrell, whose attention to detail makes me look like the sort of author who never generates a typo or continuity error (nothing could be further from the truth).

Every book I write, and indeed, my entire career, is buoyed up by the help of a certain group of friends. Jen Fulmer, Joanna Meyer, Steph Messa, Anna Bright, and Hannah Whitten are the keepers of my sanity and publishing secrets, now and forever. Lauren Blackwood and Maleeha Siddiqui are the most fun to share good news with, and true companions of the heart, as is the wonderful Bev Twomey. When I first prepared to query Pandora's story, in its unrecognizable original form, Sarah Glenn Marsh took me under her wing and taught me everything I know about revising to feedback, querying a novel, and being an author who is generous with her time and resources. Thank you so much to Sarah for her assistance and the stellar example she set.

Last but not least, I would not be the person (and therefore the writer) that I am if it wasn't for Tyler and my girls. They are the reason I keep doing this, day after day, year after year, and book after book.

As are my goats, because someone has to buy them hay.

LAURA E. WEYMOUTH

is the author of several novels, including the critically acclaimed *The Light Between Worlds, A Treason of Thorns, A Rush of Wings, A Consuming Fire,* and *The Voice Upstairs*. Born and raised in the Niagara region of Ontario, Laura now lives at the edge of the woods in western New York with her husband, three wild-hearted daughters, and an ever-expanding menagerie of animal friends. Learn more at LauraEWeymouth.com.